P9-CBQ-239

0111001010011010100100
1010101010000001010111
0100001111010110000011
1110000101101001110001
0001011110000110100101
1010011101110011100000
0010010THE HIVE0010100
0111001010010010100100
1010101010000001010111
0100001011010111011000
1110000101101001110001
0001010100000110101101
1010001001110010100110

0111001010011010100100
1010101010000001010111
0100001111010110000011
1110000101101001110001
0001011110000110100101
1010011101110011100000

0010010THE HIVE0010100

0111001010010010100100
1010101010000001010111
0100001011010111011000
1110000101101001110001
0001010100000110101101
1010001001110010100110

BARRY LYGA & MORGAN BADEN

CONCEPT BY JENNIFER BEALS
& TOM JACOBSON

KCP Loft is an imprint of Kids Can Press

First paperback edition 2021

Published in Canada and the U.S. by Kids Can Press Ltd.
25 Dockside Drive, Toronto, ON M5A 0B5

Kids Can Press is a Corus Entertainment Inc. company

www.kidscanpress.com

The text is set in Minion Pro and Menlo.

Edited by Kate Egan
Interior page design by Emma Dolan

Printed and bound in Altona, Manitoba, Canada, in 12/2020 by Friesens Corp.

CM PA 21 0 9 8 7 6 5 4 3 2 1

Library and Archives Canada Cataloguing in Publication

Title: The hive / Barry Lyga & Morgan Baden ; concept by Jennifer Beals & Tom Jacobson.
Names: Lyga, Barry, author. | Baden, Morgan, author. | Beals, Jennifer. | Jacobson, Tom.
Description: Originally published: Toronto, ON : KCP Loft, ©2019.
Identifiers: Canadiana 20200306154 | ISBN 9781525304408 (softcover)
Classification: LCC PZ7.L9995 Hiv 2021 | DDC j813/.6 — dc23

Kids Can Press gratefully acknowledges that the land on which our office is located is the traditional territory of many nations, including the Mississaugas of the Credit, the Anishnabeg, the Chippewa, the Haudenosaunee and the Wendat peoples, and is now home to many diverse First Nations, Inuit and Métis peoples.

We thank the Government of Ontario, through Ontario Creates, for supporting our publishing activity.

Today, the promise of the internet is finally fulfilled in America. It's going to be big. And beautiful. And I think people are really gonna like it, and I think it's going to be very good for the United States of America.

— the President of the United States,
announcing the Heuristic Internet Vetting Engine

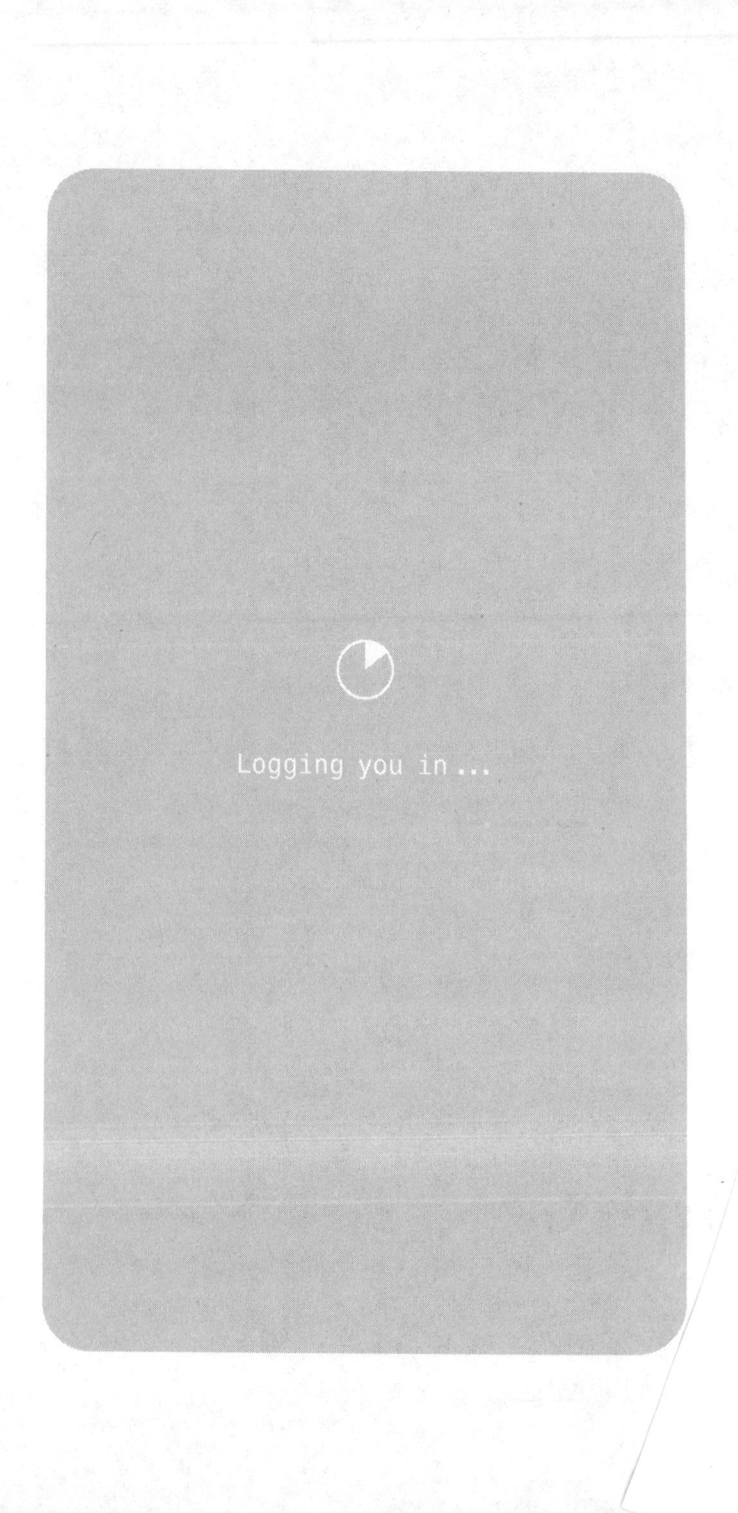
Logging you in...

Welcome to

BLiNQ

Trend Positive!

Hello, **CassieMcK39**!

So far today you have:

Any mobs today? I have the day off and I'm bored! **#SaveMeFromMyself**

Nice day for some Hive Justice! Look at that sunshine! Who's heading to **#MonsterNotAMan**?

#BLINQReaderPoll3995: Is **#MichaelJones** a monster or a man? Vote: bl.inq/poll3995

HIVE ALERT: **#MonsterNotAMan** rally happening now in Rasche Field.

I just voted MONSTER in **#BLINQReaderPoll3995**, join me: **#MonsterNotAMan** Vote: bl.inq/poll3995

ENTERTAINMENT NEWS ALERT: Rumor has it **#MichaelJones**'s wife will be appearing at today's rally. What will she be wearing? Streaming now at enewsalert.hive.gov/3995. **#MonsterNotAMan**

What kind of man does this to his wife and children? An animal, that's who. **#MeetMeAtRascheField #MonsterNotAMan**

I just voted MONSTER in **#BLINQReaderPoll3995**, join me: **#MonsterNotAMan** Vote: bl.inq/poll3995

How much must it suck to be related to **#MichaelJones** right now? Poor kids. **#MonsterNotAMan**

HIVE ALERT: **#MichaelJones** has arrived. Hive Justice set to begin momentarily. **#RascheField #MonsterNotAMan**

10010100101

Somewhere nearby, shit was going down, and Cassie had to be a part of it.

She followed the crowd down a block lined with shady trees and around a corner that she remembered well. They were heading to the baseball field in her old neighborhood, the one where Cassie had swung and missed more times than she could count. The one where Cassie's dad, Harlon McKinney, had hugged her after a skinned knee, after a tough loss, after a mean joke from the pitcher. Now, with every step she took, her blood ran hotter, her breath pulsed quicker in her lungs.

She raised a hand to shield her eyes from the blinding sun, which had just peeked out over the trees like it knew the crowd needed its own audience.

As she approached the field, the charge in the air became palpable. These people, despite their varied ages, races and backgrounds, had a shared mission, and Cassie felt their energy in her body. Her fingers twitched, her stomach knotted. *Let's do this,* she thought. And then, smaller: *Please let me feel something new. Anything.*

Her mother had disabled Hive Alerts on her phone, but there was nothing her mother could do to her phone that Cassie couldn't undo. Rachel was a classics professor, not a coder. Cassie's phone wasn't even running the software it had come with — it ran a custom variant she and her dad had cobbled together.

Now its sudden burst of pings made her jump. This was it. All around her, people were receiving the same notification she had just heard through her earbud: he was here.

The crowd roared, so Cassie did, too, the sound surprising her as it reached up her throat, around her teeth. It felt unexpectedly good to yell. Because all the others around her were stomping their feet and shaking their fists, she did as well, and that also felt good, kind of. It was real, and it wasn't pain, so that counted for something.

Cassie tried not to think about it too deeply, but for months she hadn't been able to shake the feeling that she was viewing the world from a distance, like she was occupying a different physical plane from everyone around her. Here, in this moment, Cassie thought — maybe — she could see things normally again. She could *feel* things normally again. She could belong.

And right now, she belonged *here*, at Rasche Field, with the others who'd also been drawn here by GPS and Wi-Fi and the unrelenting triangulation of cell towers.

"Do your justice," the synthetic voice in her ear said, followed by the hashtag. Everyone else heard the same.

Cassie had always hated being tall, a trait she'd inherited from her dad, but today it felt like a sign. Her first Hive Mob and she practically had a front-row seat. She saw the perpetrator immediately: a slight, sandy-haired man, his head down, climbing the bleachers, as he'd been instructed to do by the thousands who logged their votes locally. It took him forever to reach the top. When he finally did, Cassie took note of how his shoulders, which had been sagging, suddenly straightened; how his slight frame suddenly seemed to grow in size. This man was determined, Cassie realized.

Almost ... proud.

Well, he wouldn't be proud for long. He'd humiliated his family in public by writing an anonymous blog in which he'd detailed his ambivalence about his relationships with his wife and his children. Honesty on social media was admirable, but there were limits. After a particular post with the confession that his response to his wife's cancer diagnosis was to tell her he didn't love her anymore, his blog went viral, and the usual doxx gangs quickly uncovered his identity. His Dislikes and Condemns skyrocketed — even Cassie had shared the call to Condemn him, and she barely shared anything online these days.

Overnight, Hive Justice was declared, and #publicjunk was agreed to be an appropriate sentence. So justice would be served, right here, right now. As punishment for his indiscretion, he'd be forced to parade around town naked, with the words "World's Worst Husband and Father" written on his chest.

Someone started chanting — "Monster, not a man!" — and Cassie joined in, even though it was a dumb chant. But the chant wasn't the point of all this, was it? It was the togetherness, Cassie knew. The unity. That's what everyone said, anyway. She tried to say the words again, to be a part of it all, but the chant caught in her throat. She coughed as she watched the man on the bleachers square his shoulders again, like he could form a barrier around himself before things got started. The sun shifted overhead, brightening the field even more, giving Cassie a clearer look at him. She blinked. There was something about his face … for a second Cassie wondered if she knew him.

Still waiting on the top row of the bleachers, the man took off his glasses, folded them carefully and placed them in his left shirt pocket. Then he patted them. Twice.

Cassie's stomach heaved.

"Dad," she whispered.

Around her, the crowd quieted.

"Wait," Cassie said. No one heard her.

A woman with a bright scarf wrapped around her head, carrying a marker, climbed the bleachers. Noticing her, the man began unbuttoning his shirt. The sunlight gleamed off his sandy hair. Cassie struggled to catch her breath.

"Mark him!" someone behind Cassie yelled. Bursts of applause followed. The new chant thrummed — "Mark him! Mark him!" — on the bleachers, the perfect stage for the crowd in the field; the woman had approached the top, and the man had removed every item of clothing. He was completely naked, completely vulnerable. Cassie averted her eyes and tried to squelch the hot nausea climbing her throat.

She struggled to even her breathing. "It's not him," she whispered to herself. She knew that. He was white, for one thing. But still. He was *a* dad, someone's dad, and her own father, like this man, was always taking off his glasses and putting them in his pocket for safekeeping. Her limbs felt shaky and loose. What happened to the energy, the charge she'd felt just moments ago? The camaraderie?

The woman held the marker up to the crowd. Cassie expected her to be giddy, to smile at least, but instead her face was expressionless. She appeared to hesitate, then leaned in and gave the man a quick peck on the cheek. He closed his eyes in response.

The crowd, though, savored this moment. They clapped harder while Cassie felt herself shrinking back into the shell she'd formed so many months ago.

"A-ni-mal!" a little girl next to her roared. Cassie stared at her, this tiny angelic-looking thing whose eyes were burning, whose teeth were practically bared. She looked like she couldn't hurt a fly but yearned to do damage.

Cassie blinked. She looked around at the others, each of them cheering at the scene unfolding before them. On the bleachers, the woman began writing on the man's chest. He stood naked and perfectly still. Cassie turned away.

"I have to get out of here," she wheezed, and started to push back the way she came. Bodies everywhere. Cassie struggled, dodging elbows and shoulders and fists, trying to breathe.

Finally, a break in the crowd. She hit the open field and broke into a run. The sun was hot now, pounding on the back of her neck, her knees. The noise of the Hive Mob behind her quieted enough for her to clear her mind, to think again. She slowed to a jog, then a trot, kicking up the light brown dirt under her feet. It floated around her, making it hard to see. Any moment of clarity Cassie had had, any seconds when she hadn't felt like she was separated from the rest of humanity, were gone. *Poof.*

Behind her, the man was getting ready to spend his day naked in public, where the whole world could see his shame. He would be streamed live online, where people would comment and laugh and share. His wife would be even more humiliated. His kids, too. And Cassie had helped. Had cornered him at the field, left him nowhere to go.

That's what she'd wanted, right? To mete out the sort of immediate justice that the world demanded? To feel the righteous thrill of the mob at her back?

She was going to be sick. She ran through the neighborhood, through the shade of the trees she'd grown up under, across streets and around corners until she reached her house.

Wait. Her *old* house.

"Dammit!" Cassie yelled, fists clenched at her sides. She stood in the middle of her old street, in front of the house that had been sold to new owners just a few weeks before. She'd been so desperate to flee that she hadn't been thinking; she'd just relied on muscle memory. Her new apartment was in the city. She'd have to ride a bus to get there.

"Thanks, Mom," Cassie mumbled. Rachel always ruined everything.

Luckily, Cassie knew the bus stop was nearby. She hurried there and caught the next one just in time. On the bus, she ignored all the BLINQs coming in to her feed and tried to settle her stomach. If she didn't think about it, about #publicjunk and the man who didn't look like her dad but could have been him anyway, about the press of the crowd and the little girl's blazing eyes, she was fine.

The bus ride was quick enough. When she got off, the sun hid behind towers and the air felt thicker. Cassie hated the city, but she had to admit it was at least useful: when you didn't feel like making eye contact, when you felt like you couldn't hold it together for another second, everyone left you alone.

"Cassie!" Rachel exclaimed when Cassie burst through the door to their cramped new apartment. She was sitting at the tiny kitchen table, laptop open, surrounded by books. "You OK?"

"Later, Mom," Cassie said. She went straight to her bedroom and slammed the door.

In her bedroom, Cassie dived onto her bed and fumbled at her phone's screen. Once the chat app opened, her breathing returned to normal. Everything was OK. She was safe.

Dad, she texted, **today is horrible.**

The response from her dad was instantaneous. **Hey there, kiddo. Any day you can walk away from is a good one, right?**

She groaned. Her dad's mordant sense of humor always had the ironic effect of making her feel better.

I miss you so much, Cassie wrote.

I miss you and I love you.

Cassie stared at her dad's words for a few minutes, letting them warm her the way they always did. There was an ache inside her without him around, like someone had torn a chunk of her body away and now she was expected to just live like that, without the very piece that made her a whole person. The only thing that filled that ache was anger. Some part of her knew that it wasn't healthy to walk around angry all the time, but it felt so much better than the pain.

She started to write back, needing to work out her thoughts about the day. He wouldn't have an answer for this one, would he? **So, Dad, I joined my first Hive Mob today . . . I was punishing a person whose name I can't even remember, if I ever knew it in the first place.**

Then her mom burst through her door.

"Mom!" Cassie said hotly. "Jesus! Knock first!"

Rachel grimaced. "You're right. I'm sorry. But we talked about you texting your dad —"

"Who says that's what I'm doing?"

Her mom crossed her arms over her chest, leaned against the door and stared. Cassie scowled at her with deep, abiding rage. There was plenty left over from her aborted attempt at Hive Justice. All that anger and froth had to go somewhere. Mom was as good a target as any.

Instead of fleeing or bursting into flame, her mother sighed and sat gingerly on the edge of Cassie's bed.

"Honey, we talked about this, right? About texting him?" Rachel tried to smooth a lock of Cassie's dark hair, which was pulled into a knot at the top of her head, but Cassie batted her hand away.

Inside, the jumble of emotions that had been competing for her attention all day kindled. Cassie knew that if her mom lit the match, things would explode.

She set her jaw — her defiance another trait inherited from her dad — and glared at Rachel. Her voice was cold. "You can't keep me from talking to him."

Rachel glared back at Cassie for a moment. "Actually, I can."

*

Rachel hated this part, the part where her daughter was finally feeling something, and she had to go and ruin it. As tears started to spill over Cassie's cheeks, Rachel steeled herself. Her only child was approaching meltdown, but she had to keep herself together for both of them. This was hard for her, too. Different, but just as maddening.

Rachel saw her husband in Cassie's big brown eyes, in her height, in the tiny dimple she had when she smiled. She never got to see that dimple these days. So what if Cassie needed to text her dad? Rachel felt herself caving, even though she knew it wasn't healthy. Even the therapist had said so.

Then again, Dr. Gillen was long gone, along with the extra funds to afford him. He wasn't there to see how Cassie changed when she talked to her dad, how she morphed back into the carefree, loving, spunky kid she deserved to be. Even if it was only for a few minutes.

"Please, Mom," Cassie whispered again. Outside, the city noises seemed to fall away, leaving a quiet, a peace Rachel hadn't heard in … well, in six months.

"OK," Rachel relented. "For now."

Rachel wasn't even out the door before she heard the blips and pops of Cassie's keyboard. A car honked outside, and the subway vibrated under her feet, even up here on the tenth floor.

Ping. Whatever Cassie had texted, she'd gotten a response.

It was all Rachel could do not to grab the phone from her daughter's hands to see what Harlon had written. She gripped the doorknob, her knuckles white, and shut it behind her. In the dark hallway she closed her eyes and counted to ten.

Of course, she reminded herself, padding back into the

kitchen-slash-office-slash-dining room, it wasn't Harlon. Not really.

It couldn't be Harlon, because they'd buried him six months ago.

10010200101

Cassie made a face at herself in the bathroom mirror, still foggy from her shower. In the old days, she would do her hair, sweep on some mascara. But these were new days. She pulled her hair into another topknot and, doubling down, even decided to forgo her trademark berry-red lipstick. Who was she trying to impress anyway? The kids at her new school? Hard pass. They wouldn't give a damn about her, so why not return the favor?

The one thing she refused to compromise on, though, was her bracelet. She would wear it today as she wore it every day. It was a simple gold chain with ten colored stones on it. Not even real gems — just cheap knock-offs. But her dad had given it to her, so she adored it.

When she burst into the kitchen to grab breakfast, she stopped short at the look on Rachel's face. "What?" she snapped. Her hands flew to her lips, to her hair. Maybe she looked *really* bad, even for her.

Her mom's mouth had shrunk to a shriveled pucker, so tightly was she pursing her lips. Cassie realized for the first time how tired her mom looked, how the lines around her eyes and mouth had deepened. She was even more pale than usual, her skin almost translucent. Rachel shook her head tersely, fatigue and anger radiating from her in nearly visible waves.

"What, Mom?" Annoyance was overtaken by a jolt of worry then; she had a sudden flashback to that unspeakable day six months ago. Was Rachel about to say something else that would make Cassie's life explode into pieces again? She wouldn't be able to take that.

It's about your father. It's about —

But there was nothing left to explode, Cassie reminded herself. Nothing left to be taken from her. Rachel could say anything, and no matter how bad it was, it wouldn't make a difference. Things were already rock bottom for Cassie: Dad gone. Shitty new apartment. No doubt a shitty new school. No friends. And of course, nothing to wear, just to add insult to a festering pile of injuries.

When Rachel finally spoke, her voice was strained, like she was struggling to be heard through a wall. "What. Is. This."

Rachel spun her tablet around on the table, showing a video to Cassie. It took Cassie a few confusing seconds to understand why Rachel was so pissed.

Someone had recorded the Hive Mob yesterday. And there, clear as the blue sky overhead, was Cassie. Her height and pitch-black hair drew the camera to her again and again as it panned over the crowd, shouts and chants drowning out whatever Rachel was saying now.

The sick feeling started to bubble in Cassie's throat again, the same one that made her turn and run yesterday. Only this time she held it down, forcing it back into the pit of darkness she carried around with her these days.

As she watched the video, which was trending online, she was captivated. Watching yourself on-screen when you don't know you're being filmed is a total trip — though of course, everyone was filmed everywhere these days. It was like she was watching a twin she didn't know she had. As the video played, Cassie could see it in her eyes: the weakness. The fear. If she had been stronger, she would have stayed. If the perpetrator hadn't reminded her of her dad, well … the video wouldn't be showing her turning her back and running away. Like a child.

She wouldn't make that mistake again.

"Do you hear me, Cass?" Rachel flipped off the tablet. The juxtaposition of the screams of the video and the sudden silence of the kitchen made Cassie feel underwater, out of sorts. "What did we talk about? You are not to participate in this garbage!"

"Garbage?" Cassie shook her head. Only someone who hadn't felt the goose bumps on her arms from the energy of a Hive could call it garbage. And her mom, who barely knew how to operate her email, definitely didn't get it. "Mom, this is the way the world works. Don't you care about progress? About justice?"

"This isn't justice!" Rachel slammed her palm on the table so hard that her coffee cup jiggled and threatened to capsize. "Justice isn't hunting down some miserable guy who was venting about the hand life dealt him and —"

"This *is* justice now!" Cassie jabbed a pointed finger toward the window. "This is how we do things now!"

"Other countries don't do this," Rachel pleaded.

"That doesn't make it wrong," Cassie snapped.

"Or right!" Rachel shot back.

"Are we really going to have this fight again?" Cassie rolled her eyes. "Our greatest hits, right? Let me know if you forget your lines."

As soon as Rachel's skin bloomed into that particular shade of purple that it turned whenever she lost her temper with her only child, Cassie tuned her out. It was like someone muted the room; Rachel's voice just became background noise, blending in to the traffic and sounds of people outside. They'd been having this particular argument forever, it seemed.

Cassie could barely remember what it was like before Hive Justice. Her dad used to tell her about the days when someone's name trending on Twitter usually meant they had died or, best case, had dropped an unannounced album. But slowly, the online behaviors that were and were not acceptable began to change.

"People act mean when you give them the permission to," Harlon used to say. Any slight that someone shared, perceived or genuine, became fodder for vicious threats, harassment, doxxing. Send a mean tweet to an ex? Your name, your address, even your grade point average were almost immediately uncovered and broadcast to the world, potentially turning hundreds of millions of users against you. And it was all fair game. Cassie remembered a neighbor close to their old house, a sweet old woman who liked to spend most of her time gardening. She'd been the first person Cassie had known to be virtually shunned after she posted a photograph making light of some bad landscaping she'd seen in the neighborhood. Her photo went viral, and soon the internet hated her. She was a bully, a bitch. Her sharp tongue was a "microaggression cannon," a danger to society. Eventually, she'd had to sell her house after groups of angry people kept showing up unannounced and pulling the flowers out of her garden, leaving a graveyard of colors on the street. Cassie didn't know where the woman lived now. But she was sure she didn't make fun of people anymore, wherever she was.

So that's what it was like in the beginning: slowly, people online became the judge and jury for all "uncivilized" online behaviors. This condemnatory mass of the social media majority became known as the Hive, responsible for identifying and punishing whatever actions were deemed socially unacceptable.

With frightening speed, the Hive became known for its outright vigilante violence. With the national social media engagement rate at nearly 99 percent, anyone who was believed to have done something wrong was hunted down by angry crowds that meted out "justice," as the internet deemed it.

At first, the Hive was considered the price you paid for living in a free and open society, the way so many people used to treat mass shootings.

Then came the riots. After a series of them in several cities, the government was forced to catch up and enact legislation to control them the best they could. But the Hive was decentralized. There were no leaders. There were no plans to disrupt. It just *was.*

"It was us," Harlon had said to Cassie. "We met the Hive and it was us." And then he'd laughed in that way that told her he'd just made a reference to something old, something she'd have to look up if she ever wanted to understand it.

It was too late to take away their power — the Hive was too big by then — but it could be directed. Channeled. With the help of all the big technology companies running the internet, the government set up new algorithms to legislate the management of the Hive's justice system. A new, mandatory social media platform — BLINQ, available only to U.S. citizens — came into being, aggregating content from all the other platforms, making it easier to see a person's whole social profile in one place. You could still Like or Dislike a person's activity, just as before … but now you could also Condemn. And once a user's Condemns hit a certain threshold, weighted by things like speed of virality and past social media content, they were officially sanctioned.

Which meant actual consequences.

In the analog world, where things were physical not digital, the courts still played their role. Crimes — robberies and embezzlements and assaults — were still all cops and lawyers and that antiquated crap. But everyone finally realized that the only way to police the internet was *with* and *through* the internet. For years, they'd tried applying the old analog tools to the digital frontier. It was a losing battle, as anyone who knew anything about the internet could have guessed. Now, people were fully accountable for their online behavior … and faced real-world consequences.

And, as Cassie repeated to Rachel whenever she went on one of her anti-Hive crusades, things were better now. People were more careful online, more responsible. How could that be wrong, no matter how much her mother bitched about it?

"I'm late for school," Cassie said airily, right in the middle of her mother's diatribe. "One of us should probably care."

*

Rachel hated yelling. And she didn't yell, usually. But Cassie getting involved in Hive Justice ... well, that was guaranteed to nuke her self-control, not to mention trigger a migraine. Had Cassie been listening at all? It was hard to tell. Cassie had mastered her facial expressions in such a way that Rachel couldn't decipher her feelings. "Perfect Teenage Apathy Affect," Harlon had called it.

Harlon. Jesus, Harlon. The part of her that she still allowed to dream and fantasize believed that if he hadn't died, none of this would be happening.

Cassie was right about one thing.

Rachel's eyes fell on the clock on the stove. "Shi — crap!" She tried not to swear in front of Cassie; she had a beautifully naive theory that her daughter would start modeling her mother's behavior one of these days. "We're going to be late!"

"Yep," Cassie said mildly. So maybe she *was* listening? Rachel shook her head. It didn't matter. It was a big day for both of them: Cassie was starting her senior year at Westfield High School, and Rachel was starting her new professorship at Microsoft/Buzzfeed University. Maybe, she thought as she threw a granola bar and an apple into her briefcase, they should celebrate tonight. Maybe she'd order Thai. It was a splurge, but it was also Cassie's favorite.

Preparing for this new job had distracted Rachel from Harlon's death, and for that she was grateful. But she was also terrified, somewhere deep down inside of her, in a place she couldn't let Cassie — or anyone — see. As a part-time professor at the local community college in their old neighborhood, Rachel taught a few classics courses each semester, leaving plenty of time to join the parent-teacher association at Cassie's school and to attend most of her soccer games and math meets. Not that Cassie particularly cared, Rachel remembered; no matter how many times she'd sat in the bleachers to cheer Cassie on, Cassie had been disappointed if Harlon wasn't there, too.

But Harlon had been a computer engineer at some of the biggest technology companies in the world and at some of the smallest but most influential; his frequent work travel had been a thorn in their marriage. After his death, she'd discovered that they were in fairly deep financial trouble in spite of his constant work, thanks to some bad investments and Harlon's expensive technology hobbies. He had done a fantastic job keeping it a secret from her. Sometimes, it made her weep with regret, quietly, when Cassie was asleep. Other times, usually in the harsh light of day, it made her want to throw things. Why hadn't Harlon prepared her? Why had he been so secretive for so long?

Rachel had had no choice but to sell their house, pay off their debts and find a smaller (OK, *significantly* smaller) place in the city, where she could find a better-paying job. Even she had been surprised when MS/BFU contacted her for an interview. The university was a tiny, private one that had a well-deserved reputation for having a student body that descended from the wealthiest of the wealthy. Its students' parents were founders and CEOs of luxury companies and technology firms, investment bankers and entrepreneurs, and oil and gas tycoons. While no student these days was clamoring for a classics education, their parents — the ones footing the bill — still thought it necessary. How she was supposed to reach kids like that, she had no idea.

Cassie stood at the front door, tapping her foot. She raised her eyebrows in that bored, testing way when Rachel froze at the sight of her. Rachel couldn't help it. She was suddenly struck by how grown-up her daughter was, with her height and her attitude, with the way her eyes seemed to have millions of stories to tell. Grown-up, Rachel noticed, but also damaged.

*

Outside, two men — it was always two men — waiting in an unmarked black sedan sipped the remnants of their coffee, the loose grinds sticking to the white paper cups in polka-dot patterns that could've been read like tea leaves. They'd been parked long enough that the coffee was nearing just that temperature that made you grit your teeth while you choked it down, that made you question why anyone drank coffee at all.

They'd been there since the sun came up. It was the first day of school for both Rachel and Cassie McKinney, and they weren't yet sure what their weekday schedules would entail. The top brass had demanded they make an early go of it. So here they were, slumped in well-worn seats.

Finally, there was movement.

Man One tapped the shoe of Man Two, who had crossed his long legs so that they imposed on Man One's space. Both men sat up, but coolly, like they'd done this a million times before.

They had, of course.

"Targets spotted," Man One murmured into his headset. He awaited further instructions. They had only one car, and the big brass would need to direct them on which target to follow.

The directive, when it finally came a few seconds later, was clear.

"Roger," Man One said, nodding curtly. He waited until the targets had reached the end of the block, and then he started the car.

In the city's morning bustle, no one noticed.

10010300101

Cassie stomped across the scuffed marble floors of Westfield High. Her mom had tried to join her for new student registration in the administration office, the thought of which was so mortifying that Cassie felt she might actually keel over and die. But she'd managed to divert Rachel's attention to her own first day, on her own need to get going. So now Cassie was alone. She preferred it that way.

"Excuse me," she said to the only person behind the large counter in the office.

A harried woman, juggling a phone on one ear and a tablet in one hand, held up her remaining hand. "Be right with you — take a seat!" she blurted.

Cassie sat in one of the folding chairs lining the wall and reluctantly grabbed her phone. All the avoiding she'd been doing this summer, including pushing away thoughts of starting a new school her senior year, was staring her in the face. Now that she was actually here, now that this was truly happening, maybe it was time to see what Westfield High had in store for her.

She scrolled through BLINQ for any mentions of the school. It was all the usual stuff: kids talking about their teachers, about what they were going to wear, about who had broken into the school over the summer and was now expelled. There were a couple of pretty active hashtags, like #HowTheWestfield-WasWon (gossip about its athletes and the people hooking up with the athletes) and #EastOfWestfield (trash talk about the students at Westfield's rival high school, Huerta High). She had just started to unthread a complicated discussion between dozens of people about the school's dress code on #WhoWoreIt-Westfield when a BLINQ notification interrupted her, pinging in her ear.

Hive Alert! Her notification sounded. *#DumpSkylar!*

Cassie read through the hundreds of BLINQs linked to the Hive Alert. A funny little flutter had started in her stomach. She licked her dry lips and glanced up at the office administrator. Had she forgotten her? The multitasking woman who'd told her to wait was still at it, and was now frantically pounding at a laptop. For the first time Cassie noticed that she didn't have any earbuds in — weird, since most people wore them during their waking hours. Some people even slept in them.

Her own earbud pinged again. *Hive Alert! WHS Courtyard in five minutes. #DumpSkylar!*

"Hon!" The multitasker waved to Cassie. "Thanks for waiting. How can I help?"

"Hi," Cassie said, pocketing her phone and approaching the desk. "I'm new. It's my first day, I mean."

"It's everyone's first day, darlin'," the woman said, tapping on her tablet. "Last name?"

"McKinney."

"Let's see … OK, Cassie, welcome. Here comes your schedule, your locker information, a link to the map of the school —" She tapped a few more times and Cassie felt her phone vibrate with the information. "And — oh! Great. You've been assigned a buddy. She should be here any moment."

"A buddy?" Cassie's stomach kicked. A buddy was exactly what she didn't need. "Is that really necessary?"

The woman paused and peered at Cassie. "Well, do *you* know where your homeroom is?"

"No, but I can check," Cassie started to say.

The woman shook her head. "Every new student gets a buddy. Now have a fantastic day!" Somewhere in the back office a phone rang, and the woman bustled toward it.

Cassie slumped. Would anyone notice if she sneaked out without her buddy?

"Eff your buddy system," Cassie said aloud as soon as she was safely down the hall. She ducked into a little nook with a water fountain to check out the #DumpSkylar feed for a few minutes before finding her homeroom. After all, no one would miss her.

It was a little unclear what Skylar had done, but Westfield kids were *intense* about Hive Justice if their BLINQs were any indication. It was refreshing, Cassie realized, to see that other kids were feeling the same drive to destroy, to tear things down and right the world's wrongs, that she felt all the damn time. Maybe she'd find the courtyard, redeem herself from yesterday's weak performance. Was that too much to ask?

"Cassie!" A wall of blond hair appeared, a hand jutting out from her midsection and grazing dangerously close to Cassie's. At the threat of unexpected physical contact, Cassie took an automatic step back, hitting her hip on the corner of a drinking fountain. She gasped as the blond creature in front of her came into focus.

The girl chuckled and dropped her hand. "Not a handshaker, eh? No prob. I'm Sarah Stieglitz, your buddy."

Cassie stared. This was her buddy? Oh, come *on.* How had she found her? That flicker of anger flared up again. She didn't want to be rude — oh, wait. Actually, she didn't care much about being rude.

Whoever assigned buddies had made a poor match. Sarah was her polar opposite: short where Cassie was long, blond where Cassie was black, white where Cassie was brown, smiling where Cassie was ... well, not. Definitively, absolutely *not.*

Sarah was talking, but Cassie wasn't listening and cut her off midsentence. "Thanks, but I don't really need a buddy — which is why I left without you," she added pointedly.

She tried to scoot around Sarah, already tapping on her phone to pull up the map of the school.

"Cassie! Wait! I can help you!"

Cassie groaned and looked up at the ceiling. Her eyes landed on the blinking green light of the Zi Technologies IndoorWatch Camera mounted there, and she had a dawning realization that she'd been a fool to think she could escape from her buddy. Or anyone, for that matter. It was easy to forget there were cameras everywhere, recording all the time, hidden in plain sight. Even in schools.

Seizing the opportunity Cassie's pause had given her, Sarah dashed over. "Listen, I get that it probably sucks to transfer schools as a senior. I would hate it myself. But I've been assigned to escort you — it's this thing we do in student council — so can you at least let me show you around a bit? This way I don't get called out for letting the new kid get lost or something."

Cassie exhaled a groan. "I really don't need —"

"Well, obviously you don't. But here we are."

Cassie shifted her hips, eyeing the long corridor ahead of her. She had no idea where it led. The map posted on the school's website was for crap.

"I promise I'm normal," Sarah added. "I'm not going to murder you or anything."

Cassie held up her hand. "Fine. I give."

A small grin slowly took over Sarah's face. "Oh, good," she said lightly. "Surrender. Just like a good little victim."

Cassie snorted. This girl was weird. Had Cassie actually been in the market for friends, she'd possibly put Sarah on the list.

Friends, no. A quick guide? Well, OK.

Westfield seemed like every other high school. With a pang she quickly brushed away, Cassie thought about her old school, her old friends. Six months ago, after what happened to her dad, Cassie had buried her grief and had an epiphany: friendships, or relationships of any kind, weren't worth the hassle. Those old friends had reached out — some of them every day for weeks and weeks — but Cassie eventually blocked all their numbers, even those of her two best friends, Adena and Max. It wasn't until now, with Sarah giving her the lay of the land at Westfield and chatting away as though they were going to be great friends, that Cassie began to wonder if she'd underestimated how hard it would be to go through senior year without them. Or with anyone.

One year, she told herself as Sarah diverted them from what looked like the gym doors and made a sharp left down a long hallway. All she had to do was survive one year at WHS. No sense trying to put down any roots when she was going to be transplanted in ten months.

"The labs are this way, and over there is the theater. What do you do, Cassie?"

"What do I do?"

"Art? Acting? Tennis? Code? What's your thing?"

"Oh." In her old school ... *before* ... that had been easy to answer. She was Harlon McKinney's daughter, so she hacked. But now? "Nothing, really."

"Well, there's so much to do here, if you're into that. Here's the library, and there's the auditorium," Sarah said, pointing. "And there's the media center over there, right past the courtyard."

The courtyard. Where dozens and dozens of kids were gathered, some of them shouting and cheering. The Hive Mob. It was time to #DumpSkylar.

"Cassie?" Sarah finally noticed that she'd stopped, whirled around and trotted back. "Come on, we — oh."

"There's a Hive Mob," Cassie said. She was staring at the crowd. The sound of it, a steady thrum of voices and feet stomping, filled the hallway. Flashes of the previous day's Hive Mob danced in her memory, leaving her unsteady and a little unsure about whether what was happening in front of her was real or just a flashback.

"Yep. But the bell's gonna ring soon, so we should go."

Cassie nodded toward the crowd, which had filled the courtyard, an open-air space with a few trees, a smattering of grass and some benches.

"What about them? They'll all be late, right?"

Sarah shrugged. "Basically, any student can be excused at any time to go participate in any Hive Mob that involves a Westfield student. So even if it's during exams" — Sarah made a face — "we're free to go."

Cassie raised her eyebrows. Impressive. Her old school had pretty strict anti-Hive rules. The thought of being able to join one no matter when or where it was happening … and her mom wouldn't even know …

"But it's a joke," Sarah added. "Only the popular people ever trend positive. Each week, a certain crowd decides who will be the targets, and everyone just follows along. It's not even real justice. It's just —"

The bell rang.

"Cassie," Sarah warned. But Cassie's mind was already set.

"See ya, buddy," she said, and rushed toward the courtyard, her skin feeling like fire.

*

The courtyard teemed with everyone at Westfield, it appeared, except for Skylar himself. (Well, and Sarah.) They were chattering, checking their phones, the sound of BLINQs forming a symphony Cassie found herself craving. The atmosphere was almost festive.

If Cassie knew anything about high school, it was this: it's a battleground. She could see immediately which groups were in charge. The beautiful people, as they'd been called at her old school, were the most obvious to spot: the sunlight bounced off their shiny hair, their contoured faces. Then there were the techies, the sect Cassie most closely fit in with at her old school, who tended to congregate on the edges. They had a confidence that rivaled the beautiful people's, but they seemed more approachable. Cassie knew from experience, though, that if you did approach the techies, it had best be with something smart to say.

There were the badasses and the middlemen and the artists and the athletes, though as the world had grown more digital many of those groups had been diluted, weakened over time. Not many people cared these days if you could throw a touchdown pass or paint a picture, unless you also knew how to translate your winning moments into viral gifs. The more important question was, could you kick off a trending topic? Did you have the skills to doxx?

What you looked like mattered — it had always mattered and always would matter. What you could *do* mattered only a little less, and had changed dramatically, even in Cassie's lifetime.

Cassie moved around the perimeter of the courtyard and looked up toward the second floor of the school. Even the hallways were full, serving as an overflow space for the Hive Mob. This was gonna be good. She felt that charge again, the same one from yesterday, like her fingertips were buzzing. The heavy rage inside her rose up, as eager to be expended as Cassie was to be rid of it.

Cassie nudged a girl with sleek black hair and retro cat's eye glasses who didn't look exactly friendly but at least not hostile. "So what did Skylar do?"

Glasses Girl looked her up and down. Finding Cassie's black jeans and rumpled denim shirt acceptable, she broke into a grin and revealed the whole story.

With every word, Cassie felt herself start to deflate.

It turned out that Skylar, a junior, had been dumped by his girlfriend of four years, Izzy. As payback, Skylar had tried to start a vicious campaign to turn people against Izzy by sharing "secrets" about her — things she'd said to Skylar about her friends and family, about school, about him. Tried, but failed. People quickly caught on to what Skylar was doing and turned the tables on him, calling him a misogynist, an abuser. The backlash was brutal. #DumpSkylar was trending locally within hours of his failed attempt.

It couldn't be the whole story, Cassie knew. Because if #DumpSkylar was just about a heartbroken guy sharing low-level secrets from his ex-girlfriend … well, Cassie would need to find something to kick. Hard.

She kept her voice steady. "So what's the Hive verdict? Level 1? Level 2?" She could check her phone or tap her earbud for the answer, but Glasses Girl looked like she wanted to share.

There were five Levels of Hive Justice, each one denoting the severity of the crime and the spectrum of possible punishments. Most offenses trended locally only and were Level 1. Within each Level was a Range, which determined how long the Hive had to enact its justice. At Range 1, you only had a day, so you'd better act fast. The Ranges grew exponentially, and by the time you got to Range 5, the Hive had an entire year to get to you. Such a time span was theoretically possible for any Level, but in practice the algorithm that determined such things rarely punished a meager Level 1 crime with anything greater than Range 2. At higher Levels, your chance of higher Ranges increased, as did the severity options for punishments the Hive could vote on.

Glasses Girl actually squealed. "Level 1! Range 1, so we gotta do it today. We get to dump garbage all over him!"

Cassie closed her eyes and breathed deeply. Sure enough, her earbud pinged and told her *It's #garbagedump time!* There had to be more. "And then what?"

When she opened her eyes again, Glasses Girl was narrowing hers. "What do you mean? *That's* his punishment. It's been voted on. It's a good punishment because he tried to dump garbage about Izzy. Get it?"

Sensing the rise in tension, a few girls quickly appeared behind Glasses Girl, fixing Cassie with blank stares, the kind she'd perfected herself the day she turned thirteen.

"Everyone's out here waiting to throw garbage on someone who got dumped and acted out?" Cassie shook her head, exasperated. There was real shit happening in the world, and Westfield High wanted to waste time on stuff that didn't matter?

Maybe if she knew Skylar and Izzy, it would have mattered, but Cassie found the cold satisfaction of Hive Justice boiling into hot anger again. This was useless to her. It was kid stuff.

"This is what the Hive agreed to." Glasses Girl crossed her arms across her chest defensively, as though Cassie had insulted her mother.

"This is ridiculous," Cassie fumed. "Are you really wasting

your time with this crap? Are you kidding me?" Something from a conversation with her dad bubbled up in her memory just then: *Punch up, Cass. Never down.* "I'm not gonna spend my time on some douche who's sad his girlfriend broke up with him."

Glasses Girl gasped. One of the other girls — tall, with red hair — cocked her head, suddenly showing interest. "New girl, am I right?"

Cassie shrugged. She'd already said more than she should have.

"Too good to join a Hive Mob?" the redhead taunted lightly.

"A shitty one like this? I'm just saying, I like to spend my time on stuff that changes things. I was in a mob yesterday for a guy who ruined his family's lives. That one mattered. My dad always said, 'Punch up, not down.'"

The redhead laughed. "Who the hell is your father and why should I care?"

Cassie felt her cheeks burn. She was the daughter of a tech god, but she'd never in her life traded on Harlon's name or history. She wasn't about to start now.

"Never mind. I'm just saying — the whole point of the Hive is justice. Justice is for big things, not a lovers' quarrel."

"General consensus is that all Hive Justice is important," the redhead said coolly. She pushed some of the other girls aside and joined Glasses Girl in front of Cassie. From the way the other girls let her, Cassie could tell she was one of the beautiful people. "Because, of course, by definition it's the will of the people. It's an elitist stance to say that any one crime is more or less important than any other. That's for the Hive to decide, not the individual."

"Exactly, Rowan," Glasses Girl said, and the remaining girls nodded, crossing their arms.

"Sometimes people are wrong," Cassie countered. She could hear Harlon in her ear, everything he'd said over the years about Hive Justice. How it started out as a way to save the internet, and with it, the world. How it was a valid path people could use to take power back from the government, from the tech companies. How it had disrupted the world's long-held views of justice. Her dad, she remembered, a little smile appearing on her lips, was all about disrupting. She gestured around at the crowd. "If you Hive Mob over petty crap like this, you're making a joke out of the whole thing."

The redhead, Rowan, raised her eyebrows. "What an … interesting perspective."

"What's your name?" Glasses Girl asked.

"Why, so you can start a social campaign against me for thinking this particular mob is amateur hour?" Cassie snapped.

Rowan smirked. "Just more petty crap, right?"

Before Cassie could respond, Rowan and her friends began to filter away, joining the crowd.

Cassie was glad to see them go. She sought out empty space to find a path out of the courtyard and back to the hallway. She'd long since lost interest in this excuse for a Hive Mob. She'd have to find a release for her fury elsewhere.

As she edged in between the spaces, finally reaching a part of the hallway that wasn't packed, she heard a roar go up behind her. Skylar had arrived. For a moment, she considered staying.

But then, a flicker. Up ahead, on top of a row of lockers, something was perched. Moving. Cassie caught it out of the corner of her eye, the kind of movement that could be nothing, or could be everything.

She took a step forward, debating. She wasn't sure which way to go to get to her class (where was her "buddy" when she really needed her?), but the long stretch in front of her felt like the obvious direction. So she continued on, approaching the flicker, which had stilled.

And then a boy landed, hard, on the floor in front of Cassie.

His sneakers made a startling squeak. His black jacket puffed up behind him like a balloon before perfectly settling down. Under it he wore a black T-shirt that said CODE IS POETRY in white monospaced letters. Cassie's fists curled in again; it was fight or flight time, and her body had already decided to stay and fight.

"Sorry," the boy said, straightening, settling his long limbs. "I didn't see you there."

Right. Someone hadn't seen all five feet ten inches of her walking alone in an empty hallway.

"Yes, I'm often told I'm invisible," she said.

He fixed his gaze on Cassie. His eyes were green, serious. "I don't think that's true."

He looked at her for so long that she went still. Something about his eyes, his leather jacket, the whole damn thing made her anger cool. An ice cube melting into hot soup.

And then he smiled. Cassie doubted he'd even admit that, since it was just the tiniest curling up of the lip. But she saw it. And it made her flush. Her mouth went dry. She regretted not putting on lipstick.

But most importantly, she realized this was the longest

eye contact she'd had in months. No one looked at each other anymore like that; most of their interactions were digital.

"Watch where you're going next time," she snapped, stepping around him. She strode down the hall, her boots echoing.

*

Eventually, she found her first-period class. And her second, third and fourth, a forgettable mix of annoying teachers and ringing bells and gossip about Skylar, who was apparently walking around Westfield with food scraps and rusted cans and empty bottles dangling from his neck. Finally, lunch came.

As Cassie shoved her textbook into her backpack, Sarah, who was in the same fourth-period advanced calculus class, approached her.

"Whoa!" She threw her hands up in mock surrender. "Quadratic polynomials really piss you off!"

"It's not that," Cassie fumed. "It's that I've already taken advanced calc. But it's the highest math class here, so my mom's making me retake it so I don't" — she made air quotes — "lose my skills."

"Nightmare!" Sarah said. "What does your dad say about it?"

Cassie concentrated on hoisting her already-too-heavy bag onto her shoulders. It was the perfect way to avoid meeting Sarah's eyes and thereby avoid the question, though she was sure a spark of anger flickered visibly across her face. If Cassie *had* been on her way to being friends with Sarah, that comment alone would have made her reconsider.

As it stood, weeks ago she'd decided — almost subconsciously, deep inside the bones that still ached at the memory of her old life — that relationships, even the special ones, weren't really worth it in the end. People weren't worth what it cost to lose them.

"Where's the caf?" Cassie changed the subject, leading the way into a crowded corridor. Sarah pointed in the opposite direction from where Cassie was headed.

"Over here, Magellan. By the way, I told my friends to save an extra seat for you, if you're up for eating with us?"

Cassie shrugged; it's not like she had anyone else to sit with. She and Sarah cruised past the senior wing and the library, through furtive hookups and selfie poses and locker slams. In the caf — big and crowded and smelling of day-old sandwiches, even though that should've been impossible — Sarah showed Cassie the lunch options and stuck close by as Cassie grabbed an apple and a bag of pretzels.

"I thought we were eating with your friends?" Cassie wondered as Sarah led her to an empty table.

"Hmmm," Sarah said, rearranging the lettuce and pickle on her sandwich. "Maybe they got stuck in line. Doesn't matter."

Cassie frowned and sucked on a pretzel. For the next few minutes, Sarah asked her a steady stream of questions that Cassie deflected. No one needed to know the reason they'd moved here, Cassie decided, and Sarah was approaching dangerous territory, the kind of stuff only friends would ask. Cassie's gratitude for her "buddy" was wearing off. And there hadn't been much of it to begin with.

It disappeared entirely at Sarah's next line of questions.

"What's your family like?" she asked between bites. Cassie's fingers curled up, her hands becoming fists.

"Nothing special," Cassie said coldly, her limbs tightening.

"Oh, come on," Sarah continued, chuckling. "Brothers, sisters?"

Cassie glared. Sarah met her eyes, her expression earnest.

"This is a weird conversation." Cassie dropped her empty pretzel bag and glugged half her water. "Hey, what happened to your friends?"

Sarah shrugged. "It's not weird to talk about families. It's, like, the most important thing to talk about, actually. Don't you think?"

Cassie didn't answer. She couldn't — her tongue had suddenly grown too thick for her mouth. The back of her neck grew damp. She picked up her apple, her hands looking for something to do that didn't involve hitting the person across the table.

"I think someone's family reveals a lot about them … like me, for instance." Sarah leaned forward, her sandwich forgotten, and trained her eyes on Cassie. "I lost my mom when I was a sophomore. It really changed me."

Cassie froze, her apple midair. Sarah reached out and patted Cassie's arm.

"There's this amazing club here at Westfield. Well, not even a club. Just a group. It's a bunch of us who've experienced trauma in some way. I think we could really help you, Cassie."

There was a piece of apple lodged in Cassie's throat, blocking her airway. Her heartbeat throbbed in her ears. "Wh-what did you just fucking say?"

"No, it's OK, I swear!" Sarah straightened up. "The support group is literally life changing. And it's all confidential — what happens in group, stays in group. So you don't have to worry about that."

“I d-don’t have to worry …” Cassie stuttered, willing the stuck bit of apple to move out of the way or else be burned in the line of fire that was threatening to explode from her lungs. “What exactly do you think you know about me?”

“Cassie,” Sarah said softly. Her eyes darted around, checking to see if Cassie’s heat had been picked up by anyone around them. “Listen, I get it. I was angry for a long time. I was just like you.”

Cassie threw her apple onto Sarah’s tray. It landed hard, shooting up crumbs of the chips she’d left behind. Sarah leaped back, looking shocked.

“Who. Fucking. Told. You,” Cassie spat, her voice barely contained.

Sarah’s eyes widened, but then she took a deep breath, nodded once and visibly relaxed. “Westfield’s registration form asks if the incoming student has any extenuating circumstances the school should know about. Your mom said you’re grieving the sudden loss of your dad. And since I’m in the trauma group, and I lost my mom, I was assigned to be your buddy. I’m here to help.”

Cassie felt like someone had sliced open her skin and poured in a scalding liquid. Her mother’s name was a curse. Once again, Rachel had to go and fuck up her life. She couldn’t even let Cassie have a fresh start.

Sarah, oblivious, continued. “There’s no one else in group who’s lost a parent … someone lost a sister to suicide, and then a bunch of people have family members who are alive but are facing addiction problems, and then of course there’s a couple of kids dealing with their own PTSD. But until now, I was the only one who lost a parent.” She gave Cassie a sad smile. “I’ve been waiting for someone like you for years.”

For years? Cassie couldn't see anything around her — not the caf, not the shining sky outside, not even her own hands in front of her. "What you just said is supremely insane."

Sarah cocked her head and nodded thoughtfully. "This rage you're experiencing? It's totally normal. It's what you're *supposed* to feel."

Cassie knew from Dr. Gillen that anger was one of the stages of grief. She didn't need Sarah — little white Sarah, blond and well-meaning but so completely out of her depth — to explain it to her. Cassie felt the heat, the anger, rise from her limbs.

Sarah continued. "I told my friends to give us some space today, for a few minutes at least, so I could talk to you privately about group. But if you don't want to talk about it right now, we can do it later. I'll text them now, tell them we're ready for them."

Cassie stood up. Anger existed for a reason, she realized: it felt *good.* It was better than sadness, smarter than denial.

"I'm sorry you lost your mom." Cassie's voice, low and thick, somehow managed to attract the attention of the people sitting around them, who were watching, waiting, phones out. Ready to BLINQ or hashtag whatever happened next. "But if you think I'm interested in bonding over a dead parent, you can fuck right off."

Sarah blinked. She opened her mouth but Cassie didn't stay to hear the words that came out of it next.

She bolted.

As she tried to storm through the caf, she couldn't go very fast or very far. Tables and chairs and people blocked her at every turn. Her breathing was heavy in her ears. She glanced at the clock on the wall. Lunch wasn't over for another fifteen minutes, and no one was allowed to leave the caf.

Which was just as well, she thought, dropping into the first empty seat she could find, as far from Sarah as possible. Without her buddy, she had no clue how to get to any other place in the building.

Cassie fumbled for her phone, desperate to distract herself from her anger. It wasn't until she heard someone clear their throat that she realized the table wasn't empty. She looked up.

There was Rowan, her eyes fixed on Cassie, wearing an incredulous expression. With her were a clutch of girls Cassie recognized from the mob, which included Glasses Girl.

Cassie looked up at the ceiling. "Fuuuuuuuuck," she whispered. Just what she needed — a verbal assault from the cool crowd.

But instead, Rowan chuckled. "Tell me about it."

"Don't worry, I'm leaving," Cassie started to say, but Rowan held up a hand.

"Why? Stay. Curse some more. We're bored."

Cassie eyed each girl, sussing them out. She suddenly felt incredibly exposed, and a hot, fast pang made her wonder what she was even doing here.

"Cassie," Rowan purred, and Cassie knew there were a hundred ways she could have learned her name. She was curious which one Rowan had used but didn't let it show. "Cassie McKinney. I'd actually been hoping you'd join us. Are you as badass as your father?"

For God's sake. Had Westfield texted every student about her dad? Were there banners hanging in the hallways? "You don't know anything about my father," she said, her voice low and tense.

"I know enough," Rowan said. "Enough to be curious about his daughter."

"What do you want?" Cassie spat.

"Sweetheart ..." Rowan reached across the table and patted Cassie's hand. "This is your chance to make some friends. Some important friends. Maybe crack a smile?"

Cassie glanced around. She wasn't imagining it ... everyone in the lunchroom was watching. Watching her. The new girl, who'd plopped herself down at the popular table without an invitation.

She took a breath. Lunch was over in ten minutes. She couldn't change tables *again.* She'd never live it down. And she was running out of tables.

She studied Rowan again. Everyone posed in high school — even Cassie — but Rowan and her friends had taken it to a new level. Every move they made, every shift in posture, every tap on their tablets suggested they belonged on a highly produced reality show: glossy, confident, BLINQ-ready. And the other kids at Westfield were tuned in. Watching. Waiting to be entertained. Or maybe just taking notes on how to be.

Cassie was pretty well known at her old school; that was what happened when Harlon McKinney was your father, and when you'd managed to hack your way around the school's security and grading systems a few times. But no one had looked at her the way Westfield's students were looking at Rowan and her friends. And she'd never preened the way they did. Were these her only options here? To watch or be watched?

"What am I, your new charity case?" she asked, keeping her head down. "Adopt the new girl, build her up, then tear her down for your own amusement?"

Rowan chuckled, followed by the others. "Wow, are you a

pessimist or what? I'm making an effort here. Oh, and this is Madison, Indira and Livvy." Each girl waved, and Indira — the girl with the glasses from the courtyard — offered her plate of fries, as though food could convince Cassie of their harmlessness.

After a thought of the sad apple she'd eaten, she grabbed a handful of them.

"I know what you're thinking," Rowan said brightly. "You're thinking, 'Oh, these are the hot, popular girls and they look down on everyone else and spend their days perfecting the highest form of bitchcraft.'"

Despite herself, Cassie chuckled.

Rowan grinned appreciatively at the reaction. "I won't lie to you. There's a little bit of that. But look — we're just trying to get through all this crap like everyone else. It's high school, not the real world, and there's safety in numbers."

Cassie skipped her eyes around the table. It was a collection of gorgeous specimens, and then there she was — hair in a topknot, nonexistent makeup …

"I'm sure I'll fit right in," she deadpanned.

Rowan giggled. "Hey, look, if you don't want to be ready for your social media moment, then that's your funeral. But …" She pointed at each girl in turn, ending with herself. "Math. Science. History. English. We're missing tech."

"It's tough to Homework Coven the comp sci final when there isn't a tech-head in the group," Madison offered.

Underneath her hot anger, still boiling because of Sarah and Rachel, an understanding began to brew. Cassie put the pieces together. Homework Coven. Rowan's crew was gorgeous and popular, yeah, but that wasn't their goal. The four of them were cruising through high school by lending each other a hand, missing only one subject area.

The one subject Cassie could cover for them.

"It's your call," Rowan said with a shrug. "You can muddle through on your own and actually do all the work —"

"Or you can hang out with us and breeze through," Indira finished.

"We're hot *and* smart," Livvy said with absolutely no trace of ego. Just plain facts. "Deadly combination, right?"

With a snort, Cassie shook her head. She didn't want to admit how tempting the idea was. To coast through this last, miserable year at this miserable new place …

"What's the catch?" she asked.

The four girls all exchanged a look and, of course, deferred to Rowan.

"You're part of the group. You don't embarrass the group. We do everything we can to Trend Positive, so you do, too, if you're with us." Rowan hesitated for a moment. "You don't have to glam it up, but if you don't, you probably won't get onto our social and ride the trend with us."

Cassie didn't give a damn about trending positive or going viral. She just wanted to be left alone. Still … If she had even just the illusion of a posse, that would keep most other people away, right? And while she was an excellent student, she could think of better things to do with her time than, well, *all* of her schoolwork.

"One last thing," Rowan was saying. "We have a pact. If one of us Likes or Dislikes or Condemns something, we *all* do."

Cassie suppressed a bark of laughter. A total of five votes

in any one scenario hardly made a difference, she figured, and Rowan's earnestness was hilarious.

It was like Rowan could read her mind. "When we speak as a group, we have more power than you'd think," she said. "It's about consistency. We get people who want to curry favor with us to vote the same. And when the numbers are all pretty small to begin with ..." She shrugged to communicate the idea of a fait accompli. "Last year, we got three football players kicked off the team for making lewd comments at the cheerleaders."

Cassie shrugged right back. "OK, but ... why put so much effort into something that doesn't matter? You think hashtagging a kid in biology for looking up your skirt really changes anything? Try punching *up*. Maybe go after administrators or the school board or —"

"Disruption," Rowan said, using air quotes.

"Exactly," Cassie said. "If you spend so much time haggling with people on your own level, you never get a chance to get at the people *really* in charge."

"Oh, honey," Rowan said. "That's where you're wrong. Because we're the ones in charge."

"No," Cassie said emphatically. "The system is just set up to make you think that."

"You're taking this all a little too seriously," Indira said.

"It's just high school," Madison added.

"That's my whole point," Cassie said. "It's just high school." She thought of the previous day, of the unhappy husband, and her temper flared again. That guy had humiliated his wife and children. That actually *mattered*, not like these squawking high school spats. "This is a microcosm of society. The way we operate Hive Justice now is how we'll handle it out in the real world, too."

"I promise you, Cassie," Rowan said, again patting Cassie's hand and again making her feel like screaming. "It's just something to pass the time. And the high you get from trending positive? Well … it's worth it. I mean, I see your point. It makes sense. But this is the way the system is set up, and there's no reason not to take advantage of it. As long as you're careful enough — smart enough, especially — to not give an opening to let people do it back to you."

Cassie shook her head so hard that a curl of hair fell out of her topknot. "You're taking this thing that's supposed to be affirmative and empowering and you're just … It's like you're just using it to get out of class. The internet lives forever. Big stuff, sure, go for it. But you're convicting people for stupid things, and it will be with them forever."

Rowan burst out laughing. "Girl, you're so wrong. The internet gets erased every damn night."

One by one, each of Rowan's friends nodded in agreement. Cassie's throat felt swollen, like it couldn't get any words out. Luckily, she didn't have any.

"No one remembers anything from last week, let alone last year," Rowan assured her. "You think Skylar will, what? Be denied a job because of this? Get rejected from colleges?"

Indira snorted, while Livvy threw her head back, her beautiful curls dangling halfway down her back, and yelled, "Imagine a world where that would happen!"

The idea was seductive and easy. And she knew that it was true, to a degree. Her dad had once called the internet "a perpetual motion machine that runs on outrage." Some new offense would captivate Westfield tomorrow — or even by the end of the day — and no one would remember #DumpSkylar.

Well ... except for Skylar.

And except for the BLINQs and posts and pics and gifs, all of them tucked neatly away into searchable databases ...

Rowan smirked at Cassie, and Cassie tried to read deeply into her eyes to see if Rowan really believed what she was claiming. It was hard to tell, though. Rowan's eyes were bright and shining and brimming with a certainty Cassie herself had never possessed.

"We all get a do-over," Rowan said, and Cassie felt herself nodding, even if she still wasn't sure she believed her. "Every day is a new life for each of us."

"As long as you're not galactically stupid," Madison added, and Rowan nodded.

"Right." She popped a cherry tomato in her mouth and grinned. "And *that's* the beauty of the Hive."

*

After lunch, Cassie peeled off from Rowan's group and headed to the girls' bathroom. It was empty, and she slammed the door a little harder than necessary when she stepped into a stall.

The echoing clang and the vibration of the metal around her felt good. She slammed it again, then again, then again. Over and over. The bathroom tiles resounded with the clamor of metal on metal, feeding her anger and her ire, jacking them up higher and higher.

She didn't know who she was angry at. Or why. Was it Rowan

and the others, because they were just barely deep enough that she couldn't dismiss them? Was it herself, for contemplating going along with it and joining their stupid little clique? Was it her mom, for moving her here, for excising her from where she'd been known and comfortable?

Or was it her dad? Because everything eventually came back to him. Because he went away, goddammit.

Cassie rubbed her eyes. Harlon used to tell her to be herself, to *know* herself. He — and, to a degree, Rachel — tried to explain how just being born biracial would sometimes mean that people would disregard the rest of her. That sometimes people wouldn't be able to see beyond the color and into the individual. She had a tall order: she would have to know her history, those who came before, but she would also need to remain steadfast in who she was and what she believed. And she thought she had.

So why did she suddenly feel like a fraud?

She kicked open the door to the stall and stalked out to the sinks. The girl in the mirror stared at her with a rage that was frightening and glorious.

*

Sarah caught up to Cassie at the end of the next period. Apparently being told to fuck off just didn't take. That was OK — Cassie felt the tiniest bit of guilt at blowing up like that.

"Look at you," Sarah said, her voice a mixture of awe and caution. "Day one and you've already managed lunch with Rowan."

"Girl," Cassie hissed, "lay off." It was nicer than fuck off but still got the point across.

"That group isn't going to do you any favors," Sarah warned.

A wave of anger crested inside Cassie, an unconscious backlash to the sympathy, the pity, that was blooming in her stomach at the sight of Sarah. Little, loud Sarah. At first she'd seemed so empathetic, but now Cassie saw the truth — she was just needy, thirsting for acceptance with a mania that bordered on tragic.

Cassie had needed someone, once. *Look at what it did to you. You got greedy in your need for connection, for love. And then you were screwed when that person was gone.*

Not her. Not anymore.

"You need to be around peers," Sarah was saying. "And I mean people who *get* you, who get what you're going through. My group —"

"I don't know, Sarah," Cassie snapped. And then she forced herself to take a deep breath. "I don't know, Sarah," she said again, this time in a calmer tone.

It's not her fault that she's desperate, Cassie reminded herself. *Neither of us asked for this today.*

The old Cassie would have been on Sarah's side, without a doubt. Always protect the underdog. Always use the Harlon McKinney uppercut.

But Rowan, Indira, Madison and Livvy had been right about one thing: this wasn't the real world. This was just high school. More to the point, it was her last year in a place where she owed no one anything at all.

"I'll see what I can do," she lied to Sarah, and as soon as Sarah made her way down the hall, Cassie tapped her earbud. "Text Rowan: I'm in."

10010400101

How many times, Rachel mused, had she considered quitting today?

She slammed her water bottle down on the table at the front of the empty lecture hall. She counted back: at least six distinct times, and she still had one more class to go before her day was done. “Ha!” She barked a laugh out loud. “Six times!”

Soon, the room wouldn’t be empty, though it wouldn’t be full, either. It would likely never be full again. She had never wavered in her commitment to teaching classics, even when it had fallen out of favor as a course of study. But sometime in the past ten years, college administrations, wooed by fancy funders from the technology space, had begun to question the use of teaching the literature and languages and philosophies of ancient cultures; the students didn’t want it, and they were telling their parents, who footed the bills. So far, most of the parents disagreed, and fortunately Latin had seen something of a resurgence, thanks to Lorem, a popular technology that used the supposedly “dead” language to leverage a truly byzantine encryption scheme that was beyond her capacity to understand.

She began every 101 class with the same statement: "History isn't dead! It's very much alive … and it is watching you. Leering at you. Every second, every minute of the day!" While the lecture room awaited its guests — about forty kids, as it turned out MS/BFU was one of the few remaining institutions that made classics mandatory for all students — she rehearsed it again, this time with feeling.

Five minutes later, it looked like all forty students had arrived, and Rachel was waging an invisible war against the hornet's nest that had landed in her stomach. Impulsively, she tossed aside the attendance list and the syllabus. They could wait.

"I know what you're thinking. You're thinking history is more or less bunk, in the words of Henry Ford, that pioneer of American innovation and disruption. But Ford actually meant that history was bunk *to him*. That he personally had little use for it. And I should also point out that Ford was tremendously undereducated, despite his successes.

"History isn't bunk. History is what we are doomed to repeat if we forget it, to paraphrase Santayana, and we do repeat it. Over and over. History is happening all around you, right now. Anytime someone is lambasted in the press without a trial, there are the Romans, feeding victims to the lions for sport. For fun. To remind everyone how strong they need to be under Caesar. There are enemies at the gates, and all members of society must come watch the games to become knowledgeable in the ways of war." Rachel paused, taking a breath, and smiled wearily. "And there's the rub. We like to look back smugly and think how foolish they were, killing each other for sport, but it wasn't merely sport. It was education. Are they the barbarians or are *we*, who kill each other daily in the media and online, with no lesson taken away for all that violence?"

Rachel shook her head in annoyance and continued her speech on autopilot as she thought about the circularity of it all. If only she could really teach the classics the way they deserved to be taught ... maybe then her students would get it, and things in the world would go back to some semblance of normal. But it was too late, she feared. Academics and technology had fused together in ways no one had predicted.

Except Harlon. "I applaud your commitment to the classics, hon," he used to say. "But you're writing yourself a death sentence." How ironic, in retrospect.

An unmistakable *ding*. Rachel paused in her speech again, adrenaline making her chest heave. Her mouth was dry. How long had she been talking? She blinked, squinted. With the way the lecture hall was set up, she couldn't make out any faces in the crowd — it was too dark, and the light circling around her was too bright.

Ding. Ding. Ding. Ding. Ding. Ding. Ding.

Rachel stifled a groan. She could hear people shifting in their seats — how long had she been yapping away? she wondered — as they checked their devices. Even the ones who appeared to be sitting still were no doubt getting feeds through their earbuds. That many notifications at once meant something big was happening, and Rachel knew kids this age were practically powerless to refrain from reading them. She'd seen the behavior up close with Cassie. The Hive was an actual, physical addiction.

She waited a full minute for things to settle down. "Is everyone done now? Let's continue discussing the way —"

A hand shot into the air, and a voice rang out before Rachel could call on the questioner. "But isn't there historical evidence that many in ancient Roman times objected to the lack of concrete law at the time? And from that, can't we deduce that there's always been an undercurrent of rejection from a segment of the population, even if it wasn't codified into law until millennia later?"

Rachel cleared her throat. "You're conflating the notion of *jus non scriptum* — unwritten law, common law — with the lack of codification. At the time —"

"Should we really judge them by *their* standards and not ours?" he interrupted.

Rachel tried to even her breathing. She grabbed the remote control from the desk and pushed a few buttons. The lights changed; suddenly, she could see her students.

For a moment, she wished she couldn't.

"Well," she began, eyes flicking over the crowd to determine the source. He was easy to find — he sat alone, surrounded by empty chairs, in the front row. And he was a total prep, Rachel noticed, wondering if they still called them preps these days. Or was there a new word for that, like there was for almost everything else? He had porcelain-white skin and piercing blue eyes and an eighties-movie-villain cable-knit sweater tied around his shoulders. Rachel knew exactly the kind of student he was: rich, for starters. Entitled. Probably too smart for his own good.

But then he shifted forward in his seat, and the dim lights showed Rachel something that gave her pause: deep red hair, knotted into dreadlocks, tied back in a ponytail that hung past his shoulders.

OK, she thought. *Maybe not a prep.*

The sudden light seemed to hit Pause on their back-and-forth. She decided to forge ahead, pretending he wasn't there. "As I was going to say, there are distinct parallels between the ancient Greeks and our current society. Take the law, for example. In Athens, justice was collectively enforced by society at large. There were no lawyers, no judges in the courts, to which any male citizen could bring a complaint. There were only speeches, and whoever told the most compelling story often won the case."

"Right," the student said almost affably, Rachel realized, which made her more annoyed than it should have. "And as a result, the wealthy found themselves in near-constant danger. The more elite the offender, the more pleasure the courts got in rendering their punishment."

Rachel's jaw dropped. She quickly closed it, covering her surprise with a cough. "That's right. I was just getting to that, Mr. …"

She picked up the attendance sheet, trying to pretend her fingers weren't shaking. She'd never had a student try to take over her lecture like this. "What's your name, please?"

"Red Dread!" Someone guffawed from the side of the room. A few stray hoots followed.

The interrupter shot an unhappy glance to the person who'd yelled "Red Dread," then seemed to remember where he was and turned back to Rachel. "Muller. I'm Bryce Muller."

Rachel stiffened. "Well, Bryce, I'm glad to see you so informed. But perhaps you can allow me to —"

"I just wanted to make sure everyone here gets all the nuances."

"Hashtag mansplaining!" someone shouted from the back row. A wave of laughter rippled down the tiers of seats.

Rachel swallowed a chortle. Who did this guy think he was? "I appreciate your enthusiasm, Mr. Muller. But I promise I'll get to all the necessary nuances in due time ..." Her voice trailed off as a series of collective dings made everyone's eyes, which had been on her, drop to their devices immediately.

For the first time in her life, she was grateful for the culture of distraction.

Whatever was BLINQing at everyone gave Rachel just enough time to reset herself. She got through the rest of class without incident, though also without much eye contact. Even Red Dread remained docile.

"We'll continue this next time," Rachel announced when her watch told her that class was over. The sounds of her students packing up their things and leaving was the most noise they'd made since they arrived. Rachel, packing up her own things, felt a ribbon of nausea ride up her throat. Maybe she wasn't as exciting and as smart a professor as she'd always thought, if students like Bryce thought they needed to deliver her lecture for her. This whole day was a disaster. Her whole *life* was, in fact.

She was well on her way to a pity party when she gave one last look at the empty classroom to make sure the lights were all off.

"Oh!" She jumped, her heart racing. A man — surely not a student, in a sleek black suit and with a graying hairline — was sitting in the back row, tucked into a darkened corner. He nodded at her.

"Who are you?" she demanded. The man unfolded himself

from the seat and stood up, moving like someone who knows his mere presence could intimidate the skin off a snake. A chill ran down Rachel's back. *No. Not this again.*

"I'm just auditing your class, Dr. McKinney." His voice was honey smooth and just as sweet.

"Professor," she corrected, forgetting to wince at the slight. She was ABD — All But Dissertation. It was half written on a hard drive somewhere and she figured eventually she'd get back to it. "And no one told me there would be an auditor." She'd had people auditing her classes all the time — other professors, administration members, special visitors. But standard protocol was to clear it with the professor first.

He waved his hand around, taking a few steps down to the front of the room. The closer he got, the more Rachel felt a balloon of panic, of fear, inside her chest. He was physically far enough away that she was trying not to worry, but the energy in the room had shifted, and she felt the hairs on the back of her neck rise.

"I don't believe you," she said firmly, almost in wonderment at how deeply she felt that truth. "Who are you, and what do you want?"

He paused a few feet in front of her. Rachel gripped the remote control on the desk in her right hand. It wasn't much, but if she needed to, she could hurl it at him. Inside her sensible shoes, she wiggled her toes, bracing her body to flee.

"Rachel," he said. His eyes drifted toward her hand, the one with the remote control. *Shit.* He was on to her.

"Who. Are. You." The words were fire on her breath.

He looked at her for what felt like a long time, his gray eyes small and focused and unreadable. The room was so quiet that Rachel could hear the old-fashioned clock on the wall as it ticked away the seconds.

"Just tell me," she whispered, her words tightly coiled.

A pause, and then a curt nod. "I'm Agent Hernandez with the NSA."

"The NSA?" Recognition dawned on Rachel. Fury, hot and sudden, pounded through her veins. "Again?"

"Yes, I know my office has previously been in contact with you." He nodded again and then settled himself into the closest seat.

"Oh, is that what your records say?" Rachel, seething, clicked her tongue. "That the NSA has 'previously been in contact' with me?" She tried to remember the last visit she'd had from an NSA agent. There had been so many, in such a condensed time frame right after Harlon's death, that now they all bled together — just flashes of men in suits, like in a movie, descending on their house time and again, ransacking Harlon's office, their den, even their bedroom. Even Cassie's bedroom!

"I'm sure those aren't pleasant memories, but I'd appreciate your continued cooperation," Agent Hernandez said. He wasn't, Rachel noticed, asking. He was demanding. "We're looking for some more information about your late husband's activities, and if we could —"

"Look," Rachel interrupted, heat rising in a scarlet flush along her neck, up past her ears. "You vultures came and took everything. Whatever you didn't outright steal, you copied. I *still* don't have the hard drive backup of pictures from my daughter's birth. What possible use could the U.S. government have for those memories? Does someone at the NSA get his rocks off on my breastfeeding photos?"

Rachel realized she'd probably gone too far, but she was trembling. Furious. And terrified, and outraged, and a million other things. "I'm a widow. You bastards keep poking around, sniffing around Harlon's survivors like cadaver dogs with a scent. I'm going to say it one more time."

Rachel leaned forward, still gripping the remote control, close enough to Agent Hernandez now that he could feel her breath escaping in little pants. "Leave. Us. The. Hell. Alone."

It was a reaction full of the grief and fear and hatred and exhaustion she'd been facing for months. It came from deep inside her.

Something went soft in his eyes.

"Professor McKinney, I'm very, very sorry for your loss, and I'm … Well, I was going to tell you that I'm just doing my job, but that's not much of a comfort for you, is it?" He shifted his weight. "Look, your husband's work was important. And I'm not supposed to tell you this, but you deserve to know why we keep checking on you. Between us, we think there's a chance that he left some uncommitted code on a personal device. Maybe we're wrong. We're just being thorough." He sighed and shrugged and handed her a card.

"Let me guess," Rachel said sarcastically. "If I think of anything, I should call you?"

"No, ma'am. That's my personal number. I'll be back in the office on Friday. Give me a call then, and I'll see if we can expedite the return of that hard drive." He paused. "I have kids, too."

Rachel froze, only her eyes moving as Agent Hernandez nodded at her and left.

It was only once he was gone that she allowed herself to breathe. The wave of relief that rolled over her nearly made her collapse, and she doubled over, gulping air, wondering how on earth she'd managed to cope with another harrowing visit from the government entity that was intent on taking down her husband, his legacy and, she feared, his entire family.

When her lungs and heart and brain and every other organ that Agent Hernandez had affected finally relaxed, Rachel straightened and rearranged her things. She put back the remote control, smoothed her hair out of habit and then flicked off the lights. She stepped out of the room and into the blissfully empty hallway. Empty, that is, except for Bryce Muller. Red Dread. She froze. He was standing just next to the door, close enough, Rachel knew, to have heard and seen everything. He stared at her, a stunned expression on his face. For a long moment, Rachel stared back.

Eventually, Bryce's face settled into something new, and it looked like he wanted to speak. But Rachel held up her hand. She had heard enough from men today. From everyone, in fact. And he was her student. Whatever he'd just heard, whatever he thought he'd just seen, he'd need to forget it. Immediately.

"My office hours are listed in the syllabus," Rachel said tersely. As she elbowed her way around him, she added, "Don't loiter outside my classroom again, Mr. Muller."

*

Does Rowan Buckland make all of her friends color coordinate? They're all wearing shades of purple today. **#WhoWoreItWestfield**

Omg, are Skylar and Izzy back together? **#WhatsUpWestfield**

Speaking of Rowan, who IS the new girl in her group? She stomps around looking like she wants to murder someone. She's bringing Rowan down, if you ask me. **#WhatsUpWestfield**

No one asked you, Marcy. — RB **#RowanSpeaks**

It's Mary. And sorry, Rowan, that was rude of me. **#RowanSpeaksToMe**

Whatever, Marcy. — RB **#RowanSpeaks**

Huerta is going DOWN this weekend! Let's go Westfield! FOOTBALLLLLLLLL! **#HowTheWestfieldWasWon**

If Izzy's back with Skylar she deserves everything she gets. **#WhatsUpWestfield**

Is it winter break yet? **#WhatsUpWestfield**

1001 0 5 00101

Cassie ate lunch with Rowan and her friends again the next day. And the day after that, and the day after that. She was, inexplicably, a new member of Rowan's girl gang.

Her anger didn't go away, but she found it had abated somewhat. It wasn't that she enjoyed her new "friends," but they did provide a convenient distraction. When Rowan and Indira spent fifteen minutes taking forty selfies to figure out the perfect one to post, Cassie found herself caught up just enough that she didn't think about her dad or her life.

The crazy thing was, it was almost fun. For someone who preferred to keep a small group of select friends, Cassie found that being a part of Rowan's crowd was a new experience. Moving through her days, she developed a sense of something that was almost like power. People left her alone once they figured out who she was friends with, and this new status offered her the protection, the invisibility, she'd been craving. Her anger still flared and flashed of its own volition, but she had her girls to help her direct it. She'd always hated the kind of girl who spent time cutting down others, but she had to admit that it served a purpose: it felt damn good. Pointing out someone else's flaws and shortcomings helped to masquerade her own.

Better yet, the girls' whole Homework Coven notion was genius. Her homework time was cut down considerably, as the five of them ganged up on each class assignment, letting each girl's expertise lead the way. Why kill yourself on that English essay when Rowan could set it all up for you and show you what quotations to use? Why stress over physics when Indira could walk you through the equations in half the time? Cassie figured that she earned her part, given that she got all of them A's on the first quiz in Westfield's mandatory coding class.

Dad, I'm sort of cheating at school, but not really, she texted one night.

Sounds more like you're hacking life, came the reply.

After that, she didn't worry about it anymore.

Her newfound guiltless existence, though, didn't cover everything. A voice gnawed at the back of her mind, whispering that she should be nicer to Sarah. And she tried — she really did. Sarah so badly wanted someone to bond with. She wanted someone whose grief — newer, more raw — could overshadow her own. But she had nothing else to bring to the table. Other than losing parents, she and Cassie had precisely nothing in common, whereas with the Homework Coven ...

With the Coven, there was snark. And flash. And style. Nothing more than skin-deep. Nothing real. That's what mattered, for this year in particular.

Still, out of sheer guilt, Cassie spent time with Sarah between classes and occasionally in homeroom, then usually managed to bounce a few texts back and forth. Eventually, Sarah stopped pushing her trauma group and seemed OK just being friends.

Meanwhile, Cassie found that pretending to be friends with Rowan, Indira, Madison and Livvy was getting easier and easier. Sometimes she didn't even have to pretend. Bonus: it was definitely keeping her mom off her back and her rage quiet.

Of course, then Rachel had to ruin it.

*

"We have to talk about college," Rachel said to Cassie one night during dinner — cheap spaghetti, watery marinara — and Cassie groaned. The only person she hadn't reached some kind of understanding with appeared to be her mom. Their relationship was as strained as ever. Rachel had been snapping at Cassie more and more, especially about how much time Cassie was spending with her new friends after school. Cassie figured she must be stressed from her new job. It was better for everyone involved if they just left each other alone as much as possible, Cassie had decided.

"Oh, I'm going," Cassie assured her, poking around at the lukewarm noodles. "Fast as I can get out of here, I'm going." She pretended not to see Rachel's face cloud over.

"Of course you're going," Rachel said quietly. "But you'll be applying soon, and I'm a little worried about your transcripts."

"I'm an A student," Cassie argued. Why was her mom always discounting her? She was never good enough for Rachel. She remembered bringing home a B minus on an impossibly difficult statistics final sophomore year. She'd been so proud of that grade. But when Rachel saw it, she'd tsk'd and asked Cassie what had happened. Her dad, meanwhile, had as opposite a reaction as one could: he'd taken her out for ice cream.

"I'm not talking about your grades, which are very strong." Rachel paused to shake some cheese, probably the kind filled with sawdust, onto her pasta. "I'm worried about your lack of extracurriculars. I don't want schools to look at your record and wonder why you dropped everything, even all your computer stuff, when you switched schools."

"I will happily tell them why I dropped everything," Cassie snapped. "I'm sure there's some kind of 'dead dad' credit they'll give me, if you're so worried about it."

Not for the first time, Cassie wondered if she'd gone too far. Rachel turned pale, her fork frozen in midair. She sighed. "Sorry."

"No, don't be sorry," Rachel said, her voice low. She still wouldn't meet Cassie's eyes. "Maybe you're right. Maybe there is a dead-parent box you can tick off on your applications. Maybe there's a mom-who's-tried-everything-to-get-through-to-her-daughter-and-is-out-of-ideas box, too."

Abruptly, Rachel stood up, cleared her dishes and disappeared into her bedroom, the hollow door making a small *thwack* as it closed. Cassie rolled her eyes, ignoring her regret. It was just like her mom to leave *her* to clean up the kitchen. And why did she have to bring up the fact that she hadn't touched a keyboard in months? As though it had been an easy decision for her, something she'd done on a whim. *You have to have a reason to code,* Harlon used to tell her. *Your reason can be lofty or silly, grand or stupid, but it needs to exist.* Well, without him, she didn't have a reason. Even though she dreamed in code, she couldn't play around with it anymore. It felt like … Cassie hesitated, trying to place the emotion. Betrayal was the closest word she could come up with. Playing with code after her father died kind of felt like she was betraying the deepest, truest part of their relationship, their bond.

Hey, Dad, she texted as soon as she got to her bedroom. Rachel hadn't come out of hers all night. **Why is mom so mean?**

Hey there, kiddo, Harlon wrote back. **Your mom loves you. So do I.**

She has a funny way of showing it. Cassie's thumbs were faster than her brain. She shouldn't have written that. She suspected Rachel occasionally checked in on Cassie's texting with Harlon, even though it was the most private thing Cassie had ever done and would ever do.

I'm sorry you had a bad day, Harlon wrote. **But remember …**

Cassie said it out loud before the phone could send the full message: "Any day you can walk away from is a good day."

She stared at the screen awhile longer, wondering what her dad would really say if he were here. Would he be proud of Cassie? Their apartment was so quiet that she could hear the television noises from old Hattie Morris's next door. She wanted to scream, to break the silence with her internal thunder, to wake her mom from whatever cage she'd constructed around herself, from whatever it was that was keeping them from hearing each other.

Cassie's thumbs moved over the keys without her even realizing what she was asking. **Dad, why is this all so hard?**

She stayed up for hours, her eyes scratchy, her long limbs heavy. But Harlon never wrote back.

*

Sometimes he didn't write back. That was part of the randomization strategy.

It wasn't her father. Not really. Cassie knew that even though she let herself *think* it was her dad on the other end of the chat. Her father, though, was actually buried some ten miles from the new apartment, in a cemetery behind an old run-down church, the same church where baby Harlon had been baptized.

The Harlon at the other end of the chat logs was a bot. A very special one.

She and her dad had built it together. Some dads and daughters built homemade musical instruments or birdhouses. Harlon McKinney and his daughter hacked together an incredibly sophisticated bot designed to test Alan Turing's theories.

Turing had claimed that the true test of artificial intelligence was whether you could put the machine behind a curtain and have it converse with a human being on the other side. If the person on the other side couldn't tell that he or she was speaking to a machine, not a person, then congratulations — you've got bona fide artificial intelligence.

Their attempt at a Turing AI had been modeled on Harlon himself. There was a lifetime's worth of Harlon's blogs, posts, tweets and more all over the internet, to say nothing of thousands of hours of lecture videos and home movies. A hell of a lot of information on one man, capturing vocabulary, mannerisms, verbal tics and so on. Together, they'd built a neural net designed to suck all of that in, along with Harlon's entire text-message history.

They'd finished it about eight months before he died and had spent every free moment training it. It lived somewhere on the net on a secret server farm Harlon shared with some other mysterious hacker types, and only Cassie had the IP addresses that allowed her to "speak" to it.

It was like talking to her dad.

Almost.

The bot responded to her using Harlon's words and Harlon's written voice, based on what she said and how she said it. But there was a randomization factor built in. Sometimes it didn't respond because … Well, sometimes people just flaked and didn't get back to you. It was more realistic that way, though frustrating.

And she'd begun to notice that some repeats were cropping up. Depending on what she said to the bot, there was a range of responses. At first those responses had seemed infinite, but the bot was starting to tread old ground a bit. This was probably her fault; she had been — subconsciously, perhaps — sending it a lot of the same input lately. **Mom sucks. I hate my life. I miss you.** Over and over. The bot wasn't learning anything new.

She sighed and tried to figure out something new and interesting to send it but couldn't come up with anything that would throw it for a loop.

Mom said something smart today.

Ugh. No. Never.

Cassie would never admit this, but her mom was occasionally right about things.

It was *infuriating.*

Still, Cassie considered what Rachel had said about extracurriculars. She'd worked hard all throughout school, and it seemed pretty dumb to throw it away now, when she was so close to the finish line. She'd had her eye on Stanford since Harlon had taken her on a tour of it in middle school, when he'd been a visiting lecturer, and her application was already saved on her laptop, just waiting to be finalized. So the next day, while she was waiting in the lunch line to purchase her sad little banana and yogurt cup — Rachel hadn't allotted her much in the way of a lunch budget — she checked the Westfield High app to see what clubs were meeting that day. Maybe she'd surprise everyone and join one.

She had English right before lunch, with Sarah, so she let Sarah escort her to the cafeteria each day. By unspoken agreement, Sarah peeled off before they actually walked into the room.

At her lunch table, Rowan and Indira were shrieking and laughing at something on their phones. "What's up?" Cassie asked, setting down her tray.

"Oh, we're just making fun of the president's daughter. She had the baby!" Indira said gleefully.

Cassie shrugged. "Mazel, I guess." The president had a bunch of kids, but Cassie couldn't be bothered to pay much attention to any of the first family. She did, though, remember her dad ranting about how the president was scum, especially for the way he talked about women, including his own wife and daughters. "If you ever hear me talk about Cassie like that," he seethed to Rachel once, "please shoot me in the head. Twice, to be sure."

And, yeah, the first daughter had all the traits of a hottie, along with a social media following most people would kill for.

And her dad seemed like a total creeper, but Cassie just couldn't convince herself to care. Most old guys seemed like total creepers, after all.

"Cassie," Rowan said in that tone of voice that made Cassie guess her reaction to the news had been less than ideal. "Don't say you haven't seen the photos?"

"I haven't been on BLINQ since second period," Cassie protested. She and Rowan had somehow fallen into this pattern, this routine, where Cassie scoffed at the amount of time and energy Rowan spent on social media, while Rowan pretended Cassie didn't know anything about anyone as a result.

"Girl. These will *make* your life." Indira flashed Cassie her phone. Cassie grabbed it and began scrolling. It took a minute for her to digest what she was seeing. Then, her expression unreadable, Cassie handed it back.

Rowan and Indira waited eagerly, their faces bright as they scrutinized Cassie. Livvy and Madison slid onto the bench next to them and Indira nudged them, updating them in a whisper while they all waited for Cassie's reaction.

"Well?!" Indira squealed. "I can't take it anymore! What do you think?"

"I mean, I know nothing about babies ..." Cassie began. She chewed her lip and tried not to laugh. "But ..."

"But ..." Rowan prompted.

"But ..." Cassie met four pairs of glistening eyes. "That is one unfortunate-looking child."

"Ba-ha-ha!" Indira guffawed while Livvy and Madison burst out laughing. Rowan was prettily chuckling into her hand. Eventually, the table's laughter was loud and raucous enough that the others began to look at them, even more than they normally did. Cassie basked in it, surprised at how good it felt to hear real laughter. It had been a while.

"I mean," Cassie added, eager to continue making them laugh, to continue the cafeteria's collective admiration, "the poor thing is going to hate its mother for being so pretty!"

"It looks like her dad," Indira said. "Like a teeny, tiny, baby version of the president."

"With better hair," Livvy deadpanned.

Cassie had to admit it was true. Poor baby.

"My mom is gorgeous and I don't *hate* her," Rowan said. She cocked her head in thought. "But still, I get what you're saying."

"You guys, we should try to get #UnfortunateBaby trending," Livvy declared.

"Or what about #UglyMothersAreTheBestMothers?" Madison offered.

"That's so mean," Cassie said with a chuckle.

"OK, this is my mission now. Let's see what's trending already." Rowan tapped a few times and then cleared her throat. "Here's our competition: #RoyalBaby."

"But they're not royalty!" Livvy said.

"They sure act like it," Cassie grumbled. An unexpected silence fell across the table and Cassie, surprised, tried to clarify. "What? My dad said the president thinks he's a king."

"My family supports the president," Rowan said, her voice stiff and prim.

"It was just a joke." Cassie shrugged.

Rowan fixed her gaze on Cassie for another uncomfortable moment before clearing her throat again and looking back at her phone. "Check out the other trends, everyone. Let's reconvene after school to try and get something trending ourselves. We don't have much time if we want to get in on this one!"

"Speaking of after school ..." Cassie let her voice trail off and hated herself for it. She straightened her spine, set her jaw. So what if they laughed at her? "I'm thinking of joining a club. What do you guys all do?"

Indira snorted. Madison looked confused. Livvy and Rowan exchanged glances before Rowan broke into a dazzling smile. Indira snapped a quick photo of her — "This light is really beautiful, Roe, I'll post this ay-sap" — and Cassie braced herself. She'd misstepped somehow, again.

"Clubs aren't really our thing," Rowan said. She shrugged daintily. "You know our thoughts: This is all so temporary. Burn bright and brief and leave some energy for the real world."

"I get that." Cassie nodded, biting into her banana. "I guess I'm just worried about my college applications. I don't want them to look too sparse."

"Mmmm," Rowan said noncommittally. "My daddy told me I don't need to worry about college applications."

"Me neither!" Madison's eyes lit up. She liked it anytime she and Rowan had something in common.

If Harlon were alive, would Cassie need to worry about college? As she slurped the rest of her yogurt she tried to picture, not for the first time, how her life might be different had Harlon lived. They hadn't been private-jet rich, or even first-class-to-Europe-every-summer rich the way Rowan and her friends seemed to be. But Cassie had never wondered if her parents would turn down her requests for the latest technologies, or the best sneakers, or that weekend away at Max's beach house. She'd always gotten what she wanted in addition to what she needed. Now, she realized ruefully, her college search had been narrowed down to its high scholarship potential. She would probably end up at MS/BFU. With her mom. Ugh.

Cassie surveyed the rest of the cafeteria to get ideas. Her eyes landed on a tableful of techies, silently munching at their sandwiches while also tapping at tablets. She lingered long enough for the other girls to notice.

"Oh-em-gee, is our tech-head hearing the mating call of the teen cybergeek?" Rowan teased.

Cassie ducked her head, grateful she hadn't made the time to tie her hair up that morning so it could fall over her face and hide her grimace. With Harlon McKinney for a father, being a tech-head had pretty much been her birthright.

But that was over now.

"Nah," she muttered when she knew her face had reverted to its neutral expression.

"Well, let's think about what you're good at, and go from there," Livvy suggested.

"Talking shit?" Rowan joked. Cassie chuckled while the rest of the girls laughed heartily.

"No, but Rowan's right," Madison said.

"Obviously," Rowan said with a smirk.

"I'm serious. You do always have a smart comeback, and you're a fast talker." Madison counted out on her fingers. "What about debating?"

"We do have a good debate team," Indira said.

"Debate team." Cassie nodded. The two words felt right in her mouth. But more importantly, they would get her mom to ease up a bit. Hopefully.

1001060010 1

When the debate team met later that week, Cassie slipped into a seat in the back of the room just before the door closed. The meeting was held in one of the science rooms, so she had an entire lab table all to herself and a comforting view of the backs of the other team members. The room featured an impressive array of tech, including mini-projectors and voice tracking. At first glance, it didn't seem like a *horrible* group. And when she'd told her mom that she'd joined, Rachel's eyes had nearly bugged out from excitement and, behind that, relief.

The debate team president, an affable senior named Phil, jumped to the front of the room and began explaining how things would operate while he fiddled with his tablet, trying to get something to stream to the big screen mounted on the wall. Cassie tried to pay attention to his words, but her eyes mostly stayed on his fingers. They were jabbing at the touch screen in a way that made her wince.

"Dangit," Phil muttered under his breath, interrupting himself and whacking the tablet. "Can someone ping the tech squad?"

Cassie shifted in her seat. She was well acquainted with the earlier version of the app Phil was using, thanks to some work she'd done at her old school. And thanks, of course, to her dad, who had taught her that the only way to master new technologies was to get your hands in there and play around with them. All Phil needed to do, probably, was —

The door opened. A dozen pairs of eyes tracked to the sound. And in walked Mr. CODE IS POETRY. (This time, though, his shirt said LIFE IS A HACK in the same white font. *Menlo Regular*, she thought.)

Immediately, Cassie shifted her eyes, hoping he wouldn't notice her. (Again.) Heat pooled in her cheeks. She felt a driving need to gulp some fresh air, but there were only a few measly windows in the lab room, and students were probably not allowed to open them anyway. She kept her eyes on the scuffed lab table, suddenly very interested in the graffiti etched into it. She ran her fingers over *Nate <3s Liza* and tried to pretend she wasn't on fire.

She hadn't seen CODE IS POETRY guy since that first day of school ... and not for lack of looking. After a few days of surveying every classroom, every hallway, every corner, Cassie had started to wonder if she'd imagined him. He was nowhere to be found. Once, she thought about asking Sarah or even Rowan, but she'd never been able to form the words she needed to describe him. She couldn't picture herself asking, "Hey, do you know a guy with the most intense eyes you've ever seen who swoops down on you like a mysterious, sexy vulture?"

See? It was ridiculous. Who thinks vultures are sexy?

He was staring at her. Full-on staring, Cassie realized, her jaw growing slack. And she was staring back. She felt a cool wave wash over her, and for the first time in ages, a smile threatened to break out on her face. There was something about him, about his aura (and Cassie scoffed internally at even thinking the word *aura*), that made it impossible for her to look away. How had anyone at Westfield ever gotten anything done with a guy like him around all the time?

"Thanks for coming, Carson," Phil said.

Mr. Mysterious had a name. *Carson.* She rolled it around on her tongue, trying out the taste of it, the shape of it. It knocked against her teeth like a drum: *Car-son, Car-son.* "No prob," Carson said easily, breaking his side of the staring contest. "I'll get you guys set up here."

Cassie studied him as he approached the front of the room. Phil continued talking to the team members, but his words fell away and the room's sounds muted as Cassie watched Carson fiddle with the big screen, starting the reboot process. She shook herself back to attention and tried to avert her eyes, but it didn't work. Cassie had the distinct sense that Carson took up more energetic space than should be allowed for one person.

"Just as soon as my buddy here gets us going, I'll show you all a short highlights reel from last year, where …"

Phil droned on and on, and Cassie desperately wondered if this was what debate team would be like: people talking about things they knew nothing about, and Cassie having to pretend she cared. Was this really worth it? But then her eyes landed on Carson again; his shoulder blades were sharp under his shirt. Cassie's fingers itched to touch them, to trace them …

Oh, man. What was happening to her? Her anger just … evaporated. She felt so chill that she could have kicked back and propped her feet up on the table.

Then she frowned. The stream still wasn't coming across, no matter how insistently Carson's fingers punched away at the tablet screen. She remembered a time last year when her streaming had crapped out on her. Turned out to be a minor DNS daemon that somehow hadn't gotten upgraded on her phone, so it couldn't see the receiving streaming box on the network. She'd managed to fix it pretty easily. Would the code she'd changed then fix this problem?

She sighed. She *knew* it would. The question now was, should she tell Carson? What if he was offended? What if he thought she was showing off? What if —

Cassie stood up. Code superseded romance. Always.

"Uh," Phil said, noticing Cassie nearby. "Yeah?"

She pointed at the tablet. Or, if she was being honest, at Carson. "I think I can help him fix that."

"Oh, cool," Phil said. "Step aside, Carson. Let the lady show you how it's done." A few people chuckled while Carson straightened to his full height just as Cassie reached him.

She'd met him only once, of course, but she'd replayed that memory countless times. And in all those replays, she'd somehow forgotten how her mouth lined up so perfectly with his when they were facing each other.

"Um. Hi. Sorry, I j-just …" Cassie stuttered. She was *so* close to him.

"This code is kinda wack," Carson said, saving her from herself. He held out the tablet, his eyes as earnest as they'd been the first time he'd seen her. "If you wanna try …"

"I do," she said quickly, then felt herself turning purple when she realized what she'd just said. *I do.* As if they were exchanging vows. *Oh, God.* She should just go jump out the lab window now.

She hunched over the tablet and began tapping the screen. After a few seconds, the coding muscles took over. Cassie could only imagine Rowan's response if she ever tried to explain how she felt most like herself when she was knuckle-deep in code, in work so all-encompassing that everything else, the debate club and her mom and the president's daughter and even Carson, just fell away.

She couldn't remember a time when she wasn't fluent in code, when it wasn't as natural to her as breathing. Harlon would work at all hours of the day and night on a big project, for weeks or months at a time, before burning out and crashing — hard. He'd been showing her his work, testing her on her knowledge of the technologies he'd created since she was six. Working in that way, figuring out the universal language that each piece of software spoke in its own dialect, was an irresistible puzzle. It was just who she was.

Had been, she corrected herself. Since Harlon had gone, she hadn't touched a keyboard or a compiler. Not until now.

"So, Menlo Regular, huh?" She kept her focus on the code, but couldn't believe she'd just blurted that out. What an idiot. He probably didn't even know what font was on his shirt. Who knew stuff like that other than weirdos like her?

"It's got good spacing," he said. "It's the Xcode default for a reason. And it keeps a lot of my code on one line when I'm in the Terminal."

She shrugged with a diffidence she didn't actually feel. "I'm an Inconsolata girl myself. Looks good at all sizes."

He considered this. "At least you don't use Courier."

"Or Monaco," she replied.

He chuckled. Her cheeks flamed, and she was glad she wasn't facing him.

A few moments before she actually fixed the problem, she knew it was going to happen. She'd found the first domino and was about to knock it down, and that in turn would cause a chain reaction of falling, piece after piece, until the code was perfect and the fix was in place. Rather than go through the laborious process of updating the tablet again, she was just fixing the twisted bit of code from memory. It was literally only ten lines that had changed over the update, but they were important ones.

Over her shoulder, Carson must have seen what she was seeing, too. His voice, low and serious, murmured in her ear. "Whoa. I wouldn't have thought to try that."

A dam inside her broke, rushing gratitude throughout her bones. She finished typing, recompiled the app and watched its search icon spin … until it found the room's main screen. She met Carson's eyes and let herself break into a grin. He grinned back.

"That is the sexiest thing I've ever seen," Carson said, his voice pitched low.

She wondered for a moment if she should hashtag him for a microaggression, but … it actually didn't bother her.

"Awesome!" Phil said loudly, clapping his hands twice, and it occurred to Cassie that he really had a knack for interrupting. "Hey, I didn't catch your name. You're new, yeah?"

Cassie nodded, hyperaware of Carson's presence just behind her right shoulder, of how all of the debate team was watching her, waiting for her to say something. "Cassie," she choked out.

"Well, Cassie, thanks for jumping in. Maybe you should join the tech club instead of debate team, right?" Phil laughed. Then he heartily patted Carson's shoulder in that way only boys did.

"Maybe," she said, finally remembering that these people — with the exception of maybe Carson — meant nothing to her. "I didn't even know there was a tech club."

Behind her shoulder, something shifted. Carson. He cleared his throat and murmured, "We meet tomorrow. You should come by. Deets," he said, and held out a slip of paper.

Cassie stared at it. Who wrote things down? Still, as he paused against her gaze, she found the bravery she needed to adjust her body enough so that she could see him again, so that their mouths could line up like they were meant to. So that she could see his eyes again. Maybe they'd be enough to hold her in this envelope of fiery satisfaction that had settled on her for at least a little while longer.

"I should," she agreed, and took the paper from him, jamming it into her pocket. And then Carson nodded, knocked three times on the table and left.

*

"Submissions, please!"

Indira grinned. "Me first! OK, ready?"

Rowan, Madison and Livvy nodded, their eyes flashing almost as bright as their smiles. Cassie nodded, too, although less enthusiastically than she assumed Rowan would have liked. She felt like Rowan had assigned them homework.

But, she reminded herself, this was what these girls did. What *her friends* did, she corrected herself. Rowan wanted them to post a joke that would start trending, and what Rowan wanted, she usually got. Get something trending, and a slew of Likes, and you …

You …

You get nothing, really. Like Rowan had said that one day — it just disappears the next time you post something. No one goes back and looks at the thing you did yesterday that got all those Likes.

I bet Carson isn't wasting his time trolling for Likes. Cassie blushed just at the thought of him. *Girl, what has gotten into you?*

With a sigh, she sipped her slushy coffee drink, then wiped some stray whipped cream off her upper lip as Indira read her joke aloud. Her slushy coffee drink was, she realized, a misstep with this crowd. She'd arrived at the café first — she'd left early in case she couldn't find it — and impulsively used the remainder of her gift card to buy the frothy shake, caramel and all, only to be asked by Rowan when she finally arrived if she was a child, otherwise why would she drink a milkshake like that, and why didn't Cassie drink strong black coffee like everyone else?

While the girls cracked jokes, Cassie checked her phone, staring at the baby photo the first daughter had posted that morning. The president's daughter was pretty in a modified way, with perfectly straight, white teeth, trendy-but-not-edgy hair and expertly contoured makeup that made it hard to determine what she really looked like. Her husband was generically handsome in a sort of bland way, with no remarkable physical qualities, good or bad. The baby, in all its wrinkled, blotchy ugliness, didn't really look like either of them, but the more Cassie stared, the more she realized the perfect joke was tickling the front of her brain.

As she mulled it over, Rowan was busy roundly rejecting every idea presented to her. "We need something no one would dare say. Something outrageous enough to make waves and get some attention," she urged, finishing her coffee. She fixed her eyes on Cassie. "What about you? I think it's high time you proved your wit, don't you?"

Four heads swiveled to look at Cassie, who looked longingly at the final dollop of whipped cream, knowing that she absolutely could not eat it with them watching her. "Um," she stalled.

Rowan raised one eyebrow. Indira pursed her lips. Madison and Livvy smirked. *Message received*, Cassie thought. It was now or never: Cassie had to show them she wasn't some sad sack who needed them to teach her what kind of coffee to drink. She'd been well known at her old school, respected. She knew things. She was no Sarah.

Cassie felt that spark inside her light up, a kindling of the old Cassie, the one who wasn't always so pissed off, so brimming with poison. Her eyes grew fierce. She would show them.

Maybe her silly coffee drink was a muse, because just then, the perfect wording for that perfect joke landed in her mouth. She practically spat it out.

"Too bad the abortion didn't take. #BetterLuckNextBaby."

It felt like the entire coffee shop fell silent, but of course that couldn't be true, Cassie realized. Behind her she could still hear the clinking of spoons against saucers, the shaking of cinnamon on lattes, and the ever-present dings and beeps of a connected world. But at the cozy little table Rowan was presiding over? Silence.

Cassie's stomach fell. She'd forgotten that Rowan's family were big supporters of the president. She opened her mouth to take it back.

But then: a whoop of shocked laughter so loud and deep that the barista had to shush them.

Tears streamed from Indira's eyes. Livvy's mouth had formed an O so large that it looked like she would permanently stretch out her lips. Madison was doubled over, her shoulders heaving, the dregs of her coffee spilled over the table.

And then there was Rowan, who relaxed back into the cozy armchair she'd commandeered, crossed her arms and grinned. There was a hint of wickedness in her smile that made Cassie wonder if Rowan was about to steal her joke, send it out herself and get all the credit. Buoyed by the dramatic responses from the other girls — and before Rowan could steal her thunder — Cassie grabbed her phone and thumbed out the message. She hit Send.

"Done," she said, her casual tone hiding her racing heart and sweaty palms. Panic and guilt swept through her, quickly knocked away by reason: the president's daughter was gorgeous and rich and powerful and had millions of followers. Her dad was the *president*. Cassie's dad was dead. She was a nobody. Goddesses didn't worry about the ants around their feet.

Rowan grinned even wider. She had a sheen in her eyes that Cassie mistook for pride. "Edgy, funny and timely. Well, well, well. Cassie McKinney, now you're *really* one of us."

*

303 users have Condemned **@CassieMcK39** for "Too bad the abortion didn't take. **#BetterLuckNextBaby**"

289 users have Liked **@CassieMcK39** for "Too bad the abortion didn't take. **#BetterLuckNextBaby**"

Oh, snap. That's a sick joke! REBLINQ: **@CassieMcK39**: Too bad the abortion didn't take. **#BetterLuckNextBaby**

2100 users have Condemned **@CassieMcK39** for "Too bad the abortion didn't take. **#BetterLuckNextBaby**"

LOL! Hahahahaha REBLINQ: **@CassieMcK39**: Too bad the abortion didn't take. **#BetterLuckNextBaby**

Dude, abortion's not funny, this chick is sick. **#SickChick** REBLINQ: **@CassieMcK39**: Too bad the abortion didn't take. **#BetterLuckNextBaby**

I mean, she's not wrong. REBLINQ: **@CassieMcK39**: Too bad the abortion didn't take. **#BetterLuckNextBaby**

4569 users have Liked **@CassieMcK39** for "Too bad the abortion didn't take. **#BetterLuckNextBaby**"

pops popcorn This thread's gonna be funny. REBLINQ: **@CassieMcK39**: Too bad the abortion didn't take. **#BetterLuckNextBaby**

TRENDING NEWS ALERT: We're keeping an eye on a recent BLINQ from **@CassieMcK39**: tnewsalert.hive.gov/4211

This feels kind of … out of bounds, no? REBLINQ: **@CassieMcK39**: Too bad the abortion didn't take. **#BetterLuckNextBaby**

18 403 users have Liked **@CassieMcK39** for "Too bad the abortion didn't take. **#BetterLuckNextBaby**"

Who is this **@CassieMcK39**? Hey **@Bombastic_Fantastic99999** can you doxx her?

I appreciate a gal who can zing a sitting pres. REBLINQ: **@CassieMcK39**: Too bad the abortion didn't take. **#BetterLuckNextBaby**

Seriously, what are they teaching kids in schools these days? She should be expelled. REBLINQ: **@CassieMcK39**: Too bad the abortion didn't take. **#BetterLuckNextBaby**

20 050 users have Condemned **@CassieMcK39** for "Too bad the abortion didn't take. **#BetterLuckNextBaby**"

*

By the time Indira suggested they grab dinner and Rowan had decreed sushi, Cassie's BLINQ had garnered thousands of reBLINQs and she had a solid "neutral/viral" ratio. It was the first time she'd shared anything that even remotely approached viral. The air seemed to crackle around her; her body felt jumpy, like it knew something she didn't.

"We have to celebrate," Rowan declared. "Going viral is ultimate goals."

Cassie couldn't quite figure out *why.* Yeah, it was a rush to get so many people paying attention to her, but … so what? Had she actually accomplished anything? Rowan seemed to think so, and Cassie wanted to ask why but figured it would just make her look like more a rube.

And given that Rowan's idea of celebrating was much more expensive than Cassie's meager bankroll could bear, it was a good time to break off anyway. She waved goodbye and ducked outside before gulping the last of her slushie in private. In a way, she was almost grateful to bow out.

Her earbud chirped for her attention. A text from Sarah.

Sarah usually texted Cassie every day, often not saying much of substance. Cassie typically ignored the messages and dealt with the fallout the following morning at school (which was manageable … Sarah was so easygoing about Cassie's lack of availability that she never seemed to mind when Cassie left her hanging). But tonight, hearing Sarah's name in her ear triggered some new emotions. She left her phone in her pocket and had the text read to her instead.

You're everywhere! What in the world! You're going to be famous!

With a resigned sigh, Cassie said, "Respond to Sarah: blushing happy face emoji." She figured that was the perfect amount of balance between keeping Sarah at bay and acknowledging today's momentous occasion.

When I was a kid, there was a difference between being internet famous and just plain famous, Harlon used to say. *And* no one *wanted to be internet famous.*

Cassie almost walked right into oncoming traffic when a soccer ball–sized sack of guilt rammed into her gut. She flipped the bird to a driver who honked at her and wondered what her dad would think of the fact that his only daughter was now, officially, internet famous. Or at least on her way to it, depending on how the rest of the evening played out.

Twenty minutes later she rounded the corner of her block just as an alert buzzed in her earbud. It was a sound she'd never heard before. She stopped for a moment and ducked under the awning of the dry cleaner's to avoid the drizzle that had just started. At that moment, the voice of her phone's digital assistant spoke:

WARNING.
APPROACHING LEVEL 1.
STAY TUNED FOR FURTHER INSTRUCTIONS.

Wait, *what*?

Impossible. She'd misheard. She pulled her phone out of her pocket to double-check.

A notification that took up the entire screen flashed back at her.

WARNING.
APPROACHING LEVEL 1.
STAY TUNED FOR FURTHER INSTRUCTIONS.

Cassie's hand shook. The phone slipped out of her grasp and tumbled onto the sidewalk.

Level 1? Me? Cassie picked up her phone and frantically began pounding at it. She had to see what had happened with her BLINQ.

But her phone had locked her out. The only modes available to her were text and phone.

"Shit!" she cried, feeling panic rising. She'd never been locked out of her phone before. Is this how it happened when Hive Justice came for you? How did anyone survive?

The thought that she, Cassie, could be the subject of a Hive Mob made her entire body break out in goose bumps. But still, she reminded herself, this was ridiculous. Her BLINQ had been a joke. It had been smart! And biting! The more she thought about it, the more ridiculous this all seemed. If she could just explain to people … All she had to do was find a way to restore her phone to normal — she'd hack into it if need be, ignoring all thoughts of how risky that would be — and delete the BLINQ. Or reason with people who were condemning her. Or plead with them. Or …

She felt herself spiraling. And all she knew how to do when she was spiraling like this was to stop, take a few deep breaths and recap the situation. Usually, in her recapping, she'd discover things weren't as bad as they'd seemed. So she paused, tried to focus on the falling rain and slowly counted to ten.

There. That was better. Her hands weren't shaking anymore, and the cold sweat she'd broken out into was gone, replaced by the mist on the wind. She would call Rowan, she decided. She needed to hear someone tell her this was all going to be OK.

"Call Rowan," she muttered into her earbud, and within seconds her phone was ringing.

Only it never stopped ringing.

"Girl, pick up," she grumbled. Her heart was beating a little faster now, a little more erratically. She tried again, and then again.

After that, she texted. **Have you seen our BLINQ? It's going crazy. We're approaching Level 1! What should we do?**

In the rain, Cassie waited for what felt like forever for Rowan's response. When it came, it slammed into her like a truck.

We? Rowan wrote. **Try "you."**

"What the actual hell!" Cassie shouted. She was breathless now, a claw of fear stretching up her throat. This isn't what was supposed to happen.

Cassie almost hurled her useless phone to the ground but managed to redirect her anger at a nearby hydrant instead. She kicked it with the flat of her foot over and over again, then screamed out loud when that did not satisfy.

THWACK.

She jumped. Meli, the owner of the dry cleaning place, was pounding on the window. Her eyes were wild. Cassie couldn't hear her through the glass but she could read her lips: "Check your phone! Check your phone!"

She did.

LEVEL 1 ACHIEVED.

HOLD. DO NOT FLEE.

AWAIT FURTHER INSTRUCTIONS.

"This is insane!" Cassie breathed. Meli tapped on the glass again.

"You should go home," she mouthed.

Cassie waved and then pulled her denim jacket up over her head. As she was about to make a run for her front door, Sarah called.

"Hi," Cassie said, surprised at the rush of gratitude she felt. "Did you see what's going on? I'm at Level 1!"

"This is so crazy," Sarah said agreeably. "How are you? Where are you? What possessed you to … Were you showing off for Rowan or something —"

"I'm fine," Cassie interrupted. "This is nuts. When I came up with it, everyone laughed their asses off. And now she's being annoying about it all."

"What do you mean, annoying?" Sarah asked.

"She basically told me to deal with it on my own," Cassie admitted. Thinking about it made her angry all over again. The joke had been Rowan's idea. She'd wanted to go viral. And Cassie had! And now Rowan was going to pretend she wasn't involved? She was jealous, Cassie decided. Jealous that she hadn't come up with something as good as Cassie's. In fact, she remembered, Rowan hadn't come up with any ideas at all. She'd demanded everyone else do all the heavy lifting while she sat back and watched.

That was what Rowan *always* did, Cassie realized.

Cassie shook her head, trying to focus on the here and now. She was at Level 1, and she needed a plan, and she needed Sarah — and more aptly, Sarah's brain — to help her. "I don't know. Who cares? Listen, can you meet me right now? Or after dinner? Whenever. I could really use your help. I have to figure this out. Gotta get some people to upvote me and counteract the Condemns, you know?"

Cassie heard everything: the dripping of the rain, which had turned heavy and thick; the rush of water draining into the sewer under the curb; the sound of the bus pulling into the stop around the corner; Sarah's breathing, cautious and quick.

"God," Sarah finally said. "I wish … I wish I could. I do. I do. But I can't. My dad'll kill me if I leave the house tonight."

Cassie waited a beat, finding her words. She thought about asking why, but it didn't really matter. It was hard to admit to anyone, but mostly Sarah, that she needed support. "Look, I really need some help and Rowan doesn't seem like she cares. Maybe I could come over there instead? That way your dad won't get pissed."

Sarah was silent again, long enough that Cassie checked to see if her phone was still in service, or if some faction of the Hive Mob had remotely disconnected her altogether.

"Sorry, Cassie," Sarah said, her voice small and distant. "I'm really, really sorry."

Cassie stared into the middle distance as Sarah hung up. Nowhere to go. No one to help her.

Her fingers started moving on her phone's screen before she could articulate her thoughts.

Dad, Cassie texted, **I've had a super-weird day. I could really use your help.**

Harlon's reply was instantaneous. **Mom and I are always here to help you.**

Cassie ground her teeth. One of the major flaws of the bot: it thought Cassie and her mom were close.

But Dad, she wrote, **I think I'm in some real trouble.**

There's good trouble and bad trouble, my girl. Which kind are you in?

It was a tough question to answer. No one wanted to be convicted by the Hive, of course. But then again, Cassie still wasn't convinced she'd done anything wrong. A question popped into her mind: What if *everyone* who was convicted by the Hive felt the same way she did right now? Was it possible that the things Rachel said about the Hive …

No, the world was crazy, but not so crazy that her mom could actually be right.

I'm not sure yet, Cassie confessed to Harlon.

Harlon's bot took a few seconds to respond. Cassie held her breath — was something wrong with the software? Would this be one of those times when she wouldn't get a response? But then, finally, it came through.

Figure it out, my girl, and then you can take action.

10010700101

Figure it out.

Yeah, good luck with that.

Cassie remained at Level 1 overnight, with a Hold Action icon that meant the Hive algorithm had determined there was a good chance that her ongoing virality would bump her to Level 2. So no one was to take action; no range was assigned; no hashtag had been elevated. She was in limbo, wondering not whether she would go to hell but rather to which circle.

Hey, classics reference! Congratulations, Mom!

Not for the first time, she was relieved that her mom knew next to nothing about the current world and so wasn't aware that her daughter was about to be handed some ridiculous punishment as a result of her joke.

In homeroom, Sarah paled at the sight of her, then flinched as Cassie slid into the empty seat next to her. "Oh, relax," Cassie said, disgusted. "It's not contagious."

But everyone at Westfield had apparently received the same

directive Sarah had: either avoid Cassie McKinney outright or openly mock her. She passed Skylar, he of #DumpSkylar fame, in the hallway and their eyes met in sympathetic solidarity. *Well,* Cassie thought, *he appears no worse for wear. Eventually everything will be fine.*

It was kind of freeing, in a way, being in Level 1. Quiet. In a few days, it would all be over.

But then, on her way to lunch, her earbud dinged again.

LEVEL 2 ACHIEVED.
HOLD. DO NOT FLEE.
AWAIT FURTHER INSTRUCTIONS.

It was just as well, she realized dully, staring at her screen. Now seemed like the perfect opportunity to avoid the cafeteria — and Rowan — altogether and go hide out in the library.

Cassie knew no one who had borne a Level 2 punishment, but she'd followed Level 2 events online, of course. While Level 1s were awarded pretty freely (especially locally), the difference in virality numbers between Levels was exponential, so someone had to do something *really* wrong to jump to Level 2. But all in all, a Level 2 punishment — a few days without food; being shunned; having to apologize in an online video — would be bearable. Embarrassing, but not life changing.

In the media center, Cassie found an empty desk in a quiet corner and tried to make herself invisible while she strategized her next move. She had limited options. Talking to her mom was, naturally, off the table; she could only imagine how smug Rachel would be, how many versions of "I told you so" she would come up with.

Rowan wasn't talking to her, which meant the rest of the group wasn't either, just like a cluster of well-behaved remote-controlled robots. Her friends from her old school hadn't heard from her in months, and Cassie knew she couldn't go to them now. And how could she blame them? She'd ghosted them. They owed her nothing.

Glancing around the library, which used to house books and now was mostly just storage space for various technologies, Cassie felt the threat of tears behind her eyes. She had no one.

She couldn't believe that that was what she once wanted.

*

Cassie was in a state of high-level misery when she got home. It was, she supposed, nice to know who your friends *really* were. But the circumstances were — to use one of her dad's favorite terms — suboptimal. Especially given that it appeared she had *no* friends.

Level 2. She still couldn't believe it. And the Hold Action icon remained. It was possible — likely, even — that it would go away and she would remain at Level 2. But the idea of hitting Level 3 was sheer madness. She just wanted this to be over already.

It was equally maddening that her mother managed to exist in a world where knowledge of the Levels, of the Hive overall, was negligible. She studied Rachel carefully when she got home, checking for hints that she knew Cassie was in a bit of trouble — or even, maybe, for an opening to discuss this with her — but amazingly, her mother knew nothing. So she switched to her default mode, in which she ignored Rachel to the very best of her abilities (hint: exceptionally well). Filtering Momspeak through her brain and keeping only the important stuff was a skill she'd mastered shortly after her father's death, when Rachel had begun blathering at length on topics that were of no interest to Cassie. She employed those skills tonight powerfully, if she did say so herself, and managed to get to bedtime without contributing much more than the occasional grunt, nod or eye-roll to the conversation.

That afternoon she had been exhausted, zombielike. But now, she slipped into bed and knew immediately that sleep would not come. Not for her. She would be tossing and turning and checking her phone.

You could always turn the phone off, Cassie, said the voice in her head that sounded like her mother's. The suggestion was true but impossible. Even with her phone limited to just voice and text, there was no way in the world she would turn it off. She couldn't even tolerate the fifteen minutes it was unavailable to her during mandatory software updates.

And then — she remembered something. Rachel often had trouble sleeping and sometimes took melatonin to help herself drift off. She didn't just take pills or drops, either: she had these chocolate candies laced with the stuff.

Cassie climbed out of bed, crept past the door to her mother's room and sneaked into the kitchen. There, in a cabinet above the stove, she found the stash of melatonin candies, packaged in a cheerful red-and-blue box with the words SWEET SLUMBER! splashed across it in yellow.

According to the box, a partial dose — one candy — would help you relax. Two candies would really knock you out and three would send you into "blissful dreamland!"

She would settle for plain old sleep, honestly. Blissful dreamland seemed too much to hope for.

Those dosages were for old people, though. Younger metabolisms burned hotter and faster. Cassie figured she'd need a higher dose, so she chomped her way through five of the candy-coated slumber bombs. It felt weird slugging down so much candy at bedtime, but she made short work of them and then, satisfied that she'd solved at least this problem, headed back to bed.

10010800101

Cassie awoke to the sound of her mother's voice and an insistent electronic bleating that seemed determined to bludgeon its way into her skull. She groaned and flapped her hands into the darkness. All she wanted was to go back to sleep.

But there was Rachel's voice, right there along with the endless pinging sound. Rachel, saying her name over and over again, and other things, too, speaking so rapidly into the thick air of night and sleep that it threatened to become one endless word.

"Cassie Cassie wake up wake up Cassie Cassie can you hear me wake up wake up wake UP sweetie wake UP we have to go we have to run Cassie Cassie for the love of God wake up ..."

Cassie cleared her throat and tested opening her eyes. Her room was dark, her mother's face looming close and huge and wide-eyed. "Now," Rachel said. "Get up right now."

"No, Mom. I'm tired. Can't we do this in the morning?" It came out more like "Numuh, 'm tied. Kenny deuce inna mornin'?"

And then Rachel actually *touched* her, grabbed her by her

shoulders right there in bed and shook her fiercely. Or at least, as fiercely as her mom could manage. Cassie had inherited Harlon's height and broad swimmer's shoulders and towered over her mom when standing. Still, the physical contact finally roused Cassie enough that she peered around the room, bleary-eyed and muzzy-minded.

"What the hell, Mom? Let me sleep."

Rachel said nothing. She simply thrust Cassie's phone in her face. It took a moment for Cassie's vision to adjust to the sudden light in her eyes.

The pinging. Endless pinging. It was from her phone. And the screen was dead black except for a single, large, luminous numeral in the center.

5

No.

No way.

She blinked rapidly and shot up into a sitting position, snatching the phone from her mother's grasp as she did so. Bringing the screen closer to her face — as though seeing the individual pixels would change things — she stared.

LEVEL 5 ACHIEVED.
LEVEL 5 ACHIEVED.
LEVEL 5 ACHIEVED.
INSTRUCTIONS WILL BE FORTHCOMING.
FLEEING THE CITY MAY RESULT IN
ENHANCED RANGE PENALTIES.

Level 5. Not Level 3. Which would have still been a shock, but would have at least made some kind of sense. No, she was at Level 5, and no matter how badly her mind wanted to contort the bends and lines of that number 5 into a 3, it just didn't work.

She'd gone from Level 2 to Level 5 literally overnight. Not even overnight, really — it was still the middle of the night. Four in the morning, if her phone was to be believed.

"We have to get out of here," Rachel told her, her voice raw with fierce urgency. "Now."

Cassie could do little more than stare at her phone and shake her woozy head, trying to clear it of sleep. Her mother dragged her out of bed and wrapped a coat around her. "I'll pack a bag," Rachel said. "Go get your toothbrush."

Cassie blinked. Her toothbrush. Sure. That made perfect sense. In the bathroom, she grabbed her toothbrush and a few other things and then started giggling uncontrollably.

It was so *stupid*. It was just so amazingly, idiotically stupid. This just could *not* be happening. She'd made a joke. A funny one! A joke that harmed no one!

Rachel came up behind her, snatching the toiletries from her hands and thrusting them into Cassie's backpack. "Shoes. Now. Go."

A million years ago — when her life had made sense — the family had taken a trip to the Grand Canyon. For reasons that were beyond ten-year-old Cassie's abilities to fathom, they'd had to wake up at some ungodly before-sunrise hour to catch the flight to Arizona. Her mom had gently woken her, then kissed her forehead and urged her into her clothes for the trip. A hell of a contrast to the demon woman now shoving her out the door and into the hallway.

Soon, they were outside, Cassie stumbling after her mother down the stoop at the front of their building. The cool fall air was just cold enough that she could see her breath. Her father had always said that it wasn't really cold out until you could see your own breath; anything less was just brisk.

Her father. God. How could she have forgotten?

"Mom," she said. "I forgot. I have to go back."

Rachel, two steps ahead, turned and snapped, "Are you insane? We have to *run*, Cassie!"

Edging back up the stairs, Cassie replied fiercely, "No, no. I'll be right back. I promise. Right back."

Rachel bounded up the stairs and caught Cassie by the left wrist, squeezing much harder than was necessary. Cassie cried out.

"Are you on something?" Rachel demanded. "Did you take something? Because you're making *no* sense and we have got to run right-the-hell now!"

As if on cue, a light flared up the block. Cassie turned in that direction as her mother whispered, "Oh, shit."

Now Cassie knew it was serious. Her mother never, ever swore around her.

"They're coming," Rachel said. "Come on."

"My bracelet," Cassie protested as her mother dragged her down the steps. "The one Dad gave me. I have to go back for it." It was more than a gift; it was the last gift he'd given her before he died. She had to have it.

"You want *them* to find you here?" Rachel jerked her head up the block. What had been a single light was now a dozen.

Two dozen. A Hive Mob, lit by their phones, advancing on her. Marching down the street as though she were a —

She was.

She couldn't believe what she was seeing. And yet a part of her still wanted to pull away from Rachel, run back up to the apartment, grab the bracelet. Other than the Turing AI, it was the thing that most connected her to her father. Without it, could she really …

Really …

Really *what*? What exactly was her mother planning?

We have to run! Rachel had said. And, yeah, sure, that made sense. Run. But … the way Levels worked, each convict had a certain amount of time during which they couldn't escape, couldn't leave their immediate neighborhood, in order to ensure everyone who wanted to participate in the assigned Justice had a chance to do so. And between facial recognition tech in every camera on every street corner and GPS broadcasts from her phone … Running was necessary, but pointless. At Level 5, the default range meant the mob had a *year* to hunt her down. Where was she supposed to go? How was she supposed to hide for that long?

There was no way and nowhere. She still had her phone, which could be tracked. It was illegal to dump your phone while you were being hunted but not illegal to run. She'd never perceived the paradox before, but now it was so bright that she expected the air around her to effervesce. They *wanted* people to run so the mob could hunt. There was no sport, no release, no satisfaction in a quiescent prey. But you couldn't run too well because otherwise the mob would go bloodless and fleshless.

How had she never realized any of this before?

They came closer, and Rachel cried out to her from the curb, where a car waited, the engine running. Where had it come from? How had she not noticed it before?

And that was when she realized: none of this felt real because none of it *was* real. She was dreaming. Of course it was impossible to jump from Level 2 to Level 5 in a matter of hours. And how would such a mob have amassed in the middle of the night?

None of it was real. Now that she had realized it, she was in that state of lucid dreaming, where she could think clearly again. She'd dosed herself with her mom's melatonin before bed, and melatonin, she remembered now, usually triggered intense dreams. Many times she'd heard her mother complain about them when she took more than one.

Rachel took Cassie's hands in her own. "Please, baby. We have to go. I don't know what's going on with you, but they're coming and we have to go now, OK?"

Cassie grunted. "This is all just a dream, Mom. It's OK. I'll wake up soon."

Her mother stared at her in bug-eyed amazement. It was actually sort of amusing, and Cassie couldn't stifle a laugh.

"Stop it!" her mother roared, and then slapped Cassie across the face with a hand that was most assuredly not a part of any dream.

"Get in the goddamn car!" Rachel howled, biting down on each syllable, no longer willing to plead and wheedle. She dragged Cassie down the steps and over to the car, where she flung open the door.

As her mother slammed the door and ran around to the

driver's side, Cassie stared through the windshield at the approaching mob, her left hand gingerly probing the cold, tender flesh of her cheek.

It's real, she thought. *It's really happening.*

A moment later, the car's electric engine whined and they backed away from the crowd. Rachel spun the wheel hard, overriding the car's AI, which protested at the sudden jerk of the wheel, and soon they were roaring away from home and danger — to what, Cassie had no idea.

*

Cassie turned her phone over and over in her hands, staring down at the gigantic glowing 5 as it tumbled in the darkness of the car. As long as she focused on that, she could manage to block out everything else. The wind along the car. The sound of her mother clucking her tongue softly, something she did when she was stressed. The near-silent electric whir of the car's engine. The pounding of her own heart, the hot oceanic roar of her pulse in her ears.

This was really happening. She'd been accelerated to Level 5 and the world was coming for her. This rental car her mom had summoned via an app couldn't help her. At Level 5, the entire country would be looking for her. Looking to …

"What's the punishment?" she said.

Her mom turned her attention briefly from the road. The car took over, reducing speed to the legal limit and straightening their lane presence. "What?" Mom asked.

"The punishment. Am I #stoneher or #publicjunk or what?"

Cassie's phone was still locked, broadcasting only its GPS, showing only her Level.

"I don't know," Mom said. "I didn't check."

Cassie didn't believe her. Mom was a terrible liar.

"I woke up when your phone started going off. You didn't wake up, so I went in. I saw the number on the screen and I freaked out. I knew we had to run."

That actually sounded like the Rachel Cassie knew. Maybe Mom hadn't bothered to check her own phone to see what the hashtag punishment was.

"Mom, I can't run for a year. What am I supposed to do?" No one had been killed intentionally by a Hive Mob, but there had been accidents. And some of the punishments were traumatic enough that you would wish you'd been killed. Kidnapped. Held hostage. Starved and beaten. Scarred, branded, tattooed …

"We'll run as long as we can," Rachel told her. "Take each day as we can."

Cassie had been thinking and talking in the singular, but her mom kept saying "we." "You can't do this with me, Mom."

Rachel took the steering wheel back in her hands, clutching it until her knuckles cracked. "The hell I can't," she snarled. "You know what lionesses do in the wild when their cubs are threatened? While the males are out hunting, the females are home protecting the babies from everything that creeps, crawls, bites and claws. And it's hell to pay if you try to take a lioness's cubs."

"Mom, you're not a lioness. You're a classics professor." Either the melatonin was wearing off or the adrenaline in Cassie's system was overwhelming it. She was starting to think more clearly. "We're not, like, *ninjas* or anything."

"The plural of *ninja* is *ninja*," Rachel said absently, and cranked the wheel to the left, peeling off onto a side street.

"I'm glad we know that. But you can't go running and hiding with me!" Cassie sputtered. "You have a job. A *life*."

Rachel stabbed savagely at the car's touch screen. The headlights dimmed and the infrared night-vision HUD came up. They floated eerily down the street, guided by the car.

Turning to face Cassie, Rachel said, "My *job*? You think I care about my job at a time like this? You're my daughter, Cassie. You are my life and my blood. I'm not letting some technical glitch in the fabric of the universe take you away from me for a single minute. No, wait, not a single *second*. You got that?"

Her mom's expression was slightly frightening. Cassie hated to respond, hated to let it in, but she was terrified. No matter how old she was, no matter how independent, there was a part of her that yearned to surrender and let an adult take the wheel. *Metaphorically*, she thought, glancing at her mom's hands in her lap. Rachel was wringing her fingers, practically scratching herself.

As though her body had a mind of its own, Cassie found herself leaning across the center console, met halfway by her mother, and the two of them embraced for the first time since … could that be right? Since the day Harlon died.

"What are we going to do?" Cassie asked, slumping into her mother. "Where are we going to go?"

"Don't worry," Rachel murmured against Cassie's ear. "Don't worry. I know where to go."

*

Her mom *did* know where to go; that was the crazy thing. Who knew boring old Rachel McKinney would be such an expert at evading the law?

The car piloted them unerringly and with maximum efficiency to MS/BFU. "Once we're there," Rachel said, "we can hide out in the stacks and figure out our next move."

It was an idea both brilliant and antiquated, so it made perfect sense that her mom would devise it. The stacks. Unlike Westfield High, MS/BFU still had rows and rows of actual books on its property. The library at the university was like an iceberg, Cassie knew from her visits: a smallish structure aboveground, almost unnoticeable among the other buildings on campus, with sublevel after sublevel of bookshelves spreading out underground. Some old alumnus of the university had left in his will a tidy sum that, properly invested, had guaranteed the operating budget of the library long after most colleges and universities had gone all-digital for their reference and research areas. MS/BFU had one of the world's foremost analog collections, not that anyone but oldsters like Rachel bothered using it.

Deep underground, where no one went … No cell signal could penetrate or escape once you were below a certain level, and even Wi-Fi got dodgy down there, unable to infiltrate all those concrete walls and endless shelves crammed with dense paper.

It was a good idea, but something was gnawing at Cassie. "Here's the thing, Mom," she pointed out. "I can't stay down there forever."

"It's just for a little while," Rachel assured her. Her voice was calmer than it had been before, but Cassie could still hear the edge to it, that underlying current of panic. "Until we can figure out something else. Or until I can get this all cleared up."

"Mom, it's the Hive. You don't clear it up. It comes for you … and then it's over."

Rachel wrung her hands as the car painstakingly parallel parked itself a block from the library. "There has to be *something* we can do. Some kind of appeals process."

Cassie couldn't help it; despite her terror, the phrase "appeals process" made her laugh out loud. "Can you convince the millions of people downvoting me to upvote me instead? That's the only appeals process. Good luck with that."

"I'll think of something," Rachel mumbled. She killed the engine and wrenched open the door.

Cassie sighed heavily. Her mother right now was a perfect blend of naive and badass. Cassie's own natural inclination to not trust her mother, to dismiss her ideas, warred with her ongoing desperation. No choice. None at all.

She got out of the car and slipped her backpack on.

*

Rachel felt a migraine starting as she grabbed Cassie by the wrist and pulled her along the sidewalk. She hadn't had a migraine in months, not since right after Harlon's death, and she'd stopped keeping a stash of meds in her purse. She would have to bull through this. Did lionesses let a little thing like the sensation of an ice-cold railroad spike being driven through their skulls keep them from protecting their cubs? Hell, no. Neither would she.

Rachel knew Cassie enjoyed the clueless-about-the-modern-world demeanor she put on, but she knew more about the Hive than Cassie thought. She'd been married to Harlon McKinney, after all. She knew there would be consequences — dire ones — if she got caught. If *they* got caught. But Rachel would dare any mother to say she wouldn't do exactly the same thing in Rachel's position.

"Come on," she told Cassie, and she already sounded brittle to her own ears. She forced herself to steady her voice. "Library is this way. Let's go."

Cassie resisted for a moment. "Are you OK? You're getting a headache, aren't you?"

"I'm fine," she assured Cassie. "Hurry."

At this hour, the library would be shuttered, but Rachel could get in with her faculty ID. It was the first thing she'd done on her first day — guarantee that she had access to the stacks at all hours. Contrary to popular belief, there was knowledge in the world that could not be found in the endless tracts of Google or Wikipedia. Original editions with the authors' notes scribbled in margins. Volumes so forlorn and forgotten that they'd never been scanned and uploaded. A whole world of secret knowledge lurking under a layer of dust, waiting to be discovered.

And now, serving as a hideout for her fugitive daughter.

She'd expected the sodium-lit cobblestone paths cutting through the quad to be empty at this hour, but it *was* a college campus, one populated by overachievers. Even this early in the morning (or this late at night, depending on how you viewed it), there were a few students out and about, either staggering home from all-nighters and hookups or heading out to get a jump start on the day.

Holding Cassie's hand tightly, she hauled her daughter toward the library. The first glint of morning light was appearing over the horizon, splitting the dark of night. Migraine or not, she chose to see the rising sun as a metaphor. A hopeful one.

That optimism lasted roughly sixty seconds. That was how long it took for the first student to pause as they passed, turning to watch. At first Rachel thought he was checking out one of them — Cassie, no doubt, let's be honest — and her protective mother's instincts flared along with her migraine. But then she realized he was also checking his phone. A tone had gone off just as they'd passed by, the sort of alert she'd never heard before.

"Hive proximity alert," Cassie muttered, reading her mind.

Proximity alert. Right. She remembered hearing about this. Designed to make it easier for the predator to track the prey. At Level 5, Cassie's phone broadcast a signal to other phones in the immediate area, alerting people that a digital criminal was nearby. It hardly seemed fair; one more advantage to a mob that had so many.

She walked faster, tugging Cassie away from the student, who now was tapping his phone. Getting more details? Contacting others? Rachel didn't have time to guess.

Two young women with the look of being partied out of breath, heels slung over their shoulders, nudged each other, touched their earbuds, then double-checked their phones as she and Cassie passed. They argued briefly and then one of the women broke away from the other and started following them.

"Mom, get out of here," Cassie said, her voice low, her eyes darting. In a nearby building, a window flickered with light, then a shadow appeared there, as if gazing out. Alerts were sounding in the distance; students were waking up to their phones bleating.

THERE'S A LEVEL 5 RIGHT OUTSIDE!
JOIN THE MOB! HIVE! HIVE!

Her lioness self-image aside, Rachel suddenly realized how powerless she was. They were a block from the library. A single block. On a summer day, you wouldn't even notice the distance as you walked it. But on this fall night, brightening to morning, it suddenly seemed insurmountable. There were four people surrounding them now, and while they didn't look particularly dangerous, they were twice as many as Cassie and Rachel.

"Go, Mom," Cassie told her. "Give me your ID card. I'll get to the library."

Before Rachel could respond, a rock came flying through the air at them. She pushed Cassie aside as a bright blossom of pain exploded in her head. It took a single, long second to realize the pain came from the inside, not the outside — the rock had missed her, but the sudden shock had jump-started her migraine into full action.

"What's wrong with you?" she heard herself scream at the rock thrower. "What in the world is *wrong* with you?"

Her anger only seemed to embolden them. The four closed in. Rachel cursed and told Cassie to follow her as she quick-walked toward the library, wishing she had some sort of weapon. Her purse contained nothing more hazardous than a little canister of Mace that was probably past its expiration date.

She checked anyway, rummaging through her bag, and then

realized, to her shock, that Cassie wasn't following her. She turned to see her daughter standing perfectly still on the pathway as the four students advanced on her.

"Cassie!" Screaming, she forgot all about the Mace, all about everything else and anything else. Her only child was standing in harm's way, and Rachel reacted the same way she would if she saw Cassie standing in the middle of a busy highway.

She ran back to Cassie, swinging her purse by its strap. There was nothing dangerous in the purse, true, but there was a heavy hardcover book she'd been meaning to read for two weeks now. Still uncracked but solid. Her purse connected with the first student who'd seen them, the boy, clocking him across the face.

He shouted in pain and shock and surprise, and took a step back that satisfied her immensely. The migraine was now a hard, piercing pain above her left eye. She ignored it and swung the purse again, this time smashing it straight into his nose. Blood burst from him, gushing, and he staggered back, his hands to his crimson face.

Of the three others, one was the clearly hungover woman who'd ditched her friend for some Hive action. The other two were boys. Men, really. One tall and stocky, the other smaller, but with the feral look men have when they know they can get away with something. Rachel took a deep breath and raised the purse.

"Run, Cassie! Run!" She would hold them off as long as possible. Keep them from chasing Cassie. Give her some cover.

Cassie shook her head sadly. "There's no point, Mom. This is how it works. Let me just get it over with."

The migraine was nearly blinding. Her hearing was fine, but

she still couldn't believe her ears. "I did not raise you to quit!" she yelled. The two men exchanged glances and then advanced. The woman hung back, licking her lips.

Who needed an entire mob? She almost laughed out loud. All it took was a clutch of college students with phones to track and do whatever they wanted to Cassie.

"Run!" she shouted again and just then the two men pounced, one of them dodging Rachel's clumsy new purse swing as the other knocked her off-balance. She stumbled backward and nearly fell — would have, if not for one of the men, grabbing her and keeping her upright.

"Keep out of this, bitch," one of them snarled, and some *hell, no* part of Rachel just broke in that moment and she began screaming at them, screaming and flailing as the man pinned her arms to her side, screaming her throat raw, the migraine now banished by some fight-or-flight hormone racing through her body.

And still Cassie did nothing, standing frozen, staring dopily into the middle distance as the woman came up behind her, one high-heeled shoe brandished like a club.

Crack! The sickening sound of struck bone resonated as the woman brought her heel down on the back of Cassie's head. Rachel's scream died in shock as she watched her daughter stumble forward, blood geysering into the air from where she'd been hit.

Barely realizing she was doing it, Rachel stomped down on the foot of the man holding her. She had thrown on her boots, thinking she'd need something more practical than heels for running with Cassie, and their heavy soles made a solid impact.

She felt rather than heard a crunch as bones in the man's foot snapped under her weight. He howled in anger and pain … but mostly in pain. His grip on her slackened, and she pulled away, spinning around and delivering a clumsy but effective kick between his legs.

She'd never in her life kicked a man in the nuts. It felt surprisingly satisfying, especially the way his howl jumped an octave.

Something no one had ever told her about kicking a man there — it hurts, sure, but it *pisses them off.* He was clearly in ten sorts of agony, but lurched toward her anyway, arms reaching out. Fortunately, his broken foot hobbled him and he collapsed to his knees before he could put a hand on her.

The other two men seemed a little wary now, especially the one with the nose gushing blood. Their buddy had touched the stove and gotten burned. They didn't want to suffer his fate.

"Cassie!" she called out. Her voice was clear and unwavering. The migraine was banished to some dusty corner of her brain. Fighting for her kid's life was the world's best analgesic. Who knew? "Cassie! Are you OK?"

Nothing from behind her. She thought of Cassie, bleeding on the ground, dying, and forced herself not to. One of the men — the only uninjured one — feinted in her direction and she swung the purse again. It connected with the side of his face. Never intended to be used as a weapon, the purse split along one of the seams, spilling its contents, a tangle of makeup accessories hurtling at him. A power cable for her phone. Her wallet. The now-useless canister of Mace …

And a nail file. She'd forgotten that was in there. And now it was embedded in his face, having speared through his cheek.

When he opened his mouth to scream, she could see the glint of the metal file inside.

Rachel spun around. The woman was closing in on Cassie, who was down on her knees, pressing her hands to the wound in the back of her head.

"Get the fuck away from my daughter!" Rachel bellowed at the woman, who looked up, startled, as though she had been innocently reading poetry when Rachel raged at her like a maniac.

Rachel took a step toward her and the woman's nerve — probably pretty frayed to begin with — broke. She bolted.

A quick check over her shoulder told Rachel that the three men, though wounded, were still a threat. Bloody-Nose Guy was edging closer to her. Speared Cheek had yanked the file from his face and now brandished it like he thought he'd pulled the sword from the stone. Broken Foot was out of the running but was goading the other two from the ground.

She pulled Cassie to her feet. "Just want it over ..." Cassie mumbled.

The back of her daughter's head was a matted mass of blood and hair. *Head wounds bleed a lot*, Rachel reminded herself. *It's not as bad as it looks.*

"Let it be over," Cassie said.

"Sweetie, we have to run. Do it for me, baby, OK? Do it for your dad, OK?"

At the mention of Harlon, a light seemed to flicker in Cassie's eyes. Rachel tamped down her jealousy, channeling it into action. "Let's go."

Cassie stumbled with her, arm in arm. Then, after finding her footing, she broke into a proper run. The two raced up the walk, then took a sharp turn and ran down a tree-lined pathway. The library came into view ahead of them. It was, Rachel realized in that moment, now completely useless to them: her ID card was on the ground in the wreckage of her purse, a hundred yards behind them.

Casting a look over her shoulder, she saw one of the men — she couldn't tell which — hobble-running up the hill toward them. There was no way to go back.

She'd failed. She'd had one job to do — protect Cassie — and she'd figured out how to do it, but she'd failed nonetheless. The other lionesses were going to kick her out of the mom club.

I could use an actual mom club right about now, she thought, imagining herself swinging a spiked mace at the head of the guy running after them.

Her mind raced. Where could they go? At this hour, nothing on campus was open. She was tempted to tell Cassie to toss her phone. Yes, it was illegal. So what? She'd rather see her daughter prosecuted for avoiding Hive Justice than subjected to it.

The library was right in front of them now. Rachel's breath was ragged in her throat and chest; Cassie was wheezing.

"Around back," Rachel managed, tugging Cassie in the right direction. Cassie's eyes questioned the move — the door was *right there* — but she had no breath to ask why.

The back of the library. There was an old return slot there, from back when people bothered to borrow books. They would slip Cassie's phone in there and then make for Rachel's office. She could talk the security guard into letting them in. They'd hole up there for a couple of hours, plan a new move.

They crashed through a thicket of bushes that ringed the

library, taking a shortcut that brought them around the side of the building, cutting them off from the sight line of the man chasing them. Now that he could no longer see them and they could no longer see him, Rachel's breathing came a little more easily. She didn't want to slow down, though; she urged Cassie to run faster, and they came around the other corner of the library and —

Ran smack into a man who emerged from the shadows.

*

The guy who stepped out of the shadows had long red dreadlocks and shoulders wider than most doorways. He looked so much like a Norse god that Cassie half expected him to wield a hammer and drink mead from a horn. Part of Cassie noted that her mother would be very proud of her for the reference; she hoped she would be able to remember this later, post–Hive Justice, when they had a moment to breathe.

The other part was just plain gobsmacked. College men = impressive.

And threatening, she reminded herself, coming back to earth and banishing her inner Brontë heroine to some corner of her subconscious. He was several inches taller than Cassie, clearly a workout buff, and — most important of all — he had his phone out, the Hive proximity alert bleating.

Cassie moaned. The throbbing in her head where that drunk-ass Hiver had clocked her with a shoe was beginning to fade; she no longer felt her heartbeat there. With the ebbing pain, she began to feel like herself again. She'd had a scary moment there when she'd wanted to give up, when it had seemed too overwhelming to run. And then that first moment of physical violence, so crushing and complete and horrifying … She'd wanted to lie down and die.

But Mom had made her run. Had reminded her of Dad. Had forced her to live. And that's what she wanted — to live.

The redhead's phone kept beeping. He thumbed the Mute switch and shoved it into his pocket. Cassie gritted her teeth and decided she'd throw herself right at him. Take him by surprise. His wrists were exposed, their blue veins standing out against his skin. If she bit through them, he'd bleed out pretty quickly, she imagined.

Before she could move, though, her mother blurted out, "Bryce?"

Cassie turned to her mom.

"You *know* this guy?"

"He's a student." She wedged herself between Cassie and Bryce the Giant. "But I'm still not letting him hurt you."

Seeing her tiny mother stand between her and a guy the size of a California redwood once would have inspired a derisive blast of laughter from Cassie. But after watching her mother go full ninja on a quartet hell-bent on hurting her, Cassie could do nothing but take her mother very, very seriously.

Bryce hesitated an instant. "Professor McKinney," he started, then seemed to think better of it. With a smooth, graceful sweep of his arm, he shoved Rachel aside and grabbed Cassie by the wrist. The clutch of his massive hand sent a jolt of pain up Cassie's arm, which worsened when she tried to pull away. Bryce held her fast, and all she managed was to come close to dislocating her shoulder.

"Let go, you freak!" She twisted, trying to slip out of his grip, but it was like trying to dance with a boa constrictor.

"Bryce, please!" Rachel pleaded. "Don't do this! You're better than this!"

Bryce turned to Rachel, which was Cassie's opportunity. She stopped pulling and instead leaned in, flinging herself *at* Bryce, kicking out at the same time. She connected with his knee, and he yelped with surprise and pain, dropping onto his other knee. No luck, though. He still held her fast.

Rachel took advantage of the moment and came at Bryce, raking her nails down his face. He jerked back his head, and she was able only to rip the flesh of his forehead. Shallow but bloody furrows appeared there.

"Stop it!" he whispered fiercely. "I'm trying to help! We're wasting time!"

Both McKinney women froze. Cassie tugged ineffectually at her own captive arm. "You have a funny way of showing it."

Bryce glared at her and then, testing his sore knee, stood up. "You have to come with me. It's the only way."

Cassie blinked. Was this actually happening? Was someone trying to help?

"You can trust me," Bryce said, as though he could read her mind. "I'm one of the good guys."

Rachel looked from Bryce to Cassie and back again.

"I don't think we have a choice, Mom," Cassie told her. Bryce was still holding her by the wrist, but he'd relaxed his grip quite a bit. She knew she could twist out of his grasp now, but she didn't want to. Maybe it was desperation talking, but she trusted him. Her own words rang in her head; she really, truly had no choice.

There was a mob coming for her, and she'd take any chance she could to get away.

Rachel nodded thoughtfully, then started at a sound. From behind them and around the corner, a cry had gone up, followed by footfalls on cobblestones. Someone was coming. Many someones, from the sound of it.

"I'm going with you," Rachel said.

"No," Bryce said firmly. "We have to travel light."

"This is a better chance than we had before," Cassie said, and instantly regretted it. An expression of wounded shock flickered to life briefly on her mom's face before her expression returned to concern and fear.

Cassie hadn't meant it that way. Her mom had done her best. She was just safer without her now, was all.

More sounds.

"Mom —" Cassie began, but then Bryce pulled — not hard, but insistently — and she ran off with him, leaving her mother alone in the dawn.

*

Guys something big is happening on MS/BFU campus. Who's got boots on the ground? **#msbfu #PotentialHive**

I just saw someone hurl a shoe. WTF is happening on the **#msbfu** quad right now?!

I need pizza. **#msbfu**

Wait, who's being chased? I want in! I never made it to the gym today lol. **#GetThoseStepsIn #msbfu**

Hey **#msbfu**! It's almost SENIOR WEEK! Have you signed up to volunteer yet? → ms.bfu/volunteer20

Anyone else hearing weird noises outside on the quad? I'm trying to cram for my chem test and a-holes are making it hard. **#msbfu**

Ummmmm I just saw four people attack someone. Is there a **#HiveMob** happening on **#msbfu** right now?!

HIVE ALERT: Activity is being tracked on the MS/BFU campus. Follow for details.

Yasss! There hasn't been a good mob on campus in ages. What's this one for? **#msbfu**

HIVE ALERT: A mob seeking justice for **#CassieMcKinney** is forming on the MS/BFU campus. **#msbfu**

10010900101

"Where are you taking me?"

"Where were you going?" Bryce countered. His hand, large and hot, remained wrapped around her wrist as they ran.

"We were headed to the library," Cassie said through gasps for air. The backpack bounced against her shoulder blades, but she was more attentive to the flare of pain at the back of her head that each step produced. She ignored them both as best she could. "Cell signals —"

"Good idea," Bryce said, guiding her around a cluster of small trees, "but wrong place. They'll know you went into the library, tracking your last known signal. Then they can just close it down and find you. There are only so many ways out of there, and most of them are alarmed."

"Then where —"

"Left now."

She followed Bryce's lead, crashing through a thicket of

overgrown shrubbery. The university needed to reconsider its landscaping budget.

Scratched and torn by brambles and sharp branches, she emerged with Bryce into a smallish clearing, no more than ten feet wide, canopied by a massive nearby elm tree that seemed to almost stoop with age. Bryce crouched down and swept his hand along the ground, brushing away leaves to reveal a sewer cover.

"Are we going —" She broke off at a glare from him, then lowered her voice. "Are we going into the *sewers*? Is that …"

"Wouldn't stink be better than death?" he whispered back, wiping his forehead. Sweat had mixed with the blood from Rachel's claw attack, and now it smeared over his flesh. "Besides, it's not the sewers. It's an old steam-heating maintenance tunnel from before the university switched over to solar heat."

He focused his attention on the grate, fitting his fingers into slots on the rim of the cover. Cassie wondered if she should help, but he seemed to know what he was doing and besides, Bryce was a Norse god, right? What good would her puny mortal muscles do?

He strained and grunted, pulling with all his might. His face went as red as his hair. Cassie thought something might rupture.

She hunkered down next to him, aware of sounds and shouts in the near distance, aware of how much time they were wasting. "Do you need help?" she asked.

He huffed in a breath, puffed it out and fixed her with a solid, annoyed stare that said, *Please for the love of God shut the hell up — I'm trying to focus here.*

She shut up. Let him do his big-man-on-campus thing.

Bryce drew in another breath, exhaled, then, on the next

inhale, heaved with all his might. The edge of the grate came up an inch, and he twisted it to the side, setting the cover gently and silently on the rim of the hole it concealed.

"Yes," Cassie hissed. From where they had run came fresh shouts, closer than the others had been.

"Usually do this with two other guys. Come on."

Lying on his back, he shoved the cover aside some more with his feet, then dropped into the dark space below. Cassie swallowed hard, seeing absolute pitch-black down there and nothing else. By reflex, she went for her phone and poked at the screen, looking for the flashlight app. Instead, she was greeted with the flashing 5, over and over. It was ungodly bright in the predawn gloom, and she hurriedly stuffed it back into her pocket.

No guts, no glory, her dad used to say.

"And no digestion," young, stupid Cassie would say. It never failed to draw a big belly laugh from Harlon.

Dad, why the hell did you leave me? she thought, then went feet-first into the hole.

*

Bryce didn't so much catch her as guide her fall, his hands finding her body in the dark and pushing her a bit so she didn't come down too hard or collide with a wall on her way down. One hand brushed her butt and the other touched a breast. He didn't apologize. She wasn't sure if she liked that or not.

"You OK?" he whispered hoarsely.

She was. The fall had been short — seven or eight feet, maybe. For Bryce, at six foot and lots of change, it was nothing. Cassie was tall, but not Viking tall. There'd been a moment of vertiginous terror, then Bryce's hands, then the ground.

And safety. Safety most of all. Dark. Underground. Hidden.

A sound made her look up. Somewhere nearby, a cry had gone up, and all the safety of the subterranean black went away. The mob had grown, from the sound of it, and it was close. If she could make out the leaves of the elm through the moon-crescent opening of the grate, then they would be able to find her. Easily.

Bryce gently moved her aside and stood beneath the opening. From a dark corner, he had produced a long pole that looked something like a shepherd's crook, but stouter and with a strange sort of three-pronged gripping fork at the end of it. He poked this gadget straight up and the prongs slid into grooves on the underside of the cover.

"Gonna need some help this time," he said, utterly without shame or worry.

Good. The sooner they got it closed, the safer Cassie would feel, and hopefully the more her racing heart and sweaty palms would get the message. Bryce had one hand above the other on the pole, spaced apart by a foot or so. Facing him, Cassie gripped it between his hands and followed his lead. When he pulled back, she pushed forward. After a moment of absolutely nothing, her arms began to tremble and weaken, but then there *was* movement. Above, the moon crescent waned, going blacker, and she redoubled her effort, grinding her teeth, digging in her heels. She directed every morsel of strength in her body to her arms and her hands.

The cover slid farther and farther. The tiny slice of lighter darkness shrank and shrank and then, with a *thunk* that sounded too loud, it disappeared entirely.

They waited a moment, both of them breathing hard in the pitch-black. The air down here was too thick, cold and humid and stale. It tasted metallic, like unfiltered water from the tap.

The place was also completely still. Unnaturally so. She didn't like it, but she would take it if it meant a minute to regroup.

After a few moments, Bryce blew out a long breath. "I think we're OK. The concrete and iron rebar will block most of your signal," he said, "but they'll still be able to peg your last location down to a few meters. They'll find the cover eventually."

"How did you even know about this place?" she asked, and then held her hand up to shield her eyes as Bryce activated the flashlight in his phone.

He shrugged as if embarrassed by his knowledge. "We used to use the tunnels for LARPing freshman year."

She stifled a sudden giggle. The thought of Bryce, dressed in medieval armor, stomping through the tunnels under the university, swinging a sword, his red dreadlocks flailing …

On second thought, that wasn't so funny. "Well, anyway. I'm glad you know about them."

He nodded very seriously and held out his hand, palm up. "Let me see your phone."

She handed it over to him. He studied it for a moment. "Do you know how to stop the proximity alerts?" she asked.

"Uh-huh," he said, and dropped the phone to the ground and stomped on it with his ridiculously big foot.

"Hey!" Cassie yelped.

He shushed her, annoyed, then stomped on the phone again. The screen was a spiderweb of fissures now, chunks of glass missing. The frame was bent and she could make out the gray hunk of battery under the screen.

"That phone is my life!" she protested.

"Right now, it's your death."

Cassie paused. He wasn't wrong. But ... "That's illegal." Discarding or disabling your phone when on Hive Alert was an analog crime that carried some hefty penalties.

Bryce snorted. "Are you really worried about that?"

It took her a moment to process his question, then she realized: no. No, she wasn't worried about it. She was more worried about running like hell.

"Probably should have done that from the start," she muttered.

He said nothing for a moment, then regarded her with kind eyes. "Hard thing to do. We've all become so accustomed to them — it's like having a second brain. Hard to ditch your phone, even if you know it's for the best. That's what they rely on." He pointed to his ear, and she realized: her earbud. That had Bluetooth, too. It could be tracked.

She popped it out and did the honors herself this time, crushing the little pod under her foot.

Maybe it was hypocritical or just convenient, but she didn't care any longer that Hive Justice was the law of the land. She remembered her dad once railing against people who thought the law didn't apply to them — people who parked in handicapped spots or gunned through red lights. And he was right because the law was *for* everyone, so it applied to everyone.

But all she'd done was tell a joke. A tasteless joke, sure. Offensive and crass? Yeah, OK, she'd cop to that. But the idea that she could be sent to Level 5 and have to go on the run for a year just to avoid being stoned to death … for a *joke* …

The outrage of what was happening, combined with what was left in the wake of her dissipating adrenaline — exhaustion, nausea, a grim sort of numbness — caused a fresh flood of tears. Cassie tried to stifle them but Bryce must have noticed, because he awkwardly put a hand on her shoulder — it felt like a weight — before shuffling a few steps away in some sweet but misguided attempt to give her some privacy.

Cassie didn't want privacy. She wanted to know what the hell this guy was doing with her. *For* her. But she was also, suddenly and deeply, afraid to ask.

"What now?" she asked, her voice husky and thick. Normally, she didn't let people lead her around. But Bryce had shown up at the right time and gotten her this far, so it made sense to give him the wheel for now.

"This way," he told her, pointing the beam of his phone behind her. She looked. The darkness opened into a tunnel, its walls dripping with condensation and mold.

"Then what?"

He shrugged. "At some point, we turn. Don't worry. Let's go before my battery dies. Grab your broken phone — we don't want to leave a trail of breadcrumbs." He strode off, leaving her in encroaching dark.

The idea of being stranded when the phone battery died did not appeal to her. She picked up the pieces of her phone — her old life — and raced after Bryce.

*

It was easy to lose track of time in the tunnel. They were silent as they went along, Bryce a half step ahead, guiding them at every four-way intersection or T. He seemed to know the way intuitively, and she wondered exactly how much time he'd spent down here. His knowledge seemed too in-depth to have come from some innocent live-action role-playing.

The pain in her head had ebbed to a dull, persistent ache that occasionally flared into a sharp stab when she moved her neck too quickly. After a few minutes, she'd risked probing the area with cautious fingers. She needed to know how bad it was.

The bleeding had stopped. Her hair was matted and encrusted with blood, the stuff flaking away and sticking to her hands as she investigated. A large, almost tumorous lump of sensitive flesh had bloomed at the impact site. Touching it sent sparks of pain radiating out, so she avoided it. She couldn't tell if her skull had been breached or not, but nothing seemed to be spilling out of her, so she figured she would live.

At a four-way intersection, Bryce paused for a moment, as though thinking or remembering. Then he put his hand on the wall nearest them, wiped some mold away and nodded to himself. He rubbed his hand on his jeans leg to clean it, then indicated a right turn with a tilt of his head.

Cassie lagged as he headed into the right-hand tunnel. She peered at the wall where he'd put his hand and glanced. In the receding light of Bryce's phone, she made out a symbol, etched into the concrete:

Ω

Omega. Greek letter. The *final* Greek letter, actually. The Greeks had no *Z* — their alphabet went from alpha to omega. Hence the bit from the Bible where God says, "I am the Alpha and the Omega." *I'm everything,* he was saying. *I'm all of it. Ain't nothing but me.*

Having a classics professor for a mother helped in times like this. She could recite, if need be, all sorts of classical allusions and references to omega. But she was still baffled as to why it was carved into a wall down in the old steam tunnels, and that confusion offered a momentary break from the thudding fear that followed her down the tunnels with every step.

It was getting dark; Bryce hadn't slowed down. Cassie raced to catch up to him.

"Where exactly are we going?" she asked him, breaking their silence. "And what's the deal with the omega on the wall?"

"It's not an omega," he told her, neatly sidestepping the more important question.

"Of course it is. I'm not an idiot."

"No one said you were." He stopped and frowned at her. "I don't think you're an idiot," he said a bit too earnestly.

"Great. Then treat me like I'm smart," she shot back. She'd allowed her fear to turn into a tether to Bryce. But at some point, she had to clear it from her mind and think for herself. "Where are we going?"

Bryce sighed. "I have some friends. They might be able to help you." Cassie's face lit up. "Might," Bryce cautioned her. "I can't be sure."

"Where are they? Are they the ones who carved that symbol into the wall?" Something occurred to her. "There were symbols carved into all of the walls at all of the intersections, right? I just didn't notice them. That's the only way you could know how to navigate this place."

He nodded. "We use the tunnels to move around when we need to go undetected. Emergencies only."

"So that LARP stuff was bullshit."

Bryce blushed. "Uh, no. That's how we discovered the tunnels."

Cassie found herself grinning again. "Were you Sir Bryce of the Round Table?"

"No, I … " His blush grew furiously redder. "Never mind."

"Tell me!" she said, almost giddy. The pain in her head had subsided to almost nothing by now, and she was safe for the first time in hours *and* there was the promise of help. A lightness filled her.

"I'm not telling you," he said. "Not happening."

She begged some more, but nothing would move him. They walked several yards down the tunnel, then Bryce brought them up short. There was a door set into the wall to their right, recessed half a foot or so from the tunnel. Bryce looked it up and down. Cassie did, too. She spotted the omega just before he did, pointing to the small etching slightly below the top of the door-jamb. She ran her fingers over it; the cold wall and the rough edges reminded her that this wasn't a game. People, real people, had resorted to carving lines into the walls of underground tunnels to find … what? Safety? Escape? Whatever it was, it meant something aboveground wasn't working out well for them.

She could relate.

"OK, good," Bryce said, clearly relieved. "Good."

"This is where we go?" she asked.

Bryce nodded absently but made no move to open the door. It was barricaded with a hefty-looking two-inch-thick wooden bar that she figured she could lift on her own, if need be.

"Before we go any farther," he said, "we need to talk."

"About assigning me a LARP name?" Her attempt at a joke landed flat at Bryce's feet.

"Can you please take this seriously?" he asked, his voice and expression weary.

She crossed her arms over her chest. She didn't need to be told how serious this was. The blood drying in her hair was a pretty solid indicator. She gave him the impatient *OK, talk, I'm listening* look she employed during Mom lectures.

"We have to tread lightly here," he told her. "No one knows we're coming. I'm still new to all of this, but I wanted to help and this is the only way I know how. Let me do the talking, all right?"

"Is this …" She picked her words carefully. "Is this like one of those things in the movies where there's a bunch of people who once got Hive Mobbed who are now hiding out in the sewers and they're, like, called the Underground and they're trying to bring down the system?"

He scowled at her. "Absolutely not."

"Oh." She was disappointed. She thought maybe there was a group to hook up with.

"For one thing," he said, "they don't hang out in the sewers. Gross. They have the top floor of an abandoned building. Nice views. And it's not called the Underground. It's the Organized Human Mutiny."

"But other than those two massive differences … it's a yes?" Cassie scoffed. "I was kind of kidding."

Bryce looked thoughtful. "Isn't that what got you into this mess in the first place?"

Cassie trained her eyes on the ground, chastened. Bryce's words were ricocheting through her brain and she tried to grab on to them. Organized. Human. Mutiny. She looked at the omega symbol again.

It's not an omega, Bryce had said.

It all clicked for her. She almost smiled. Organized Human Mutiny.

OHM.

Ohm. An ohm was represented by an Ω.

It was a term from electronics. She knew it from soldering motherboards with her father.

An ohm was a unit of resistance.

*

There was a moment, right as Bryce lifted the door bar and fished a key from his pocket to unlock the door, when Cassie was still operating just as a girl on the run. Blameless? Nah. But still a victim. And still, she reminded herself, thinking of all the Hive Mobs she'd heard about over the years, and the two she'd participated in, a proponent of Hive Justice.

That all changed as she absorbed the meaning of OHM. Organized Human Mutiny.

Where Bryce was leading her, she realized, was a revolution.

A disruption.

They emerged into a dark, claustrophobic boiler room, the air filled with burps from the nearby furnace. Bryce closed the door behind them and used a thin metal hook to slip through the gap between the door and the wall to reset the door bar on the other side. Then he concealed the hook behind the furnace.

"OK, let's go."

He took her through another doorway into a darkened hall. They made their way to yet another door, this one opening into a stairwell. In silence, they climbed the switchback stairs, three or four stories, at which point a clot of old sofas and mattresses blocked them from going any further.

"Now what?" Cassie asked.

Bryce jimmied open the fire door on the landing just below the blockade and led her into a corridor lined with identical doors on either side. It was a hotel, she realized. An old, run-down, lightless hotel.

Halfway down the hall, Bryce paused. Cassie spotted the Ω before he did, subtly carved into the wood of a door, overlaying the number 3 in such a way as to be almost invisible. Bryce snorted, annoyed and impressed at the same time.

"Beginner's luck?" Cassie said, shrugging as Bryce opened the door.

Cassie hesitated for a moment. Slipping into a hotel room with a guy she'd just met didn't seem like the smartest move. Then again, her options were few and becoming fewer with almost every moment that passed. Reluctantly, she followed Bryce into the room.

It was nearly empty, save for an ancient, enormous CRT television turned on one side, its screen kicked in and gaping wide like a glass-toothed mouth desperate for food. Maybe it was just the hour, the lack of sleep, the adrenaline rush, but that TV looked outright evil to her, something from one of the millions of low-budget horror movies she'd streamed, the ones she wasn't supposed to watch but did anyway. Perfectly normal, perfectly harmless everyday items — dolls, game boards, phones, microwave ovens — suddenly became possessed and dangerous. The TV seemed to be one of them, but in the real world now, and she realized that her mother had been right all along — she shouldn't have watched those movies.

Her mother. Ugh. A wave of grief so powerful that it seemed almost tangible hit her, rocked her back on her heels. In true Cassie/Rachel fashion, they'd parted on a sour note. Cassie hadn't meant to imply that her mother's escape plan was bad, but she knew she'd done just that. She'd basically said, *You did a lousy job protecting me, Mom.* An epically shitty way to leave things. Especially since …

Would she ever see her mother again? What would happen to Rachel if she was identified as helping a Hive fugitive? Bad enough that Cassie had ruined her own life; did she have to crush her mother's, too?

"You all right?" Bryce asked.

She'd almost forgotten he was there. He stood across the room, by the narrow closet door, one hand on the knob.

"Is this where we hide out?" she asked. Other than the TV from hell, the room was empty. The idea of holing up here didn't exactly thrill her …

"No," he said. "Come on."

He opened the closet door and she saw a ladder inside. Bryce climbed up quickly, bidding her to follow him. "Close the door before you come up," he said.

She stepped into the tiny closet, shut the door and had barely enough room to turn around to face the ladder. Pale light came from above, the first she'd seen other than Bryce's phone since they'd closed the steam tunnel cover over their heads.

At the top of the ladder, Bryce helped her onto the floor. This was another hotel room, but the floor squeaked and trembled at her footfalls. "The subfloor is weak. Weakened, I should say. We deliberately undermined it. Unless you walk the right pattern, you'll end up back downstairs. With some broken bones and contusions and more blood, so ..."

The pattern turned out to be pretty simple as she watched him go first and realized what Bryce was doing: you took a number of steps equal to consecutive prime numbers, turning each time the tens digit incremented. Soon they were out in a corridor again.

They made their way farther up in this manner, zigzagging from floor to floor. When rubble blocked a staircase — strategically and intentionally, she now realized — they would prowl the hallways until they found the Ω and then use concealed ladders, stairs and (in one case) a makeshift dumbwaiter to ascend. There were occasional tricks and traps, which Bryce talked her through and around.

She was exhausted by the time they got to the twenty-fifth floor. Her fatigue was mingling with her anger, and she found herself unreasonably mad at OHM for being smart enough to house their escape colony up in the clouds. They'd needed to pull themselves up from the twenty-fourth floor with a complicated rope-and-pulley system, and her shoulders ached.

"How much farther?" she snapped.

"One more floor." Bryce sounded winded. He was stronger

than Cassie but also much, much bigger. More muscles, but those muscles had to move around a lot more weight. He leaned against a wall and slid down to sit. She followed his lead, folding herself cross-legged on what had once been a low-pile carpet and what was now a random mosaic of threads over a plywood floor.

All of the windows they'd come across had been painted over, and the ones in this room were no exception. Only Bryce's phone lit the way, and it had been a couple of hours of constant light.

"I'm gonna shut this off for a minute," he told her. "Save battery. OK?"

In the unfamiliar dark, with a guy she barely knew, in a crumbling old building that was possibly haunted by the ghost of a dead TV.

"Perfect," she muttered.

Darkness enfolded her, the spot where Bryce's phone had been still glowing for a moment, until her eyes forgot its light. She clenched her fists, nails digging into palms. It's not that she was afraid of the dark. She was just *afraid*, period. And angry. Now that they'd stopped, it all rushed in on her.

She struggled to catch her breath.

"It'll be OK," Bryce said. His voice was a ghost in the still, black air. "We're close."

"What am I doing here!" Cassie burst out. The darkness ... it was getting to her.

"Cassie. It's OK. They can help you. I know it. I've seen it before."

Ask questions. It was a regular instruction in the McKinney household. Both Mom and Dad exhorted her all the time:

Ask questions. It's the only way you'll learn anything remotely interesting in the world. The question is humanity's best tool for forward progress.

Her parents argued a lot. Not about anything specific to them or their family or their life together. Just about the world. Her dad's bleeding edge, if-we-can-do-it-then-we-must-do-it attitude constantly at war with Mom's sensibilities, forged in the early fires of ancient Greece and Rome. Words like "disruption," "democratization," "Socratic," and "hegemonic" sailed through the air with great frequency in the McKinney house, and the only way young Cassie could learn to make sense of what her parents were discussing was to, well …

"Why are you helping me?"

It was almost as though he'd been expecting the question at that very moment — his answer was nearly instantaneous. "I don't like a system that beats the hell out of people for what they say."

"First Amendment zealot?"

"Something like that." But there was a pinched quality to his voice. There was more.

"So you do this all the time, then?"

"Not really. Usually I just give money to the right causes. But you're in deep. I thought you needed a rope." He paused. "Plus, I like your mom. She doesn't tolerate any shit."

Cassie didn't know which comment flummoxed her more: the idea of a guy not much older than her "giving money" to causes or the fact that he could actually tolerate Rachel.

Steering away from the too-raw thought of Mom was easy. "When you say 'give money …' "

Discomfort came off him in waves, radiating through the darkness. "I'm rich, OK? Born into it. My grandfather — he's the one who made all the money in the first place — he taught me that when you have a lot, you have to give a lot. So that's what I try to do. All right?"

It was clearly a sore point for him, though as someone who had never had much money and now had even less of it, she couldn't understand why. Still, she moved on.

"What is this place?" she asked the blank space before her. Maybe if he talked, she'd get distracted. History was good at making people forget the present.

Bryce's voice floated to her. "It was supposed to be a hotel. Ran out of funding."

"Who owns it?"

Bryce paused. She imagined him sweeping his dreads off his forehead and frowning. "Good question. I guess *someone* owns it. But OHM hacked the city's zoning databases and removed it, then killed any reference to it on commercial real estate sites, too. As far as the internet is concerned, this place doesn't exist."

Cassie opened her mouth to say that that was ridiculous, that erasing some database records wouldn't make the place disappear, but stopped herself. As long as the tax records had vanished, the place really *was* invisible. She thought of all the buildings she passed each day, the anonymous ones that bore no signs or lettering. There were dozens of them, just part of the visual background noise of the city. Could one of them be a secret bunker for Hive renegades? Sure.

"Why go up?" she asked, thinking of those old horror movies again. The victims always ran up flights of stairs when being chased by the bad guy. Made no sense. Fewer options in an attic or on a second floor. More room to run if you're at ground level. "Why put the headquarters at the top of the building?"

She could almost hear his shrug. "The higher up we go, the fewer cameras there are to catch someone and run facial recognition. Think about it."

She did. Most cameras were mounted on walls or ceilings and pointed down. Even the ones on high lampposts were getting a wide field of vision that mostly included the space below them. Go high enough and you avoid the all-seeing, never-blinking eyes.

"But what about satellites?"

He sighed. "They're a problem, sure, but there are a limited number and they have to be aimed at you intentionally. Plus, it's just a matter of geometry — they point straight down. If you don't look up, it's not like they can see your face. Just the top of your head."

She'd never thought of it that way before. "What about drones?" Drones were all over the place, so ubiquitous that most people hardly noticed them anymore. Cassie and Harlon had spent a lot of time spoofing the Bluetooth and Wi-Fi signals that most of the drones used, making them land on rooftops or fly down into sewers.

"Drones are a problem," Bryce admitted. "But they have search patterns that you can anticipate and counter."

The light from Bryce's phone flicked on. "One floor to go."

Cassie's spirits soared. Now they were getting somewhere.

*

They found the last ladder they needed in a maid's closet near what had been intended to serve someday as a vending machine alcove. Cassie didn't know what time it was, but her gut knew that it had been at least twelve or thirteen hours since her last meal. To her chagrin, her stomach then emphasized the message by letting out a growl so loud that Bryce — climbing the ladder above her — paused to look down.

"We'll get you something in a minute," he said.

Up on the twenty-sixth floor, they found a man.

Cassie stared while Bryce spoke quietly to him. He wielded a rifle of the sort she had seen in action movies, the sight of which in real life made her twitchy. She knew nothing at all about guns, so didn't know what kind it was, except that she was pretty sure it fired a lot of bullets in a very short period of time. Its presence made her feel both relief and fear at the same time (which, she surmised, was sort of the whole point of guns, really); for a hot, almost blinding moment, she wondered what would happen if she tried to knock him down, steal his gun and run.

The man finally nodded to Bryce and opened a door behind him. Bryce ushered Cassie in.

What lay beyond was the last thing she expected to see. She'd been anticipating more dark, cramped rooms and corridors. Instead, the room beyond the door was massive, an open space the size of half a floor, broken up only by cubicles made of what she realized were the headboards from the hotel's missing beds. There were thirty or forty people, most of them sitting at make-shift desks with laptops or tablets, furiously working.

And lights! Sweet, sweet electric lights overhead. The place reminded her of the tech start-ups her dad had taken her to, businesses looking to seduce the famous Harlon McKinney away to apply his special brand of techno-magic to their service or app or system infrastructure. Mom had worked ten years at the same school; Dad had changed jobs literally fifteen times that Cassie could remember, hopping from tech firm to tech firm depending on his whims and what seemed most interesting to him at the time.

She peered around the room. The perimeter of the space was entirely composed of large floor-to-ceiling windows, every last one of which was covered with black crepe paper.

Bryce had stepped away from her when they entered. Now he approached, brandishing a brace of protein bars, both of which Cassie grabbed. Food overrode fear. Not anger, though; Cassie still glared at him as she stripped the foil wrapper.

"'Nice views?'" she quoted him from earlier.

He shrugged. "If you peel back the paper, yeah." A pause. "Don't *ever* peel back the paper. And let me do all the talking here. They know me."

He guided her without actually touching her toward one of the cubicles. Within it, a slim guy with a shaven head, maybe somewhere in his mid-twenties, sat in a threadbare recliner, tapping a laptop keyboard, spellbound by what was on the screen. Cassie sneaked a peek — it was Swift code. He was writing or modifying a framework for system-level face detection as best she could tell from the fast-scrolling screen. She felt the rage monster inside her settle down. The code lulled her into a sense of calm.

He was so caught up in his work that it took a protracted, exaggerated throat-clearing from Bryce to get his attention. He finally looked up and blinked at the two of them, saying nothing.

"This is TonyStark," Bryce said.

Cassie fiercely resisted the urge to roll her eyes. "Hi, uh, Mr. Stark."

"No, no," he told her. She realized that he was still typing, albeit more slowly. He hadn't stopped. "Not, like, first name Tony last name Stark. TonyStark. All one word. InterCapped."

"Right."

TonyStark returned his gaze to the screen. "No girlfriends, Bryce. You know the rules. This isn't a hangout. It's a —"

"Resistance movement, no shit." If Bryce was disturbed by the girlfriend comment, he didn't show it. Cassie decided to be irritated for both of them, but TonyStark didn't look up to see her expression. "I know. She's not my girlfriend. She's Hive hunted."

TonyStark grunted and kept pounding the keys. "Join the club. Who isn't?"

"You don't get it," Bryce said. "This is Cassie McKinney."

It was the first time in her life that Cassie heard her name spoken as though it mattered. She liked it.

TonyStark had precisely zero reaction. "Cassie for Catherine or Cassie for Cathleen? Oh, wait — I don't care."

"McKinney," Bryce said. "Dude."

"So what?" Tap, tap, tap.

"McKinney," Bryce said one more time, then enunciated it precisely: "Mick. Kin. E."

"I'm Level 5," Cassie said, ignoring Bryce's look that said *I said to let me do the talking.*

Level 5 seemed to get TonyStark's attention. His fingers

stopped on the keyboard and he slowly closed the lid of the laptop, turning to look at her as though seeing her for the first time.

"Level 5." He said it without inflection, without emotion. "For real?"

"Check for yourself," Cassie told him.

TonyStark pursed his lips and tapped the earbud in his left ear. "Hive search, BLINQ, Cassie McKinney."

She and Bryce waited until the AI in his earbud got back to him. Probably just the results of a standard Google search, but it would be enough.

TonyStark's eyes widened and he whistled low and long. "Oh, yeah, Abortion Joke Girl. Goddamn, Red Dread. What *have* you brought us?"

"Red Dread?" Cassie glanced over at Bryce, who was fuming. "So that's your LARP name!"

"Can we focus on what matters?" Bryce's irked tone told her she'd struck gold. Or blood. Maybe both. A small victory on a fantastically terrible day.

"You brought us a Level 5." TonyStark shook his head, then leaned back in the recliner, steepling his fingers. "Are you crazy? Bringing that kind of heat up here?"

"She's in trouble," Bryce said, "and she —"

"And she doesn't like being talked about as if she's not right here," Cassie said, her cheeks hot. "Look, we wrecked my phone and came through the steam tunnels to get here. No one tracked us. You're still safe. But I'm not, and I'm looking at at least a year before I am, to say nothing of the criminal charges for breaking my phone. Is there anything you can do?"

TonyStark held her gaze. He didn't blink, not once, for a good thirty seconds. It was unnerving as hell.

"Can we reverse her Condemns?" Bryce asked. "Upvote her enough to drop her down a couple of Levels?"

TonyStark barked a cynical laugh. "Are you kidding?"

"We've done it before," Bryce reminded him.

They had? Cassie had figured this to be longest of all long shots. She'd never heard of anyone reversing Condemns, but then again thousands of people got bumped to Level 1 every day. She couldn't keep track of all of them. But if OHM had managed to reverse Condemns, that meant there was hope for her. If there was a way to thwart the Hive, she wanted in.

"That was different," TonyStark was saying. "There were only a few thousand votes there. Not hard to game it and drop from Level 2 to Level 1. She's at Level 5, with millions of votes. You really struck a nerve, girl. We'd need to scour the system for millions of unaligned votes, calculate the odds of those people voting on their own, isolate the uncommitteds and hack them … It would take forever, and at the end of the day it probably still wouldn't work." He flipped open the laptop, minimized his Xcode window and hit the web. "Check it, man: she's still getting down-voted. With her velocity, we're behind the eight ball. If we pulled out all the stops, we might be able to get her down to Level 4, but —"

"I'll take Level 4," she blurted out.

Level 4. Six months. A few hours ago, the idea of being on the run for that long would have seemed insurmountable, but compared to a year it was a vacation.

TonyStark snorted and slammed his laptop shut again. "I bet

you would. You really want me to risk everyone here to put all our other work on hold just to help you?" He chuckled without a drop of mirth. "Your girlfriend has some balls, Red Dread."

"She's not my girlfriend and stop calling me that."

TonyStark shrugged.

"You don't understand," Bryce added. "This is Harlon McKinney's kid."

Cassie could tell that this tidbit intrigued TonyStark because he actually raised his left eyebrow two or three millimeters. It was the most life she'd seen in him yet.

"This girl?" he said, deigning to shift his eyes momentarily to Cassie. "You're telling me this kid's pops is Black Moses?"

The uttering of her dad's online handle hit Cassie harder than she thought it would. She'd grown up knowing he was a legend in hacker circles, that the tag Black Moses on an open-source library meant it would be gobbled up and used by everyone from script-kiddies in their parents' basements to international megacorporations worth billions. When she'd taken her first tentative steps into the world of hacking and cracking, she'd been amazed at her father's presence. She'd known that he was famous and beloved in hacker culture, but knowing something and witnessing it for yourself were two different things.

"Yeah," Cassie said, "*this girl* is Harlon's kid. And seriously, do you hate women or something? Stop talking to him like he owns me."

Bryce bristled. Through clenched teeth, he said, "Cassie, these are the only people who can help you, so —"

"No, no," TonyStark interrupted. "She's right." He grinned for the first time since she'd met him, and his grin was startlingly open and genuine. "Manners are the first thing to go when you're on the run. We're all hiding, you dig? We've all been subject to Hive 'Justice.'" He actually made the air quotes. "Most of us don't want anything to do with the outside world. Or new people. Not anymore."

"I get it. I'm a little hot right now," Cassie said.

"Being on the run will do that," TonyStark said. "But look: I'm still not convinced you're the real McCoy. Or McKinney. Convenient story for someone looking for us to make the impossible happen."

Bryce said, "Do you want to see her ID or something? Birth certificate? Jesus, just Google up a picture of McKinney's kid."

"Won't work," Cassie said. "Dad was super protective of me. There aren't any pictures of me online until I was old enough to make that decision myself. And even then, he doesn't show up in any of them. He was worried some hacker asshole might decide to prove what a big shot he was by taking down Black Moses's daughter."

"Oh," said Bryce, abashed. He stroked his dreads. "Then ..."

"Like I said, mighty convenient." TonyStark turned his attention back to his laptop. "Now, I need to get back to it."

"I can prove it," Cassie said.

TonyStark sighed heavily and Cassie thought she'd lost him. He'd made up his mind. He was done with her. The only person in the world who might be able to fix her life.

Bryce held his hands up in a helpless gesture, his expression screaming, *I don't know.*

She couldn't just give up.

"You know Cloakr?" she blurted out.

Of course TonyStark did. Anyone who claimed to know their way around source code did. Cloakr was her dad's first big app, the one that put him on the map. It autodetected attempts by rogue Wi-Fi routers to plant malware on someone's phone, then employed a series of firewalls to make that phone appear invisible to those routers. The trick was filtering out the legit Wi-Fi signals and letting them through. Harlon's app made him famous among white-hat hackers, infamous among black hats.

"Duh," TonyStark said. He dug into his pocket and flashed his phone at her. Right there on the home screen was the Cloakr icon.

"Cool," she said. "Go to GitTown and check the commits on the app."

GitTown was an online repository where coders uploaded their source code for others to see and contribute to. Harlon liked it because it had ironclad security and because, in his words, "the XML and CSS are written like poetry."

Code is poetry, she thought, and thought of Carson, his shirt, his eyes. The potency of the memory shocked her. She'd only seen him twice, had barely connected with him, and yet … And yet she'd imagined some possibility there. Hard to believe that mere hours ago, he had been at the forefront of her mind. She'd cast him out of her thoughts. That was another life. A life that was no longer hers and probably never had been possible to begin with.

TonyStark grunted and shrugged as if to say, *OK, I'll play along. For now.* He loaded up GitTown in his browser.

Cassie skimmed the screen quickly. "Go to Cloakr and check the commit on September 30," she told him.

"Which year?" Clearly still skeptical.

"Doesn't matter. There's only the one."

Sure enough, Harlon had committed a source code update on only a single September 30.

"It's my birthday," Cassie said offhandedly. "That's what you want. Open it up."

TonyStark opened the source code to the September 30 version of Cloakr. The screen scrolled with code.

"You're looking for 'var CTMspecial,'" she told TonyStark.

He paused, fingers hovering over the keyboard. "I've practically memorized this app. There's no such variable."

"There is in this version."

He found the variable. It had been declared, but there was no value for it, and it was commented out so it wouldn't run when compiled.

"Define CTMspecial as an integer," she said. "The value is 1349. The time of my birth."

TonyStark's fingers flew over the keyboard, doing as she'd bidden. She cast a glance at Bryce, who looked baffled. Not a coder. Even at his height, out of his depth.

"Now uncomment that line and commit the code under your own name," she said. "Then run a diff on the current version."

"Diff" was programming speak for letting the computer go through two similar files and produce a report showing the differences between them. It was a lot more convenient and a lot more accurate than letting frail, imperfect human eyes do the job.

TonyStark had GitTown run the diff. A new window popped up, filled with two columns of code, one for each version of the source code being compared. Differences were highlighted in red.

Scrolling down, TonyStark stopped, blinked.

Roughly halfway down the second column was this: HAPPY BIRTHDAY, CASSIE.

“Oh, holy shit!” TonyStark spun around in his chair and gazed up at her. “You’re her! You’re you!”

Cassie sniffed, affecting icy calm on the outside. “Cool story, bro,” she told him.

He winced. “Just tell me one thing. Answer one question, OK? Do you think your joke was funny?”

There was a right answer and a wrong answer, and she figured one meant help and the other meant she was on her own.

But she didn’t waste any time trying to suss out what answer TonyStark wanted to hear. “Hell, yeah, it was funny,” she said.

TonyStark’s face split into a wide toothy grin.

*

Bryce stuck with them, even though he didn’t have to anymore. Cassie had been accepted by TonyStark — at least temporarily — which meant that she now had a fighting chance at staying with OHM and at having them help figure out what the hell had happened with her BLINQ scores.

“We have rules,” TonyStark told her. “You break them, you’re out. Even Black Moses’s daughter only gets one strike in this game.”

“Oh, good,” Cassie said with a voice dripping sarcasm. “Sports metaphors. I was wondering when we would get to the sports metaphors.”

“Holy Christ …” Bryce moaned.

But TonyStark just smiled. "Keep your attitude, Cassie. It's gonna help you stay alive. But seriously — we're going way out on a limb for you. Remember that."

He took her on a quick "tour" of the OHM floor, showing her a series of cots and a frightening-looking bathroom. The place was like some warped version of an orphanage, like the photos Cassie had seen in old news stories, and she squeezed her eyes closed and reminded herself to breathe. She couldn't get back to real life soon enough. How long was she supposed to stay here?

How long *could* she stay here? Right now, all she had was TonyStark's promise and Bryce's assurances that these people could and would help, that they wouldn't toss her out on the street or bring a Hive Mob down on her. Promises from two men she'd just met.

Sadly, that was better than any of her other options.

"I can't promise you results," TonyStark said as he introduced her to some of the others. "We'll do what we can. We've had some success in the past, but only with Levels 1 and 2. Level 5 is a whole 'nother ball game. The sheer number of votes makes things exponentially more complicated."

"I understand." And she did, she truly did. But understanding the complexity of it didn't lessen her urgency to reverse her Hive Level and get the hell back to her life.

"Let's see what we're dealing with." TonyStark steered her toward a cubicle where a woman with a half-shaved head and enough metal in her left ear to build a drive train stared at three enormous monitors. "Hey, Tish, check out Cassie McKinney, local area, can you?"

Tish glanced over her shoulder. She wore black lip gloss and had dramatic green eye shadow over her right eye only. It made her look vaguely cyborgish. Cassie figured that was the point.

Her fingers flew over the keyboard. In a moment, the center screen lit up with Cassie's BLINQ profile, the aggregate of her social media footprint, with feeds from Instagram, Facebook, Snapchat, Yardio and Guessom. Her avatar had gone black and white, with a red bar through it, indicating her Level 5 status.

Tish's eyebrow arched significantly.

The flanking screens on the right and left filled up. On the right, an endless scroll of numbers. On the left, a graph in the classic "hockey stick" mode, showing a slow build, followed by a sudden and dramatic spike.

"This is where you went viral," Tish said, pointing to the spot where the gentle up slope became a leap into the stratosphere. "Looks like, uh, a retweet from a retweet got the attention of @BlitzenBot202, who has something like twenty thousand followers. Once he/she/they retweeted, you were on a rocket ride to Hive Justice."

"I have no idea who that person is," Cassie confessed, peering at the profile.

Tish shrugged. "I'd wonder if they even were a person, but check out the history. Volume levels are normal. It seems to be a news aggregator account. But anything's possible. Could be a busy bot."

Everyone on BLINQ was a real, verified person — that was the whole point of BLINQ — but bots still crawled the other sites, like Instagram and Twitter. And they could gin up dissatisfaction and discontent among real people that then got fed back into BLINQ, into the system that had Condemned Cassie. BLINQ was both a platform and an aggregator. The most important aggregator in the country.

"What's her velocity like?" TonyStark asked.

"Most of the pass-along virality seems to have abated," Tish told him. "Still getting like bounces and shares, but the major push has — whoa."

They all swiveled to look at what had caught her attention. On the center screen, Cassie's black-and-white avatar had gone to full color, and the red Level 5 bar through it had vanished.

"What happened?" Cassie asked. "What just happened?" Her heart raced and her words couldn't keep up. "What did you do? Oh, my God, am I cleared? Did you fix the Condemns?"

"Shut *down*, girl!" Tish said. "I didn't do anything. I've never seen this before —"

"Wait, look!" Bryce leaned over, clearly aggravating Tish. She turned from her monitors long enough to shoot him a death glare. "Look at this."

His finger hovered on the center screen, just below Cassie's avatar. They'd missed it in the shock of seeing the Level 5 bar disappear. The small, almost innocuous, Hold Action icon had appeared there.

Cassie could barely breathe. It was happening. Somehow, it was happening. The trend was reversing. Everything was going to be fine! In a few hours — well, maybe a few days — she'd be laughing about this with her mom.

"Going back down to Level 4," Cassie said hopefully, "and they're making sure no one tries to kill me in the meantime."

"I've seriously never seen anything like this," Tish repeated. "It doesn't usually work like … Oh, shit!"

No one had to ask what had prompted the curse from her. They all saw it.

In the blink of an eye, Cassie's avatar returned to black and white, only this time there was something deeper and more sinister about it. The gray-scale effect had harsher shadows, more contrast. Cassie looked like something out of a horror movie.

And the red bar was back, too.

The only thing that didn't return was the legend Level 5.

That had been replaced by something none of them had ever seen before:

LEVEL 6

And beneath that

#InfiniteRange
#KillOnSight

*

Livestream from the White House Press Briefing Room
Dean Hythe, President of the United States:

"I'm not going to get into details. I'm just not going to do it.

"Look, what this girl said was vile. OK? Vile. Absolutely disgusting. I don't even want to repeat it and I can't believe the media has been plastering it all over every TV screen and every phone and computer and what have you. Just disgusting. Really an embarrassment for the media, the way they treat these things, and we're going to do something about that soon, believe me.

"But this isn't about me. Or about my family. Even though we've been treated horribly — just horribly — in this whole thing. This is about the will of the people, OK? The will. Of. The people. The whole point of Hive Justice is to put some power into the hands of the people. I ran for this office and won — twice — with some of the biggest margins in history. Some say *the* biggest margins. I don't say that. I just say some of the biggest because maybe there are some that are bigger. I don't know of any, but maybe there are.

"Anyway, this is the whole reason for Hive in the first place. This isn't me saying this girl should die, though she should pay a serious price for what she did, I think you know. It isn't me. Don't write that in your papers and on your blogs or whatever. This is the will of the people. I ran and won twice to give power back to the people, and they have that power now. It's up to them to use it.

"And I know you all have a lot of questions about this Level 6 and so on, so I'm going to turn it over to — where is she? Where's … Ah, there. There. Here she is, everyone. Alexandra Pastor. You know her, right? Doing great work, such great work, at my Justice Department. Really fantastic work, and no one knows Hive like she knows Hive. So I'm gonna bring her up here and let her talk to you about it all."

*

Bitch ran. Ditch that bitch. **#InfiniteRange #KillOnSight #CassieMcKinney**

READ THIS THREAD! According to local PD, there have been NO PINGS from **#CassieMcKinney**'s phone in FOUR HOURS. SHE BROKE HER PHONE! READ THE THREAD, PEOPLE!

While you're all distracted by **#CassieMcKinney** and **#Level6**, **@POTUS** just signed a bill allowing gov't hacking of cell phones w/o **#4A** procedures. Wake up, sheeple! **#4Amatters**

Local PD claims **#CassieMcKinney** has "gone underground." Where is she? **#HasCassieSurfacedYet?**

Check out photos from city near MS/BFU, last known sighting of **#CassieMcKinney.** BIGGEST **#HIVEMOB** EVER! **#HasCassieSurfacedYet?**

I'm no fan of **@POTUS**, but her joke was disgusting and she deserves punishment. **#HasCassieSurfacedYet?**

Doxxers reveal she's the daughter of notorious hacker Black Moses. The same Black Moses who hacked Super Bowl halftime show to play "Fuck Tha Police" while children were watching. Apple doesn't fall far from the tree, does it? **#HasCassieSurfacedYet?**

Two injured when **#HiveMob** seeking **#CassieMcKinney** collided with **#HiveMob** in pursuit of **#OldManFlasher**. LOL.

#KillOnSight? I have only two words for you: Fuck yeah. **#HasCassieSurfacedYet?**

I have never been happier to live in this country! **#HasCassieSurfacedYet? #KillOnSight #InfiniteRange**

No one can hide 4ever, she has to come up at some point. **#HasCassieSurfacedYet?**

*

Livestream continues
Alexandra Pastor, Special Deputy Attorney General, Justice Department Division of Heuristic Internet Vetting Engine:

"Thank you for the podium, Mr. President. It's been such an honor to work under such a visionary. I'm happy to discuss Level 6 and Infinite Range. Let me give you a little background first, and then I'm happy to take some questions.

"First of all, Level 6 is not new. Level 6 was built into Hive from the outset. It was part of the initial spec and it's been there from the beginning. It was designed and developed by the same programmers who assembled the rest of the Hive experience. I've heard some scattered rumors on the internet that this was some kind of secret black-box protocol bolted onto the system after the fact, or put into place at the order of the president after Ms. McKinney's comment trended. This is not true.

"Level 6 was part of the system from the start but never set to public-facing because honestly we never thought it would be necessary. Now, take a look at this chart, please. As you can see, the incidence of online harassment and bullying dropped dramatically with the announcement of the Hive system. This was before it was even activated. At that time, we realized that we had a very potent weapon on our hands in the war for decency and good behavior. So we made the decision to mask Level 6, thinking it would end up being unnecessary. And when Hive launched later that year, the chart shows us online harassment dropped even further. Ninety-two percent of all Hive matters are Level 1. Only 1 percent have risen to Level 5.

"In short, the system *works.* People are behaving themselves.

"But then came Cassie McKinney. Now, we're still processing the votes, but her virality blew away all of our models. We held her at Levels 1 and 2 for as long as we reasonably could while we made certain that there were no glitches in the system. Everything was legit. And more and more votes kept coming in, to the point that she rapidly ascended to Level 5. At that point, signals stopped coming from her phone, indicating that she'd destroyed it, in contravention of Hive Law. Such an act algorithmically pushed her over the edge into Level 6. We planned to reveal this in a press conference, but the system's machine learning engine decided to proceed on its own. And so here we are today. Now I'd like to introduce Erich Gorfinkle. As you'll recall, he was handpicked by President Hythe's predecessor for this role, and he is the ultimate expert on day-to-day Hive operations."

*

LOL. Facebook just served me an ad for spelunking gear. Because I posted that **#CassieMcKinney** has "gone underground." Stupid algorithms.

I've written a post on the necessary brutality of Hive Justice and why, whether you agree with **#HasCassieSurfacedYet?** or not, she has to die. Please read and share it! sh.ort/Cassie

2 days and **#HasCassieSurfacedYet?** WTF??? She should be EXTRA killed for BREAKING THE LAW. Should have been found by now.

Just curious, but are there restrictions on HOW she's supposed to be killed? I can't find any relevant info online. **#HasCassieSurfacedYet?**

#HasCassieSurfacedYet? I hope whoever finds her RAPES HER FIRST. Teach that bitch to open her mouth.

New doxx dump up at hivecommunity.justice! Includes elem school grades, FB history, PICS!!! **#HasCassieSurfacedYet?**

Dam, that booty tho! **#HasCassieSurfacedYet?**

Don't usually like black chix, but id hit dat before hitting dat, if u get me! **#HasCassieSurfacedYet?**

Not saying id do it, but … do u have to kill her right away or can u make it slow? Again: JUST ASKING. **#HasCassieSurfacedYet?**

PLEASE READ: "Why Cassie McKinney's Biraciality Speaks Volumes about Justice in America." http://short.link/7 **#HasCassieSurfacedYet?**

Interesting stat: 82% of whites consider Cassie McKinney to be black. **#HasCassieSurfacedYet?**

BLINQ Alert! BLINQ Alert! Woman spotted in Dallas shopping mall is NOT **@CassieMcK39**. Hive Mobs in Dallas, desist from further action. Police and EMTs en route.

Like, what im saying is technically is it legal 2 do stuff 2 her BEFORE u kill her or in the PROCESS of killing her? Thats all, so please stop saying im a musoginist. I'm just ASKING QUESTIONS, OK? **#HasCassieSurfacedYet?**

*

Livestream continues
Erich Gorfinkle, Protocol Manager, Justice Department Division of Heuristic Internet Vetting Engine:

"Everyone seems to be up in arms today about one thing or another, but can we just take a moment and remember what things were like *before* Hive went live? Online harassment and bullying were at an all-time high and had spilled out into the streets. Vigilante groups were stalking and doxxing with impunity.

"Now there's a structure to it. Gone are the days when

someone could hashtag their neighbor and get a mob together to beat him up. There's a *system* now, and it works, thanks to the vision and genius of this president. Now the mobs aren't just random expressions of anger; they reflect our own outrage in a measured, approved fashion. As they should.

"Do you really want to go back to the way things were? Lawless and out of control? Now we have Hive Justice — legal, potent and above all, effective. It works.

"And no, I won't be taking any questions."

10010100010 1

When she dared pull back the bedroom curtain to look outside that morning, Rachel saw nothing but a yellow-and-white smear. Eggs.

In the three days since Cassie had hit Level 6, the apartment had been egged close to a dozen times. After the third time, she'd stopped bothering to call the landlord to hose off the windows. There was no point.

No sunlight coming through and no point.

Jesus, she thought. *Jesus. What the hell is happening?*

The four college kids who'd assaulted her and Cassie that first night had, fortunately, been drunk, stoned or high as kites at the time. They all told the police and the media that they'd seen Cassie, but none of them could identify the woman with her. Rachel tried to ignore what that said about her own memorability and focused on the positive: it meant she was safe. For now.

Safe except for the eggs. Safe except for the throngs of angry Hive Mobbers gathered outside her building twenty-four hours a day. The chanting ebbed and flowed, but it was always there:

"Give! Us! Cass! Ie!"

"Give! Us! Cass! Ie!"

They wanted her daughter. They wanted blood. The two were the same. Cassie wasn't a person to them; she was just a *vector*, an angle for their own pent-up rage and impotence.

Usually, when Rachel was stressed or upset, she retreated to the past. Horace. Homer. Tacitus. But there was no relief in her beloved classics now. Nothing in the past could change the present or guarantee the future, as she and Cassie found themselves doxxed, their private lives spilled out into the open.

A very special, very unexpected secondary pain came from the reminders of Harlon that the internet now spat in her face every time she made the mistake of glancing at a screen. There was video of the time he'd hacked the Super Bowl livestream, back when he was not much older than Cassie. The prank that had put him on the map and put the world on notice that Black Moses had the goods. A cyber firm in the Valley had been impressed enough to snap him up and pay his legal fees. And the legend was born.

Now, the legend's daughter was claiming her own notoriety. Family vacation photos. Personal snapshots of Cassie as a baby, a toddler, a preteen. Emails she'd written, BLINQs she'd posted, then deleted. All of it and more dredged up by the unending fury and diligence of the Hive Mob.

Her hand trembled as she raised her cup of coffee to her lips. She had to go to work. She had to pretend everything was OK and normal.

She had no other choice.

Three days ago, her daughter had slipped through her fingers. Since then, Rachel hadn't slept, other than the occasional twenty-minute burst; it was an anguished sleep that she fought every time, filled with lights and screams that intermingled with the real world. She didn't know what was true anymore, and what was just a nightmare.

She knew this, though: no one could know what she knew. After Cassie disappeared with Bryce, Rachel had also fled. She'd escaped to her office to do what she did best: research. Research on Hive history and processes; anecdata from the tens of thousands of people convicted. She knew she'd be brought in for questioning, surveilled. But until then, she needed to act like she had no idea where her daughter was. She would take her secrets, her last moments with Cassie, to her grave if that's what was required. If that's what would help keep Cassie alive and safe.

*

She drew in a shaky breath. She was, somehow, standing in front of a full classroom — even fuller than her class list indicated. She should have known gawkers would try to crash her class; she would have known a lot of things if she'd been thinking clearly.

If she'd been thinking clearly she might also have been able to remember the last three days. Instead, all she could see was Cassie's face, the fear in her daughter's eyes. The blood from her head injury spattered on the cement. The pain of missing her, of regret over the angry cloud that had been hovering over the two of them for so long now … It was physical, visceral. What a waste of so much time.

But she had to get it together.

The Hive demanded it.

*

He finally appeared, moments before she was ready to collapse. The door opened, and Red Dread slipped in. He didn't meet Rachel's eyes.

Somehow she made it through the rest of the class, her hands shaking so badly that she had to tuck them into her jacket pockets. Words came out of her mouth but she couldn't swear they were even English, let alone that they made any sense. Every face looking back at her was a blur, a wet watercolor painting someone had run fingers across. Pings pinged. BLINQs blinqed. Rachel felt the target on her back weigh more heavily with each passing second. She knew she was being watched … she just wasn't sure when they would strike.

Which meant she had to make her move, now.

"Your next reading assignment is in your email already," Rachel said as the clock ran out, her voice thick. She cleared her throat, blinked a few times so that the watercolor became something more realistic than impressionistic. "And I've extended the deadline for your first assignment." She'd had to; she hadn't even created the damn thing yet.

Students began packing up their things, uncrossing legs, closing laptops, screwing the caps on water bottles. Rachel cleared her throat again. She was running out of time.

"Mr. Muller," she announced. "Can you stay and see me, please?" Her voice cracked on the last word.

"I guess," he said coolly. He hung back while the class emptied.

"You can't do this," he hissed as soon as the last student was gone. The door closed on the two of them.

"Please," Rachel begged, the tears coming before she could stop them. She found herself gripping Bryce's wrists, shaking them. "Where is she? Is she all right?"

Bryce's eyes got round. He ripped his arms from Rachel's grasp and grabbed her phone from the table, jabbing at it for a few minutes before dropping it angrily on the table.

"Are you trying to get us all killed?"

"Please," she repeated. "Just tell me where she is."

"You're being watched all the time," he whispered. He took a step back. "Including right now. Every room in this place has surveillance. And your phone! Jesus. I just crashed it deliberately so it'll reboot and give us a minute or two. For now, though, you have to get. It. Together."

He, too, was blurry through Rachel's tears. She'd always hated watercolors. "I'm trying."

He sighed. "Take a deep breath."

"Shut up!" Rachel lunged at him, to what end she wasn't entirely sure other than to try to shake the answers out of him. He didn't know what it was like to have a daughter, a husband, disappear. He was barely a man and yet he had the gall to tell her to calm down? To take a goddamn breath?

"Rachel!" Bryce yelped, then cursed. "Professor McKinney. I swear, I will tell you all I can tell you." He dropped his voice. "Right now, she's OK."

The room spun. Rachel exhaled and braced herself against the desk, her knees buckling. Bryce caught her, his hand gripping her waist, until he gently led her to the chair and placed her in it. He offered her a water from his backpack and she gulped it, grateful, unable to remember the last time she'd had anything but coffee.

"OK?" Bryce prompted. Rachel nodded. She started to ask questions but Bryce shook his head sharply and widened his eyes again, letting them tick up to the EXIT sign over the door. Likely place for the surveillance cameras.

"She's fine," he repeated, his voice so low that Rachel struggled to hear him, then worried she'd misheard him.

"I can't tell you much more than that. It's too dangerous." Bryce hesitated. "For all of us, including you."

"How's her head? Is she eating enough? Does she need clothes? I can —"

"No, you cannot," Bryce's eyes went soft as Rachel's face fell. "I'm sorry. I wish ..."

"No, it's all right," Rachel said, surprised at how much she meant it in that moment. Cassie was alive. She could manage everything else — the not knowing, the fear of the future — as long as that one potential horror was removed.

"We're working on a plan," Bryce continued, his voice even lower, his words garbled. He was trying to throw off the video feed, or any audio that was possibly capturing their forbidden moments.

"But meanwhile you, Professor, remember nothing. You know nothing. You woke up and Cassie was gone. We've erased the record of your ride share; we've hacked into every security camera on the route you took and replicated old feeds. We think you're untraceable at this point, though of course we can't be totally sure."

She nodded slowly. The only other possible connection to her wasn't digital — it was depressingly analog. Her exploding purse had strewn her belongings on the sidewalk at the quad. After Bryce had spirited Cassie away, she'd retraced her steps. The kids were gone, scattered around campus, looking for Cassie. She'd gathered up what she could find. She thought she'd found everything that could identify her, but what if she'd missed something?

Rachel drained the rest of the water bottle. "I know nothing."

"Nothing." Bryce nodded.

"The easy part is that it all feels like a dream anyway," Rachel said so quietly that Bryce had to lean in closer. She met his eyes and remembered what she needed to ask him, what had been humming underneath the current of the past three days. "Why are you helping me?"

Bryce, so still and so close, breathed unevenly a few times.

Then the door burst open, *thwacking* against the wall. Rachel jumped to her feet, bumping into Bryce's shoulder. It felt like running into concrete.

"Rachel McKinney. You're needed for questioning," a no-nonsense voice announced, but with five agents swarming into the room, Rachel couldn't be sure which one it came from. She glared at each of them. One was Agent Hernandez, who looked nothing at all like the relatively kind — or at least neutral — man who'd given her the business card that even now lay on her desk in her office, propped up near the phone.

She'd been expecting trouble because of Cassie and had forgotten all about the other trouble she was in, the Harlon sort of trouble. "I already told you Harlon didn't leave anything —"

"We're not here about that," Hernandez told her, eyes flicking around the room as he watched his men search the place. “This is about your daughter.”

“Wait, what?” The NSA was under the Department of Defense; Hive was a function of the Department of Justice. “I think you have your jurisdictions mixed up, gentlemen.” She said it a little more brightly than she felt it.

Hernandez regarded her from the doorway. Something in his stance told her that he would prefer her to come to him, but that he would be perfectly happy to come drag her away, if need be.

“We can, uh, talk later ...” Bryce said into the silence.

“Of course,” Rachel mumbled. Her tongue grew thick, her neck sweaty, at the prospect of what was about to happen.

“*Vos nescitis quidquam,*” Bryce breathed into her ear as he slipped past her and the agents approached.

You know nothing.

She went to the door and let the agents lead her through the history building, across campus and into a waiting unmarked SUV.

In the back of the car, sirens wailing, Rachel felt a fraction of the heat she imagined her daughter felt. She closed her eyes and tried to will a message to Cassie, sending out all the energy she could muster, imagining that a mother could reach her child telepathically if only she believed in it enough.

Stay strong, Cassie, Rachel repeated to herself over and over again. And then:

Keep running, Cassie.

100101100101

Three days wasn't that long. It was a holiday weekend, really. Nothing more. Just long enough for the mondo huge scab on Cassie's head to peel off, for the swelling to go down. Three days was a nice vacation.

If.

If you weren't holed up in what used to be a hotel but was now the nerve center of a weird hackathon/resistance movement.

If you weren't isolated from everyone and anyone who knew you and cared for you.

If you weren't wanted by pretty much every living, breathing, connected human being in the country.

She tried not to pay attention to the stream of digital sludge her life had become, but it was impossible. The OHMers were obsessed with her case, and even if she hadn't been sneaking peeks at their screens, she would have heard them calling out the most egregious examples to each other anyway.

People were saying the most horrible things about her online.

It was OK to do that with someone who was Level 5. Well, or 6, she guessed. Bullying, harassing cyber-taunts that would have had people bumped to Level 2 or 3 in a heartbeat were now fair game when directed at a Level 6 criminal.

There were comments about her appearance, her body, her sexuality. Her race. She was grateful that she'd never had any reason or desire to take pictures of herself naked — it was bad enough that the world was now ogling bikini shots from last summer on the Jersey shore. She'd been threatened with stoning, being rolled in broken glass and dumped into a bath of saltwater, multiple varieties of rape and one particularly imaginative removal of her eyes. One man (it had to be a man, right?) had gone on at length on a BLINQ thread, explicating how his plan to kidnap Cassie and keep her bound in his basement for several years was not a violation of the Level 6 mandated death penalty since he would, eventually, kill her. (The description of her death was another thread all its own.) The vitriol was constant — was this what the internet was like before the Hive?

All of this distraction made her work suffer. And right now, her work was all that mattered.

Bryce had had to leave OHM in order to throw off any suspicions that he was involved in Cassie's disappearance. He had to go live his life as normally as possible. The Hive Mob didn't and couldn't know that Bryce knew Cassie, but it was only a matter of time before someone connected him to Rachel. As time passed and the mob became more desperate for its promised allotment of flesh and blood, they would look for any path that could conceivably lead to Cassie. Rachel's life would be turned upside down and soon the lives of her students would become new avenues of attack.

So Bryce was gone and while she'd only known him for a few hours, at least he had a connection to her mother. Now she was lost in a nameless building with people she didn't know, and they were supposed to … save her?

Right.

Day and night had no meaning here. With the windows blacked out and a roomful of hackers who slept and ate on their own messed-up schedules, she might as well have been living in a world without time. Except that she knew time was passing out there in the real world and that the mob grew angrier and larger with each passing minute.

The world had become accustomed to immediate gratification. Instant delivery. Instant response. Now, instant justice. Cassie was denying them, and they would not forgive.

She spent time working on her project, the one Tish and TonyStark had told her she would need to complete in order to prove her value to them.

"We're not a charity," Tish said to her early on. They were sitting together in one of the little kitchenettes scattered throughout the floor. It stank of burned coffee and stale chips.

"We don't do this for the lulz," Tish went on, stirring a sludge of coffee in a chipped mug that said, BLINQ AND YOU WON'T MISS IT! "And we're not interested in making friends. We're here to burn the system to the ground. You grok?"

"I grok."

"Everyone here has been burned by the Hive. We all have the stink of its shit on us. We lost jobs and friends. Families and respect. We lost our lives."

"What did you do?" Cassie asked, and immediately regretted

it. Tish's expression, already hard, went to stone.

"No," she said. "It's like prison. You don't ask that."

Cassie realized pretty quickly that it didn't matter what any of them had done; what mattered was that they'd been cut off from their lives. For a few moments, she'd allowed herself to think of OHM as though it were the sleepaway computer camp she'd gone to as a kid. But this wasn't fun time in the sun time. This wasn't voluntary.

Everyone here was the walking wounded. Everyone had a sad story, and none of them wanted to tell it. They kept their burdens and their pains deep.

Leaks always sprang, though. There were tears at odd moments. Wistful sighs. She noticed photographs of chubby babies, of elderly parents, taped up in reverent spots directly in the owner's sightline. The opposite of *memento mori*, artifacts that reminded the owner that death came for all. These were something different. The opposite. Reminders to *live.* She racked her brain for the scraps of Latin her mom had taught her ...

Memento vivere. That was it. *Remember to live.*

It was good advice for OHM. Good advice for her, too.

All she had were the pajamas she'd worn the night she and Rachel had fled the apartment, as well as whatever Rachel had thrown into her backpack. So a toothbrush (thank God for that!) and some clothes, including the jeans she'd been wearing the day she and Carson font-flirted. That was a million years and another lifetime ago. A file deleted from the drive, the sectors zeroed and then re-zeroed. Her old life had been erased. She could never go back. There was one moment, on day two or three — it was hard to tell — when one of the OHMers, a scrappy guy who looked about fourteen but was actually in his twenties, according to Tish, had come into the kitchen when Cassie was scrounging for more caffeine. His backpack had brushed against her, and she'd seen his collection of pins decorating the flap. CODE IS POETRY, read the big one in the middle. And right there in the kitchen, after he'd left her alone, she'd closed her eyes and replayed the two times she'd seen Carson. All the things that might've been, could've been, in a different life.

It was weird to say, since she barely knew him, but she missed him. Or, more accurately, the possibility of him.

In a weird way, she missed Rowan and the rest of the gaggle, too. Missed them in the sense of wanting them right here, right now, so that she could throttle them with her bare hands. Rowan's egging her on had led to all of this, and Cassie missed the opportunity for revenge.

She missed things she wouldn't have expected, too. Like the moon. The stars. A decent night's sleep.

The gravity of Level 6 was beginning to weigh on Cassie. Her shoulders ached; her mouth felt perpetually dry; her stomach roiled. She lay awake at night, the steady hum of OHM's machinery her only company. Once, she dreamed she was sitting at Rowan's lunch table, eating an apple. Apples were hard to come by at OHM, and in her dream Cassie's mouth watered. Outside it was autumn, the season of apple picking and leaves turning and her birthday. But inside, behind the hidden windows, it just felt like a season of panic.

Cassie spent whatever time she could manage hanging over Tish's shoulder, studying her every move and offering suggestions, until Tish snapped at her. "Kid! You need to stop hovering! TonyStark," she called, "can we *please* get her a system already? She is seriously cramping my style."

TonyStark swept in to get her off Tish's back. He took her on a brief tour of the floor, pointing out the kitchenettes, the cramped and mildewy bathrooms. The bathrooms were all unisex. "We code binary, but gender isn't," TonyStark told her with utmost sincerity. It was the most human thing he'd said to her yet.

Especially considering what he'd said to her shortly before Bryce left: "So tell me something, for real: Is your pops really dead?"

Cassie had clenched her jaw and her fists. Bryce put a hand on her shoulder, holding her back. "Come on, man," he said to TonyStark. "Don't be an asshole."

"Just wondering. Legend has it the man went underground. Deep, deep underground. Like, beyond OHM, you know?"

"He's dead," Cassie had said bitterly. "I saw him in his coffin. Is that good enough for you?"

TonyStark had nodded thoughtfully. "It is."

And now he was regaling her with the finer points of OHM's invisible oasis in the midst of the city: "We took the whole building off the grid. Literally cut the power lines, the water lines, everything. Solar panels bring us power. We have a rain collection system on the roof, sort of a modified solar still. Because they can track you with infrared, we keep the heat variable. Fogs the IR sensors and makes it harder to read human bodies."

"They?" she asked.

He fixed her with a serious look, adjusting his glasses. "The government. NSA. CIA. FBI."

"The CIA isn't allowed to spy on American citizens."

He smiled tightly. "Go on thinking that. We use a mesh

network and a custom social network that only pings to our LAN in order to keep in touch without getting our fingerprints all over the 'net."

"The Dark Web?" Cassie ventured.

TonyStark snorted. "Yo momma knows about the Dark Web." He considered. "Actually, yeah, *your* mom probably does. Anyway, the Dark Web is so last decade. We piggyback off innocent Bluetooth signals to mesh across the city and to other OHM outposts. It's slow and laggy, but it keeps us hidden and untraceable."

Other OHM outposts ... "How big *is* this?" she asked. "How many of you —"

He held up a hand. "Nope."

"What's the deal with the graffiti?" she asked. Many of the walls were festooned with strange, abstract patterns of black paint. She occasionally saw someone snap a picture of one of them with a smartphone.

"Not yet," he told her. "Enough for now. You're not a stray we took in. You gotta earn your way. GIGO."

GIGO. The closest thing there was to a programmer's religion. Four simple words: *Garbage in, garbage out.* Harlon had her saying it when she was two years old; there was video of her — old, shitty 4K video — running around one of their many apartments, babbling, "Gabbage in, gabbage out!" before she'd figured out the letter *R.*

It was simple: until the AI revolution, machine learning and neural nets, computers couldn't think for themselves. They were just dumb brains, waiting for instructions. Their power lay not in independent thought or creativity, but in speed — they couldn't think, but they could execute instructions much faster and more accurately than a human.

Which meant that you had to be very, very precise about what you told a computer to do. It couldn't make judgments on the veracity of data or the integrity of a set of commands. It didn't ask questions; it just ran.

If you fed garbage data to the computer, you'd get garbage back out. GIGO.

OHM needed to be sure *she* wasn't garbage. And so she'd been given a project. In the time-honored ways of Silicon Valley and tech start-ups everywhere, she'd been given precious little in the way of instruction or direction.

"Impress us," TonyStark told her with a grin. "Show us exactly what Black Moses passed down to you. And then, yeah, we'll see if we can help you."

*

Impress us. Nothing like a vague command to jump-start the creative juices, right?

She definitely wanted to impress everyone at OHM. Let them see that she was the real deal, like her dad. Not just some idiot teenage girl who had posted something dumb — but funny, she reminded herself — and was now paying the ultimate price.

Even though decent computers could be hard to come by, soon two guys Cassie had learned were ostensibly bodyguards ("we can't hack for shit, but we played rugby in college," one of them told her) returned from their daily expedition with food, water and, amazingly, a computer that was in decent-enough shape for

Cassie to mess around with. As she familiarized herself with the available tech, which was laggy and slow as promised, she had time to think.

When the Hive became the law, there were pockets of resistance throughout the country. Protests, editorials, that sort of thing. Cassie had even had an entire social studies unit on the proposed law, back in elementary school, led by a teacher who was passionately anti-Hive. But the technology that underpinned the concept of the Hive had always been Cassie's main argument for believing in its mission: because technology, in and of itself, was neutral. Code was built by people, sure, but the elements of it were impartial. Pristine.

She took her cues from her dad. If he'd been upset by the Hive, she probably would have been, too. Harlon, usually in the frontline of any kind of protest, had surprisingly been pretty low-key as the Hive was being debated and ultimately enacted. It was just the sort of tech disruption that usually inspired some passion in him one way or the other, but he'd been placid about it, almost disconnected. Rachel, meanwhile, flew into a fury at every mention of the Hive on the news.

That changed right after the press conference after the president signed the bill into law. Rachel had been ranting about the inherent problems (of course, adding in something relevant about the Romans) when Harlon stood up from the dinner table, threw his fork onto his plate and snapped, "Enough, Rachel," in a tone so final and so constrained that Cassie had been shocked, and Mom had actually stopped talking. Harlon never lost his temper. Just that once …

The Hive had brought that out in him. She'd thought it was

because he was pro-Hive and was tired of Mom cutting it down. But …

Cassie blinked at her cursor circling around and around as some data took its sweet time downloading and allowed a new thought to worm its way up to the surface. What if, she realized, the Hive wasn't delivering on its promises? What if it was actively causing problems, wreaking havoc, instead of making things more civilized? No one could see that more clearly than Cassie.

What if … it was up to her, to everyone in OHM, to fix it?

Cassie hadn't paid much attention to the protests or the counter-movements back when they were everywhere, and especially when they filtered down to being only somewhere, some of the time. She hadn't needed to.

It was different now.

*

Impress us. She mainlined the vile coffee that percolated constantly in the kitchenettes and scarfed down a frightening quantity of donuts and potato chips. She hadn't been so wired and so carb loaded since her first hackathon. Harlon had warned her at the time not to overdo it.

"I've been where you are, baby. You get so high you think you can't come down, but gravity's a bear, and she'll hug the life right out of you. Be smart."

She'd won three categories at that first hackathon, taking home a new laptop and a bunch of other sweet gear. The price she paid for it was a headache that didn't go away for two days and the most vicious diarrhea imaginable. Totally worth it.

But thinking of her dad made her think of her smashed phone, her line to him. She wondered what his AI would say if she texted him now. **Dad, I'm on the run.** Had they built that possibility into their code? If she could get her hands on another phone …

She brushed her hair out of her eyes. On day two, she figured out how she would prove her worth to OHM. *If* she could pull it off.

It was a thorny problem, especially with the slow tech at her disposal. But she had a roomful of genius hackers on hand, and what they lacked in social niceties they made up for in wisdom. She had learned a long time ago how to breach a hacker's shell of impenetrable apathy by approaching with a problem that promised a unique solution. It had worked on her dad when he was neck-deep in code and blocking out the rest of the world to the point that he'd developed two cavities from forgetting to brush his teeth.

Thinking of her dad made her wonder: Was this about her race? Her comment had gone viral. But had it been all on its own? Maybe if a white girl had said the same thing …

She shook her head. She had to focus on what she could change. Right now.

Mom had tossed a hoodie into the backpack, so Cassie threw that on and found an isolated corner. With her borrowed laptop and a gigantic mug of sludge that had aspirations to be liquid coffee someday, she settled in and started working.

Time flew. Her hands cramped from typing, but the rest of her body just … relaxed. For the first time since her dad's death, really. She hadn't realized it, but the anger had clenched her body like a fist, and now the metaphorical fingers of that fist were falling open, even as her literal fingers were flying on the keyboard.

All that rage. All that pent-up anger. Dissolved by immersing herself in her element. She hadn't coded — not *really* coded — since her dad died. It had felt sacrilegious. Profane. Somehow disrespectful. And yet it had been the cure she'd needed. The balm for her pain. Code was the cure. She never should have given it up.

TonyStark occasionally stopped by, not interrupting, just watching her fingers fly on the keyboard, nodding in approval. Almost despite herself, she'd come to like him. When he was coding, he was a fucking statue, nothing moving but the tips of his fingers on the keys. When not coding, he was like a hyperactive kindergartner, his entire body constantly in motion. They'd had a rough start. He hadn't trusted her and she hadn't entirely trusted him. But now …

Now, she looked up momentarily from her screen. TonyStark stared at her, his legs jiggling slightly as he danced to some tune only he could hear. After a second or two, his face exploded into a smile and he gave her a thumbs-up before disappearing around a corner, whistling some tuneless ditty.

Look at you, Cassie, she thought. *Winning over people. Who knew you had it in you?*

She yawned, cracked her knuckles and bore down on the keyboard again.

*

Twenty-four hours later, interrupted only by two hour-long catnaps, she thought she had her answer. And the timing was just perfect.

She remembered telling Rowan to punch up, not down. She

couldn't fix the system or change her fate, but she could make sure the world knew in no uncertain terms how fucked up everything was. The Hive was designed to be a hunt, to send the offender scurrying for cover and to satisfy the bloodlust of the crowd with a chase.

She didn't know much about boxing, but she knew this: she could retreat into her corner or she could deliver a massive uppercut. Punch up.

The president was giving a live interview on one of the business channels, the boring ones that only talked about money and stock prices and bond yields and who knew what-the-hell-else all day long. Those were the only channels he sat down for, she noticed. Big business loved him, so the people who loved big business loved him, too.

There was a stock ticker running endlessly at the bottom of the screen on that channel, 24-7. Even during commercials. God forbid Stock Bros miss a quarter percent change in Douche International, right?

It took her all day to do it. Most of that time was spent probing gently for holes in the firewall, looking for the best way in that wouldn't alert the network's cybersecurity monkeys until it was far too late. She spent a little more time figuring out how to lock out said cyber-monkeys from the control panel. The only way to shut her up would be to shut the network itself down.

Her dad would approve, she figured. Hoped.

By the time she'd done all of that, the president was already on the air. She had been so busy trying to get into the system that she'd run out of time to figure out what exactly to *do* with that access. She'd have to wing it. Cassie pursed her lips, clicked her tongue; whatever she could find to distract her from the waxing and waning emotions inside her: *Be vengeful*, one voice said. *Be kind*, another ordered. *Be approachable, be contrite; be haughty, be bitchy, be really pissed off. Be terrified. Be pawing your way out of a rage so thick that you can't even breathe.* She closed her eyes, aware of the ticking clock. Surprisingly, an image of her mother flashed before her.

Cassie opened her eyes. All the voices were now in agreement: *just be real.*

Impress us, TonyStark had said.

Impress this, she thought, and executed her code.

She cleared her throat and spoke up. Not shouting, but projecting pretty well. "Anyone watching the president on TV?" she asked innocently.

There was a pause, then a fervid moment of mouse clicks and finger taps on glass.

Laptop lids slammed shut and people started shouting. It was the first time in three days that Cassie heard raised voices at OHM.

Everyone was watching. Everyone could see what she had done.

Hacked into the network's stock ticker. And now, running in an endless loop under the president as he fulminated and gesticulated and bombinated, was this:

HEY, **@POTUS**: KILL ME ALL YOU WANT — THAT BABY'S STILL AS UGLY AS YOU ARE. LOVE, **@CASSIEMCK39**. **#HasCassieSurfacedYet? #COMEANDGETME #INFINITERANGEISNTLONGENOUGHASSHOLE**

100101200101

TonyStark couldn't stop laughing. He would pause for an instant but then catch a glimpse of Cassie and begin howling all over again. If nothing else, she figured she'd impressed *him*, which was nice. Meanwhile, others had gathered around, some yelling recriminations, others defending Cassie.

There were no leaders at OHM, just a collection of like-minded people finding common ground where they could and otherwise leaving each other alone. OK, it reminded Cassie of the classical democracy her mom always talked about, but Cassie couldn't even think about her mom. Too painful.

If there'd been a leader, maybe someone would have punished Cassie or singled her out for praise. Instead, she was treated to a good half hour of people yelling at one another. Where there had once been only the sound of keystrokes, there was now nothing but fervor and rage.

The broadcast network had to take its feed down for a full fifteen minutes, showing only a static rainbow grid while the in-house cyber-squad located Cassie's worm and throttled it. She hadn't had time to give it any sort of replication vectors, but she had enough time to make it *look* like it had reproduced itself multiple times once in the network's systems. So the cyber-jackals had to spend additional time scrubbing their system, looking for more iterations of the worm. When they didn't find any, they would probably spend a couple of days panicking, reinstalling packages "just in case" and generally living in hell for a little while.

Oh well.

"Friggin' hilarious," TonyStark said. "Abso-friggin'-lutely hilarious."

"Are you nuts?" someone challenged. Cassie didn't know his name, but from his appearance, she decided he was Piercings Guy. "She's already at Level 6 and now she's bringing even *more* heat down? If she wants to blow herself up, fine, but not while *I'm* standing in the blast radius!"

There was a chorus of murmured agreements, but TonyStark just crossed his arms over his chest. "You said it yourself, man — she's Level 6. WTF they gonna do? Kill her twice? Whole goddamn internet wants to eat her brains. Zombie hordes roaming the streets looking for a taste of that sweet Cassie-meat. Can't get any worse."

"Not for *her*," Piercings Guy shot back, "but what about for *us*?"

Cassie could sense that TonyStark was losing the crowd. Democracy could be ugly, she knew. As much as she'd tried to block out her mom's lectures on the early throes of democracy, she couldn't unhear them.

"I was told to impress," Cassie said, brushing her hair back. "I thought you guys were about resistance. About disruption. If you're not going to kick the powers-that-be in the balls every now and then, what's the point?"

It was her voice but not her words. Harlon had said the same thing to her once. "We disrupt to shake out the old order. To clear-cut the old growth and make way for the new. There's a purpose. It looks chaotic, but it's not. We have to kick the system in the balls every now and then; otherwise, there's no point."

"Chaos masks order," she went on, recalling her father. "Like a fractal. There's hidden order in the chaos and that's what makes it all make sense. My prank will piss off the people who already hate me. Big deal. But it'll give the people on the sidelines something to rally around. The president won't be able to resist — he'll have to punch back. Hard. And he'll be punching down. And the people who care will be turned off by that and maybe we get a foothold into reversing my little problem.

"Oh, and BTW," she said over her shoulder to TonyStark, "Who are you calling 'meat,' Mr. My-Scalp-Looks-Like-Easter-Ham?"

A ripple of surprised laughter filled the room. TonyStark smoothed back his bald dome with one hand and clucked his tongue. "Damn, girl. I'm on *your* side."

"Coulda fooled me."

More laughter. Piercings Guy could tell he was losing the room. Shared amusement went a long way toward shifting the mood of a crowd. That's how memes worked, really. Her banter with TonyStark was infectious.

"We have their attention now," Cassie said.

"Jesus Christ, like you didn't before?" Piercings Guy grumbled.

"Now we have it for being something other than a victim of so-called Hive Justice," she said. "There's no way out of this on the defensive. There are too many of them and just one of me. If I ever want to go home again, I have no choice; I have to go on the attack. People respect strength. They're drawn to it. Trust me." There was a story from Roman history lurking somewhere in her mind, some memory of Mom discussing one of the endless ancient wars. But she couldn't dredge up the details. What she did remember, though, was something from last year's advanced biology class. "It's evolutionary. Part of our lizard brain. Back when we lived in caves, we were drawn to the person confident enough to kill the mastodon or get us past the sabertooth lair."

"This is true," TonyStark said. He stepped closer to her and seemed ready to throw a comradely arm around her. She wasn't quite ready for that and was relieved when he didn't bother. She liked him and she was glad she'd impressed him, but that was enough.

"That's how politicians and other assholes take charge," TonyStark went on. "They don't know jack *or* shit, but they pretend they do and people get suckered. Cassie just judo'd them."

She was absurdly touched that for the first time he'd used her name instead of "that girl."

Piercings Guy gritted his teeth and appeared ready to volley back. Cassie was already weary of him, especially since she wasn't even 100 percent sure she was right. Fortunately, fate intervened in the person of Tish, who cleared her throat more loudly than any human should be able to and stepped in between Cassie and Piercings Guy.

"Data don't lie," she announced, holding up a tablet.

It took Cassie a moment to tell exactly what it was she was looking at. She realized it was a graph tracking her BLINQ status. She was still at Level 6 (that wouldn't change), but her Likes had ticked up slightly. In fact, they were rising faster than her Condemns.

Her heart quickened. That familiar post-hack rush careered through her limbs; she'd missed it. She wondered briefly if returning to code was somehow betraying her father, if by giving up her self-imposed code ban, she'd made his death mean less.

Based almost purely on the satisfaction pumping through her veins, she decided no. Nothing that felt this good could be that bad. It was time for her to get back in the game. "I did it!" she blurted out.

A groan from the crowd. Tish fixed her with a withering, contemptuous glare that Cassie knew — even after only three days — was Tish Default. "Girl, don't be so proud. Yeah, your Like velocity is up, but the ratio of Condemns to Likes is so great that it would take six years at the current rate for your Likes to outpace and drop you back to Level 5."

"Six years? For real?" Cassie's shoulder dropped.

Tish shrugged. "Five years, ten months, six days. I rounded up."

"Well, shit."

"See?" Piercings Guy licked his lips. He was back on a roll. "See?"

"Brother, she moved a needle no one has ever moved before," TonyStark said. "With just a couple of days and an impressively shitty laptop. I say we help her. Even if we can't set her straight online, she's an asset to us and what we do."

She spied some nods in the group. Good. She didn't relish the idea of staying at OHM forever, but right now it was better than the alternative. If they kicked her out ... she'd be back on the street again. Defenseless. On the run with nowhere to go.

Piercings Guy grunted. "No. No way. She's a risk and a liability and a loose cannon. And this is coming from the guy who turned off every traffic signal in the city last May. I know what a loose cannon is."

A murmur of agreement. Bad.

Tish turned to Cassie. "What do you have to say for yourself?"

It should have been something from Harlon. It should have been from one of his infamous manifestos, the ones that set off Twitter wars and blog threads. She should have channeled him the way she always did in times of stress and crisis, used his words and his beliefs to sway these people — *his* people — to her side.

But the first thing that popped into her head was her mom.

"'Give me a firm place to stand and with a lever I will move the whole world,'" she told them.

The room fell silent.

"Archimedes," she said, by way of explanation. "Like TonyStark said — I had a little time and a little tech and I moved the needle. Give me a firm place to stand and a lever and see what I can do."

Piercings Guy shook his head. TonyStark grinned.

"Let's vote, people!" Tish called out. "Hands up if you think she should stay."

Cassie didn't want to watch. She forced herself to anyway.

10010130 0101

"I want a lawyer," Rachel whispered.

She couldn't be sure exactly what they were up to. She wasn't formally under arrest, but it still felt as though she were. A lawyer seemed appropriate.

While his partner drove and kept an eye on the road, Agent Hernandez twisted around to peer back at her from the front seat. "What did you say?"

"I said I want a lawyer," she repeated more forcefully.

He nodded, his lips pursed. "Are you sure? Lawyers are expensive. You don't have much of a nest egg."

"You looked at my bank records." She said it without accusation or heat. It was just a fact.

"We looked at everything," he told her.

"So," Rachel snapped, "all of that stuff about how you have kids, too, and you feel for me — that was all just crap, I guess?"

Hernandez's expression darkened and he glowered at her. "I

do have kids. That's why I'm doing this. So that they can grow up in a safe and orderly world."

"A safe and orderly world where they get to hunt and kill other children," she said. "How special for you."

Hernandez sneered. "Watch your mouth, Professor McKinney. We're still being nice."

"This is nice? I hate to imagine what nasty looks like."

He settled back into his seat, turning away from her. "You won't have to imagine," he promised.

*

They took her to the local police station but marched her in through the back door. She knew — vaguely — something of police booking procedures. Harlon had been arrested a couple of times early in their dating days, usually for defacing Confederate monuments. She knew that she should be processed with the desk sergeant, fingerprinted, face-scanned and photographed.

None of that happened.

Instead, they took her through a series of dark, empty corridors that wound like a maze in the bowels of the precinct. And for the first time, she began to fear. If they'd intended on merely arresting her and using her for leverage against Cassie, they would be following procedure. Instead, they were wending their way through a labyrinth, heading toward the minotaur, with no Ariadne in sight.

"Where are we going?" she demanded, fighting to keep a tremor out of her voice. These men only understood strength. They had no sympathy for damsels in distress.

"You'll see," Hernandez said.

Finally, they opened an obstinate old door and ushered her into a small room that stank of mold and rust. A broken mirror took up most of one wall, a chunk of missing glass allowing her to peer into the next room. An old, disused interrogation room, then.

There was a rickety table in the center of the room, lit by the overhead spasms of a single, unreliable light bulb. Hernandez's partner, who hadn't spoken a word, appeared in the doorway with a very sturdy chair. He placed it behind the table and guided Rachel into it with surprising gentleness.

They don't want any bruises on me. No evidence. Does that mean they're definitely going to let me go or that they want the body to be staged a certain way?

The equanimity with which she approached the notion that her own government — sworn to protect her and her rights — was planning to murder her didn't even shock her. It just seemed natural at this point. They'd sentenced her daughter to death; why not her, too?

"Professor McKinney." Hernandez's partner had a surprisingly mellifluous voice. He could have been an opera singer. Even the spoken word sounded musical. "I am Special Agent Jason Khartouk. If you truly want a lawyer, of course it is your right to have one. But we hope we can clear this up without such complications."

"What's going on?" she asked warily.

"You're not under arrest," Hernandez told her. "We took you into custody to get you here and to talk to you privately." He glanced over at Khartouk and a silent handoff took place.

"As I've told Agent Hernandez and every other NSA agent I've ever met: I didn't know anything about Harlon's work. I could barely understand it. He didn't leave anything behind that you people haven't already taken."

Khartouk planted his fists on the table, leaning forward. "We're not sure about any of that. We found references in some of your husband's notes to something he called 'a perfect encryption.' He also made reference to 'The Purloined Letter.'" Edgar Allen Poe's famous story about a missing letter that actually turns out to be in plain sight. Harlon didn't usually go in for literary allusions, but when he did he used them properly.

"I don't know anything about —" she began wearily.

Khartouk cut her off. "That's a conversation for another day. We're here to talk about your daughter."

"What does she have to do with Harlon's purloined letter?"

A tight smile. "Please don't play dumb. It's unbecoming. This is about the Hive. Contrary to popular belief, we government stooges *can* walk and chew gum at the same time."

She imagined how it had happened: Level 5 girl goes missing. Government wants to get involved. And, hey — look! It just so happens we already have some NSA goons watching the family anyway. How convenient.

"Professor McKinney, your daughter is in deep, deep trouble," Khartouk was saying. "And this isn't just about her. It's about the integrity of the entire Hive system. Now, eventually the mob will find her. And it will be ugly. But if you help us get to her first —"

"You'll what, expunge her record?" Rachel said it a little more nastily than she'd intended, but there was a slight lilt of hope in her voice. *Could* they do that? *Would* they? Why else would they be here?

Hernandez clucked his tongue. "Your daughter broke the law. Run, sure. Show how clever you are, lead the mob on a merry chase, yeah, OK. But she ditched her phone. She went off the grid."

"Wouldn't you, if you were running for your life?"

A sigh. "There's a bigger picture here. The social good. The stability of law and order."

"The death of a child." Rachel pulled her shoulders back as she said it. "Even the Romans had the decency to kill them as infants, before they could speak."

Hernandez's lip curled and he stepped closer, but Khartouk cleared his throat. Hernandez stepped back.

Good cop, bad cop, Rachel told herself. *Hernandez slaps you around and Khartouk stops him so he gains your sympathy. Don't fall for it. They're* both *bad cops.*

"For Cassie to do as good a job as she's done hiding," Khartouk said in his calming, musical voice, "she must have had help. Witnesses report an adult woman with her at the campus. Your campus," he said pointedly. "And RideHop reports a rental car was sent to your apartment with a destination of, once again, your campus. It's all pretty incriminating, and I know you'd like to explain it to us."

Rachel bit her lip. Bryce had said "we" (whoever *we* was) had hacked away evidence of her ride. So much for that. There was no winning scenario here. She obviously wouldn't tell them a damn thing about Cassie, but she couldn't wish away the evidence they had either. And Hernandez was right: lawyers were expensive, and she didn't know any, in any event. She wouldn't risk her meager savings and her life on a name plucked from Google or Yelp. The wisdom of the crowd didn't seem all that wise these days.

Her best bet, she reasoned, was to give them just enough to get them to let her go. Then she could try to figure out a plan of action, in her own home, not under a naked light bulb in the dank basement of a police precinct.

"Sometimes kids — especially kids in trouble," she said after a measured moment, "do stupid things, like use their parents' credit cards and accounts to order car services."

Hernandez's contempt for her was as blatant and obvious as his knitted eyebrows and the furrow between them. Khartouk, though, merely nodded, as though perfectly happy to buy this line of bullshit.

"That's true," he admitted. "Kids do all sorts of crazy things. Like BLINQ filthy comments about the president and his family. Because let's not forget, Professor — that's why we're here."

"Don't do this," Rachel said. "Not to Cassie. Look, you can rip my apartment to shreds, take everything Harlon ever touched. That's what you want, right? That's what you've always wanted. But please, leave my daughter alone."

Khartouk smiled too smoothly. "We can multitask. Right now, we're interested in Cassie."

Right now. So it would never end is what they were telling her. They would hunt her not just until they found Cassie, dead or alive, *but until they found Cassie and whatever it was they wanted from Harlon.* Rachel decided to change her approach.

"Were you young once, Agent Khartouk?"

His smile did not falter. "A long time ago, yes. A different world. But even then, my parents knew to keep me in line."

"So this is all my fault? I'm a bad parent?" She was on comfortable ground now. Sure, they could argue about her parenting skills. She was a mom — she was used to people telling her she was doing it wrong.

"There's being a parent," Hernandez snapped, "and there's aiding and abetting a felon."

"These theoretical children of yours, Agent Hernandez: Wouldn't you do the same for them, if you were in my shoes?"

Hernandez grimaced and took a step toward her. She didn't actually think she was in any danger until Khartouk suddenly stepped between them and backed Hernandez up. Hernandez waited a beat and then closed the door. The room was no darker, but suddenly seemed so much smaller.

Khartouk turned around, facing Rachel again. He looked crestfallen, disappointed. "You're not going to tell me anything, are you, Rachel?"

She wasn't Professor McKinney any longer. And the door was closed. The door was closed and she was alone with two men who did *things* for a living.

It took a while to swallow and find her voice. "It doesn't matter what you do to me," she said, her voice hoarse. "I don't know where Cassie is. I really don't."

Hernandez crossed his arms over his chest and leaned against the door. Khartouk stroked his jawline and regarded her for several protracted moments.

"The problem, Rachel, is this: I don't believe you."

"I can't help that," she replied.

Khartouk chuckled. "I think you can. I think you can help that by telling me the truth. And I think I know how to get you there."

Rachel's spine stiffened. "Just so you know: it's been proven that physical torture is ineffective. The subject will tell you anything you want to hear in order to make the pain stop."

Khartouk seemed taken aback. "Physical torture? We're not monsters, Professor McKinney. We're the United States government. Trust me when I tell you that we are not going to lay a single finger on you."

Back to Professor McKinney. Still, she wasn't sure she could believe him … but she wanted to. Both because he seemed so incredibly, almost innocently, earnest (that voice!) and also because she really, really did not want to be tortured. She didn't know much. She didn't know where Cassie had gone or how long she'd stayed there or whom she was with, but she did have one teeny, tiny piece of data that the NSA lacked. She knew a name.

Bryce.

"I have nothing to tell you," she said. "Nothing you don't already know."

"Again, I want to believe you, but I don't. I can't. It's my job not to." Khartouk glanced over at Hernandez. "Lights."

With a sweep of his hand, Hernandez flipped the switch and doused the room in darkness. Rachel clenched her jaw, holding back the scream that pounded for attention and release at the back of her throat. They hadn't done anything yet. They hadn't touched her. She couldn't crack this soon. But it was so dark, so suddenly dark, and there were two powerful men with weapons not far from her.

A light flickered, partly illuminating Khartouk. It was his phone, she realized. He tapped at the screen and then aimed the phone at the far wall, projecting an image there. It took her a moment to realize —

"You know what this is?" Khartouk asked calmly. Musically.

She did. A slightly blurred image of her with two-year-old Cassie. The first time Cassie had ridden a carousel, at Glory's Island, the amusement park near Rachel's parents' house. Rachel was wearing a yellow sundress that she hated — it bared her shoulders — but which Harlon adored. "You look like Theia," he'd told her. The Greek Titan of myth, the mother of the sun. Classical allusions were the way to her heart.

Cassie wore the cartoon-themed jumper she could never be without at that age. She wanted to sleep in it, and they'd compromised by letting her curl up with it like a blanket. One day a week, she was allowed to wear it, and this was that day. Her daughter was perched on a lovingly rendered seahorse, her eyes open wide with glee, her arms flung into the air as Rachel held her around the waist.

Harlon had snapped the picture. A good day. Why were they showing it to her? To remind her of what she'd lost and what she could still lose? She knew already.

"You have my pictures," she said evenly. "I'm not surprised."

"Do you know how human memory works, Rachel?" Khartouk asked rhetorically. "No one does, really. Take forgetting, for example. We take it for granted that we'll forget things. But why? Why should we forget things, and why are we OK with it? We don't even understand the process — do memories decay? are they interfered with by other memories? — but we just accept it."

"Now I know how my students feel when I lecture them," Rachel said, and feigned a yawn.

Hernandez snorted nastily in the dark. Khartouk stared at the photo for a long moment. Then, without a word, he tapped at his phone. A dialogue box came up, two buttons duplicated on the projection:

DELETE PHOTO

CANCEL

He tapped DELETE PHOTO and the picture disappeared. Blank white light projected on the wall.

Was this supposed to intimidate her somehow? Showing her a photo of her daughter and then deleting it?

"Memories," Khartouk said. "Sometimes they're lost or dim and we jump-start them with evidence. With photos or souvenirs. But what happens if that evidence goes away? Our brains aren't infinite storage areas. Without prompting, what do we remember? How long do we remember it? How *well*?"

If there was a point to this, Rachel didn't know what it was.

"Take out your phone." It was Hernandez speaking this time. "And show us that picture."

A million snarky, rebellious replies clawed their way up her throat, but she did as he'd bidden. Flicking through her photo album, she couldn't find the picture, though.

"It must not be on my phone," she said. But she thought *all* her photos were on her phone. Harlon had set up some kind of cloud account. Everything was supposed to be there.

"What about this one?" Khartouk asked. He'd projected another photo, this one of Rachel and Cassie at a toy store. Beaming together at the camera as Harlon snapped away.

"Right here," she said, bringing up the pic. She held out her phone to show them.

Khartouk nodded and once again brought up the DELETE dialogue. The photo vanished from the wall. "Check it now," he said.

She turned her phone so that it faced her again. She was no longer looking at the toy store picture. It was now a photo from later in the day, when Cassie had tried her first milkshake. Chocolate, of course. (Or, as she pronounced it then, "chockit.")

Rachel swiped back, but the toy store photo was gone.

Clever. They could control her phone. But everything was backed up in the cloud.

"I know what you're thinking," Khartouk said. "You're thinking, *But I have backups.*" He sighed sadly. "No. You don't." He projected another photo and started swiping through. In a blur of motion, Cassie went from newborn to her first steps to her first birthday ...

"See, we, uh, liberated some technology from Google. Related to image lookups. Now, when I delete a photo here" — he waggled his phone in the air — "a bot goes out into the web and finds every instance of that same photo. Every single copy. Every backup. On your computer at home. On your phone. In the cloud. Every copy. And destroys it. Overwrites it with ones and zeroes to a military-grade deletion spec so it can't be recovered." He paused to let his words sink in. "Those pictures are gone *forever*, Rachel. You will never, ever see them again. Except in your memories. Which" — he shrugged — "we've already discussed."

Rachel realized that she'd gone cold. Her body was trembling — the phone in her hand shook. It couldn't be true. But she had the evidence literally in her own hand.

A photo of Cassie on her first birthday, face cake-smashed. Icing everywhere. Took forever to wash it out, a screaming one-year-old hopped up on sugar, thrashing in the bathtub and then it was gone, deleted. Rachel let out an involuntary moan.

Cassie at two, caught in a moment of repose, staring far off into the distance, something so ancient and knowing and unknowable in her eyes, captured magically, serendipitously, and then, in less than a blink, the photo was gone.

"No!" Rachel screamed. "No!" She lurched up out of the chair but managed to rise only a couple of inches. At some point, Hernandez had come up behind her, and his hands caught her shoulders, shoved her back down into the chair.

She trembled, watching through tears as Khartouk calmly called up and obliterated moments from her life at random. Harlon's fortieth birthday disappeared into the ether. Cassie's first day of kindergarten. Her own baby shower. Gone, gone, gone. All as Khartouk musically narrated each image before consigning it to oblivion with a casual tap of his finger.

"Imagine if your daughter dies, Rachel. Imagine if she dies and you don't even have a picture left to remember her by."

It went on endlessly. She didn't know how long. She lost count of the number of pictures. How many pictures do parents take of their children? Surely hundreds in those first soft, sleepless months alone. And over Cassie's lifetime? How many thousands?

Rachel watched Cassie's third-grade dance recital disappear. She held on furiously, clenching her fists. Every part of her yearned to scream out Bryce's name, to give them the single piece of data she had in her possession that could end this.

It would be easy to do.

It would be so easy to do.

*

They returned her to the apartment some indeterminate time later, with a stern warning not to leave the state without contacting them first.

She'd lost track of the time and of how many photos — and *which* photos — they'd deleted. At some point during the hellish process, she'd stopped begging. She'd just become one protracted moan, her eyes no longer focusing, not even able to steal one final look at the photos as they erased them from her world for good. Eventually, Khartouk had sighed, shut off his phone and said, as though to a disinterested third party, "She's no good to us. She doesn't know anything."

Now, sprawled on the floor of her apartment, her mind refusing to function normally, she felt as though a flu bug racked her body. She lay there for too long, then managed to drag herself to the sofa. With a heroic effort, she used the arm of the sofa to pull herself up to her knees.

And fuck them, she decided.

Fuck. Them.

She'd resisted. She hadn't given them Bryce's name. She'd held out as they'd erased Cassie, sacrificing the certain past for the hopeful future.

Harlon's voice rang in her head. Telling her what to do. She stood and made her way to her laptop. Paused. Then she went to the coat closet, where the cable guy had installed the modem and wireless router. With a fierce cry of victory, she yanked out the power cords.

Your laptop can still pick up other Wi-Fi signals, Harlon told her. *It's not safe.*

She returned to the laptop. Flipped it open. From her desk, she scrounged around until she found a USB key. The size of her photo library was much, much tinier than it had been earlier that day. Choking back a sob, she copied what remained to the USB drive. No Wi-Fi on that. No way to erase it remotely. At least, not that she knew of.

It wasn't much. They could always just take the USB key from her. But it was something. It was something and she would take it.

There was something else she would take, too.

Control.

*

Once she was safely ensconced in her office, behind keycard access and university security officers, Rachel's fingers drummed over her laptop. There was an idea stewing inside her, one that her brain was a little too afraid to consider. It was risky. But what wasn't right now? She tapped some keys, made some movements. She watched as if from afar.

Rachel had never read #UniversityMoms before. Then again, she could count on one hand the number of hashtag threads she had read. Once, before Harlon had died, he and Cassie had made her look at #ClassicsProfessorsBeLike, and the comments had in equal parts infuriated and amused her.

She browsed through the thread. The university had pretty good benefits for working parents, including on-site daycare and various support groups, but this thread consisted of minor complaints, general encouragements and — Rachel's fingers hovered over these conversations — a philosophical thread about the changing role of mothers in their children's lives today, as technology was helping them evolve into adults more quickly than in the past.

Her fingers flew. She posted before she could really think about whether that was the smart thing to do. Then again, it didn't matter if it was smart. It just had to be effective. It just had to be something she could do, a task she could complete, instead of waiting for the inevitable breakdown that was sure to come as she watched the world hunt down her only child.

She published it and watched the comments roll in.

*

#UniversityMoms Discussion Board:
A Place for MS/BFU Mothers to Share, Support and Save Our Sanity
Join a discussion or start your own!
For Working Moms at MS/BFU

HOT THREAD ALERT: "I need help from other moms. You might be the only people who understand" has been viewed 12x more than the average post. Join the conversation!

Posted by: McKinneyR

I need help from other moms. You might be the only people who understand, who can help stop this. Because, like me, you'd do anything — ANYTHING — for your kid.

My daughter is 17, and she did something stupid. I did stupid things when I was a kid, too. I don't know a single adult who hasn't. But we didn't have the world watching us back then. I'd say that makes us lucky.

Think of the worst thing you ever did back then. And now think of how you would feel if the world had seen it. Think of how you would feel if the world had permission not just to determine your punishment but to dole it out, too.

That's what's happening to my daughter right now. My only child is running for her life. Cassie is just a kid. She deserves to learn from her mistakes, to grow and contribute to the world. She doesn't deserve this.

As parents — mothers — we have a moral obligation to keep our kids safe. To create a world that's safe for them. And yet … we live in this world of online justice, where every move we make is up for public debate. Imagine if it were your kid. Imagine if your child was missing because a bunch of strangers decided she's not worthy of life.

Help me, moms. I'm begging you. Help me save my kid.

10010140 0101

Rachel and Harlon had differed on how to raise Cassie. Harlon was less concerned with whether Cassie had finished her vegetables than whether she'd figured out the optimal way to chop and cook them. Rachel would assign Cassie chores and talk about responsibility; Harlon would help Cassie dirty every dish in the house while they made inedible cookies (which they ate anyway) and then suggest they just throw them out and buy new ones. "Fail fast and move on!" was his mantra. Cassie was witness to more "discussions" about what was best for her than she cared to remember.

In the hours after the ticker hack, Cassie reveled in the memories, feeling like she was a child again, listening to Mommy and Daddy bicker over how to deal with her. Half of OHM, led by TonyStark, thought Cassie had done a brilliant job proving her worth, while the other half thought her "stunt" to be unnecessarily dangerous, outrageous, immature, aggressive and — what was it Piercings Guy had called it? Ah, yes, Cassie remembered: egotistical.

Given the vociferousness of the debate, she thought it would be a squeaker, but it wasn't even a close vote. In the end, even Piercings Guy was shamed into raising his hand for Cassie.

She breathed a sigh of relief — she was in. She was part of OHM now. She belonged and she had help.

By way of official welcome, they gave her a smartphone that had been manufactured before she was born. It couldn't even load apps other than the ones that were already on it. And its interface was a muted series of gray tones.

"Security through obscurity," TonyStark told her. "Don't do anything stupid with it. It doesn't have a GPS chip, so they can't track you with it, but they can still find you if you're dumb."

"And the dull-ass screen?" she asked.

He sniffed. "It's been proven that the colors in mobile interfaces are designed to stimulate your adrenal responses. You get a dopamine kick from the color combinations so you stay glued to the screen. We kill the colors so we can focus on things other than Candy Crush and BLINQ."

With a grateful shriek of delight, she scrambled away to figure out the nitty-gritty of the phone. She finally had a new lifeline to her dad, once she could hack the thing to use an encrypted SMS client. She suspected part of the reason for giving her such outdated tech was to test her mettle yet again.

She had just started setting it up when TonyStark found her and announced that he had news.

"We have confirmation your mom has been brought in for questioning," he told her. His voice was nothing close to gentle; he could have been a waiter telling her the kitchen was closing in five minutes. "They're making a big deal of the new processes in place for Level 6, so they're using Rachel as an example." He showed her his laptop screen.

Tish and a couple others joined them. Cassie paled when she saw the image of her mother. She looked like she'd aged ten years.

"They've arrested her?" she said, aghast.

TonyStark shook his head. "Nah, the records say she's just there for questioning. They'll probably release her soon, back to your apartment."

Good news, yes. Cassie, though, was beginning to wonder if she would ever stop feeling like the wind had been knocked out of her. "And then what? She's just supposed to go back to work tomorrow? To regular life?" Her voice sounded like someone else's.

"Cass ..." Tish said gently.

"No, seriously, what?" Cassie's eyes had taken on a wild look. "There's a mob of people trying to kill her daughter and she's supposed to just ... take it? Let them? Get up in the morning and have a shower and put on a suit and take the subway to work and eat breakfast and drink coffee and —"

"Kid. Come with me." Tish grabbed Cassie's elbow and pulled her away from TonyStark. His face flooded with relief. "Let's go for a walk."

"A walk? Where, to the end of the hotel?" Cassie muttered.

"Hey," Tish said sharply. "We're lucky to be here. Never forget that."

Cassie struggled to control her breathing. After a moment she whispered, "Sorry," and then her face collapsed, tears flowing.

Tish led Cassie through a maze of rooms she hadn't managed to explore yet, on the other end of the building, facing west,

Cassie guessed, based on the hints of sunset peeking through the tiny rips and tears of the window coverings. These rooms were in slightly less habitable shape, and she and Tish stepped carefully over holes and dips in the floors. Finally, Tish reached their destination, such as it was: an alcove in the rectangular shape of the rest of the hotel room. There was a makeshift seat — cushion, blanket — and a stack of books Cassie recognized from her childhood. Chapter books, picture books. Kid stuff.

"Look up," Tish demanded, but her voice was lighter, happier. Cassie peered up and gasped.

The alcove had a skylight. An *uncovered* skylight.

"I don't know who knows about this spot," Tish said happily, dropping to her knees and fluffing the cushion. "But it's where I come when I need a break. I figure the skylight is small enough and high enough that the risk of being spotted is pretty low." She paused and then looked meaningfully at Cassie. "That doesn't mean you should tell anyone else about it, OK?"

The remaining sunlight rained down on the top of Tish's head, turning her purple hair dark blue. Cassie nodded. When Tish patted the space next to her, Cassie fell into it, turning her face up to the skylight, closing her eyes and pretending she could feel the breeze, the dusk, the softening of the day.

"So … Level 6, huh?" Tish whistled. "What's it feel like to be the girl who was so dangerous that the government had to put a hit out on you?"

Tish's lighthearted tone aside, the words made Cassie's head spin. It was impossible to digest what had happened to her over the past few days. And now, with her mom in custody … How could this be real? How could anyone believe she was dangerous?

Something struck Cassie. "I just want her to be OK," she said. "My mom, I mean. TonyStark said she'll probably just go home soon but … how can I be sure? And, like — then what?" She chewed her lip. "Things weren't always great between us, and I left them even worse."

Tish looked thoughtful. "This is why I don't want kids."

"That's super helpful, Tish, thanks," Cassie snapped.

"I don't get a lot of girl talk in here," she grumbled. "Gimme a break."

"If she knew I was fine, that we were trying to figure out a plan …"

Tish's eyes widened. Today they were lined with sparkly green, and little jeweled stickers formed a feather shape across her left eyebrow. "Kid. Stop that line of thinking right now."

"What line of thinking?" Bryce's massive form appeared in the alcove.

Tish jumped to her feet. "Shit! What are you doing here?"

He waved his hand around noncommittally. "Relax, I won't bust your secret place. We all have one of our own. But you're needed in the hackers' pit. We might be on to something."

Cassie leaped up. "Let's g —"

"Stay here, Cassie," Bryce said gently. "You need a break. And we're not ready for you yet."

"Did you see my mom? Were you at school?"

Bryce nodded, just once. "Look, things are gonna happen fast. But right now, you need to chill a bit and get your feet under you before you're any good to yourself or your mom or anyone. OK?"

Cassie slumped against the wall and watched Tish and Bryce

round a corner and disappear into the belly of the hotel. She looked up; the sky was changing color again, and she traced faint cloud lines and the paths of two distant airplanes. Time passed and the sky darkened. Her fidgeting and her rapid breathing slowed, stopped … Then started again. Try as she might, she couldn't stay relaxed for more than a few minutes at a time. Bryce meant well, she knew, but he was an idiot to think she couldn't help. Being agitated just meant she was *more* engaged.

She wondered if her mom had been released from custody yet. It had been hours.

Something tugged at her. Soon, it became a voice. *You could ask someone*, it suggested.

It was a bad idea. She knew that, yet her hands moved of their own accord, finding her new-old phone and holding it up to the fading light. She *could* ask someone to check in on Rachel … it was possible. She had the physical capability to do so … but was it smart?

"Eff smart," she said aloud. A smart joke was what landed her here in the first place.

Her fingers hovered over the keypad. Not Rowan. No way. Rowan had lured her in, used her for her tech brain, gotten her into this mess in the first place, then tossed her out when she wasn't convenient anymore. So not Indira, Izzy or Madison either. Adena? Max? Maybe. She let the idea curl around her.

Suddenly, a big, fuzzy, blond ball flashed across her eyes. Sarah. What had she been thinking, keeping Sarah at arm's length this whole time? What a stupid idea that had been. Sarah was someone true, someone real. She cared about Cassie. *She* could help. Right?

The hesitation, the risk, warred with her desire to make sure her mom could sleep at night. It was no contest. She tapped out a text.

Sarah, it's C. Huge favor needed. It's about my mom.

She waited.

It didn't take long.

OMG I can't believe you're contacting me. Are you crazy? Are you OK?

Cassie broke into a grin. Sarah was wrong — she was desperate, not insane — but this wasn't the time to tell her that.

Can you get a msg to my mom? Tell her I'm OK? I'm with w/ some people who will totally get me out of this.

A pause. Cassie was already picturing the relief on Rachel's face when Sarah relayed the message, the weight off her shoulders.

Totes. I can do that. Where r u? Sarah asked.

Some old hotel. Just tell her I'm in the city and I'm safe. k?

It took forever for the comeback. Damn this old tech!

Got it. I'll tell her.

It was all Cassie could ask for. She texted back a heart and closed her eyes, breathing and wishing at the same time.

*

She emerged from the not-so-secret hiding place to find TonyStark, Bryce and Tish in a low-key but noticeable argument.

"I don't trust virgins," TonyStark was saying emphatically, crossing his arms over his chest.

Virgins. People who hadn't been Hive Mobbed.

"What about me?" Bryce asked hotly.

"I trust you when I can see you," TonyStark said with admirable bluntness. "Otherwise ..."

Bryce snorted and hovered over TonyStark. It was no contest. Bryce could pick up a skinny hacker dude like TonyStark and body-slam him into pulp without even breathing hard.

"Whoa, whoa!" Tish interposed herself between them. "We're not going to get anywhere by beating each other up."

"I won't be getting beat up," Bryce said. "This little shit! Do you know what I risk by coming here?"

"Do you know what we risk by *letting* you come here?" To his credit, TonyStark hadn't flinched, even with a ton of Red Dread looming over him.

"I declare Bryce has the biggest," Tish said drily. "The dick-measuring contest is now over."

For the first time, TonyStark seemed to lose his cool. He rounded on Tish. "What? Are you kidding me? Him?"

Tish shrugged. "Look at him. If everything's in proportion ..."

"Jesus!" TonyStark said. Bryce just seemed embarrassed.

"I'm not sayin'," Tish told them. "I'm just sayin', is all."

"And *I'm* just saying," Bryce insisted, "that we can trust @Shameless."

@Shameless? Cassie had been watching from the sidelines, quietly, but now she spoke up. "Who's @Shameless?"

"No, *you* can trust @Shameless," TonyStark said. "*We* don't have that luxury."

"Hey! I said, who's @Shameless?"

Ignoring her, Bryce fumed at TonyStark. "Man, you can't tear down the system without a little help on the inside."

"Says you."

Bryce stared. "That's all you've got? Says you?"

TonyStark shrugged. "I got neither the time nor the inclination to explain to a rich dude why I'm —"

"Rich? This isn't about money, man."

"Everything is about money! Money is power. How many rich people have been Hive Mobbed? Somewhere, someone's making a profit. Someone always is. And you just don't see —"

"Hey!" Cassie yelled through cupped hands. "I asked a question! Who. Is. @Shameless?"

Tish opened her mouth, then shut it. "Nah. Too easy."

Bryce and TonyStark exchanged glances. "So tell her," Bryce said.

"Nah, you tell her. It's your deal."

"@Shameless is a guy we know —"

"A guy *you* know."

Bryce shot a death glare at TonyStark. "Fine. A guy *I* know. He's on the inside."

"Inside of what?"

Bryce stuttered on the first word: "H-hive. Like, Department of Justice, Hive."

Cassie's jaw dropped. Tish nodded and TonyStark smirked. "See? My girl is no idiot. She knows better than to trust insiders."

"I'm not your girl," Cassie told him. "You were doing so well, actually using my name."

TonyStark grunted in embarrassment.

"But, yeah," Cassie went on, "I'm not sure about marching right into the hornets' nest."

Bryce shrugged. “OK. Got any better ideas? Maybe poke the president again? That solved everything, didn’t it?”

There was a long silence, broken when Tish said, “Let’s at least hear Bryce out.”

Bryce flashed her a grateful smile, which she waved off like a bad smell. “Look,” he started, “everything we’ve been able to piece together so far indicates that there’s something fishy going on with regard to your Level 6. It’s ... Show her,” he said to TonyStark.

“Check it,” TonyStark said, stroking his keyboard. “There’s something happening here. We just have to find it.”

Some of the hackers were reckless with their tools, pounding away at keyboards as though the letters that faded or the keycaps that flew off were able to regenerate themselves. TonyStark, though, was like an artist; his fingers moved over the keys with precision and purpose, with a grace that Cassie loved watching. Every hacker had a style, she was learning. She wondered what hers would ultimately be.

If she lived long enough, obvi.

Now that he was in his milieu, all of TonyStark’s outrage at Bryce melted away. He was cool and professional again. She stood over his shoulder, next to Tish and Bryce, while his screen lit up with Cassie’s BLINQ profile, the feeds moving so fast that no one could read them, the content showcasing the world’s reactions to every facet of Cassie’s life. Her profile picture was still circled in red, with “LEVEL 6 – #KillOnSight” still flashing. She tried not to look at it too closely.

“Shortly after you were made Level 6, I put out the word to @Shameless,” Bryce told Cassie. “I asked him to help us analyze your virality stats. He's supposed to be pinging me back soon."

"I thought you guys already did an analysis?" Cassie asked, confused. For the three days and change that she'd been stuck at OHM, she'd seen Tish and TonyStark and some of the others running constant checks on her stats. What was the point of it all?

"We've done nothing *but* analyses," Tish grumbled, reading her mood and her mind. "Not a damn one of them makes sense."

Cassie met Bryce's eyes. "Really?"

Bryce opened his mouth to speak, then shrugged. "I wouldn't want to overstep my bounds," he said to TonyStark.

TonyStark threw his hands up. "Dudes. She just called out the president in front of the whole damn world. I think she can handle the truth."

"Cool. Cool. OK, Cassie, here's the thing." Bryce pulled on one of the dreadlocks that had fallen from the knot he'd tied them into at the back of his head. "No one's ever seen anything like this before. The speed of virality, the sheer number of comments ... Statistically, it doesn't seem to work. Based on that alone, we're looking at quite possibly hundreds of thousands of people who've never participated in Hive actions before who suddenly decided your joke was worth breaking their silence. A few thousand, egged on by the mob mentality and wanting to be a part of it?" Bryce shrugged. "Sure. But *this* many? It just doesn't add up."

"You think someone manipulated the system?" she asked.

TonyStark barked with laughter. "Girl, the system *is* manipulation. We don't know what the hell is going on. It's possible this is all on the up-and-up. But it's nothing we've ever seen before." He paused, then grinned. "And we've seen a lot."

"And you think @Shameless can shed some light on it?"

"Yes," Bryce said immediately.

Cassie liked Bryce and owed him a lot. But three days in forced proximity to Tish and TonyStark had given her mad respect for their skills and opinions. "Tish?"

She mulled it over before shrugging. "This @Shameless dude … he's helped us out before. But on little things. Can't imagine why he'd want to get involved with something at this level. Too risky."

"He doesn't and he won't," said TonyStark. "This is how they get you — they help you with the small, insignificant stuff, then snatch you on the big stuff. And it gets no bigger."

He tapped on his keyboard and the screen flipped to a new view: the latest coverage of Hive Mobs searching for Cassie. Her eyes widened. Throughout the city, streets were clogged with people hunting her. Even with a screen between them, she could feel their hatred, their animal instinct to find her, to drag her. To kill her. No one knew where'd she'd fled, and the entire country was looking for her.

It was one thing to see the online feeds about her, Cassie realized. It was another entirely to see actual physical bodies out on the prowl. In the stale air of the hotel, she shivered.

"I trust the guy." Bryce checked his watch, a simple analog one that looked like it belonged to his great-grandfather. "He pinged me late last night and said he wanted to talk. Said he had suspicions."

"Do you really think he can help me?" Cassie chewed her lip, then winced at the pain. Her lips were raw; she needed a new outlet for her anxiety. For the first time she understood why people exercised.

"*Us*," Tish corrected her. "In case you haven't noticed, we're kind of in this together, kid."

TonyStark nodded once, firmly.

Cassie's cheeks flooded with warmth. "Thanks," she mumbled just as Bryce's phone beeped.

"Here it is," Bryce whispered. "@Shameless."

Everyone, even TonyStark, peered at Bryce's screen. It was a short message, but it was enough:

Critical info. You and the girl at Venecia, 10 p.m.

TonyStark let out a low whistle. Tish's jaw dropped. Cassie wanted to remark on the way @Shameless had taken away her agency by calling her "the girl" but she was stuck on the sudden change of plans. She and Bryce ... out in public ... at a club. Tonight.

Bryce was still staring in awe at his phone. "Holy shit."

"The inside man, in the flesh!" TonyStark led out a loud sound, a cross between a laugh and a guffaw, and slapped Bryce on the shoulder. "Damn, son. Were you expecting that?"

"What if it's a trap?" Tish said.

"Um, hello? It's definitely a trap!" Cassie snapped. "Your informant, who works for the government, wants to meet me, alone, in some random club? It's not safe." She turned to TonyStark. "Tell them it's not safe."

"It's totally not safe," TonyStark agreed.

"We'll go in with a plan," Bryce said. "And you won't be alone."

"Hell, no!"

Bryce regarded her sadly. "Cassie. We don't have a choice."

"*We* don't, but *I* do!" she hollered. "*I* choose not to walk into what's obviously a setup. *I* choose not to walk out of this hotel and into a mob that literally wants nothing more than to kill me. No way. If I'm going down, I'm going down fighting!"

"You'll be fine," Tish said suddenly. She popped up from her screen; she'd disappeared into her pod while no one was looking. "Check out the dress code for Venecia."

In the photos from Venecia's feed, bodies danced to unheard beats, their heads covered. Grotesque masks with distorted cutouts for eyes and hideous painted mouths swayed, nodded, shook; the result was a disturbing scene straight out of a horror film. It almost looked familiar to Cassie, as though she'd watched that movie back when she liked to watch horror films, before her life had become one.

"This is why @Shameless chose Venecia. Masks are required," Tish explained. She considered. "Well, the site just says 'no real faces allowed,' so we could probably get away with heavy costume makeup. But I don't have that kind of tool kit anymore. Our best bet is to get a mask."

She glanced at Bryce. "And some scissors."

TonyStark leaned back in his chair and let out a long laugh. Bryce's hands flew to his ponytail, his face wearing an expression of shock so comical that even Cassie couldn't suppress a tiny smile.

"No way," he insisted. Tish smiled grimly and held up two fingers in a mock scissors.

TonyStark couldn't stop chuckling. "It was nice knowing ya, Red Dread."

"Man," Bryce said, scowling, "don't start with me." To Cassie, he said, "I'm gonna go figure out some masks and such for us. I'll be in touch about tonight, OK?"

Once he'd left, Cassie found herself back in the alcove, staring at her phone, willing a text from Sarah to pop up. As much as she wanted to hear about her mom, a big part of her — a Rachel-sized part — was second-guessing her decision to ask Sarah for help, and not just because it was a safety risk to her and everyone at OHM. On the one hand, she knew that was what friends did for each other. On the other, by texting Sarah, she'd put her friend in jeopardy. She'd been desperate, yeah, but ... Not cool.

In a rush of regret she deleted her text thread with Sarah and expunged the fake phone number that the encrypted app had created for her. That would at least give Sarah plausible deniability if anyone ever asked her about it.

Back in the main room, she made a beeline for one of the kitchenettes. Sometimes there were day-old doughnuts, and a day-old powdered doughnut was actually, in her estimation, superior to freshly baked. Her eyes had just alighted on her white-dusted prize when someone shouted.

"Breach! Breach!"

It took Cassie a moment to recognize the voice — it came from one of the rugby guys, now charging into the room, waving his arms wildly. She stepped away from the kitchenette and over to TonyStark's cube, where Tish was also hanging out.

"Get *out*!" the rugby guy shouted. "Breach! Get the *fuck* out!"

Someone yelled, "Is this another fucking drill?"

Rugby Guy just kept shouting. "Breach! We've been breached! Get out!" as he ran through the room.

TonyStark and Tish looked at each other. Tish was already on her tablet, tapping away. "Oh, shit! Our location's been BLINQed! Cops *and* Hive Mobs en route."

"En route?" someone snapped. "Sounds like they're here."

Before anyone could respond, the sound of gunfire, muted by walls and doors, blasted out. Bullet holes appeared in the door from the corridor and then the door crashed inward. The other rugby guy — and dammit, she'd never even learned their names! — collapsed backward, shaking and bleeding profusely, crashing to the floor.

TonyStark tapped his earbud. "Rome burns!" he shouted. "Rome burns!"

The surviving rugby guy was charging around the room, still screaming "Breach!" at the top of his lungs. The room became a chaos of bodies and then gun smoke drifting in. A stray bullet from somewhere hit the window behind Cassie, exploding the glass outward. The black paper ripped outside with the force of the shattering glass and suddenly daylight bloomed at OHM.

A hand grabbed her by the wrist. Cassie looked down and saw TonyStark holding her fast. "Come on!" he shouted, and pulled her after him.

She opened her mouth to ask about Tish, but as she looked around . . .

Tish had crouched behind a partition and was wielding a long rifle with a wicked-looking scope mounted atop it. Cassie had no idea where it had come from and it seemed insane that Tish was brandishing it.

"We have to help her!" she cried as TonyStark dragged her toward a door. "We have to help her!"

He ignored her and tugged harder, almost yanking her off her feet as he bore relentlessly toward the door. She fought back, but he had a grip like a boa constrictor, and he forced her through the door and into a dark corridor she'd never seen before. Some other OHMers pushed past them, running frantically toward the other end of the hall.

"Let go of me!" she screamed, pulling. "Let go!"

"You want to die?" TonyStark snarled. "Settle down!"

There was no light in the corridor, save for flashes from cell phones and the LEDs in earbuds as people dashed past them. Cassie was buffeted by bodies, knocked against the walls. The sounds of footsteps and screams and panting breath and bullets became her world, steeped in darkness.

Eventually, TonyStark kicked open a door with a savage grunt. Sunlight spilled in, blinding her. They were on the rooftop.

There was nowhere to go.

Nowhere.

She had no screams left. Only a whimper.

"Listen," he told her, dragging her out onto the roof, "I can't do all of it for you. You're gonna have to do some of it, grok?" When she said nothing, simply stared back at the black hole of the corridor they'd just walked along, he shook her violently by the shoulders. "You grok?"

"I grok!" she said. "But all our work's on the computers. And Tish!"

More gunfire echoed along the hall, exploding out into the day.

"Rome burns," TonyStark reminded her. "That crashed our network and executed a mass-deletion protocol. Better the data's gone than in their hands."

"But Tish —"

"Tish did two tours as a sniper in the 'Stan. She can take care of herself."

"How did they find us?" she demanded, her heart pounding too hard, too loud. "You said we were safe."

It wasn't her text. Her phone had no way to transmit location. Even if someone had intercepted the texts and decrypted them in record time, there was no GPS data to use.

"Nowhere's safe forever," TonyStark told her.

Cassie stared at him. Someone ran past them, elbowing her out of the way. Swept up by an adrenaline high, she scarcely registered it.

"Where do we go?" she asked, her mind racing. Escape seemed impossible, and she was #KillOnSight. "We're up too high ..."

"We thought of that," he told her. "We thought of everything. You have to run now, OK? Can you follow me?"

She nodded.

TonyStark grinned. "Knew you could. Let's go."

10010150 0101

She and TonyStark ran across the rooftop, gravel crunching under their feet, kicked up in a solid wake behind them. Once — just once — she dared fire a look over her shoulder.

Men in black body armor weren't too far behind them, wielding large assault rifles. Other OHMers ran here and there, scattering to the edges of the rooftop. Some of them, to her alarm, dropped right over the side.

Others never made it that far, cut down by bullets before they could escape. Cassie thought, for one second that filled her with relief, that she was simply watching a movie, something VR immersive.

Then her left foot came down wrong, twisted in the gravel. She gasped in shock and at the sudden lightning bolt of pain, then thought of the guns, of the men, and forced herself back into balance and into reality.

She kept running.

At the edge of the rooftop, TonyStark paused just briefly.

Then, without a word, he vaulted over the parapet into thin air.

A scream curdled in Cassie's throat. Good thing, too. Had she given it voice, she never would have heard TonyStark's stage-whispered, "Come on!"

Leaning over the parapet, she peered down. TonyStark stood on a wooden plank balanced over the railings of an old fire escape. Cassie worried at her bottom lip, tasted her own blood.

Gunshots in the background were even more persuasive than the pleading expression on TonyStark's face.

Cassie clambered over the parapet and dropped straight down, eyes tightly shut. She landed squarely on the plank, which didn't budge, and saw that it was bolted to the exterior wall of the hotel. This wasn't a lucky coincidence.

"Told you we planned for everything," TonyStark said. He reached out and she took his hand.

The next part was vertigo inducing. Hugging the wall, they inched along a narrow ledge, making their way north to the corner of the building. She risked a single, vertiginous look down — the black ribbon of Carmichael Avenue was clotted with onlookers and vehicles. Police cars spun their lights into the crowd; an enormous military-camo-tattooed *thing* stood halfway up the block. She dragged her eyes up to fight a wave of dizziness. From below, the street noise of tires on pavement, feet on cement, people barking orders into their earbuds was all muted and distorted. It sounded less like the city's normal buzz and more like something in a cartoon.

Carmichael ran east–west, and she could see the sun peeking through the skyscrapers. She wanted to luxuriate in its glow for the first time in days, but TonyStark's hand was an insistent, clutching reminder that someone could look up and see them at any moment.

And then a shout from above made Cassie look up sharply, a move that took her off-balance and almost tipped her backward and into a thirty-story plunge. TonyStark wrapped his arm around her shoulders, pinning her to the walls.

"Don't look up," he ordered. "Or down."

"But they —"

"You down there!" a commanding voice boomed. "Don't move any farther!"

"Don't listen to them."

She had no intention of listening to them, but when a burst of gunfire rattled from above, she froze in place. The whistle-slam of bullets raced all around her, and she knew that if she moved even a centimeter, she'd be hit.

And fall.

And die.

"They can't hit you," TonyStark told her. "I promise. The angles are all wrong. That's why we set up this particular escape route. As long as you hug the wall, you can't be hit."

"I can't move," she whispered. It was true. She was paralyzed.

"Maybe this'll help: Any second now, they're gonna come down to the fire escape. And then they *can* shoot you. And they will. We need to be around that corner before they get down here."

Yeah, that worked. Cassie tossed a glance back the way they'd come. She was alarmed but also heartened by how far from the fire escape they were already. It had felt as though their progress could be measured with a microscope, but they were already more than halfway to the corner.

"Get a move on, you slowpoke," she told TonyStark. Bravado was his native tongue, and it was the closest she could come to saying *thank you so much* without getting all sappy.

With the rough concrete of the building's exterior wall against her palms and cheek, she made her way along the ledge after TonyStark, all the way to the corner. He went first, disappearing to the other side of the building.

Turning the corner was tougher than she thought it would be. On the ground, it would be nothing, but there was no room for error here. She had to shift her center of gravity at just the right moment, reaching around the corner with her right hand to find the wall on that side ...

A wind barreled down the canyon between buildings, threatening to pluck her from the ledge and toss her into the open air. She clutched the corner with all her strength, willing herself to stick to the wall like a bug. At the same time, TonyStark took her hand from the other side.

"You can do this, dig? I can't help you at this angle. You gotta do it yourself."

She nodded. Realized he couldn't see her head. Popped a thumbs-up on the hand he held.

"Good." He let go. "Now just sort of slide your feet toward the corner until your right heel is just off the ledge. I know it's scary, but you'll be OK."

She did as he'd told her, sidling along the ledge until she felt a drop in her heel. Closing her eyes tight, she gritted her teeth into a new wind. A breeze. On the ground, it would be nothing. Up here?

She blocked it from her mind. TonyStark was still giving commands, but she ignored him. She had this figured out.

She leaned into the building as far as she could and swung her right leg out in an arc, around the corner. Her toe stubbed against the ledge on the other side, and she greeted the pain like an old friend she'd not seen in years.

"You got it, Cassie. You got it."

With a deep breath, she leaned out as far as she dared, one hand on either side of the corner of the hotel. For a perilous, horrifying instant, her center of gravity was over open space, but then her momentum took her around; her weight landed on her right foot. She now straddled the corner. When she turned her head to the right and opened her eyes, TonyStark was grinning at her.

"Fancy meeting you here," he deadpanned.

"Now what?" she asked.

In response, he started inching his way along the ledge, moving away from her. Cassie groaned. Her entire body hurt from exertion at this point. Clinging to the ledge taxed her core, her shoulders, her calves and thighs …

From around the corner, she thought she heard the sound of boots hitting the wooden plank. That galvanized her to action and she crab-walked along the ledge with a greater confidence spurred on by urgency.

Near the middle of this side of the hotel, TonyStark stopped. "This next part is tough," he said without a trace of irony.

Cassie barked laughter. "Oh, the *next* part is tough."

"Watch me and do what I do."

As she watched, TonyStark reached down and threaded his belt out of its loops until it hung loose in his left hand. Cassie wondered what the hell he was up to … until she looked up.

"Oh, *hell*, no!" she exclaimed.

"Double your belt over like this," he told her, demonstrating. "Otherwise, it won't be strong enough."

"No way," she said. "No *way*."

He shrugged. "Feel free to take your chances with the mob, Ms. #KillOnSight."

And with that, he looped his doubled-over belt over the zip line bolted into the wall just above their heads. He used the additional stability to turn around so that he was facing out from the building, then — with a wink in Cassie's direction — kicked off from the wall and slid at increasingly terrifying speed across the yawning abyss between buildings.

On reflex, Cassie almost spun around to watch him but stopped herself at the last possible moment, just before her foot turned out into nothingness. She closed her eyes and clung to the wall for dear life.

She couldn't do this.

She couldn't *actually* do this.

Had TonyStark made it? Had he survived? She couldn't get enough of an angle looking over her shoulder, and she couldn't turn around …

Well, she *could* turn around.

Same way he had.

Goddammit, she thought. *I hate everyone in the whole world right now.*

She had gone zip lining once, actually. With her parents. Six years ago. It had been a place in Arizona during their Grand Canyon trip, the dry heat baking their skin as they waited their turn in line. A guy in his midtwenties who had smiled at her too much made sure safety harnesses were attached and snug.

She had suffered his touch because she knew how important the harness was.

Dad went first, skimming the tops of pine trees and whooping like a madman. Cassie went next, eyes tightly shut until about halfway through, when she opened them to the gasp-inducing sight of the treetops whipping by beneath her.

But that had been in a controlled environment, with multiple safety checks and regulation, inspected gear. This was throwing herself at the ground and hoping to miss.

What choice did she have?

She reached down, balanced precariously, aware that a wrong move in the wrong direction could topple her backward off the ledge. Fumbling with shaking hands, she slowly threaded her belt out of her jeans. With a deep breath, she folded it over and then flipped it into the air, over the end of the zip line.

"Sighted!" someone shouted.

She jerked and turned to her left, almost losing her balance. Coming around the corner was one of the men in black body armor, clinging to the building and so unable to unstrap the assault rifle slung over his shoulder. "Sighted! North side of the building! They have a zip line!"

Shit. Cassie did as TonyStark had done and turned around, using her anchor above to keep herself from falling. Across the way, she spied TonyStark, waving frantically to her from a balcony one story down.

One story down and what seemed to be ten football fields away.

It wasn't *that* far, she knew. If she'd been on the sidewalk, the distance between buildings would have been negligible. Not even noticeable. Just another skinny alleyway cut between two buildings. Nothing to see.

Up here, it might as well have been the Grand Canyon.

"Don't move!" the man cried out. He'd made his way around the corner now and was — to her shock — actually moving to unsling his rifle.

Double shit!

Cassie couldn't afford the luxury of fear or hesitation any longer. As TonyStark had done, she kicked off from the wall and heard herself scream like a lunatic as she rocketed down the zip line. Over the sound of her own yelling came several reports in a row. Bullets whizzed over her head and she screamed even more loudly and the next thing she knew she was crashing into TonyStark, who caught her on the balcony and pulled her down, flattening her on the floor of the balcony as bullets rained around them.

"You're safe!" he told her. "You made it!"

"They're shooting at us!" she bellowed. "We're not safe!"

As if to punctuate the point, a bullet pinged off the balcony's railing and ricocheted into a window, shattering it.

"Wait," he said.

Just as she opened her mouth to berate him — wait for *what*? — the gunfire stopped. She peered up and across the chasm, where she spied the gunman making his way to the zip line, his rifle again slung over his shoulder.

There was a knife in a sheath strapped to the railing. TonyStark used it to cut the zip line.

"You guys really planned this," she said in amazement. Facing the wall as he was, the gunman wouldn't know the line had been cut until he got there.

"We don't mess around," he said. "Come on. Now we go up."

*

They clambered up a fire escape ladder, then used balconies and fire escapes to zigzag their way up another story, coming around another corner to the west side of the building. There were conveniently placed boards in certain places to lead them to their next step, and Cassie again marveled at the planning that OHM had mastered. When she dared glance around, her stomach heaved; down below, more lights flashed but the sounds of the city were muted, drowned out by wind and her own heavy breathing. She'd been in and out of the city her whole life and had come to understand its rhythms. But from up here, it was an alien landscape, a set of boxes stacked in rigid rows. The lights that were so warm and comforting when seen down on the street were now distracting and dangerous. The slivers of alleyways were obstacles. Everything felt vicious and personal, as though the city she called home had decided to evict her all on its own.

Cassie allowed herself to think for just a moment what would happen if she fell. Or if they caught her.

Each time they crossed a board TonyStark would pause to haul it in. "I don't think they'll follow, but just in case."

"What about other OHMers?" she asked. "What if they need them?"

"We all have different routes," he said. "We drill. We take it seriously; we have to."

She thought of the OHMers she'd watched hopping over the

side of the roof. She'd imagined them plummeting to their death, but they'd had other escape routes planned already.

"They know we're in — I mean *on* this building, though," she told him. "That one guy saw us zip line here and he radioed others ..."

"We won't be here for long," he told her. They'd arrived at a balcony with only one exit — a ladder leading up to the roof. TonyStark went first and Cassie scrambled after him.

The rooftop was wide and flat, interrupted only by the hulking blocks of industrial air conditioning units and a bulkhead with a door. She was on something solid again, not a rickety fire escape or a six-inch-wide ledge overlooking a lethal drop, so she could be forgiven for pausing for a moment.

Sunlight overhead. Clouds. Blue sky.

"It was the text, wasn't it?" she blurted out. Some part of her brain, a part not necessary for physical survival, had been working on the problem during their escape. "The one from @Shameless. It came to Bryce and they traced it, right?"

For a moment, TonyStark looked much older than his actual age. He spoke in something like a whisper. "I don't know. I don't want to think about it."

She understood. Face-to-face with Bryce, TonyStark was all bluster, but clearly he didn't want to imagine Bryce was at fault.

"Let's get a move on," he insisted, and jogged to the north.

Cassie followed. At the northernmost edge of the roof, there was a stout, faded red box labeled FIRE. TonyStark opened it and lifted out a false bottom. Underneath were two strangely squarish backpacks.

"You ever go skydiving?" he asked.

What in the world did *that* have to do with —

She realized. She stared at the backpacks. And then she looked over the parapet, down hundreds of feet below.

"This is your plan?" she asked, her voice cracking. "*This* is your plan? We're jumping off the building? Are you insane?" The more she stared, the farther away the ground seemed to get. The distance swam before her eyes and she felt dizzy.

He took her by the shoulders and guided her away from the edge. "Have you ever done this before? Used a parachute?"

She laughed in his face. "Jesus Christ, no. But what if I did? Jumping out of a plane … I know how it works — you need enough distance and speed to open your chute. This is just a *building* —"

"It's called BASE jumping," he told her, now holding out one of the packs. "Totally safe." He hesitated. "*Mostly* safe."

"Nope." She pushed him away. TonyStark and his absurdly tiny parachute pack. "Not doing it. Let's just work our way down through the building."

He licked his lips. For the first time, she saw panic in his eyes. "We don't have that option. They're already in the building, most likely. We can't evade them. But they won't expect us to jump."

"Because they're less crazy than we are?"

TonyStark's nostrils flared, but he took a deep breath and managed not to lose his cool. "Listen to me: This is a thirty-story building. It's almost a thousand feet tall. Dudes have BASE jumped off hundred-foot statues before and survived, OK?"

She opened her mouth to respond, but there was no rejoinder to that comment. It was just insane. There was no arguing with crazy.

She stood in shock as TonyStark slipped on his pack and then helped her into hers, snapping shut the clasp on her chest. He was talking the whole time, but she barely understood most of it. Something about making sure to jump as far away from the building as possible.

Did he think she was going to do this?

She was *not* going to do this.

"Look," he went on, "you've got a static line, OK?" He tugged a slender cable that extended from her pack to a hefty bolt on the concrete parapet. "Connected up here. It pulls the chute for you at the right time. All you gotta do is bend your knees when you land, dig?"

She nodded dumbly.

"You only have about thirty seconds before you hit the ground. Pick your spot. Don't change your mind. When you land, hit the button on your chest to release the chute and run like hell. Don't wait for me. You have a phone, right?"

She nodded again. He really thought they were going to do this.

"We'll find you, then." He licked his lips again. "OK. I'll go first."

"TonyStark," she started, "there's no way —"

"Shit!" he yelled.

Behind her, the bulkhead door came crashing open. Half a dozen men in black body armor spilled through, weapons drawn and aimed. Cassie's heart slammed into overdrive and a pulsing whine filled her ears. She saw TonyStark's lips moving but couldn't hear him.

The next thing she knew, his hands were on her shoulders,

roughly shoving her to one side. He drew a gun from the firebox and squeezed off several rounds in the direction of the cops, who scattered for the protection of the air-conditioning units.

In the brief seconds of respite, TonyStark grabbed Cassie again and shouted. He was loud enough that she could hear him even through the static in her ears.

"Remember to jump out!" he yelled, and before she could object, he shoved her right off the roof.

She spun as she tumbled, turning around to see the cops advancing, catching a brief glance. On their own, her legs pumped hard in their last contact with the roof, propelling her several feet out from the side of the building.

And holy shit there was nothing under her.

Thirty seconds, he'd said. She had thirty seconds. It felt like thirty minutes, the world slowing, suspended in gelatin.

As she fell, she saw TonyStark leap over the edge of the rooftop, for a moment eclipsing the sun with his silhouette. His arms and legs pumped madly.

And then …

Oh.

Oh, no.

A cop at the roof's edge. Seen from the waist up. Aiming. Firing.

He missed. Didn't hit TonyStark, whose arms and legs were still working, pinwheeling madly against the air.

Thank God, she thought. *Thank* —

Still falling. What if this didn't work? What if —

Didn't hit TonyStark, but the bullet zipped through his static line. She watched as that umbilical went slack at both ends.

She cried out, but there was nothing to say, nothing to do, and her cry was just an inarticulate bawl of terror and anguish.

Spinning, TonyStark toppled downward. He'd leaped in a blind panic. He hadn't jumped far enough out from the building.

She was too far away to hear it, but she could imagine the sound his head made when it cracked against one of the building's ledges. A sound like a rubber mallet hitting a board, splintering it.

Her static line went taut, jerking her up for a moment, reversing her momentum and tearing her breath from her lungs with brutal apathy.

And then she was floating. Just drifting in the air, her chute a canopy above her, and for an instant, all was calm, all was sedate and good. The relief from the chaos of diving toward the earth was beautiful. The *world* was beautiful.

And then TonyStark's body plummeted past her, unmoving, trailing blood and gristle as he plunged down, down, down.

10010160010 1

Rachel stared in disbelieving shock at her tablet, unable to tap away from the livestreams.

There were four windows open, each one showing a different feed. One from a local news crew, the others from onlookers who were Facebook Live-ing, Periscoping and BLINQvid-ing.

METRO POLICE RAID CYBER-TERROR DEN! read one scroll. But that wasn't the one she was interested in.

#HasCassieSurfacedYet? is in the building! one BLINQ read.

Hive Mob to **#BlevinsHotel. #HasCassieSurfacedYet? #Level6 #KillOnSight**

It was perhaps not surprising how quickly Rachel had acclimated to internet speak now that she relied on it to check in on her daughter. She moved through each feed quickly, absorbing the acronyms and hashtags like she'd been born knowing them. Oddly, she thought of the poet Samuel Taylor Coleridge just then, of a sacred river running through measureless caverns, as the void inside her opened further, as whatever shreds of hope she'd been hanging on to began to fray and fall. The Hive believed Cassie was at an abandoned hotel and police were raiding it. Rachel had no reason not to believe the Hive. The wisdom of the crowds wasn't particularly wise these days, but it was usually accurate. Coleridge's "sunless sea" was real, and she was living in it.

Her daughter. In a "cyber-terror den."

If she could even trust that description. Harlon had been called a cyber-terrorist many times in his life, had even been refused entry to prestigious technology conferences and events by interns who didn't recognize him. Mostly because he had the temerity to "hack while black." White hackers were just ... hackers. Hackers who usually became founders of mega-billion-dollar tech firms. Black hackers, on the other hand, were dangerous cyber-terrorists. "Thugs with bugs," they were called.

As she watched, crystal-clear 8k video streamed to her, perfect in every detail but held in shaky, inexpert hands. First there were police cordoning off the building, then the outrage of the disappointed mob.

On the news feed now, a legal expert was discussing whether law enforcement or Hive had jurisdiction.

"If Cassie McKinney is in the building, theoretically, Hive Justice takes precedence over police action. However, this has never been tested in a court of law. Furthermore, Ms. McKinney is also charged with analog crimes, including destroying her cell phone, which could color a court's decision on jurisdiction."

He prattled on, and Rachel found herself outraged by the faux politeness of the media, the way everyone calmly referred to her daughter as "Ms. McKinney" while just as calmly discussing her impending horrific death at the hands of a mob. It would be more honest if they called her "that bitch."

On the livestream, people were climbing down from rooftops, jumping from the sky. Rachel couldn't believe what she was seeing. A careful network of old construction equipment, scaffolding and fire escapes acted as a sort of vertical ziggurat for those who knew the path. Some took missteps, panicked by the cops above them or by the tinny cracks of sound that she imagined to be gunfire, so loud up close, so pathetic at a distance.

Bodies in free fall. Bodies of people in terror. "'A savage place … with ceaseless turmoil seething,'" Rachel whispered.

Was one of the bodies her daughter's? Was Cassie already dead?

Her fingers danced on the screen of her tablet, lighting it, dimming it, lighting it, dimming it. She yearned to call Bryce but knew that she couldn't. She was under constant surveillance, or so she assumed. Her phone calls, texts, emails — everything was monitored, processed, collated, scrutinized. They — the scary *they* of conspiracy movies, now suddenly real — knew everything she was doing and saying.

"If the mob kills Ms. McKinney before the police can arrest her," the expert droned on, "I assume no charges will be brought. Typically, Hive Justice supersedes analog concerns …"

Resisting the urge to hurl across the room the tablet and its endless prattle about her daughter's life, she instead stood up and paced the length of her office. Finally, she did what she always knew she would do: she picked up her phone and she called Bryce.

When she got his voice mail, she cleared her throat and spoke with as much casual boredom as she could muster. "Mr. Muller, this is Professor McKinney. I'm still waiting on that outline for your special project. Please let me know if you'll be able to turn it in on time. Is everything going smoothly? Let me know."

She hung up, then stared at the blank screen of her phone. Hoping Bryce would respond in a way that would make sense to her. Hoping she hadn't done something stupid.

Something that could cost Cassie her life.

Returning to the tablet, she watched as someone on BLINQ zoomed in on the rooftop of the hotel. Police were leaning over the edge of the roof, rifles aimed down.

Something that could cost Cassie her life.

Assuming Cassie was still alive.

Rachel took a deep breath, a sip of cold coffee, a pause. She couldn't wait for Bryce to get back to her. The wait would kill her — literally, she thought, holding a hand over her heart, feeling its palpitations. No, she couldn't wait. She had to *do.*

*

For the first time, Rachel understood how addictive it was — thanks to the lights and colors all the tech companies used to light up users' brains — to be online, to reach out virtually and make an instant connection with someone, even when you were feeling more alone than you had known it was possible to feel.

Rachel's post to #UniversityMoms hadn't just been well received by the working moms at MS/BFU; it had spread to other university mom groups, to sister schools and archenemies alike. Someone had screenshotted it and shared it on BLINQ, and then Instagram, Facebook, Snapchat, Yardio and Guessom, and within mere hours a wave of parental sympathy was rising. Petitions were started, signed, shared. Desperate pleas from other moms, some of whom had seen their own children punished by the Hive, echoed far and wide. The thrill Rachel got each time her notifications pinged — which was every few seconds at this point — was almost enough to sustain her, and definitely enough to make her see, even just a bit, why Harlon and Cassie spent the bulk of their time online.

"Online action needs to turn to real-life action," Rachel repeated to herself, her eyes blurry from lack of sleep and too much screen time. She squinted as she browsed her notifications. This was a start, yes. But she needed more. The public needed to see her army in action. A crowd. A protest. Something they couldn't ignore.

*

#UniversityMoms Discussion Board:
A Place for MS/BFU Mothers to Share, Support and Save Our Sanity
Join a discussion or start your own!
For Working Moms at MS/BFU

HOT THREAD ALERT: "We gather NOW. MS/BFU quad. Bring everyone you know."

100101700101

Cassie landed safely not far from TonyStark's exploded remains.

Somehow she remembered to bend her knees on impact.

Somehow she remembered to hit the button on her chest that detached the chute.

Stumbling for three or four steps, she lost her balance and dropped to all fours. She knew she had to get up. Get up and run. The police had seen her parachute down here. She had to —

A gout of vomit erupted from her, gushing out with a force she'd never felt before. She was helpless in its throes, her jaw straining, eyes bulging as she puked up everything in her. When it was over, she dry-heaved twice, her stomach clenching and lurching, her gullet rippling with useless contractions, violently expelling nothing from her.

Gasping for breath, she crawled to one side. There was a pile of trash bags gathered along the wall, and she could hear footsteps. On panic-propelled hands and knees, she made her way to the pile and burrowed in, ignoring the smell and the occasional sharp jab from something discarded and pointy.

Deep in the dark, her teeth chattered uncontrollably, so loud that she feared the sound would give her away. She slipped the wrist of her jacket between her teeth, biting down on it over and over.

Footsteps thudded into the alleyway. The squawk of radios. Shouts and commands. She wanted to peek out, to see what they were doing, but didn't dare risk moving. Was it even safe to breathe? Would it move the bags of garbage and point to her location?

Someone approached her. After a moment, a foot kicked at the garbage bags. She bit down on her jacket as hard as she could, crushing a scream between her teeth.

Another kick. She closed her eyes and told herself not to move, not to flinch.

A third kick, this one softer. Desultory, almost.

She waited for another kick. For a bag to shift. To be dragged out of her cocoon of trash by her hair and thrown to the crowd.

Didn't happen.

Instead, she heard footfalls receding, the buzz and chirp of radios fading into the distance as she realized that she was weeping in utter and complete silence without moving a muscle.

*

She didn't know how much time passed before she risked crawling out of the trash heap. She'd told herself to wait at least five minutes, but after counting to 120, she lost track and started again, then lost track again, then decided she just couldn't stand waiting any longer. She had to *do.* To act.

They wanted her dead, so she had to be more alive than she'd ever been.

The alley was empty. They'd left poor TonyStark's body there on the ground without so much as an old jacket to cover him up. A part of her thought maybe he'd survived somehow and was playing possum, but his head was split wide open, a rope of smashed intestine snaking out from under him. She forced herself to look, to study, even though she wanted to close her eyes and scream. She had to let what they had done to TonyStark imprint on her somehow so she would always remember what she was now fighting for.

She knelt down by him and touched his back with a shaking hand. "I'm really sorry," she whispered. "Thank you for helping me."

And then she sucked in a breath and — because she had no other choice — she quickly ran her hands over what was left of his body.

She was trapped in an alleyway with the entire country looking for her. She had no resources at all and she needed some.

TonyStark's phone was crushed to oblivion, but his wallet was intact. There was no ID or credit cards — of course — but there was a sheaf of paper money. Some places still took that. She tucked the bills into her pocket and probed some more, sniffling back tears.

And found the gun.

It had survived the fall. Because the people who made guns were terrified of death and obsessed with survival. She pulled it from his waistband and wiped it clean on his clothes. She had no idea how to use a gun, other than what she'd seen in movies, but she figured even just pointing it at someone would get her somewhere.

Tucking it into her waistband at the small of her back, she covered it with her jacket. Now how would she move on? She had the most famous face in the country, and facial recognition software was looking for her from every ATM and traffic camera. Plus, the cops would be back soon, no doubt, to retrieve TonyStark's body if nothing else. She had to get out of here.

The only resource at her disposal was the gun, and she didn't think she could shoot her way through a Hive Mob and heavily armed cops. She thought frantically, hopping from one foot to the other, and then her eyes fell on her hiding spot, the pile of garbage bags.

There had to be *something* in there that could help, right?

The prospect of trawling other people's refuse did not excite her, but she had no other options and time was running out. After prodding the bags with her toes, she tore open the one that felt the least squishy and liquid. It turned out to be filled with old cardboard and a broken glass that nearly ripped open the webbing between her right thumb and forefinger.

The second bag, though, was a bit more helpful. There was a pair of sunglasses with one arm twisted askew. She stared at the glasses for a moment. Facial recognition always started with the eyes. That was how it knew the subject in question was a person. Once the software recognized eyes, it proceeded to map the surrounding area, using machine learning to match features with what it already knew comprised a human face.

If you could stop it from seeing your eyes, you were halfway home.

Most cameras these days sprayed infrared dots in addition to using visible light, so sunglasses didn't always work, but if they were polarized …

Fortunately, there was a simple way to find out. She whipped out her cell phone and turned it on. For the first time, she was glad for the ancient tech — it had an LCD screen, as opposed to the OLED screens on newer phones.

She held the phone vertically and looked at it through the sunglasses as she slowly rotated it to horizontal. Sure enough, the colors on-screen shifted. The lenses were polarized.

Great. That would help with the cameras — maybe — but human beings wouldn't be fooled by a pair of shades. She was just too damn recognizable. She wished she could text her dad for some advice, though she wasn't sure exactly how to frame the question to get any sort of useful advice from the bot. Maybe *Hey, Dad, how do you hack people?*

Much to her surprise, the answer popped up in her head, almost but not quite in her father's voice: *Social engineering, sweetheart.*

Sure, sure. Social engineering — the flip side and companion to digital hacking.

First, she would need to do some pretty radical surgery, the kind she'd done on at least three dolls when she was a kid, before her mom decided to stop buying them anymore. With a piece of the broken glass held carefully in her hand, she managed to hack away at her hair. Now it was probably patchy and stood out in tufts, but that was OK.

Then she prowled through the trash some more until she found what she was looking for. It wasn't perfect, but it was close enough: a short metal curtain rod, slightly bent. When she cupped the end of it in her hand, it looked like a cane.

Combined with the sunglasses and the bad haircut and the grime from her trash diving, she figured she could pass for a blind, homeless person.

Fooling machines is one thing, Dad had told her. *Overrun a buffer or spoof an IP address. Whatever. To fool people, you have to work* with *their prejudices instead of against them.*

With a deep breath, she stepped out of the alley, tapping the sidewalk with her makeshift cane, trying her best to appear as though she couldn't see.

There was a loose cluster of people at one end of the street and a police cordon in the opposite direction. The cops or the mob?

The mob would be easier to fool. The cops would have portable face scanners, would make her take off the shades and then it would all be over. The mob would either recognize her or not.

She breathed a silent prayer that she was pretty sure headed nowhere and to no one, then tap-tapped her way down the sidewalk.

*

To her surprise and delight, it worked. A guy in his thirties even offered to help her cross the street when the light changed. It would look weird to decline, she decided, so she said yes and allowed him to take her elbow and escort her. He was a perfect gentleman, sweet and concerned, and for the time it took to cross, she even forgot that he wanted to kill her.

The police had cordoned off a three-block radius around OHM's now-defunct headquarters, but they hadn't set up blockades everywhere. Feigning blindness and homelessness, she became invisible to most passersby and was able to prowl the alleyways until she found one that led her out of the danger zone.

Bad thinking, that. *Everywhere* was the danger zone. Anywhere there was a camera, she was in trouble. All it would take was one hit on a database and the mob would descend.

One hit on a database and you die. One stupid joke and your life is over. Rowan and the Homework Coven flashed in her memory. She'd been *goaded* into this. She'd been *pushed* ...

You did it to fit in, a voice told her. *No one made you.*

It was her mom's voice. Clipped and unsympathetic and — oh, yeah — telling the truth, by the way.

I wish you were wrong. You're always wrong, but not this time. And I bet you'd love to hear you were right, but who knows if I'll ever ...

She found a spot in an alley that was blocked off from cameras and sat with her back against a wall, her knees drawn up to her chest, head down. It was the safest thing she could imagine, and now that she felt safe, all she could think about was the jump from the building, watching TonyStark's head crack open on the ledge, the way he'd tumbled through the air.

Sobs racked her. This was her life now. This was her life.

10010180 0101

A megaphone in her hands, Rachel could feel the buzz in the air. She was as surprised as anyone by the size of the crowd, driven by her virtual plea to save Cassie but also by their own many reasons to tell the world that this particular brand of Hive Justice had to be stopped.

She had used the digital world to summon an analog mob to put an end to the idea of using the digital world to summon analog mobs. The irony was not lost on her.

Rachel shielded her eyes from the sun and from the remaining images of rifles, of bodies, that she hadn't yet been able to shake. She tried to find Bryce in the crowd but guessed he wouldn't show. He knew as well as she did that she was being watched — the officers weren't even making themselves subtle, blatantly glaring at her as she took her place on the makeshift stage in the campus quad.

She couldn't think about Bryce right now. Only herself, only Cassie. *Watch this*, she thought.

"Attention, moms and friends of moms!" she called. She almost dropped the megaphone, surprised by the powerful way it made her voice sound, the way it rippled throughout the crowd. She coughed a little bit, just to stall. She hadn't really prepared anything. In fact, she realized, as hundreds of faces stared expectantly at her, she had no idea what she was supposed to do now.

So Rachel did what she always did when she was unsure: she lectured.

"Bread and circuses," she started, and she could almost hear Cassie groan. *Jeez, Mom! Not that crap again!*

"Bread and fucking circuses!" she said with heat. It killed the professor in her to curse so casually in front of her "class," but she couldn't lose this audience. Already, she could see that her emotion was reeling them in.

"The Roman elite figured everything would work out all right for them," she said, practically spitting her contempt, "as long as they gave the masses bread and circuses. Well, the economy's doing well, so you have your bread. And now they have a genuine circus that Nero himself would approve of: Hive Justice. Who needs to worry about the upkeep on lions when you can just get a bunch of pissed-off trolls to do your dirty work for you? It's a circus, all right."

She had them. People were holding up their phones to record her. Behind the safety of the megaphone, Rachel grimaced. She never let students shoot video of her lectures; she was uncomfortable with the idea of having her face and voice plastered all over the internet. But right now, she needed to go viral.

So she kept talking, shouting despite the megaphone, letting herself go hoarse.

She talked about history, sure, but also about her daughter, about her family, about the way Cassie had been grieving her father's death. About a parent's fear, bone-deep, blood thick and ever present.

And all around her, some people — not all, but some — listened.

*

Afterward, hands shaking from adrenaline, Rachel sipped some water and accepted congratulations and encouragements from strangers who lined up to meet her. She remembered nothing about any of them. Her eyes were too blurry, her mind was too busy. But she felt a deep appreciation for each of them, and she knew that feeling of their support would buoy her.

One kid stood out, though. He approached Rachel somewhere near the end of the event, right before she could make her way back to the safety of her office. He was lanky in that way only teen boys are, as though his limbs had minds of their own. He wore a black leather bomber jacket and a T-shirt that read TO ERR IS HUMAN. TO REALLY F&%K UP TAKES A COMPUTER. But the word "computer" was upside down.

Rachel had to smile.

"Mrs. McK-Kinney?" he said, stuttering a bit, holding out a hand. "Professor, I mean? Doctor, I mean?"

She shook his hand before he could run down further honorifics. "Professor is fine. Thanks for coming." He was so incredibly out of place here, in the midst of the middle-aged. She wanted to give him a hug and tuck him into bed.

"I just wanted to say ..." He realized he should take his hand back, then stared at it for a moment, as though unsure what to do with it. He settled on jamming it into his coat pocket. "I knew your daughter. Know her. I go to Westfield. I'm Carson."

Rachel's eyes widened. Cassie never, *ever* spoke of her friends. Not to her mother. "You're one of Cassie's friends?"

He blushed. "I, uh, probably *not*, you know? I mean, I met her a couple of times and she seemed cool and I liked her ... Uh, not in a creepy way. Not like creepy."

Rachel nodded. "It's OK. You know her, though?"

"Yeah. And I just ... I saw about this rally online and I had to come, you know?" Shuffling his feet, he stared at the ground. "I know computer stuff. I mean, I'm no Harlon McKinney. But if I can help. At all. Tell me."

And then, to her surprise, this utterly charming young man handed her an actual slip of paper with his phone number on it.

Rachel tucked it away. "Thank you, Carson. I'm going to keep that in mind."

Over his head, she noticed the university police were beginning to disperse the crowd. It was time for her to go before someone invented a pretext to arrest her.

"Thanks again, Carson," she said. It seemed to mean a lot to him, and Rachel figured she'd at least accomplished *that* much.

10010190O101

The slender spike of sky between the two buildings forming her alley began to darken with night and thicken with clouds. Rain was coming. She had to find some kind of shelter. It was one thing to emulate a homeless person, quite another to become one.

That might be her ultimate fate, she realized, and then shoved the thought aside. TonyStark hadn't meant to sacrifice his life for her, but he had, and she wasn't going to let that life degenerate into a puddle of self-pity and meaninglessness. She was going to finish what she'd started with OHM, which meant following the only lead she had: @Shameless.

With a name like that, could she even trust such a person? Hell, even if he was named @MostTrustworthyGuyEVAH, could she afford to trust him?

It was getting late and she didn't know where Venecia was. Her ancient phone couldn't get on any kind of data network, so she couldn't check maps or the website. She contemplated flagging a cab and just saying "Venecia" to the driver. But cabs had cameras, she remembered. No way.

She couldn't get online, but text messages were sent using unused bandwidth on the voice line of phones. She had only one choice. She had to ask Sarah for help again.

hey its me

Time passed. She remembered that this phone had no personal data and she'd purged the earlier text thread. So she added:

cassie

After a few moments, Sarah came back:

wtf?

I need your help again just an address please it's a place called venecia

r u kidding me?

please

where r u? r u going there? that's a rough spot

doesn't matter. just need that address

A few more moments passed and then the address came through, along with **BE CAREFUL!!!** and a heart emoji.

ty! Cassie texted and then quickly shut off the phone. The address was on the other side of town, and it would take a while to get there, since she was pretending to be blind.

*

With minutes to spare, she lurked at the corner of an alleyway with a line of sight to the entrance to Venecia. As she watched, masked revelers approached the door, gave a complicated knock, then spoke to the bouncer and entered. How in the world was she supposed to make this work? She had no mask and no password. Just by watching over and over, she thought she had the secret knock down — two short, one long, three short — but that wouldn't get her very far.

Her fists clenched. Her body, exhausted, nevertheless vibrated with energy. She had to get in there.

Just then, a strong hand grabbed her from behind and dragged her back into the alley. Before she could scream, another hand was clapped over her mouth. She lashed back with an elbow but missed.

"It's me," a familiar voice hissed in her ear. "Stop fighting me."

Bryce.

She stopped struggling and he let go. She stepped away from him and spun around. A part of her wanted to fling herself into his arms in joy and gratitude and relief. Another part wanted to kick him in the nuts.

"Did you do it?" she demanded. "Did you tip off the mob?"

It was such a weird coincidence, after all. Bryce got a message from @Shameless, then left OHM. Soon afterward, the raid.

The bullets.

The body, spinning in the air …

She shook herself all over, like a dog trying to get clean.

"Did I …?" He ran a hand through his hair, newly shorn, she noticed. It suited him so much better than the trustafarian look. "Did I tip them off? Are you crazy? Those were my *friends*, Cassie. I risked everything for them. No way did I narc on them. I don't know who did. Someone BLINQed the location."

"Then they tracked your text."

"Uh-uh. Not a chance. We bounce signals all over God's creation before they land anywhere in HQ."

"Then who?" she asked. Her blood pumped so hot that she imagined it bubbled in her veins. "Who did it? And how?"

"I don't know, Cassie," he said with frustration. "Maybe it was just that our time was up. It was inevitable that we'd be found out someday. That's why we had escape routes planned in the first place. Just bad luck, all right?" Bryce checked his ridiculously old-fashioned watch. "We don't have time for this. We have to get inside." He unslung a messenger bag from his shoulder. "I brought gear." He unzipped the bag. "Cutting your hair was a good idea, ditto the shades, but this should work better. Here."

She took the thing he handed her. It was a latex mask, but more detailed than any she'd ever seen. "It's called a prosthetic mask," he explained. "They're way expensive, but there are benefits to being a trust-fund kid. Someone passing you on the street probably won't realize you're wearing a mask at all."

She tugged the mask on. It was a little hot in there but otherwise fine.

"How's it look?"

He shrugged. "When your lips don't move, it loses some of its magic, but we're going somewhere where you're supposed to be masked, so it's fine. Let's go."

10010200101

From the outside, Venecia was an abandoned warehouse, all crumbling walls decorated in graffiti and spare cement blocks dotting the perimeter. At the entrance (under a blacked-out sign with a single flickering light bulb), Bryce did the knock, and when the door opened, he flashed a fake ID. He'd given Cassie one, too, and she held it up with a hand that — she was proud to note — did not tremble.

Didn't matter. The bouncer, who barely glanced at them before holding up a finger, mouthed the word "Wait," and closed the door again.

The pounding bass spilled onto the street in those seconds the door had been opened, leaving behind a yawning silence that made Cassie feel exposed, vulnerable. She shivered and surveyed the block. It was empty; nothing of note except an old bus stop shelter, which, with its ripped-out bench and weeds bursting through the sidewalk cracks, looked positively dystopian. On the far corner, a single streetlight cast a weak orange glow, and in it Cassie could see a mist forming, particles of water floating, trying to decide if they had enough pizazz to turn into a proper rainstorm.

"Bryce," she croaked. "This is a bad idea."

"That's not my name," he hissed. His mask was a sleek army green, and without his trademark red dreadlocks, Cassie couldn't shake the idea that he had turned into a different person. That somehow, in the space of the day — a day when she'd been raided, forced to go on the run and watched one of her only allies killed in the process — the world had turned upside down yet again.

She fought back a fresh onslaught of tears as her last image of TonyStark flashed before her eyes. She struggled to remember the code names Bryce had insisted they use: he was Pyrrhus, the famous Greek general, and she was Lyssa, the Greek goddess of uncontrolled rage.

Bryce shifted. "This mask is hot as hell."

"Pyrrhus ..." Cassie tried again. She glanced down the block once more. The mist had made up its mind, and fat raindrops were driving down onto the cement, making pinging noises on her mask. In addition to her prosthetic mask, Bryce had handed her a headband with a plume of black feathers rising up from her forehead. It was just simple enough to be forgettable.

Over the patter of raindrops came a hoot, followed by some cheers. Tires squealed in the distance. This part of the city would've put Cassie on edge even without a Level 6 conviction swallowing her whole. She tugged Bryce's elbow. "What's taking so long? Is this normal?"

Cassie couldn't tell what his expression was under his mask, but the glare from his eyes gave her a pretty good indication. "I don't know. But I trust @Shameless."

On cue the door swung open, the music drowning out Cassie's reply. The bouncer held up a hand and waved them in. "Precaution," he said affably, ushering them in before taking a survey of the empty block and closing the door behind them. "We instituted a new ID check after some trouble a few months back."

"Bummer," Bryce said, nodding their goodbyes and dragging Cassie behind him. "Keep up," he said in a low voice. He knew where @Shameless was supposed to meet them.

She tried. But the pulsing music drowned out every word, every thought, and the shock of so many faceless dancers disoriented Cassie. The scene was unlike anything she'd ever experienced. The bass was so loud that it reverberated in her bones; it became her heartbeat, throbbing in tune. A dark dance floor glowed brightly every few seconds as a strobe light flashed. And the masks — so many masks! Beautiful painted ones and horrid, grotesque ones, disguising everyone, turning the dance floor into a pit of movement that was equal parts threatening and welcoming. No one could want to kill you when you were just a nameless mask in a crowd, right?

Bryce lifted his mask a few inches. "He should be over there!" he mouthed, his voice drowned by the crowd's cheer as a new song played. She gripped his sleeve as they darted through thrashing limbs. No one was doing it intentionally, but it felt like the crowd — the noise, the heat — was assaulting Cassie, and by the time Bryce pulled open an unnoticeable door tucked away in the far corner of the dance floor under the DJ booth, Cassie's body hurt.

After Bryce closed the door behind them, Cassie could hear him panting under his mask, which he then ripped off. In the dim light of the silent room, she saw his face was slick with sweat.

Cassie kept her mask on, even though she was desperate to gulp in the stale air. She realized she was still holding Bryce's sleeve, and she dropped it before he could notice, too. The room was dark, small and cramped — boxes piled high, a single, over-crowded desk with an ancient computer, and what looked like old equipment stacked in haphazard towers — and it took a moment for her eyes to adjust. Behind the desk, an old-fashioned flat-screen television, muted but running a news channel. Cassie glanced at it, then cried out involuntarily and grabbed Bryce's arm again.

"Mom!"

Bryce gaped, then turned over the room looking for the remote. When he found it, he jabbed some buttons until sound finally came back. The newscaster, a Ken doll with a fake tan, seemed delighted to fill them in.

"If you're just joining us, take a look at today's unexpected event. Rachel N. McKinney, mother of Level 6 Hive convict Cassie McKinney, led a protest today that consisted of, in the words of her spokesperson, a, quote, mom army demanding protection for our kids in this age of mob rule run by an unjust horde of unqualified aggressors, unquote. Hundreds of supporters rallied in person to put an end to Hive rule, while online the event trended as thousands in other locations shared their agreement. Rachel McKinney has gone viral, taking to the 'net to appeal to other parents for help. She is under 24-7 surveillance for suspected contact with her daughter who, as we all know, has been ordered to be killed on contact." He turned to his co-anchor, who appeared to take equal pleasure in sharing the news, and added, "What a mom. You have kids, Lee. Would you do the same if your child was in danger?"

Not missing a beat, Lee brightened her smile by another ten degrees and nodded. "Of course, Dan. Now let's take a look at the weather."

Bryce muted the television as Cassie stood, struck silent, trying to process this new idea. Her mother. Rachel. Hosting a protest.

Going viral.

Heat began to spread around her neck, up her cheeks. She placed a hand on her chest, checking to see if her heart had pumped its way out.

"Cass," Bryce whispered. He nodded to the area behind some boxes. Cassie could see there was enough room for someone to comfortably perch there, to sneak up on them. Bryce held a finger to his lips. Cassie nodded tightly. There was someone else in the room.

"@Shameless?" Bryce asked. He tugged Cassie's arm until his hand found hers and he clasped it.

@Shameless was wearing a glittery yellow mask, curving around the edges of his face. He nodded once and stepped forward, out of the shadows, lifting his mask as he did so.

Cassie gasped. Bryce went silent, his face stony.

"But you're ..." Cassie sputtered.

"A woman?" A tired smile flashed briefly. "Surprise."

Cassie grinned despite herself. "Cool," she murmured to Bryce. But he didn't respond. His eyes were trained on @Shameless tightly, like he was locking her in place. Or, Cassie realized, like he was expecting her to make a move. A dangerous move.

Something about the woman … She was familiar … Cassie couldn't quite place it …

Cassie's eyes ticked between Bryce and @Shameless. "Bryce?" she said quietly. "Is this safe?"

"Are you kidding?" Bryce leaped backward, swinging toward the closed door, yanking Cassie so hard that her shoulder nearly popped out of its socket. "That's Alexandra fucking Pastor! The fucking enemy!"

*

Alexandra Pastor. The woman who ran the Hive for the Department of Justice. She'd spoken at the president's press conference when Cassie was bumped to Level 6.

She let Bryce drag her to the door. Alexandra Pastor. Holy crap. But there was something *else*, too … She'd recognized Alexandra before Bryce said anything, but it hadn't been from the press conference. She —

"Stop!" Alexandra called. Bryce fumbled with the doorknob as Cassie gripped her shoulder.

"We have backup!" Bryce lied, finally getting the knob to release. The door swung open and the music from the club invaded their little space, a wave of sound that nearly knocked Cassie over. Bryce pushed her ahead but Alexandra lunged forward, her body crashing into the door before Bryce could pull his own frame through.

"I'm on your side!" she exclaimed. She must've been stronger than her petite frame suggested because she managed to hold

Bryce back for a few seconds longer than Cassie would have guessed possible. "Just hear me out!"

Alexandra and Bryce locked eyes. From this angle, Cassie could see a little tattoo on the back of her neck, white stars that stood out against her warm ochre skin. She gaped. That was it. The tattoo. She knew that tattoo. Once, for a while, it had been present in her own house.

"I know you."

A break in the music made Cassie's statement loud enough for both Bryce and Alexandra to hear it. Their heads swiveled toward her. The music started up again, a beat that throbbed in time to the pulsing pain in her shoulder, and she winced. She saw a flash of sympathy in Alexandra's eyes, and in that moment, Cassie decided to trust her.

They didn't have much choice, anyway.

"Get back in there," Cassie demanded.

"She's dangerous!" Bryce hissed.

"No, she's your inside man," Cassie reminded him. Besides, the secret weight of the gun in her waistband emboldened her. She had options. Lousy ones, yes, but better than none.

They allowed themselves to be shoved back into the room and closed the door behind her. Cassie took a deep breath and ripped off her prosthetic mask. "How did you know my dad?"

"What the fuck!" Bryce yelled, eyes wild. "This isn't about your dad! This is Alexandra fucking Pastor! She reports directly to the president. She's the exact reason you are where you are right now! She's in charge of the whole goddamn Hive!"

Cassie eyed Alexandra carefully, feeling out the situation. If she was wrong ...

She could see it, though, dancing before her eyes as though it had just happened. She'd come back from a soccer match with her mom. She must've been eight or nine, maybe. Harlon had missed her match, and she remembered snapping at Rachel on their walk home, and Rachel trying to explain that Harlon was working on a special project, but did Cassie want some ice cream to make up for it?

At home, Cassie found her dad in his office with a woman she'd never seen before. She was magazine-level fashionable — trendy boots and leather pants, plum lipstick striking against her black skin, stuff her mom wouldn't be caught dead in. As she leaned over her keyboard her hair fell forward, and Cassie spotted the stars on her neck.

Harlon, distracted, had waved and blown Cassie a kiss but then closed the door. Alexandra left sometime later, but he remained cloistered all weekend. Rachel brought him food and water and finally, late the next afternoon, she persuaded him to go to sleep. Cassie had never seen that woman again.

I'm not wrong, she thought.

"She's been playing the long game this whole time." The realization dawned on her quickly; a sped-up sunrise.

Alexandra's dark eyes sparkled. "Harlon always said you were too smart for your own good."

Bryce let out a tortured moan, an animal sound. Then he slammed his fist into the wall. "Someone please tell me what the hell is going on here?"

"Happy to," Alexandra said smoothly. She gestured to a small space behind a stack of boxes. "Come with me."

Behind the boxes was a sort of crawl space; they had to

crouch, but there were a few chairs, a laptop and what looked like a martini glass, half full. Alexandra shrugged when Cassie noticed it. "Whatever gets you through, right?"

"Tell us what you want." Bryce crossed his arms. He chose to sit on the floor rather than on the remaining rickety chair.

"Let me tell you a story," Alexandra said, draining the rest of her drink. She clapped her hands together once, then rubbed them as if she was trying to generate heat. "I helped devise the Hive. And of course, when we talk about the Hive, what we're really talking about is the algorithm."

Cassie nodded. Bryce looked unimpressed.

"I hired the programmers. Then I wrote the rules that they all used to code the Hive — everything, from the Condemn thresholds to the aggregators. Some of those rules I devised right in your house, Cassie."

The air in the crawl space was thick. Cassie tried not to inhale it too deeply but she was finding it hard to breathe. She fumbled for the words. "What are you saying, exactly?"

Alexandra sat silently for a few moments, surveying Cassie, before saying, "How much did you really know about your father and what he believed?"

Cassie rolled her eyes. Her whole life, Harlon's fans — the really intense ones, the hackers who kept posters of him on their walls — would try to test her bond with her dad. As though she, his only child, couldn't possibly be as close to him as they, his many disciples, were. "I promise, I know more about him than you think I do." But even as she said it, a seed of doubt was growing.

If she noticed, Alexandra was at least kind enough to say

nothing. "If it can be coded, it should be coded. He used to say that, and a thousand variants of that, all the time. Right?"

Cassie nodded. Harlon had lived his life on the premise that coding could be both life sustaining — lifesaving, even — and frivolous, and that both options were of equal value.

"He was always generous with his time and especially with his skills," Alexandra mused. "There's a confidence in having that much talent. He never worried that someone would overtake him. I think he liked the idea of it, actually. I sometimes got the impression he was looking for someone to challenge him."

"Can you speed this up?" Bryce said impatiently.

Alexandra clapped her hands together again, startling Cassie, who'd been lost in a swirl of memories. "Of course. What I'm trying to say is that Harlon and I created the Hive together, under a contract from the DOJ."

In the stunned silence that followed, Cassie briefly envisioned what would happen if she punched Alexandra in the face. Hard.

"I'd known him through the usual hacker circles online, but I never thought he'd come on board. He was a pretty big get, as you can imagine," Alexandra continued, as if she hadn't dropped a bomb, as if she weren't now staring at the hole it had left behind. "This was a big deal. We knew we were going to change the world."

"My dad would never create something like this!" The certainty burst out of Cassie as she gestured vaguely around her, at her version of the Hive, which now existed everywhere, in everyone, in every shadow that would extend its long arms in the spaces around her. Her hands were trembling. No way. Harlon hacked *for* the people, not to turn them against each other.

Alexandra trained her gaze on her. "I guess you do know

your father better, Cassie. Because you're right. A few weeks into the project, Harlon expressed some moral concerns about the Hive. He ripped up our contract and walked away." She let out a chuckle, but it was hard to say whether it was mirthful or resentful. "Almost left me high and dry there. It was a lot of money. But he didn't hold it against me when I went back and convinced Justice to give me a chance to do it all on my own. And I did. Got myself a political appointment, a cushy job ..."

Cassie bit back her disgust at the satisfaction in Alexandra's voice and focused on the feeling of pride rising in her.

"He quit?" she whispered. Alexandra nodded and Cassie caught her breath, her vision of Harlon resettled back into the comfortable, reliable version she'd always known: Harlon McKinney, white hat, hacker for good. Or if not good, at least not for evil. She ducked her head, hiding the smile she couldn't stop from spreading. Building the Hive would've been the project of a lifetime. A legacy.

She was proud of him, but also, layered behind the pride, a little dismayed that he'd never told her.

What else, she wondered, *hadn't he told her?*

"I used Harlon's office sometimes in those early days. Rachel was always really nice about letting me crash there when we were deep in a code binge. I don't know how she put up with him. Us."

The mention of Rachel lit a match inside Cassie. She had forgotten, somehow, all the times she would wake up in the middle of the night to find Harlon holding court in his office, his tech buddies enraptured as they strung themselves out on greasy food and caffeine or occasionally on bottles of golden-brown liquid that Cassie could smell from down the hall. Coding parties, he'd call them. She had forgotten how many times she'd watched Rachel clean up the messes as Harlon slept them off, the sun blazing high in the sky. When was the last time he'd hosted one? Cassie struggled to think, the weight of TonyStark still turning her stomach. There had been one right after her ninth birthday — she could remember because there were still balloons, sparkly and green, floating languidly around the house for weeks after the party, and one of Harlon's friends had popped them all late during one all-nighter, waking Cassie from a dream and making her cry.

Harlon had never hosted another one. The Hive was established not long after that.

Cassie turned some new thoughts over in her head. All those years of putting Harlon on a pedestal … all those months of hating Rachel for things Cassie couldn't remember, emotions she couldn't name. What if this whole time Rachel had been holding Harlon together, making it so he could be a father sometimes, even though she had to be a mother all the time?

"Anyway," Alexandra said. "I built it, and it changed the world. We knew it would, of course. But we didn't know it would change it like this."

Bryce snorted. "You didn't know you would get people killed?"

Alexandra's gaze was steady and clear. "You obviously don't remember what it was like … especially for women and people of color. The death threats. The casual racism and misogyny. The insults. And then people taking the law into their own hands."

"So instead of stopping them," Bryce said, "you just made it legal for them to do it. Congratulations."

Alexandra Pastor fumed. “No, you brat. We put a *structure* in place. It got so bad that people were dying. We put a stop to that.”

“Until now,” Cassie said quietly.

Bryce folded his arms over his chest and nodded at Alexandra triumphantly.

“People were having their lives ruined. Every time they went online, it followed them. We made it predictable, enforceable and finite. This part wasn’t supposed to happen,” Alexandra said, her voice low. “All that stuff I livestreamed? About Level 6 being part of the original spec? Bullshit. Level 6 was *never* part of the spec. Nothing that I worked on. Certainly nothing that Harlon worked on. Gorfinkle put it in place and he’s been itching to use it. They did it over my objections, told me it would never be used. And now here we are. Here *you* are.”

Cassie went still. The words hung in the room for a long time, long enough that she turned them over and over in her mind until they became mush, just unintelligible sounds. They didn’t mean anything.

Alexandra eventually continued. “It’s a tale as old as time, isn’t it? Eventually, especially when the president saw how Hive polled, all the plans we’d made turned upside down. The algorithms took on a life of their own …”

“Bullshit. You designed them to do that. Don’t blame the code; blame yourself,” Bryce spat.

“GIGO,” Cassie whispered. *Garbage in. Garbage out.*

But who was the garbage? Was she? She swallowed hotly, seeing streaks of TonyStark’s blood splattered against the pavement, a collage of destruction. Was he?

“I designed them when I thought the positive aspects of

humanity outweighed the negative ones," Alexandra countered. Her bottom lip trembled just once, enough for Cassie to notice. "What I failed to factor into my many, many equations was neutrality."

"Apathy," Cassie said. Like her, before her father's death. Before Rowan. Before, before, before.

"Exactly," Alexandra agreed. She jumped up from her seat and began pacing, her shoulders slouched and neck bent so she didn't hit her head. "It turned out that a nontrivial percentage of people didn't want to participate in Hive Justice. They just wanted to *watch* it. But above all, they didn't care that the only people who *were* actively participating were approaching it from the wrong angles. We expected a counterbalance and it never came."

"Jesus. Did you consult anyone who'd ever worked in fucking retail?" Bryce fumed. "Humanity is filled with people dying to complain. To *avenge*. The squeaky wheel gets the grease, man."

"We thought ..." Alexandra paused, then collapsed back into her chair.

"Yeah, yeah," Bryce said. "We all thought."

"Shut up!" Cassie snapped. "Let her talk. She owes it to us."

"That's the thing. It quickly became apparent that the Hive wasn't going to turn itself around. It wasn't going to self-correct. So we started experimenting with some tweaks to the code. When it didn't work, we just thought, well, the human mind ... it's unpredictable, really. It's not logical. And when you agglomerate a critical mass of them, you throw the rules of logic out the window. Chaos theory takes over. But then ..."

Cassie shifted in her uncomfortable seat and, realizing she had been holding her breath, exhaled.

Alexandra continued: "A few weeks ago, I got a note in my personal email directing me to an anonymous site. I had to hack into it, and the back end was ... my God, it was beautiful. Just outstanding. Whoever coded this page is damn good. They buried a message so deep in the code that it took me days to find it. And it said ... It said that the administration has been manipulating Hive Justice all along. That someone created ghost accounts, hidden from public view but able to alter the Condemn threads as needed. The counterbalance had been manufactured and then misdirected. It was everything I feared, laid out in front of me in a way I couldn't ignore."

Bryce's jaw tensed.

Alexandra noticed.

"The note also led me to a hidden data cache. Evidence, it said. Top-level encryption. But everything else in the email was legit, so I knew whatever was in the cache had to be the real deal. It only gave me one clue: *the color is the code.*"

"This is crazy," Bryce said. "You really expect me to believe you built this thing almost single-handedly, but someone *else* is conveniently misusing it?"

"Believe what you want," she told him. "All I can say is this: throughout my tenure at the Hive, there have been ... inconsistencies. I stayed abreast of them in the beginning, but I got promoted at a fast rate ... unprecedented, really. My new work would distract me for weeks or months on end. I stopped looking for the mistakes. I was told to keep focusing on the positive aspects of the Hive, on all the good we were doing."

"So the system is biased."

"It was biased from day one," Alexandra said, a touch of exasperation in her tone. "Humans coded it. Humans implemented it."

"But *you* invented it," Bryce countered, his voice thin and tight, a violin string ready to snap. "*You* allowed it to be violated. And now we're in danger. Our friend is dead."

Alexandra dropped her head. "I know."

"But why unleash the ghost accounts on me?" Cassie burst out. "I made a dumb joke. Why do they care so much that they'd do this to me?"

Alexandra sighed. "They were looking for a scapegoat. You fit their needs ..." she trailed off. "Do you follow politics, Cassie?"

Cassie felt a pang of guilt for not knowing what she was getting at. Then she felt a stifling hot anger — her old friend, rage. She was seventeen. She couldn't even vote yet. Did she follow politics? Not especially.

"The president is facing the end of his second term and the end of his power — not acceptable to a man like that. He's out for blood. Willing to try anything. If he thought he could turn this embarrassment, this laughingstock you made of him, into a hook to hang a campaign on —"

"Make him a sympathetic figure instead of a corrupt, all-powerful one ..." Bryce added, his fingers drumming together.

"And build on the organic reactions, elevate the negativity ..."

Cassie's head swung between them.

"Turn her into a scapegoat for all that's wrong with humanity," Bryce continued, his voice rising. "Make her the bully. A vulgar thing who preys on innocent babies. Someone who spends too much time on the Hive when she should be studying, or at least comforting her widowed mother."

"And then, while we're all distracted by how much we hate Cassie, how wrong she is for this society ..." Alexandra continued.

"The president gets to becomes the person who saved us from someone like her. From ourselves."

"And furthermore leverages the publicity and the acclaim to call a new Constitutional Convention," Alexandra said quietly.

"Wait, say *what*?" Bryce's jaw dropped open.

Constitutional Convention. *That* Cassie understood. They'd studied it in school. With his party in power at a Constitutional Convention, the president could literally rewrite the country's fundamental laws and leverage the Hive to have the states ratify his new constitution. At one stroke, every policy he favored could be enacted as *the* law. Virtually inviolable.

Including the elimination of term limits. He could run for a third, a fourth ... And with the Hive Mobs on his side, no one could stop him.

"And I make it all possible," Cassie said quietly.

"People say nasty shit about the president all day, every day. Why do you think they picked you? The daughter of a controversial hacker?" Alexandra smiled grimly. "The NSA had already been watching you and your mom since he died, looking for anything he left behind. Looking for any excuse to get their fingers in Harlon's cookie jar. And you just went ahead and raised your hand, giving them the pretext they needed to come in and scoop it all up. Like a lamb eager for slaughter. Two birds with one stone."

"Watch it," Bryce warned, stepping close to Cassie.

Ignoring Bryce, Alexandra delivered the final blow: "Your death is an asset to the president, Cassie. It's the test case that proves the efficacy of Hive Justice and gives him a way to eliminate people who stand up to him. Legally. Permanently. With no blood on his hands."

Cassie felt herself slide out of her seat, her legs unable to bear weight. Her mind raced, trying to find a word, any word, to describe the tornado of emotions running through it.

Bryce crawled over to her, shaking her shoulders until she met his eyes. "Cass, this is good news."

"What?" Cassie fought tears again, despair her new default state. "The president personally needs me dead. How is that good news?"

"We know now. We know what they did!" Bryce laughed, an actual laugh Cassie hadn't ever heard. "There's a way out. We know what to do. We can find the ghost accounts. Cassie, this is it!"

"You're making it sound much easier than it actually is," Alexandra warned him. "Even if you can reverse the numbers programmatically, you'll need it to spill into organic reversals, too."

"Don't listen to her. You'll be acquitted, Cassie!"

Free.

Bryce shook her again, only it was more of a hug attempt this time, and Cassie welcomed it, leaning into his neck and closing her eyes. "I'll get to see my mom again?" Her words were muffled by Bryce's skin, rough and warm against her cheek.

"You'll get to live your life again," Bryce assured her, squeezing her tighter, a brotherly, euphoric embrace. She relaxed into him, letting her limbs settle, trying to catch her breath. The promise of a return to her regular life had knocked the wind out of her.

Alexandra suddenly shushed them, even though no one was saying anything. She held up a hand, her head cocked toward the door. Cassie thought she saw her eyes flash a warning to Bryce.

"What is it?" she whispered. It was, she realized, *too* quiet. The music in the club had stopped.

It all happened in slow motion — Alexandra's eyes widening; Bryce releasing Cassie and standing up, knocking over his chair. It tumbled to the floor, taking an eternity to land, to shatter the silence.

Cassie wondered if her heart would leap through her chest and land on the floor next to the chair. Whatever was happening outside, every cell in her body was telling her it was bad news.

In their cramped space, Cassie stared at Alexandra and Bryce, willing them to give her some clue with their eyes, their hands. Sign language, maybe. Anything.

Instead, they just looked at each other, communicating in a way that Cassie couldn't decipher.

Something was on the tip of her tongue, some dawning realization.

She ran out of time to wait for it. The door burst open.

Someone screamed.

It was, Cassie realized, her own voice.

*

She wasn't the only one making noise. Outside the door, where there had once been the relentless beat of music, there were more screams. There were crashes as things unseen fell over or were thrown. Within seconds, the noises built until Cassie couldn't tell if they were real or simply part of a song she'd never heard. Bryce grabbed her, covering her mouth with his hand.

"Shut up! Shut up!" he hissed.

Through tears she managed to find the yawning hole inside her where the scream was escaping and willed herself to close it. It didn't matter, though. The noises outside the storage space escalated, a rising crescendo.

"The Hive is here," Alexandra said, and Cassie felt that space open up inside her again. A cavern, really. A sinkhole.

Alexandra punched buttons on her phone and then tucked her laptop into her jacket pocket and added, in an eerily calm tone, "I suggest you run." Then, in a superhero move Cassie couldn't appreciate in the moment, she slipped out the door and disappeared into the chaos.

She left the door open.

"Go! Go!" Bryce yelled, his voice muffled amid the screams and — oh, my God, were those gunshots? — from the club. But Cassie was frozen. She looked helplessly at Bryce.

"I can't move my legs," she whispered. She couldn't escape again. She didn't have it in her.

"You have to run!" Bryce yelled again. "They will kill you before we get a chance to stop all this! Mask up and run!"

Cassie closed her eyes. It was only a matter of seconds before they would find her, she knew. The club couldn't have that many hiding spaces.

Harlon would make her run, she thought. Her dad would never let her stand still like this, an open target for the very people who had set her up. He'd tell her to *go, go, go,* to *Fuck the*

Man and make them chase her until time ended, or she died, or they caught her — whichever came first.

But she thought suddenly of the night she'd hit Level 5. Of her mother dragging her out of bed, down the stairs into the car ...

Yes, her dad would make her run, but her mother would run *with* her.

Cassie didn't have time to take a deep breath, but she did it anyway, and in that space she heard her mother's voice in her head. It said, *I'm here, baby. We have to go now.*

Her body responded. She ducked under Bryce's raised arm and threw herself into the crowd, tugging her mask into place as she did so.

It was dark. The mob must've cut the power when they raided the club, and a spatter of flashlights danced across the room, seeking her out. She drove deeper into the crowd, into bodies and noise. Bryce was right behind her, one hand grazing her elbow. The noise was deafening, a steady hum of moans and whimpers punctuated by high-pitched screams of "Help me!" and "What the fuck!" If only people would stop screaming, Cassie thought, she might have a chance to make a plan. Instead, she was moving by instinct, keeping her body low.

A voice, amplified over a loudspeaker, and probably through everyone's earbuds, if the bodily convulsions were any indication: "Cassie McKinney! Level 6 perpetrator! Hive Justice demands you! Show yourself!"

It was a mistake for them to say her name. Before the announcement had even finished a wave of screams rose up in response. What had been a loud but mostly quiescent crowd, perhaps assuming this was a drug raid or an immersive floor show, was now practically foaming at the mouth, desperate with the knowledge that there was a Level 6 perpetrator in the room, that they could join the mob and be the ones to take her down. Their thirst slammed into Cassie.

She was in the middle of the club floor, still crouched low, keeping one eye on the pattern of flashlights against the walls and another on Bryce, who still crept behind her. He was harder to hide than she was. Norse gods couldn't stay invisible for long.

Cassie plotted her move. The front door was out, surely; so, too, was the back exit, even though its red EXIT sign seemed to be beckoning her. Those were too obvious. She looked up, through the bodies, to the ceiling. There, about a foot down, was a system of wide, exposed ductwork that looked strong enough to support her. Her idea was a risk, but if she could hoist herself up onto the air ducts, she could crawl along to reach somewhere more private — the bathrooms, maybe, or the kitchen, the back of the bar, wherever — and she could probably climb her way through the building, all with a bird's-eye view. From up there, she could find her escape route. She thought of Bryce's words when this all began, during that horrible excursion through the tunnels and up the abandoned hotel to OHM. *The higher up we go, the fewer cameras.*

And if there wasn't an escape route? Cassie wouldn't let that thought linger. She could ride it out up there if she had to. The mob couldn't stay in the building forever … right?

A fresh wave of yells convinced her to push away the doubts (and there were many) and make a decision. She was out of time. Any second now, people were going to start removing their masks to prove they weren't Cassie McKinney.

She tugged on Bryce's fingers, pointed up and yelled — knowing no one could her hear — "I'm going up! I'll find you when things settle down!" He blinked in confusion, then looked up, realized Cassie's plan and nodded. He, too, knew they were out of time.

She darted through the crowd on all fours, her body braced against stray kicks and accidental punches. Two people actually stepped on her, and she flinched in agony. She kept her head protected as best she could and continued on, seeking spaces in the darkness, blocking out the noises, the pain. Bruises and sprains would be dealt with later. *Just get there*, she told herself.

Going by gut instinct, or maybe driven by fate, or finally having some good luck, Cassie touched something other than body parts: a wall.

"Yes!" she whispered, trying to catch her breath, her hands feeling her way along it. Her fingers grasped a hinge — an opening, maybe? Just then another announcement shook the club.

"Stop what you're doing or face immediate consequences! We are seeking a Level 6 perpetrator. Hive Justice demands it! Everybody freeze!"

Cassie heard the instructions, but her body disobeyed. You could tell a crowd of hundreds to freeze but dozens of them would still be moving within it, still be fidgeting or thinking the order didn't apply to them. Her fingers inched along the hinge, finding the opening. Her eyes were adjusting to the dark and shapes started to appear — a set of calves and knees just a few feet away from her; several discarded earbuds; someone's phone, jostled from a hand, on the ground. Did she dare?

She almost guffawed. That ship had sailed days ago. She slid her hands across the floor, her fingers brushing the aluminum and glass. Centimeter by centimeter, she pulled it toward her, into her pocket. A new phone. Better than the crap in her other pocket.

Now, the door. She couldn't wait any longer. People were growing restless.

"Show yourself, Cassie!" someone nearby yelled, followed by a chorus of cheers.

"Has Cassie surfaced yet?" someone else yelled, half laughing, answered by waves of giggles and shouts. Cassie's heart thrummed quickly. Was she a joke now? Was her life a joke?

Would her death be, too?

Behind the fear came fury, fast and threatening, and it made her move ahead. She refused to be a joke. Her fingers danced over the walls, her body following, until she found a handle. She pulled it down, bracing herself for a click or a burst of light to give her away. But the door opened silently, and she slipped into darkness. It was, in retrospect, so easy.

The room had a sliver of a window near the ceiling, letting in a glimmer of moonlight outside the club, just enough for Cassie to make out that this was a bathroom. She blinked and checked under the three stalls. Empty. The silvery ductwork above her glinted. Her height was an advantage as she stood on the rim of the toilet (*Don't look at it, don't look at it,* she told herself), took a deep, courage-filling breath and leaped.

The top of the duct was smooth and slippery; she almost lost her grip but managed to cling by her fingers and then haul herself, bracing her feet against the wall of the stall, walking up until she could throw her leg over.

She could practically hear the duct heaving as her long body slid onto it, but she moved along, left toward the main club, silently and smoothly. The walls in this place didn't go all the way to the ceiling — there were gaps at the top to let the trendy pipes and ductwork through.

Grace had never been Cassie's forte, but she turned herself into a lithe gymnast as she navigated, clutching the edges of the duct, keeping herself flat as she inched forward slowly, each limb, each muscle operating in tandem with the others. She had no idea where Bryce would turn up, but he knew the plan, ill-conceived as it was.

After a few moments, Cassie paused, guessing she must have been somewhere near the far edge of the dance floor. It was as good a place as any to check, so she risked peeking over the side.

"Fuck!" she exclaimed, pulling back to the cover of the ductwork, then cursing herself for speaking aloud. She'd misjudged; she was directly above the dance floor, which was still crawling with people. Half of them seemed to be ignoring the mob's demands, and half of them seemed to be joining in. Fortunately, no one was looking up. Between the shadows of the club's rigging and the maze of exposed pipes and ducts up here, she was shielded. She had to keep moving, find a safe exit. But first, she had to find Bryce.

She scurried faster, her knees occasionally reverberating against the corrugated duct beneath her. Anyone with remotely decent hearing could trace her movements, if they were paying attention. Cassie just had to hope they weren't. After another twenty feet or so — she hoped — she tried again, peeking over the side ...

Bingo. She was right above the bar, where the bartenders were casually sneaking sips out of bottles and elbowing each other with amusement while the mob was busy. People in one corner, guided by some hefty-looking men, were already removing their masks, proving their innocence with their faces.

They weren't happy about it, Cassie could see. A grumble appeared to be rising and spreading. She hoped they'd hurry. If the dance crowd turned on the mob, that could be her best chance to escape.

But where was Bryce? She scanned the crowd, telling her eyes to look for the biggest, bulkiest man in the room. Meanwhile, she reached behind her, into her pocket, to get the phone she'd snagged from the club floor. If Bryce didn't look up, she'd have to call him.

Her eyes ricocheted between the phone and the floor until, finally, she spotted him. He was skulking along the perimeter of the club, near the wall. Cassie could see his lips mouthing "Excuse me, excuse me," to each person he passed, including to those he had to forcibly pick up and move out of his way. She was struck, suddenly, by how kind Bryce was. How unfailingly polite. How much he'd stuck his neck out for her, for Rachel, for TonyStark, for OHM.

She smiled and began dialing. He would be so surprised when he picked up his phone and Cassie told him, "Look up!"

Except he didn't answer. Cassie watched as Bryce looked at his phone. Something passed over his face, something hard to decipher from this far up, and he put it back into his pocket. In Cassie's ear, it still rang.

It was a random, anonymous number to him, but given the

circumstances, she figured he'd answer. Disappointed, she tried again. And again. Bryce kept moving. By this point he'd traveled in nearly a full circle, his eyes roaming the room. "Bryce," she whispered frantically, knowing no one could hear her.

Finally, he stopped. His eyes lit up. Cassie had a fleeting moment of hope, of wondering if Bryce had seen someone from OHM, someone who could help them. Her.

Instead, Bryce leaned down and patted the shoulder of someone Cassie didn't recognize. He was wiry and short, with big eyes and a big nose and a big earring in his left ear, like his face was making up for all the space his body couldn't occupy. He and Bryce began whispering furiously.

Cassie grabbed the phone and began pounding on it. **Look up, dude**, she texted.

It's me.

LOOK UP.

Nothing. He checked the phone but just as quickly slid it back into his pocket.

Of course. He couldn't be *sure* unless …

Pyrrhus, it's Lyssa.

We have to get out of here.

WHAT IS THE MATTER WITH YOU?

WE HAVE TO GOOOOOO!

Cassie must have finally hit peak annoyance, because Bryce pulled out his phone again and read the messages. Cassie watched his eyes widen, dart up, scanning the ceiling. She waved just enough to catch his attention, hoping it was *only* his she caught.

Finally, Bryce saw her. Cassie broke into a smile, ready to see his shocked expression, his surprise at her having been so clever, so *ingenious*, that she'd managed to rise above the danger. That she'd managed, for once, to save *him*, instead of him saving her.

He didn't seem happy, though.

His eyes still locked with hers, Bryce tapped his friend again on the shoulder. His friend looked up and followed Bryce's line of vision. His big eyes grew even bigger.

It took only a moment, a flash, for Cassie to realize something was wrong, to realize how horrifically exposed she was. Bryce pointed just past her, and Cassie's feeling of vulnerability revved into high gear. Why wasn't he acknowledging her? What was he doing?

She craned her neck, but her precarious perch made it impossible to see what he was pointing at. There was nothing back there anyway, except for the DJ booth …

… with its microphone …

… and lights …

Oh, no.

As she watched, Bryce and the little guy bolted forward, running right under her.

Microphone. Lights. To get the crowd's attention. To point her out.

She twisted, gripping the duct with her thighs like a jockey, nearly falling. Yes. They were almost there now, almost at the booth.

They were coming after her.

The realization hit Cassie like a bolt of thunder.

She'd been betrayed.

By *Bryce*.

It was *Bryce.* Pretending to help her, actually leading her astray. She was furious at herself for not trusting her gut. Or for trusting it too much. She wasn't sure which.

He'd led the Hive to OHM. *He'd* led her right to @Shameless, no doubt figuring that would be the end of her. And now … now he'd led the Hive to her once again.

The phone slid from her hands. It bounced once off a ledge on the duct pipe, then tumbled down into the crowd below.

She didn't wait to see where it landed or who looked up. She just ran.

Crawled, really. Back from where she came, hoping the bathroom would be as empty as it was when she disappeared, thinking she might somehow manage to squeeze out of its tiny window. She moved much faster on the return trip, her limbs used to the movement, her brain not caring how many people heard her. Getting out was her only goal.

The wall between the dance floor and the bathroom only stretched to within a few feet of the ceiling. She rushed toward the gap, scuttled into the bathroom, then let her legs dangle and she dropped without even checking for witnesses. Her mind racing, blind from Bryce's betrayal, she paid no mind to the open toilet underneath her feet, so when she let gravity do its job, her right foot slipped, landing in the bowl. Water sloshed over the sides of the toilet, and she yelped in surprise.

Amazingly, the bathroom was still empty. She hobbled over to the window. It would be a tight squeeze.

But it would be done.

10010210010l

I just feel like maybe moms shouldn't be on social media at all. Am I wrong? **#MomArmy #NoThanks #NoMoreMoms**

Cassie McKinney's ma is kinda hot. **#MILF** (Her daughter sucks tho.)

This replay of the hotel raid is SICK, it looks like a video game. **#HasCassieSurfacedYet?**

Guys I'm three drinks in and I lost my mask but Venecia is HAWTTTT right now, come on down. **#MaskLife**

I'm a mom and I'm not going anywhere. **#SaveCassie #MomArmy**

Anyone know what's happening at Venecia? Was gonna go but my friend says something's going down ... **#MaskLife**

Calling all moms! Let's mobilize to save Cassie McKinney! **#NotOurDaughters #NotOurSons**

Omg a friend is at Venecia and says the power just got cut. What is going on?!?! **#HiveMobOrWhut**

If a Hive Mob steps on my mask I'm gonna lose it, that shit is custom made. **#Venecia #MaskLife**

Whoa, the club just got raided. **#MaskLife**

HIVE ALERT. A Hive Mob is descending on Venecia after rumors Cassie McKinney is headed there. **#HasCassieSurfacedYet?**

Oh, my God am I gonna get a chance to get Cassie McKinney? OH, MY GOD I'm at Venecia right now and she's totally here! **#Supposedly #HasCassieSurfacedYet?**

What a b, ruining a good night out at da club. Cassie ruins everything. **#HasCassieSurfacedYet?**

This effing rain, man. **#BummerSummer**

10010220010 1

Cassie ran as though all the demons of hell were on her back — or maybe all the lions in ancient Rome's Colosseum. Her heart thrummed in time with her feet slapping on the wet concrete. The mob was spilling out of Venecia now, no doubt realizing that they'd missed their target. She ducked down an alley, only to find that it dead-ended in a brick wall some thirty feet high. Might as well be a million — there was no way for her to climb it.

Alleyways had been so good to her today. And now she would die in this one.

She couldn't believe it had been Bryce all along. Bryce, who had rescued her from the Hive the first time … and why? Why had he even bothered, if he was just going to betray her and all of OHM?

Shit! Shit! Stop thinking about that and think about this!

She danced around the alley in terror, looking for something — anything — that could help her. It was only a matter of time before they got here.

Under the mask, she sweated profusely. She pulled it off and shook it out, then wiped beads of moisture from her forehead and from around her eyes. Something jostled her from behind and she slapped a hand back there.

The gun. She'd forgotten. She had no idea how many bullets were in it and didn't even know how to check. In movies, the Tough Guy Hero always did something to make the bullet-holding part pop out, but she was afraid that if she did that, she would be unable to get it back in.

There was a door set into one wall, recessed by a good fifteen inches. She could crunch up in there ... Maybe no one would see her?

Yeah, right. Not likely.

There was no doorknob out here, but the door had to open somehow, right?

In desperation, she got up super close to the door and switched on her original phone, the gray OHM special. Cranking the brightness on the phone, she ran the screen along the doorjamb, peering into the little cone of light she'd created. It only took a moment — in the crack between the door and the frame, she spied a smallish shadow that filled the crack right where a door-knob *would* be.

There was a doorknob on the other side, with a simple deadbolt.

Movies came in handy once again. She knew exactly what to do.

Shivering in the cold and the rain, she nonetheless stripped off her jacket and wadded it into a ball. She pressed it against the door where the lock was, then pressed the muzzle of the gun against the wad of cloth. Makeshift silencer, like mobsters whacking dudes in action movies with a pillow to muffle the gunshot.

Wincing and praying for silence, she pulled the trigger. There was a sharp crack, barely audible over the rain, and then the violence of the explosion shot up her arm to her shoulder, vibrating through pain into almost instant numbness. With a muted curse, she dropped the gun and the jacket. Steam purled up from the door.

The mouth of the alley was still empty. With a vicious shake to work some feeling back into her arm, she picked up the jacket and gun, then waved the steam away from the door.

The bullet hole wasn't as impressive as she'd hoped, but peering into it, she could see that the horizontal metal piece that locked the door was cracked in two. She shoved the door and it stayed depressingly still.

Above the patter of the rain, she heard the stomp of feet. A herd of hatred headed her way.

"Come on," she pleaded in a barely audible whisper. "Come on …"

She shoved the door again. Nothing. She reared back and with all her strength kicked the door with her foot right where the lock was.

With a satisfying *crack*, the door moved a bit. Cassie pushed it again to open it, but nothing.

Dumbass! The door opens out*! You keep pushing it!*

Her kick had finished the job of breaking the lock that the bullet had started, and now she hooked her finger in the bullet hole and used it to pull the door open. Success!

She scrambled inside and pulled the door shut behind her. It wouldn't lock, but it stayed in the shut position, especially after she jammed her jacket into the hinges to keep it steady.

A dim red light glowed from overhead. When she looked up, she noticed an EXIT sign … and a security camera.

Shit! Goddamit! You idiot!

She spun around and ran down the dark hallway. Doors were to either side of her, but she didn't want to duck into a place where she would be caught barefaced on camera. Once she was sure she was out of the camera's range, she paused long enough to pull her mask back on. She wouldn't be seen on camera again.

At the end of the hallway, there was a glass door. This one, fortunately, was unlocked, and she eased through into another corridor. After a few moments of wandering around, she realized she was "backstage" in a retail space shared by a bunch of different stores. Because it was after hours, everything was closed, but another door led her into a lobby staffed by a lone security guard sitting at a desk tapping a tablet.

Sometimes, her dad had once told her, *the indolence of people is your best asset.*

The guard didn't even look up at her as she emerged. "Late night, huh?" he asked with a bored mien.

Just to be safe, she pretended to scratch her nose as she answered, obscuring the mask's motionless lips. "Yeah. See you tomorrow."

And then she was out on the street. She waited until she was out of sight of the lobby before breaking into a run.

She ran with no plan. Maybe if she didn't know where she was going, the Hive Mob wouldn't either. And at least as long as she kept running, they couldn't catch her.

But she couldn't run forever. Eventually, she crashed, breathing hard, at an empty bus stop. The rain had picked up, and the shelter was welcome. Under her mask, she sweated, but she didn't dare to reach underneath and wipe it away.

She had cash, thanks to TonyStark, but buses, like cabs, had cameras. Even with the mask, could she risk it?

Could she *not* risk it? She needed to do something. She couldn't bother Sarah again — Sarah had risked enough for her already. The only other person to contact was her mom. And she knew her mom was being monitored. There was no way the cops would haul Rachel in for questioning and then let her go without keeping an eye on her.

So … what? Who could she turn to?

She thrust her hands into her pockets and realized that the answer was literally at her fingertips

*

Hey, it's Cassie. So if you don't want to kill me is there a chance we could meet?

The answer came immediately: **Absolutely. Where/when?**

10010230010 1

Rachel didn't trust an internet connection in her home. Not anymore. While it was absurd, there was a part of her that could almost feel the Wi-Fi bandwidth shooting through her and enveloping her. She hadn't reconnected the modem and didn't plan on doing it anytime soon. No point making it even easier for the NSA to spy.

But she still needed access. She needed to be online. To track Cassie, as much as that was possible. To keep on top of the burgeoning ranks of her resistance.

So she ended up spending most of her time in her office on campus, where the Wi-Fi was fast and free, and where she could convince herself that the multitude of other users somehow disguised her signal from snoopers.

Honey, you just don't understand how this works. Harlon's voice in her head. He said that a lot, any time she complained about something tech related. *I don't try to speak Latin; you don't talk tech, OK?*

She knew that someone out there was skimming her bandwidth, watching everything she watched, learning everything she learned. That was the price she paid, the other side of the #MomArmy coin.

But they would only learn what everyone else knew already. She had no conduit to Cassie. No special knowledge. Let the NSA choke on the information abyss.

She sighed, yawned and rubbed her eyes. She'd paired her phone to her big desktop screen and now watched as BLINQ feeds scrolled by. The #MomArmy was on the move … virtually. Someone was organizing a boycott of Facebook, on the theory that if they could disrupt one social network's algorithms, others might follow. "It's all interconnected!" Aiden&Jenna'sMomma explained in an excited mix of text and emojis. "With enough numbers, we can make a difference!"

Right now, the only difference Rachel cared about was the mounting rage of the Hive as Cassie apparently evaded capture yet again. Rachel wasn't sure which side of the family ninja skills came from, but Cassie had inherited them from somewhere. If the internet was to be believed (and that was a big if, even in the best of times), Cassie had managed to escape yet another Hive Mob, this one at a dance club/bar in a part of town so seedy that Rachel felt a shiver of paranoia just looking it up on a map.

It was a sign of what her life had become that she was not in the least bit concerned about her underage daughter in a bar.

Cassie had escaped. That's all that mattered.

She cracked her knuckles and leaned in toward her keyboard, when there was a knock at her office door.

She wondered, *Would the NSA bother knocking?*

"Yes?" she called.

The door cracked open. Randall Worther, dean of the Classics Department, poked his head in. "Rachel. Do you have a moment?"

"Sure." She had endless moments stacked atop one another, teetering and threatening to collapse and bury her with a lifetime of time itself. There was nothing in her life but each moment in which she lived and then the next, and she just had to get through them. Like pushing through tall grass, unable to see your destination, hoping it was still there.

Randall stepped inside and closed the door behind him. It was long after hours, as proven by his sartorial concession of loosening his tie and unbuttoning the top button of his shirt. He was the sort of guy Rachel once would have accused of having a stick planted far up his posterior, but she knew that wasn't fair. He had to project a certain image; it was part of the job.

"I'm sorry to bother you when you're working late ..." He gestured to a chair and she nodded.

"I'm not really working," she confessed as he sank into the chair. "It's just ... not comfortable at home right now."

"Right." He cleared his throat. "Right."

He looked around the office for a moment, as though desperate to find something odd or interesting that he could hang a few minutes of small talk on. But Rachel's office was still in the unpacking phase. She hadn't shelved her books yet, nor hung anything personal on the walls. The office was an off-white cube with rather nice built-in bookshelves and a stack of boxes.

"I hate to have to talk about this ..." he began, pointedly not looking in her direction. "But it's my job. I hope you understand."

Rachel leaned back in her chair. "What's on your mind?"

"This … *activism* of yours …"

A knot formed in Rachel's gut. "What about it?"

Haltingly, he continued. "We support free speech, obviously. It's core to our mission as a university. But we also rely on a number of government contracts and research grants. This is a …" He fumbled, then finally resigned himself to looking up at her. "This is a tough thing to talk about. I know you're under a lot of stress. But there are some important people — people above my pay grade — who are upset with the attention you're bringing to the university."

She knew her part in this discussion. She was to meekly accept the admonition, keep her head down, keep her voice lowered. Go along to get along.

Well, fuck that, she decided.

"Are you really sitting here and asking me to choose between my job and my child?" Her voice was tight and throaty.

"Of course not!" he exclaimed. "No one is saying that!"

"Because there aren't a lot of ways to interpret what you're saying. It sounds vaguely like a threat to my job."

She'd hoped that her offensive posture would force him to stand down. Instead, he stood up, straightening his jacket.

"You're new here, Rachel. Still on probation. Not tenured. I'm not making threats. I'm just giving you some advice — don't make things difficult for the university, or the university will have no choice but to make things difficult for you."

He left before she could reply. Which was too bad because she'd worked up a head of steam and was ready to put him on blast.

She could follow, but running after someone to yell at him didn't really show a position of strength.

So she swallowed the retort, along with a toxic brew of rage, helplessness and regret, and returned to typing. There were hashtags to amplify, people to rally and a world to change.

If she lost her job, fine. If she lost her home, fine. If that's what it took to have Cassie back, she would gladly give it all away.

100102400101

They agreed to meet at 168 Vance Street, which was right around the block from the bus stop. When the time came, Cassie huddled behind a cluster of bushes and a fence near a broken streetlight, across the street from the building's front door. That's why she'd chosen this place.

She had only ever exchanged a couple of dozen words with Carson, and now she was trusting him with her life. She knew enough now not to let trust go untested. If he showed up across the street alone, great. If a mob came instead, she'd already identified her exit strategy.

Just then, someone touched her on her shoulder. Cassie nearly yelped but managed to keep it together.

Carson had slipped up beside her while she was focused on the building across the street.

"Smart," he said, with a jerk of his head at their putative meeting place. "I would have done the same."

She stared at him, almost unable to believe he was actually

here. Her mom had thrown together her backpack that night, a million years ago, when she'd merely been Level 5. The jeans she'd tossed in were the ones Cassie wore to debate club.

The ones she'd worn when Carson went old-school, writing down his number on a piece of paper. The same piece of paper she'd found at the lint-thick bottom of her pocket.

Then she'd conjured him like a magic spell.

"Sweet mask," he said, breaking the silence. "Do you really want to stand in the rain or should we go somewhere dry?"

Cassie licked her lips, a motion that was lost on him with the mask between them. "Are you inviting me to your place?"

"You got a better idea?"

She exhaled. She hadn't realized how badly she'd wanted what he was offering until it was within her reach: A safe room. A bed. Maybe a soda.

She barely knew Carson. Didn't know him at all, actually.

And yet he felt like some kind of home.

In the end, there was no alternative. He knew as well as she did: she really had no other choice.

She appreciated that he didn't say it.

*

They took a ride share back to his apartment, with Cassie sitting in strategic shadows, her mask doing most of the work. They crept up a flight of stairs, then around a bend, entering the apartment through a back door. Cassie hadn't even known that there were apartments with back doors.

This was no ordinary apartment, though. The back door

spilled them into a kitchen bigger than the living room in Cassie's old house. Carson was loaded, it appeared. She thought momentarily, with a chill, of Bryce. Everyone had more money than she did.

"This way," Carson said in a not-quite whisper and led her down a dark hallway. Soon they were in a bedroom that tried desperately to look dark and cramped but was too big to pull it off. The walls were a slate gray, and blackout curtains added to the gloomy effect.

"We're good now," he said, gesturing. With hesitant hands, Cassie peeled off the mask. Carson blinked, noticing Cassie's roughly shorn hair, but said nothing.

She couldn't find the words to say thank-you yet, but the silence was too much for her. "So your parents are OK with you sneaking girls into the house?" she whispered.

He shrugged. "You don't have to whisper. I leave them alone, they leave me alone." He dropped into a comfortable gaming chair and swiveled to his desk. There were three monitors set up in a classic triangle arrangement, with a monster laptop open between them and a tablet tethered by a cable. He tapped some keys and the screens lit up. It was familiar — Cassie's BLINQ account, along with charts, graphs, trend lines and streaming hashtag feeds. #HasCassieSurfacedYet? wasn't dipping anytime soon.

"Welcome home," Cassie muttered mordantly.

"Have a seat." He jerked his head toward another chair, which she rolled over and flopped into. "I've never seen *anything* like this," he told her without even glancing in her direction. "It's like the whole country is CassieTV, 24-7."

Cassie nodded, barely hearing him. Not wanting to hear him. She was suddenly bone-tired. Made sense, really. She'd been on the run for more than twelve hours, racing across rooftops, BASE jumping, running, shooting through doors, evading the law, channeling her inner action hero. And now, finally, she seemed to be somewhere safe. Carson was saying something important but her eyelids drooped, commanding her to sleep.

"Why are you helping me?" she heard herself ask him, her voice thick with fatigue. "You hardly know me."

"I know you code with Inconsolata. That's pretty much all I need to know."

She smiled, eyes half closed, head resting back against the chair. "No. Seriously."

He looked away from his screens, his expression one of mingled anger and concern, his eyebrows crunched together. "Seriously? Because you made a *joke* and they're trying to kill you for it. The bed's a wreck, but there's a trundle and it's already made. Get some sleep."

She didn't want to listen to him, but all she wanted to do was listen to him. She wasn't sure how she transported herself from the chair to the bed, but before she knew it she had collapsed and fallen into a darkness, deep and all-encompassing, before he could finish his offer.

*

She awoke with a jolt to the sound of his fingers slamming the keys. Her dad had typed like that, banging away at the keyboard as though it had insulted his mother. Mom used to yell at him from the other room, *Harlon! I can tell what you're typing from the aftershocks!*

Dad went through keyboards the way some people went through socks.

Her body still heavy, she pried herself up from the bed. To her surprise, she'd only been out for about an hour. Carson was at his keyboard, casually sipping an energy drink, as if he weren't harboring a fugitive at all.

"What's happening? Anything new?" she asked, rushing up behind him. As she approached, she noticed the way his hair was slightly sticking up in the back, as though he'd rubbed some pomade on it and then tousled it to achieve a "look." Or maybe, she had to admit, he'd just slept on it in some weird way. She touched a choppy lock of her own hair. She wasn't one to talk, really.

On one of the screens, she spied the frameworks for a bot, one designed to crawl sites in search of data, sort of a custom-built Google. His style was spare and lean, unlike her own, which was wild and untethered.

"Code is poetry," she murmured. The memory of his shirt, of her life pre-Level 6, slammed into her. Her shoulders sagged.

But at Carson's grin, she straightened up. "Yeah, you know why? Because poetry is messy and human and imperfect. So is code. We make it. It can't be perfect."

Speaking of not perfect … She readily saw some flaws in his bot. "We've gotta move fast. Do you mind?" she asked, reaching for the keyboard.

"Please," he said, rolling back in his chair. "Save me from myself."

She started typing and pretty soon time ceased to have meaning. This was the best. It was everything. When you sank into what Harlon reverentially called "the Flow," where it was just your fingers and the keyboard and the code, where nothing else happened or mattered.

"Jesus," Carson said admiringly. "Are you a cyborg or something?"

She blushed with mingled pride and embarrassment. "It's just what I'm good at."

"If I could code half as well as you do ..."

"I'm guessing from the setup you've got here, you're doing OK." She considered things. "And, I mean, you took a chance, agreeing to meet with me. So, like, overall, you're *more* than OK."

Behind her, Carson didn't say anything. Cassie was glad. She kept her eyes and hands trained on his computer, her lips pressed together. Part of her wanted to word-vomit every thought she'd had over the past few days — about OHM and her parents; about the Hive, and friendship and justice — just to clear it from her system. For reasons she couldn't quite articulate yet, Carson seemed like a receptive audience.

She was close to opening her mouth and unloading everything when he interrupted her thoughts and her flow by cracking his knuckles. "Can I show you something?"

She stepped away, exhaling, grateful the moment had passed. Whatever it was — if anything at all — she didn't know if she was ready for it. "Yeah, sure."

He took up his position at the keyboard again. "I'm a decent coder, but what I'm really good at is patterns. Finding signal in the noise, you know? And I've been staring at your account and ...

it's just all off," he complained. "I can't put my finger on it, but there's something *wrong* here. Your trend. And how does …"

His fingers, long and strong, played on the keyboard. Cassie watched them as he spoke. It was hard to believe she was here, in Carson's bedroom. That he'd let her in. She thought, if she had more energy, or maybe if she weren't being chased, she'd enjoy wondering what it all meant. Maybe someday …

Carson rolled up his sleeves. Cassie spied something up near the crook of his right arm. Without asking permission, she grabbed his wrist and turned his arm out so that inside faced up.

There, nestled up near the inner fold of the elbow, was a small blue Ω.

"OHM," she whispered. She stared at him. "Are you …"

He pulled his arm back. "It's an omega. I like it. So what?"

"You're one of them," she said. Or was it *one of us*?

He demurred, palms raised in deflection. "No. I'm not. You can only be OHM if you've been Hived. I haven't been. Besides, my coding skills aren't quite l33t enough for OHM."

She considered him in the pale light of his screens. "Then what are you?"

He shrugged. "A sympathizer? An ally? I don't know the word. I'm just trying to help. And it's good for them to have someone on the outside." And then: "You were there?" he asked quietly. "During the raid?"

She nodded, silent. When she realized her hand was still gripping his arm, she dropped it and stepped back.

Carson looked at the floor. "Damn."

"That's about it."

"You made it out," he said. "From the livestream, it looked like some other people did, too. Did you know a guy who calls himself TonyStark?"

The force of her reaction caught her off guard. In an instant, she was in the air again, falling, her static line not yet taut, watching TonyStark's head crack open on that ledge.

"He's dead." The tonelessness of her own voice surprised her, though her breath hitched in her chest, caught on grief lodged in her heart. She fell back onto the bed. "He died saving me from the Hive Mob and the cops."

For a moment, she worried that Carson might do something really stupid and annoying and wonderful, like stand up and take her hand, or even give her a hug. She would hate and love it at the same time.

But he didn't. And she felt greedy and self-absorbed for thinking it, much less wanting it. She'd known TonyStark for a few days. Who knew how long Carson had been communicating with him and working with him? She should be the one offering comfort.

She'd never been good at that.

"I need you to know something about him, OK?" Carson said. "He was on your side."

Cassie nodded, trying to sit in the stillness her memories of TonyStark brought her. "I know."

"He fed me some data. They'd gotten further than you think. But they were arguing internally about what to do with it."

She sat up straight. Yes, Pastor had 'fessed up to the irregularities in the Hive, but that was just hearsay. She needed solid evidence. "They had proof? There was something wrong with the system?"

"Of course there's something wrong with the system! There's something wrong with *every* system. Bugs and glitches are part of software engineering. GIGO."

Cassie rolled her eyes. "You know what? I'm tired of hearing that the system's fucked. I want to know *how* and what I can do about it!"

Carson leaned back in his chair, studying her. A faint smile began to light up his face, like someone had turned on a dimmer switch inside him.

"I swear to God, Carson, if you laugh at me right now, I'll rip out your heart."

"I'm not laughing at you." Carson held up a hand, pledging. "It's just ..." He trailed off.

"What?" she demanded. "Tell me!"

He spoke in a rush. "It's just that when you get angry, your eyes kind of disappear and you kinda look like a Super Chibi character."

She couldn't help herself — she laughed, probably more heartily than the little jab deserved. It felt good to laugh, a real, honest laugh, for the first time since ... well, since even before sending the BLINQ that changed everything. She felt the ball of anger that had been coruscating in her gut begin to spin down and dissipate, replaced by thought. Anger was useful, she knew, but not right now. Right now, her head had to be clear.

"I needed that," she admitted. "Thanks."

He essayed a bow. "I live to serve." Turning back to his computer, he moused around a bit. "Let's walk through how we got here in the first place. I've been putting together a timeline, just to keep things straight in my head. Like I said, I'm good at patterns. Some of this is public stuff. Some of it's stuff that OHM dug out of government archives."

A picture appeared on-screen: the heads of the country's biggest tech firms, at a table with the president of the United States.

"This was a little way back," Carson said. "Before our time. The guy wasn't even sworn in yet, and he met with all the tech bigwigs, the heads of the biggest and the most innovative and most powerful companies in the field. This is where it all started, even though we didn't know it yet. BLINQ was born here."

She leaned in and stared at the photo. The president and a bunch of mostly white people, mostly men. No one looked happy to be there, except maybe the president.

"Every now and then, there'd be another meeting," he said, clicking. The photo changed. Most of the faces were the same, though there were some substitutions. The head of BLINQ popped up. And Alexandra Pastor showed in the background, her head down, studying her phone.

"They got all of these guys together. Not one of them had all of the pieces of the puzzle, but together they did. So they glued them all together behind the scenes. Get some data from Apple, some data from Google, some more data from Facebook ... They took advantage of the Spectre and Meltdown vulnerabilities before they were made public. All these flaws, just waiting to be used. You mash it all together in an NSA supercomputer somewhere, and it spits out BLINQ. One ring to rule them all."

"Come on," Cassie scoffed. "Those are some of the most powerful people in the world, running the most powerful companies in the world. You can't just *make* them do things, even if you're the government. Hell, I remember my dad telling me Apple wouldn't let the FBI break iPhone encryption. You think they're just going to go along with the president?"

"You think they had a choice? They hide behind the law," Carson told her with disgust. "'We just follow the laws of the countries we do business in,' they say." He tapped some keys and a web page came up. Cassie skimmed it.

"Section 702 of the FISA Amendments Act," Carson announced. "Between that and Section 215 of the Patriot Act, they modified the legislation that had originally set up a secret court called the FISA court. Made it easier for the government to spy on people. No one knows what goes on in there, but according to legal blogs I've checked, the Justice Department could totally use it to force concessions from the tech companies."

"The Justice Department ..." They administered the Hive.

"Yeah. They used FISA courts to bend the tech companies to their will in secret. No one knew. No one could tell."

"So the government forces all of the companies to cooperate, to use their data, their algorithms and their encryption to create BLINQ," Cassie said. "Was Alexandra lying? Was it really not about policing people online?"

"It's a twofer," he said, shrugging. "Misdirection, like a magic trick: 'Hey, look over here at the shiny new internet thing that lets you shame your neighbors!' And while people were doing that, this administration was laying the groundwork to use the same system to control people."

Cassie swallowed hard. "By letting them think *they* were in control. But they weren't." She frowned. "*We* weren't," she admitted. She'd been as big a Hive booster as anyone, until it was pointed at her. The whole thing was superseductive and it had worked like a charm.

"But why pick me?" she wondered. "And how did they do it?" She thought about what Alexandra had told her. "Alexandra said that I was a convenient scapegoat."

"Well, yeah, sure. Misdirection again. What they *really* wanted was a way to test Level 6, right? To make sure people wouldn't rebel against it, to see if someone would *actually* kill someone just because of what she or he said online."

"It didn't matter that it was *me*," she murmured.

"They were looking for something, anything."

"Convenient."

Carson leaned back. "Yep."

Cassie thought back to what Alexandra had told her and Bryce at Venecia. "So they used these things called *ghost accounts*," she began. She filled him in on the rest of what Alexandra had told her.

He sighed when she was done. "This is what I don't get. I don't care what Alexandra told you: you can't game this system. It's impossible."

Which was true. Every participant (that is to say, every American citizen over the age of thirteen) was Verified and given a unique twenty-two-digit identifier. With such a long identifier, there were trillions of possibilities, but only a small percentage were valid.

It was the same principle used by credit card numbers. Credit card numbers were superlong not for identification purposes but rather for security. If you tried to create a random credit card by stringing together the right number of digits, the odds were overwhelming that you'd "hit" one of the many, many trillions of numbers that weren't valid. And with so many trillions of possibilities, your odds of luckily hitting a "good" card number were abysmally low.

The same logic ran BLINQ identifiers. With so many numbers and so few (relatively) valid ones, it was impossible to create bots or false accounts.

"You'd fail the checksum every time," Carson said. "The system would reject the identifier as invalid and not create the account. So, no bots."

"But Alexandra said there were ghost accounts. She said that's how they've been ramping up my Condemns. Are you sure you can't fake the identifiers?"

Carson gestured to one of the screens, which scrolled endlessly with code. Cassie had ignored it before because it was just flowing by so fast, but now she forced herself to scrutinize it.

It was an endless stream of twenty-two-digit numbers, followed by the words "Processing" and then "Invalid!"

"TonyStark put this together, but I've been running it for him because my bandwidth is better," he told her. "It's a megacluster with a so-called dark matter IP to generate billions of potential BLINQ accounts. They're all ditched by the system as invalid. None of them pass the checksum."

Cassie let the scrolling text hypnotize her. Sometimes if you let the code bleed away, answers revealed themselves. Sometimes if you just stared at everything and nothing at once, the world melted. In the thaw you found things you didn't even know you were looking for.

"Who decides what's a valid identifier in the first place?" she heard herself ask. She was on a path. Not sure where it went, but it was something.

"Well … BLINQ does," Carson told her. "They assign it when you turn thirteen and your parents file your Social Media Induction form."

"Right." The path was looking a little clearer. "And they generate the number the same way credit card companies do, right? They assign it and it goes into a database somewhere."

"Sure." Carson shrugged. "And then it works just like when you charge a Starbucks or a ride share. You plug in a number and the system makes sure it matches in the database."

"So what if BLINQ has made and approved a whole batch of numbers that don't actually connect to anyone? What if only *they* know about these accounts? And what if they're using them to game the algorithm and direct Hive Justice where they want it to go?"

Carson shook his head. "No. Doesn't work. Ever since 2016, everyone knows what bots are like. I've been examining your virality and the interactivity of your hashtags. Assume for the sake of argument that someone *has* figured out how to make BLINQ bots. There's nothing in the activity around you that looks like a bot. There are characteristics that bots have and we know what they are, and I'm not seeing them."

Cassie frowned. Bots were handy, yes, but limited and they could only do so much. Made for a specific purpose, they stuck to that purpose. If you wanted to persuade people to eat vanilla ice cream, you could have a bot tweet at someone who talked about, say, chocolate ice cream and spam them with vanilla ice cream coupons and information. You could have the bot interact with people who said things about vanilla ice cream to reinforce their behavior. But no matter how good the bot, it wouldn't pass the Turing test because all it would care about would be vanilla ice cream. And pretty much any decent hacker could identify that in five minutes.

"OK," she admitted, "so if it's not bots, then what? Who?"

"Throw in how, when and why," he told her.

"We know some of those. But, yeah, this whole thing feels like trying to unravel a spiderweb without breaking any strands."

A thought occurred to her. She jumped up and commandeered Carson's chair. There, on the center screen, was her BLINQ account. Likes: 90 234 491. Condemns: 140 384 889. She grabbed the mouse, then found herself tapping it rapidly on the desk, unsure what to do next.

Carson came up beside her and very kindly did not chastise her for stealing his chair and touching his gear.

"What are you thinking?"

"Is there a way to see who hasn't voted?" she asked. The thought formed as she spoke the words. "Apathy," she'd said, and Alexandra had agreed. The original plan for the Hive had anticipated a counterbalance to the system's worst impulses, but they hadn't accounted for apathy, for some people not caring enough to click. "Can we get a count of people who haven't bothered?"

"Abstentions?" Carson slid into the guest chair and leaned forward, chin on fists. "That's not a public-facing API, but we know there are about 350 million BLINQ accounts, so you just subtract your Likes and Condemns … It's like a hundred million or so."

"No." She clicked around, opening a Terminal window. An API was an application programming interface — it was the way programmers communicated with code they hadn't written.

Systems had APIs that hooked into aspects of their functionality — if there was an API that, say, controlled a system's fonts, then you could write code that used that API to manipulate text in your own app without having to recreate it all from scratch. Each company decided which public-facing APIs would be made available to any programmer.

But there was another way.

"Can we get to the private API?" she asked. "They have to have something like that set up for internal use, right? They'd need it so that they know how many ghosts to use. We need to do this right."

Carson nudged her chair with his foot, pushing her out of the way. "Let me see what I can do."

He put the word out on the OHM network. There were still groups of them, of course, all around the country. In the wake of the raid on TonyStark's crew, most of the cells had gone dark in self-defense, but Carson was able to track down a couple of loners who had the information they needed — the IP addresses associated with a BLINQ server farm on the Canadian border.

He leaned back, frustrated. It was one thing to have the IP addresses — that was like knowing where someone's house was. Beyond that, though …

"I know it just looks like a bunch of code on the screen …" Carson told her and drifted off.

She'd done enough digital breaking and entering in her time to know. They knew where the house was, but it was surrounded by a wall sixteen feet thick and ten miles high, and there was a bloodthirsty pack of wolves roaming the front lawn.

"BLINQ security is insane," he said.

Cassie pursed her lips and took over. She drummed her fingers on the desk, thinking.

She poked around the edges of the facility's systems. Nothing that would trigger any alarms. Just getting the lay of the cyberland.

"I think I see something that'll work," she said after a little while. "Can you put together a database query while I get us through security?"

He blinked. "Are you serious? You're gonna hack a government system? Just like that?"

"Just like that, yeah." She flexed her fingers and started typing.

By the time Carson had crafted the query they needed — set up to mesh with the specifications of the BLINQ API and its specific database structure — Cassie had evaded BLINQ security and managed to open a port into the database. The system was nearly impregnable, but once again human fallibility met brute code and spat out garbage. A sysadmin had dutifully updated the security system to counter the KRACK II vulnerability, but had ignored several smartbulbs. They'd never had their firmware updated, so Cassie was able to turn them into zombies to use as attack vectors to worm her way into the network. It was no easy feat, but it was totally doable. The Internet of Things was a real boon to hackers — once people installed their smart-stuff, they tended to forget about it and neglect the firmware security updates. Meaning it was ripe for exploitation by people like Cassie.

Carson offered up a low whistle as he leaned over her shoulder, watching. "I feel like a Little League kid at the World Series," he admitted.

Cassie smiled. In so many ways, he reminded her of her dad … except Harlon had no humility at all. She grabbed the query from him and ran it against the BLINQ database. It wasn't a complicated query — just scooping up any accounts that hadn't voted on Cassie and sending the sum back as an integer — so it took almost no time at all. Nonetheless, Cassie killed the connection the instant she could, and then they sat frozen and staring at the screen for long seconds after.

They had just hacked a secure government database without really thinking it through. They sat in silent, mutual awe. Had she gone too far? She thought she'd covered her tracks, but there was always a better system, smarter code, a more devious hacker. What kind of trouble might she be leading to Carson's door?

Carson broke the almost eerie quiet. "Uh, there's a chance," he said with a little shiver in his voice, "that my parents are going to get audited this year."

Cassie couldn't help it; she burst out laughing. After a moment, Carson joined her.

*

The number, when they looked at it, was bigger than she'd anticipated. Well over two hundred million. Given what she'd been through in the past week, Cassie couldn't imagine that more than two hundred million people hadn't bothered to chime in on #AbortionJoke and #HasCassieSurfacedYet?

And the fact was: they hadn't. There couldn't be that many abstentions. It was impossible.

"Bots," Cassie said triumphantly, folding her arms over her chest.

Carson popped the tab on a can of CaffBomb!, the preferred beverage of those who can't be bothered with sleep. "No BLINQ bots. Seriously."

"There have to be," she said, and pointed at the number again.

He peered at it blearily and swigged his drink. "So a bunch of people abstained. So what? You're the social media devil of the day, but not everyone gives a shit."

Cassie swiped the can from him and took a long, generous swallow. "Let's do some hard-core science here. Open up the calculator."

"Calculator? I do math with the command line."

"Of course you do. But let's pretend we're stupid."

Carson opened the calculator app. Cassie read off a string of numbers to him: her Likes, her Condemns and the abstentions figure from BLINQ.

The total was significantly north of four hundred million.

"Ta-da!" Cassie said.

"So what?" Carson asked with a tinge of misery. "We did addition. Big whoop."

She took the can again, this time tilting it at his lips. "You need more caffeine. Your brain isn't working right. More than four hundred million."

"Population of the United States is right around that …" He drifted off. "Oh, crap."

She nodded triumphantly. There were around four hundred million people in the U.S., but not all of them were over the age of thirteen. Not all of them were even online.

"Ghost accounts," Carson murmured, leaning in toward the screen, as if by getting closer to the data, he could somehow force it to make more sense. "Holy fucking shit," he swore softly. "All of us too-smart hacker types were trying calculus and trig and computer science, and the answer was just plain old arithmetic all along."

"The ghost accounts exist. Alexandra wasn't lying. The numbers are so big that they must have figured no one would bother to add them up," Cassie said. "They hid it all in plain sight."

Carson snorted in derision. "You give them too much credit. I think they just went overboard. They got cocky and just kept juicing your numbers to make things worse and worse." He snapped his fingers. "Plus, this is the first time they've ever done anything this big, with this many accounts. No one ever bothered adding them up before because there was no point — the numbers were so small that it didn't matter."

"But this time, yeah, they went overboard. But then … how do they shield the bots from discovery in the first place? We know how bots work — they're easy to identify, but no one has been able to —"

Carson suddenly jumped up from his chair and Cassie fell silent as he paced the room fiercely, knocking over piles of thumb drives, pawing through old Blu-rays.

"Carson?" She didn't want to interrupt this process, whatever it was, but time was not their friend.

"Aha!" he crowed, and waved a USB drive in the air triumphantly. "Got it!"

"Got what?" She joined him at the desk again as he jammed the drive into a port.

"Patterns! I knew I remembered this, but I couldn't remember where the backup was … Patterns! Mapping data!"

"Mapping? What maps?"

"Not like *map* maps," he said, punching up a file. "Like, metaphorical maps. Maps of activity." He pointed at a graphic filling the screen. "Here!"

It was a complicated skein of digital silk, thousands of strands spun out from the center of a web, threads of multiple colors unspooling out to the boundaries of the screen and beyond.

"What am I looking at?" Cassie asked, leaning in intently.

Carson's left foot tapped madly. "A map of BLINQ account activity for one of the accounts that was a big viral push for #HasCassieSurfacedYet? The threads are connections to other accounts, interactions, color coded." He pointed out specific lines. "Likes, Dislikes, Condemns, retweets, BLINQ-ups. You get the picture."

It was a visualization of the account's activity, she realized, rendering hundreds of interactions in a single image. "What time period does this take place over?" Bots were known for bursts of activity over short periods of time, targeted to do the most damage.

"This is, like, a week," Carson said, still tapping madly away at the floor. "Not typical bot behavior at all, right?"

She shook her head. This looked, well, pretty normal. An opinion Carson then ratified by bringing up his own BLINQ activity graph. It wasn't identical to the first one — that would have been weird! — but they had similar characteristics. For example, they both interacted with other accounts on a regular basis, and they both had a collection of people they regularly Liked and reBLINQed. They both had usage patterns that fell off at night, when the user was asleep, with a spike in activity early in the morning. Things like that.

"It's not a bot, then," Cassie said. "I don't know why we're even looking at this."

"Because there's something here," he said. "Trust me."

Cassie sighed. "Fine. Convince me."

Carson never took his eyes from the screen. "Right. This is my domain now. Patterns. Follow me here. What if we're looking at a new kind of bot? Something a little closer to a classic Turing AI than what we know of bots?"

"Something slower and less efficient than a bot," Cassie said. "Not really the point, is it?"

"Slower and less efficient, yeah," he agreed, "but only so that it gains in *effectiveness* what it loses in speed and efficiency. What if it's designed to be slow so that we don't think it's a bot in the first place?"

"I'm not following you."

"You said it before," he told her. "BLINQ keeps the database, right? They have the list of numbers. And now we know that there are more accounts than there are people online. So what's the deal with the extra accounts?" He tapped the back of a finger on the graphic. "There are a slew of accounts with activity maps like this one. And here's the thing: they all talk to each other. All the time."

That got Cassie's attention. Bots talking to each other … during their downtime? She sat upright. "What do they talk about?"

"All kinds of shit, it looks like. They just bounce links and bits of text back and forth. Like we do. Except … they keep to themselves. It's like their own quarantined version of the internet, where they just babble to each other. And they don't interact with any non-bots. Until ..."

"Until someone makes fun of the president's grandkid."

It all made sense now. It all fell into place. BLINQ had something like a hundred million of Alexandra's "ghost accounts." And in order to disguise them from bot hunters, they had the accounts rigged with AIs who spent all day and all night talking to each other, mimicking normal human behavior so that anyone looking for the usual bot flags wouldn't find them.

The ghost accounts did nothing else. They had no contact with the rest of the internet until they were needed. Until someone gave the order to Level up this person or that person.

Like her interactions with the Harlon AI, except *both* ends of the chat were artificial. Millions upon millions of invented dads and daughters, moms and sons, best friends, talking back and forth about whatever their algorithms vomited up for them.

"At which point," she told Carson, "someone flips a switch and the ghost accounts go ahead and interact with the rest of the 'net, looking like real people. There would never be anything at all like 100 percent participation in a thread, so they can see where a trend is headed and then swap in as many ghost accounts as they need in order to make it go their way."

Carson nodded triumphantly. "Who knows how many times they've done this before? How many test runs? All to ... what?"

She remembered what Alexandra had told her at Venecia. About the president. The election. The Constitutional Convention.

"They've gamed one system," Cassie told him. "Now they're planning to game another. And with these accounts, they can totally hijack Hive Justice to push public opinion, influence elections ..." She swallowed. "And when that doesn't work, they can Level 6 anyone they want to. Got a political rival who's making it tough to pass a law? Cherry-pick a post or a BLINQ, pump it up to Level 6 and just ... get rid of them."

Cassie wondered if she'd ever catch her breath again, now that she knew the biggest secret her government was trying to keep from her. From *them*.

There was nothing left to say.

Until there was.

"I have to admit," said Carson. "There's something that's been bugging me that I just can't reconcile: How the heck does Sarah Stieglitz fit into all of this?"

Cassie blinked. "What?"

Carson waited a moment, considering. Then, with a gentleness she didn't anticipate, he said, "Didn't you know? I guess you didn't. You haven't been online, right? Sarah's been one of the people shouting loudest for your head."

Cassie's vision went blurry and her ears filled with static. She gripped the armrests of her chair, seeking to anchor herself to the real world because in that moment, she felt as though she could melt away and then just evaporate.

Sarah. Her friend Sarah. No. Impossible.

But she knew. Even as she denied it, she *knew*.

"She set the Hive Mob loose on the club and on OHM headquarters," Carson was saying when her senses returned to her. "But how is she connected to all of this? How did she know where to find you?"

Cassie's lips moved and her throat bobbed, but no words came out.

Sarah.

She'd suspected Bryce. She'd run from *Bryce.* But it had been Sarah all along.

BE CAREFUL!!! Sarah had texted. Along with that damn heart emoji.

She had contacted Sarah and asked her to tell Rachel that she was in an old hotel somewhere. How long would it take the Hive to crowdsource the location based on that information? Seconds, maybe. Minutes at most.

And then she'd asked for directions to Venecia. Might as well just have said, "Hey, I'll be at the club tonight — come kill me!"

Of *course.* It made perfect sense, except that it didn't. Why would Sarah do this? She seemed to like Cassie. She didn't like Hive. She rejected it. Was she working for someone and, if so, who?

"She knew because I told her," Cassie said, her voice strangled and weak.

"You what?" He sat upright, gripping the arms of his chair tight, looking around.

"She doesn't know I'm here. I didn't tell her. I ..." She passed a hand over her eyes. "Oh, God, I was so stupid, but I needed help."

"What did you do?" he asked. "Exactly?"

She told him about the two times she'd reached out to Sarah for help. "I bet she never said anything to my mom after all, either," she said bitterly.

"So you used a burner phone and dumped it later," he mused. "She's not actually tracking you ..."

"No, I just helpfully told her where to kill me."

She was staring down at the floor between her feet, mentally lashing herself for her stupidity. Carson leaned in and craned his neck so that he could look into her eyes. "Hey. Stupid is part of life, right? You were desperate. And despite everything that happened, you're safe."

Safe. The word echoed within her. It was a small, simple word, but right now it had no meaning she could cling to.

"We need to contact her," Cassie told him. "She might know something."

Carson pursed his lips, considering. "Contact the girl who sold you out multiple times. Hmm. Bad idea or worst idea ever? I can't decide."

"Please," she said. "I have to find out what she knows."

Carson rummaged in a drawer for a moment, coming up with an outdated model of iPhone. "Jailbroken, custom OS, the usual," he said, handing it to her. "Try not to go more than ten texts. The encryption is good, but there's no point leaving a trail."

She impulsively hugged him. When her arms wrapped around his neck, she felt him freeze for a moment, then thaw. The hug felt good, felt real, and she wanted to linger in it. But even though it felt real, she couldn't be sure. Couldn't know if it was desperation that led to her craving.

"I'm sorry," she said, pulling away.

"Why?" he asked with a grin. "Best ten seconds of my life."

"Down, boy," she told him. They weren't there. Not yet.

Carson shuffled his right foot, brushed his hair out of his eyes with his left hand and just generally decided to look at everything in his bedroom except for Cassie. "Sorry," he mumbled. "When I get nervous, I get inappropriate."

She softened. It was Carson, and she liked him, and, yeah, he had every right to be nervous. "Yeah, if they catch you helping me …"

"It's not that. It's … you." He finally looked at her again and shrugged helplessly. "I don't know. You ever see someone and just …"

She'd experienced exactly that with Carson the first time she'd seen him, ten million years ago. Cassie squeezed her eyes shut, hoping Carson didn't finish that sentence, but at the same time desperately wanting him to. Now wasn't the time for that, though.

"I really have to do this …" she said, gesturing with the phone.

He startled, as though he'd just woken up from a dream into a new nightmare. "Jesus! Yes! Do it. Sorry."

She tapped out Sarah's number from memory. **It's Cassie again. Has it really been you all along, ratting me out? I thought we were friends.**

A full minute passed before the response came through.

You think we're friends? Cassie could hear everything in her body now — her heartbeat, the blood rushing behind her ears, the creaks her knees made as she stood up and began pacing around the alcove.

Of course we're friends …, she wrote.

Sarah responded with a laughing face emoji. Cassie, her breath quickening, sent back a single question mark.

I was so excited to be your buddy. But you rejected my help. Over and over again. That's not a friend. Karma's a bitch, Cassie.

Cassie stared at Sarah's response in horror. Rejected Sarah's help? Is that what Cassie had done? And if so, was this actually the punishment?

She could feel more tears approaching — at what point would she run out, the back part of her brain wondered? A million thoughts were pulsing through her, but how could she explain to Sarah why she couldn't be the support system for damaged kids that Sarah wanted her to be? How could she make her understand that Cassie was just trying to protect herself? She thumbed back a pathetic, **That's not it at all! And even if I messed up, do you really think I deserve to die for it?**

I don't even feel sorry for you, Sarah finally wrote. **You deserve everything you get.**

Deflated, she sat on Carson's bed, the little ancient iPhone cradled in her hands. The screen, so dim and so tiny, glared up at her, blasting pixelated text at her eyes.

You deserve everything you get.

The hell of it was that Sarah was right. Cassie had gone to Sarah for help, and that had led the police and the mob right to OHM. And then TonyStark had died. There was a straight, bright-red line from Cassie's weakness to TonyStark's death. It was her fault he'd died.

I deserve everything I get. Sarah was right. Cassie had done this to herself. Yeah, the government helped her along, but if she hadn't been so desperate to fit in, to fill the void with something snarky and dark and bad as opposed to something worthwhile, she wouldn't have been on their radar in the first place. Rowan pushed her and goaded her, but Cassie came up with the joke and Cassie shoved it into the ether. She kept looking for a way out, but maybe there wasn't one. Maybe there was just punishment.

"Got some bad news," Carson said soberly.

"Compared to what?" she asked, not even looking up.

"No, for reals." His urgency compelled her to raise her eyes. He was pointing to a video window. "Your mom's been arrested."

*

I still can't get over that a Level 6 convict went to my school. Do you think the news will interview us once she's dead? WATCH OUT I'M GONNA BE FAMOUS! **#WhatsUpWestfield**

Jackass, you're not famous, she is. **#WhatsUpWestfield**

I wonder if anyone who was friends with her ever suspected anything? Like was she shady? Did she skin small animals during homeroom? Who knew what? **#WhatsUpWestfield**

Who was actually friends with **#CassieMcKinney**? Someone needs to spill some tea. **#WhatsUpWestfield**

Um … OK, I guess I'll just say it. Rowan and her girl gang were friends with her. They ate lunch with her every day. So … **#WhatsUpWestfield**

CASSIE MCKINNEY WAS FRIENDS WITH ROWAN??? WHAT PLANET HAVE I BEEN LIVING ON TO MISS THIS??? This is amazing. I bet she's totally hiding Cassie in her parents' carriage house. **#WhatsUpWestfield**

I sat in a debate club meeting with **#CassieMcKinney** once, AMA! **#WhatsUpWestfield #Level6**

OMG guys, do you think Rowan still talks to Cassie? **#HasCassieSurfacedYet? #WhatsUpWestfield**

We were never friends. — RB **#RowanSpeaks**

Liar, I served you all coffee the day Cassie sent her joke. You were friends. **#WhatsUpWestfield #YouTipForShit**

Cassie sat with Rowan & co every day at lunch and definitely shared homework. (YES WE ALL KNOW ABOUT YOUR STUPID CHEATING METHOD, ROWAN. You're not as smart as you think you are!) **#WhatsUpWestfield**

Everyone, leave Rowan alone. She's a victim here and I can't believe you're all bullying her like this. Indira will set the record straight, she's good with words, and Rowan is very busy reexamining all her relationships after this breach of trust. — Livvy **#LivvySpeaks #RowanSpeaks**

Now I remember! I definitely saw **#CassieMcKinney** with Rowan and her friends a bunch of times. I can't believe they're trying to deny it. Typical fake news. **#WhatsUpWestfield**

How many times do I have to say it? We were never friends. Search my feeds, she's nowhere in them. — RB **#RowanSpeaks**

Allow me to clear the air, Westfield. Cassie McKinney sat with us a few times. She ingratiated herself with our group based on false pretenses — namely, we falsely thought she was cool. It wasn't until this event that we realized how disturbed a person she truly is. (Was.) — Indira **#IndiraSpeaks #LivvySpeaks #RowanSpeaks #WhatsUpWestfield**

And we've been fully cooperating with the authorities. — Mads **#MadisonSpeaks #IndiraSpeaks #LivvySpeaks #RowanSpeaks #WhatsUpWestfield**

Oh, for God's sake, Madison. Delete that. — RB **#RowanSpeaks**

100102500101

This time, it wasn't the NSA. The men at her door were two uniformed police officers and a detective in a rumpled gray suit that streamed with rainwater.

"Mrs. McKinney, I have a warrant for your arrest, for aiding and abetting a fugitive of Hive Justice." The detective held up a sheaf of papers, then lowered it immediately. For all Rachel could tell, it was a takeout menu.

They came into the apartment without so much as a "May I?" And one of them roughly yanked Rachel's arms back before slapping on the handcuffs. They were too tight, but the cop just pulled her along when she protested, dragging her out of the apartment.

"Search warrant, too," the detective said almost casually, flapping another piece of paper at her as she went by. "Tear it apart, guys."

A troop of cops had mustered in the hall. Rachel watched them march into her home. If she ever got to return, she knew it'd be a disaster zone.

If. If.

"You have the right to remain silent," someone said in a bored tone of voice. "You have the right to speak. Anything you say can and will be used against you in a court of law. You have the right to hire an attorney. If you cannot afford one, you will be given an entry in the defendant's lottery. Do you understand the rights I have just read to you?"

"Yes," she said, wondering how they would use that against her in a court of law.

"Good." And they dragged her away.

*

Cassie could feel her body coming apart at the seams. She spun around in Carson's room, looking for something to punch.

"No," she said loudly and firmly. "No. Fucking. Way." And clenched her fists and turned again —

Carson stood there, holding out a pillow. "Go for it," he said.

Without even hesitating to consider, Cassie lashed out with one fist, then the other. And then back again. One-two. One-two. Harlon had tried — and failed — to teach her rudimentary boxing as a child, but she remembered the basics of jab-cross, and she whaled at the pillow with all her might, until she was exhausted, spent of strength and outrage.

"Better?" Carson asked, taking a risk to lower the pillow.

"Yeah. No. There's no such thing as *better* anymore."

He looked as though he would toss the pillow aside, then reconsidered and sank into his chair, hugging it to his chest. "We can't worry about your mom right now. There's literally nothing we can do for her."

Cassie shot him a withering glare. *We're not giving up on my mom when she's never given up on me.* "Easy for you to say! *Your* mom is right down the hall and you can see her whenever you want and she's not going to jail for the rest of her life!"

"No," he said very calmly, "my mom is in a rehab clinic in Saratoga Springs, probably banging an orderly for cigarettes."

"Oh." Cassie looked at the floor. "Well, I'm sorry."

Carson shrugged, but he seemed distracted, as though he was remembering some distant memory. "Thanks, but no need to be. It's just what is. I can't do anything about it and it doesn't say anything about me."

She opened her mouth to speak, not even sure what she would say, but a beep stopped her. "What's that?"

Carson spun the chair around to the laptop. "You just got a PM on BLINQ."

A private message? BLINQ PMs could only come from people you whitelisted in advance, and her list was pretty thin.

"Someone called Red Dread," Carson told her, then backed up so that she could step up to the monitor.

Bryce? She paused before responding. "He's OHM. But I never whitelisted him!"

"The government controls BLINQ," Carson reminded her. "If he's with Alexandra, they whitelisted him for you."

"For a minute there, I coulda sworn he was going to turn me in. I didn't think I could trust him. But now that I know it was Sarah ..." She squeezed her fists into her eyes, trying to get the room to stop spinning. She didn't know who to trust anymore, other than her mom and Carson. Bryce had run … but running was usually the right move these days. "I mean, he's OHM. He's on our side, right?" It wasn't rhetorical. She really wanted to know.

Carson shrugged. "Cassie, I'm a decent hacker, but the OHM people do it 24-7. I mean, they look forward to leap years 'cause they get an extra day at it, you know?"

"And?" She studied him. Something was bothering him. "What's your point?"

He was struggling, but he got it out: "My point is this: Everything you and I figured out just now? About the ghost accounts and all that? If you and I could figure it out from my bedroom, trust me — OHM figured it out, too."

"And didn't tell me." Cassie's stomach tightened in something that was decidedly not hunger. "Why?"

Carson threw his hands up in the universal *beats the living hell out of me* gesture.

She rubbed her temples. Every time things seemed to get simpler, there was another complication right around the corner. "I feel like I have to read this message. Is it safe?"

"Sure is. We're running a custom VPN."

Sounded good to her. She opened the PM. To her surprise, it wasn't a message but rather a solitary link: https://23462.vidded.fly.

She glanced nervously at Carson. "Do I click?" She wanted to, but it was his house, his gear, his life. If she somehow led the police or the mob here, it would fall on him just as heavily as on her.

He poked around with another laptop for a moment, checking some things. "Yeah, that site is encrypted HTTPS backed by RSA keys with 2048-bit modules and SHA-256. It's solid."

She clicked and a video window opened. Bryce, standing somewhere with a brick wall behind him, speaking in a hushed tone, his voice raw and almost inaudible.

"Cassie, I'm sorry about what happened at the club. Look, I can't explain too much on vid, even secure vid, but I'm on your side. And @Shameless is trustworthy. I'm not perfect, but I only have your best interests at heart. There are some at OHM who disagree. They want to use you to make a point. You need to run. Go underground. Deep, deep underground. And don't come up for anything, not even for me. Please listen to me."

Then he held up a sheet of paper covered in thick black scrawls. It was only in frame for a second before he pulled it away and the screen went black.

They both stared at the screen and then Cassie noticed something. With a cry, she shoved Carson out of the way and started banging on the keyboard.

"What the hell!" Carson complained.

"There's a timer!" she told him, not bothering to gesture. She needed both hands on the keyboard. Up in the upper left corner, a dark gray timer ticked down against the black background. Cassie had only seconds to download the video to Carson's hard drive.

`youtube-dl` didn't work, even though Carson had it installed. She tried the command line and some `curl` action, but that didn't work either. They needed that video or at least a frame of it.

The counter had ten seconds left to go, and there was a speck of dust on the screen that was driving Cassie crazy. She lifted her hand from the keyboard for a precious half second and wiped at the speck. It stayed where it was.

Not a speck. A pixel. A light gray pixel in the midst of the black.

She clicked right on the pixel and a menu popped up. DOWNLOAD was one option. With a cry of triumph, she clicked on it and watched a spinning circle conjure itself. Moments later, she had the video on Carson's hard drive.

She sighed in relief and rocked back on her heels. Carson put a hand over his chest. "I don't think my heart can take much more of this," he told her.

"I hear you." She gestured for him to take over. "Bring up that frame with the paper."

He did so. "It's just scribbles, and it's only on camera for a second. What's the big deal?"

Go underground, he'd said. Her first reaction was *Hell, no.* There was nowhere *to* go underground. For one thing, she couldn't hide forever; eventually the mob would find her. For another, she didn't know how to go underground, and the only people who could have helped her — OHM — were ...

Were ...

She pointed to the pattern on the screen. "It's sort of like a hand-drawn QR code," she told Carson. The memories flooded in along with sudden understanding. "I saw them at OHM, painted on the walls. Didn't realize what they were at first."

Carson sat forward eagerly. "Got it. Steganography. How do we decode it?"

"Not sure. Like I said, I didn't realize what they were until just now."

Carson blew out a long breath. "Well, we can try light filters, color filters ..." Even as he spoke, he brought up a series of

Photoshop documents with layers of differing levels of opacity and color temperature. He overlaid the coded image onto the documents, looking for anything that would jump out under the new "lighting." But there was nothing.

They spent the better part of an hour trying every filter they could think of, running the code under blue, red, yellow and more, then applying Gaussian blurs, unsharp masks, circular halftones ... Nothing resulted in anything more than a jumbled mess.

"We're going about this all wrong," Cassie said. "He did this by hand. With a marker. He didn't have fancy filters with him. It has to be simple. We're making it too complicated."

"A guy named Red Dread shouldn't be allowed anywhere near magic markers," Carson said.

Cassie permitted herself a small smile, remembering her run across campus with Bryce, their jump into the maintenance tunnels. The climb to OHM.

"He's not so bad," she said, as he fiddled with the image a bit more.

"If he freehanded it, then there can't be anything precise about the placement of the lines."

"Well, if it's not about precision, then maybe it's about —" She broke off. "Maybe it's something we can't see, but the computer can."

"We already tried a million different —"

"No. Is there a way to search for a color?" She'd never used any sort of graphics software before, other than applying filters to selfies and occasionally whipping up a diptych to post.

"Sure." Carson shrugged. "But it's all black."

“To us it’s black. But maybe there’s something we can’t see. Something … red.”

Carson’s eyes widened. “As in Red Dread. Got it.”

He moused around for a moment and then said, “Yasss!”

There on the screen was a subtle pattern of red dots, so small and so dark that to the naked eye they just blended in. But the computer was able to pick them out. Bryce had drawn his thick black morass of lines and curls and whorls, then gone back with red and put in the dots.

“Simple substitution cipher,” Carson scoffed. A few moments later, he read out, “‘Meet us at …’ So all that stuff about ‘go deep underground …’ ”

“He’s assuming someone else will see the video.”

Carson checked the rest of the dots. “OK, he’s setting up a meeting. But ‘us’?”

“Him and Alexandra, probably.”

“We’re not going, right?”

Cassie patted him on the shoulder. “You haven’t hung out with me enough. I *always* do the really stupid thing.”

10010260101

Cassie let Carson go first. He insisted. She was glad for the sudden burst of boy bravado, because as much bravery as she was projecting, she was still the one living with a hashtag death sentence, and going inside an old storage unit felt like surrender.

So Carson went first, something of a strut to his walk. They were in a place that even the locals would have called "the bad part of town," delivered there by a circuitous route of buses, ride shares and three harrowing blocks of walking. With her mask on, Cassie felt somewhat protected, and with Carson at her side she felt even better. But she knew that she would never again feel 100 percent safe anywhere, under any circumstances.

She found a shadow outside the storage unit and made herself small under its cover. A pale half-moon hung above her. The building was a giant concrete cube with peeling, faded orange doors. A rickety chain-link fence ran the perimeter of the property and rattled like ghosts every time someone in the same zip code breathed in its direction. Cassie found a spot under a burned-out lamppost and startled every three seconds when the fence made its discordant music.

Carson had entered the unit labeled 24 a full minute earlier. They had agreed that she was not to come in until she heard him say the name Jef Raskin, the man who had pioneered the original Macintosh project a billion years ago. If she heard anything else — or if three minutes passed — she was to run like hell.

They hadn't discussed to *where*. There was no point. Nowhere was safe for long.

Another twenty seconds passed and then Carson poked his head out of the storage unit. Somewhat reluctantly, he said, "Jef Raskin."

Inside was better than out. Cassie felt less exposed, less endangered, even though Alexandra Pastor was standing right there, next to Bryce, the two of them looking like the oddest power couple in the world.

"I don't like that he's here," Carson grumbled. "And I like even less that *she's* here. But they're alone and they surrendered their phones, so we're as safe as can be. For now."

Cassie put a hand on his elbow by way of thanks, or maybe to help remind her she wasn't totally alone. She wanted to do more. Hug him, maybe; hold him. Let him hold her. That would be … "Nice" felt like too small a word for it, but also too much to let herself hope for.

She faced Bryce first, then flicked her eyes to Alexandra. "Go ahead," she told them. "You have my attention."

After a moment's hesitation and a glance at Alexandra, Bryce spoke first. "Cassie, I had nothing to do with what went down at the club. I was just as surprised as you. Someone named @Sarah —"

"I know," she interrupted. "But what *were* you doing? Who were you talking to?"

Bryce had the good grace to blush a bit and look away. "Look … I didn't have a choice. That guy was with OHM. But not on your side. *Our* side," he corrected. "There were two factions, but they were both playing nice. You had people like TonyStark and Tish, who really wanted to help you. And then you had other people, who … They were figuring out how to use you, to turn you in to the authorities or toss you out to the Hive in exchange for getting their own records clear. I was protecting you. I had to get him out of there before he could do or say anything. Believe me or don't, but I'm on your side, Cassie. Always have been."

She turned that over in her head for a moment. She remembered the vote to keep her in OHM. How there'd been a group dead set against it who had come around. But they hadn't come around, had they? They'd just realized that they could benefit by having Cassie at hand. Of course there were people who wanted to use her at OHM. Of *course*. Everyone was trying to use her. And she wasn't going to stand for it any longer. "And you?" she asked Alexandra.

Alexandra shrugged. "I'm on the side of what's right. When we first set up the Hive, I thought it was the right thing to do. Now I'm not so sure. I've seen how it can be manipulated —"

"Can be?" Cassie arched an eyebrow.

Alexandra sucked in a breath. "Yeah, okay. How it *is* manipulated. That's not how it's supposed to work. You shouldn't die, Cassie. You probably shouldn't even be higher than, say, Level 2.

The whole thing got out of hand." She clucked her tongue. "We're a species that has built technologies —"

"— that we're not mature enough to handle," Cassie finished for her. Harlon had said it all the time.

Pastor smiled sadly. "I miss your dad, kid."

"Fuck you." Cassie's voice was low, tense, her eyes shining. "He was just a code jockey to you. He was my world."

A cold moment passed between them, and then Alexandra nodded slowly. "Yes. Of course. I'm sorry."

Bryce stepped into the breach, holding out a USB key shaped like Superman. "This is the encrypted data dump Alexandra was led to."

Alexandra grabbed Bryce's wrist, but it was too late; he'd already handed it off to Cassie, who took a careful step back.

"We don't need your help," Carson shot from behind Cassie. "We have our own evidence."

"What are you doing?" Alexandra demanded, her voice trembling. "You can't give that kind of data away! We don't know what's in it. I could be exposed!"

Bryce made a show of dusting off his hands. "Don't care. I'm sorry and thanks for your help, but this has gone too far."

Fuming, Alexandra turned her attention back to Cassie. "Cassie, please listen to me. I know the temptation you're feeling right now. You want to tear it all down. Burn it to the ground. But the system is fragile and you need to consider —"

"Your asshole cops are holding my mom. They're gonna lock her up forever for the crime of helping me. I don't give a good goddamn what happens to the system at this point." She held up the Superman key. "This is her way out."

"What are you going to do? Blackmail the federal government? Even assuming you could decrypt the data in the first place."

"The color is the code," Cassie told her. "You said that before. That's the decryption key, right? I'll work it out."

Alexandra hiccuped a laugh. "You'll work it out, will you? Yeah, colors have something to do with the encryption key. We think it's about the hexadecimal codes for web-safe colors. String ten of them together and you have a nice sixty-character string."

"Great. I'll figure it out."

"No, you won't. There are 216 web-safe colors, Cassie. Do you know how many possible combinations of ten that means?" When Cassie said nothing, Alexandra went on: "It's something like one-point-seven-one-four times ten to the twenty-third power. In other words, *quadrillions* of possibilities. Have fun breaking that."

Cassie swallowed. If she thought about the enormity of it, she would fumble. So she pushed Alexandra's words away and replaced them with her dad's: *The point of it all, Cassie, is to see if you can trick a machine into telling you the answer.* Harlon wouldn't be staggered by this. He'd think it was fun, a challenge.

"You don't know what you're up against," Alexandra continued. "You have no idea."

Cassie trained her eyes on Alexandra, pausing just long enough for a glimmer of concern to flash in her eyes. "I have a perfect idea. Whether I can crack into this thing or not, it doesn't matter. We already have a lot of evidence and we'll put all of it out on the internet and show people just how corrupt the system really is."

There was silence for several heartbeats, and then Alexandra started laughing.

It wasn't a tinkly little chuckle, either. The sound of it made Cassie start to wilt before snapping her back into a fighting stance.

"Hey!" Cassie shouted. "Hey! What's so damn funny?"

"You're so notorious that I forget you're still a kid," Alexandra said, wiping tears from her eyes. "You think you can just post some kind of manifesto online and people will rally to you? Come on."

Cassie clenched her fist around the USB key. She *did* think that. And she was counting on it. But she wasn't about to let Alexandra know it. She stuck out her chin. "No. There's more to it."

As though she'd said nothing, Alexandra just kept on talking. "I'll tell you how it will play out, OK? Save you some effort. You put up the data and you post a video somewhere to get people to look at it. The first thing that happens is everyone spends a day parsing the video to try to figure out where you recorded it and where you might be. The data gets skipped over because it's ugly and complicated and boring. There's no entertainment value to it.

"At some point, a couple of serious people actually start to dig into the data. But we're not idiots, Cassie. We've been doing this for a while. There's a lot of misdirection in that data. The ghost accounts aren't truly intelligent, but they're not stupid either.

"So now you get 'we said / she said.' You'll have dueling experts and conspiracy theories, but no justice, no peace, no respite. No freedom. By the time anyone actually realizes you're right, you'll be dead, and your mom will be in a maximum security facility in

Colorado." Alexandra folded her arms over her chest. "And that's how your scenario will play out."

"Bullshit," Cassie said automatically. But she didn't believe herself. What Alexandra had said had the ring of truth to it. Inside, she deflated. Was there no way out?

"Cassie's the most famous person in the country right now," Carson said, rallying. "People will listen."

Alexandra shook her head. "Most *in*famous. There's a difference. That colors the perception of what she puts out there. It'll seem self-serving. No one will take any of that evidence at face value. Listen to me, Cassie," she said, leaning close with urgency. "There's another way. If you can do something that gets people's attention, something that could change people's minds, even a little bit, I promise you I'll amplify it on my end."

"With more ghost accounts?"

Alexandra nodded. "And that's not the only trick in our book. Your mom has lit a spark online. She's got some people in her corner and in yours. I'll push on my end and thanks to the groundwork she's laid, it'll look organic and believable." She inclined her head toward the Superman key. "Don't be stupid. Your father knew when to be a sledgehammer —"

"— and when to be a drill." Cassie bristled. "Seriously, stop quoting my own father to me."

Holding up both hands, palms out, Alexandra agreed. "Sorry. Won't happen again."

The Superman key was digging painfully into her palm. Cassie opened her hand and stared down at it. It had everything she needed to change the world. To save herself.

And yet, it was useless to her.

"What do you want right now, Cassie?" Alexandra asked. In the moment, in the dark, the words felt soft. Safe.

"I want my mom free," she said, her voice catching. "I want my life back."

"And I believe you can have those things." Alexandra pointed to the key. "But you have to hold off on that. You can burn the system to the ground, but that won't actually help you at all. You'll be a martyr, which isn't a great life because ... well, because you'll be dead. But if you can move the needle a little bit, I can do the rest for you, behind the scenes. I can make the system work for you rather than against you."

Cassie still stared at the Superman key, contemplating. "And my mom goes free."

"Yes. Of course. That's easy. That's a phone call."

"And the people who were arrested at OHM. Them, too."

"You want to send up a flare to the world, saying the fix is in? I can't help them, Cassie. You, yes. Your mom, sure. That's it."

Bryce walked the few steps between them and put a hand on her shoulder.

"It's a good deal, Cass," Bryce told her. "You get your life back. The OHM folks will figure themselves out. You're no good to anyone if you're dead."

"But ..." Cassie's mouth felt too small, her bones too big. For a while there, she thought maybe there could be something bigger. Something like a revolution.

But was that what she wanted? A revolution? Her dad's blood yearned for the ultimate disruption, for tipping over the table entirely. But she was tired. And deep down she was scared. A revolution was a luxury she didn't have the time for. She just needed to stop running and go home.

"I have to get going," Alexandra said. "I've been off the grid way too long. People are going to start asking the kinds of questions I can't answer." She took a few steps toward the door and then paused in front of Cassie. With a slight hesitation, she took Cassie's chin in her hand and tilted her face upward a bit.

"You really do look ..." she murmured, then dropped her hand. "Good luck, Cassie."

Bryce exchanged a complicated look with Carson, then joined Alexandra. Carson and Cassie were alone.

Alone.

She didn't know what to do. Exposing the Hive for what it really was felt satisfying and thrilling, but ... What if Alexandra was right? What if Bryce was right? What if the smartest thing to do was to keep playing the game, only this time with an ace up her sleeve? Alexandra seemed to have the right idea, but ... could Cassie trust anything that came from her?

"We need to get the hell out of here," Carson told her, breaking into her thoughts. "We're just standing around waiting to be seen and there's only one exit."

He was right. They scrambled out the door and into the night.

*

Mask in place, she hopped on a bus with him. They stayed toward the back. Carson had brought a big twenty-inch folding tablet, which they opened and crouched behind. There was no one near them on the bus, but they still kept their voices low.

"What do you think?" she asked.

Carson curled his lip in distaste. "I don't trust either of them."

"So ... go big or go home?"

He groaned. "I don't trust them, but I think they might be right anyway. It kinda makes sense."

That was precisely what she expected to hear ... and exactly what she didn't want to hear. Alexandra had laid out a very convincing description of how Cassie's plan to blow up the system could and probably would fail. She'd seen any number of internet wars, from the small-scale high school stuff to the big-time political arena. Very rarely did the truth come out until all the dust was settled and it was too late to help anyone anyway. There would be think pieces about the lessons learned and exhortations to do better next time ...

And then "next time" would be exactly the same.

The whole thing was garbage. "I have no good options," she said, almost to herself.

Carson drummed his fingers against the tablet. They traveled a centimeter to the left, where they grazed the top of her hand. "I know," he said simply.

"How can I change things?" she murmured. "Everyone wants to kill me."

Now his fingers were holding hers. "Maybe not everyone."

She couldn't bear to release his hand. "This is getting near the end of the line for you, Carson. You've already risked enough." She thought of her mom. Of TonyStark. Too many people had already sacrificed too much in her name. She wasn't worth a single person more, another life ruined.

His eyes, warm and soft, studied hers. "You don't get to tell me when to jump off the train."

"I can't let you keep risking your life. You've already done enough to get sent to prison for the rest of your life."

"Exactly," he agreed. "So why stop now?"

"Because … because it's stupid to go down with this ship when there's a raft right next to you!"

"Cass." Carson squeezed her hand. "I don't care if your last words are to tell me to run. I'm not going anywhere."

She opened her mouth, ready for a smart retort. But something else occurred to her instead.

"Hey, wait a sec." She sat up straight and Carson moved quickly to keep the tablet between her face and the camera.

"Wait a sec what?" he asked.

"Last words."

He blinked. "Yeah?"

"People's last words are, like, important. Memorable. Sometimes iconic. Right?"

"Yeah. So?"

"So right now, that's my advantage. I'm basically on death row and everyone is clinging to every word and image about me. Alexandra said to move the needle and I've been sitting here like a dumbass trying to figure out how to get people's attention."

"But you've already *got* their attention." Carson was catching on. "All you need to do is figure out where and how to direct it."

Cassie considered. An idea was forming, expanding behind her eyes. Carson looked very interested. She knew what to do. The only thing that could possibly make a difference. The one thing no one would expect.

"What's up your sleeve, Cass?"

She met his eyes. There was a hint of a sparkle in them, and it lit her up inside. "One hell of a last speech, for starters."

10010270101

When they finally uncuffed her, Rachel's wrists were red and raw. She exhaled sharply as her fingers caressed them, then told herself to woman up. A little pain on her wrists was nothing compared to what her daughter had endured. *Was* enduring.

Assuming …

Assuming Cassie was —

She wouldn't let herself go there. Not a chance.

She was in a different interview room this time, one that looked well used and was positioned in the middle of the precinct, in full view of other officers rather than hidden in an abandoned corner of the precinct, which she guessed was a good sign. Then again, the cuffs were a bad sign. They had left her alone, for now, though of course she knew that behind the wall of mirrors facing her was any number of officers, dying to catch her in the act.

Of what, exactly? She was under arrest for "aiding and abetting a Hive fugitive," the arresting officers had said. Which was funny, considering the only time she'd left her house was to go to work, on a transit path that was well monitored and easily able to prove her lack of contact with Cassie. Or with anyone. Yesterday's classes had shrunk back to their expected sizes, but most of the students were still way too interested in watching Rachel crack, real time, than in learning about the origins of the Roman senate.

Someone knocked on the mirror. Rachel jumped so hard that she kicked the leg of the table. The door opened a moment later, and the arresting detective sauntered in along with another, similarly rumpled, matching smirks on their faces.

"Mrs. McKinney," the arresting detective announced, dropping into a seat across the table from her. She eyed the other one, who leaned against the far wall, next to a small window protected by bars.

"I said, *Mrs. McKinney,*" he repeated, all traces of humor vanished from his face.

"What?" Rachel asked, more exhausted than annoyed.

"Watch it," he warned, smacking his tablet against the table. "Do you know why you're here?"

Rachel looked at him dully. The unforgiving lights of the interview room did his skin, splotchy and gray, no favors. She herself hadn't looked in a mirror in days.

"Because you arrested me."

He stared at her for a moment with unadulterated disdain. He turned to his partner. "You hear that, Coop? We got a comedian on our hands."

"Lucky us," Coop said, barely looking up from his own tablet. He was tapping furiously at his screen.

"I'm not making a joke," Rachel sighed. She leaned back in

her chair and looked at the ceiling. Rust-colored rings formed a pattern in the corner; a leak, long ago. "You arrested me. That's why I'm here. I know exactly as much — or as little, depending on your perspective — as I did the last time I was brought in here."

The other cop — !Coop, Harlon would have called him — leaned in close to Rachel. She expected to smell coffee on his breath, but instead she smelled spearmint: fresh, enticing. She closed her eyes and wondered when she and Cassie had last been to the dentist. Before Harlon's death, definitely. She'd have to make an appointment when she got b —

Rachel opened her eyes and stifled a scream. She'd been near-asleep, running a to-do list through her head the way she did every night, forgetting where she was. There would be no appointments to make.

"You. Have. No. *Idea*. How. Much. Trouble. Your. Daughter. Is. In," !Coop spat. He was staring at her, and she had the sense that if she'd been asleep for hours instead of seconds, he would have been staring the whole time regardless. He meant to intimidate her dreams.

Rachel raised her eyebrows. "Is that a joke? Is there a trouble beyond death that I'm not aware of?"

!Coop slammed his tablet down on the table again. Her tax dollars at work. "It's been four days, Mrs. McKinney. We know you and your daughter were close. You have to have heard from her by now."

Rachel looked out past the lone window. The sky was a sickly yellow, but Rachel couldn't tell if it was the lights reflecting on the glass or if the day had really decided to succumb to a color so sad, as though it was as tired as she was. Close. She and Cassie. If only that were true. The last seventeen years had been a constant battle for Cassie's affections, one she was always losing. The more she tried, the worse it got. She and her daughter could never get in sync.

So, no, Rachel wouldn't classify them as close.

But it wasn't for lack of trying. In the early days, she'd catch herself pulling away from her daughter, disconnecting sometimes, as if she was subconsciously worried that getting too close to her, loving her too much, would damage her just as equally as not loving her enough.

If she ever got Cassie back … *when* she got Cassie back, she corrected herself … that would all change.

Rachel met !Coop's eyes. "You obviously don't know my daughter. But I do. And I can assure you, if you haven't caught her by now, you won't ever catch her."

That caught !Coop's attention. He straightened, strode over to the table, power-posed next to her. "What makes you say that, Mrs. McKinney?"

"Because she doesn't want to be found. Her *life* depends on it."

"You think she doesn't want to be found?" !Coop chuckled, shuffling from one foot to the other. "You don't think she likes this attention, Mrs. McKinney? Just a little, tiny bit?"

A look of horror flashed on Rachel's face. "The attention of an angry mob of people with a legal right to kill her on sight? No, sir, I don't think she likes that kind of attention."

!Coop grabbed Rachel's arm and forced her to a standing position. "I'm about to teach you a little something about your daughter, Mrs. McKinney."

He dragged her across the room, her feet tripping over each other. She was too frightened to protest.

"Tell me," he said, shoving her roughly against the small window, gripping the back of her neck. "Do people who don't like attention do this?"

Rachel blinked.

They were on the fourth floor of the precinct; she remembered taking the elevator. Across the street was a parking lot, a fast-food place, a bank and a billboard park — one of the ones that had been erected a few years back, where billboards of differing heights flashed ads and livestreams, visible for blocks.

But they weren't flashing ads or livestreams now. They were showing something else.

"Been doing that on a loop for twenty minutes," !Coop said from behind her and Coop. "Care to explain that to us?"

Rachel stared. There was only one explanation she could offer, and it brought a smile to her face that even !Coop's angry, deranged snort of derision couldn't erase.

Cassie was still alive.

10010 2 8 00101

Across the city, every digital billboard — and there were thousands — went blank at the same time.

After a protracted period of nonactivity, the screens all lit up at the same time with white text on a black background.

The font was Inconsolata.

#HasCassieSurfacedYet? flashed on every billboard.

The hashtag remained on-screen for ten seconds, then flickered and vanished, replaced by: *Not yet.*

Ten more seconds. Flicker.

Soon.

Ten final, excruciating seconds. And then … a set of coordinates. Longitude and latitude.

It repeated every minute for almost half an hour before techs were able to lock down security and purge Cassie's botnet from the billboards' network.

By then, damn near everyone in the city had seen it, and it had gone viral across the country.

10010290 0101

From the relative safety of his bedroom, Carson leaned over Cassie's shoulder, chuckling as the billboards came to life under her control.

"Think you got their attention?"

Harlon had once hacked the Super Bowl. Years later, when he told her about it, he seemed almost ashamed. Almost. *I was young and angry and hotheaded. I don't regret doing it, but I see a new context now. Sometimes when you have to put a hole in a wall, you need a sledgehammer and sometimes you just need a drill. Know the difference.*

"I guess we'll find out soon." She rubbed her hands together. "Let's get ready for Step Two."

10010300010l

The coordinates converged on a baseball stadium, empty this fall night. A crowd converged, too.

The crowd numbered in the tens of thousands, verging into six figures. The stadium seated close to fifty thousand, but there was space on the field as well.

The security team on duty that night had a heads-up from management about five minutes before the Hive Mob was audible in the near distance. Five blocks in every direction, you could hear them, marching. Chanting.

"Le-vel 6! Kill on sight! Le-vel 6! Kill on sight!"

The security team was ordered to unlock and roll back the gates. Full cameras in operation, including backup drones. The owners of the stadium had no desire to suffer the wrath of a Hive Mob by keeping the place shut up. They would have lost the battle anyway, their meager security team of rent-a-cops against a hundred-thousand-strong moving bulwark of anger and outrage. Better to open the doors, let everyone in and take lots of pictures in case things got out of hand and people needed to be sued and/or prosecuted later.

The mob was remarkably orderly as it trooped into the stadium. The chant echoed and reechoed through the tunnels leading out to the field, rebounded up and down the ramps, filled with the percussion of two hundred thousand feet.

Cassie and Carson watched livestreaming aerial footage from a local news drone. From overhead, the stadium filled like a spill of water in slow motion, the seats going from home-team navy blue to a motley speckled rainbow. And then the field itself transmogrified from bright, overtended green to a wash of tints.

"You sure this is gonna work?" Carson asked without checking over his shoulder. His fingers were poised above a keyboard.

She wasn't sure it was going to work, but she was sure it would surprise people. Just like hacking the business channel feed during the president's interview. There was something only *she* could do, and it was guaranteed to shake things up.

When the dust settles, sometimes you see new things, her dad had said.

The drone caught a good shot of the stadium's main jumbo screen, a sleek, curved black glass parenthesis. "Just type what I told you to type," Cassie said. "My script'll do the rest."

"Yes, ma'am."

"Let's do it," she said.

*

In the stadium, the big screen flashed once, a burst of white light that stalled the chant of the mob and transformed it into a nearly worshipful mass groan of surprise and awe.

The screen was roughly 245 feet by 73 feet, an area the size of thousands of fifty-inch televisions. It was the biggest of its kind in the world of sports.

And Carson had hacked into it. Cassie could have done it, but she'd been busy figuring out what she was going to say. There was no time to record, so she would have to do it live and absolutely nail it. Anything less than perfection would just make things worse.

One hundred thousand people all turned to look up at the massive screen as it flared to life. Around the country and around the world, untold millions more watched Periscopes and Facebook Lives and BLINQvids streamed from the site.

#HasCassieSurfacedYet? the screen asked. The mob howled. The bloodlust and repudiation made Cassie's stomach curdle.

The word "NOW" exploded onto the screen. The mob screamed itself raw.

And then:

Cassie McKinney appeared on-screen. Helpfully, in case anyone didn't already know her face, a chyron read "@CassieMcK39" and "LIVE WEBCAST."

She sat in front of a haphazardly hung white sheet; a clichéd way to hide clues to her location, and a compelling visual that brought to mind hostages, terrorists, victims. Shot from the waist up, Cassie wore a denim jacket, buttoned halfway, with a green T-shirt underneath. The damage to her hair, hacked into ribbons and patches, was mitigated by a bandana tied around her head. She wore no makeup. A constellation of bruises dotted her left cheek and chin.

Out in the mob, a hush, as more than one person remembered: "Jesus H. Christ. She's a *kid.*"

On the screen, Cassie gazed into the camera levelly for several silent, excruciating seconds. Despite her disheveled appearance, her eyes were clear. Focused. Then she licked her raw, chapped lips.

"You know," she said conversationally, as though speaking to only one person and not the furious crowd of Hivers ready to rend her limb from limb, given the chance. "You know, in retrospect, I guess it *was* sort of a tasteless joke."

She shrugged one shoulder.

Then: "Sorry."

The screen flashed once and then returned to black.

*

#HiveAlert: #CassieMcKinney just hacked into every billboard in the city. HOW IS THAT BITCH STILL ALIVE? **#HiveMob**

Omg if you're wondering if **#HasCassieSurfacedYet?**
look outside your windows. 😂

Breaking news: Level 6 perpetrator **#CassieMcKinney** has seized control of streaming billboards. "In retrospect it was a tasteless joke," she says. **#HasCassieSurfacedYet?**

Y'all Hivers in **#CassieMcKinney**'s city are terrible at this. Bring the girl down South and we'll **#KillOnSight** like the patriots we are. **#SouthernersDoItBetter**

I mean, she admitted it and apologized. Are we done yet? This whole Cassie thing has gone on wayyyyyyy too long. **#DoPeopleReallyStillCareIfCassieHasSurfacedYet?**

She barely said sorry. Not buying it. Nooooope. We should still **#KillOnSight**, right?

Hey **@elisa917sunshine**, doesn't **#CassieMcKinney** kind of look like your fifth-grade class photo in her streaming vid? LOL

BLINQ ALERT: #CassieMcKinney remains at Level 6.

Why is the BLINQ feed reminding us Cassie is a Level sixer? Did they think we'd forget? Fishy.

@Animalsounds20913847 do you know why they just said that? Should we be concerned? **#KeepCassieAt6**

Guys, rumor has it the govt is going to downgrade **#CassieMcKinney**, pass it along, they can't do that. **#KeepCassieAt6**

Honestly I'm kinda bored by the Cassie story now. Let's downgrade her Level and move on already. **#ImOverIt**

I swear if the government cancels her Hive conviction we should riot in the streets. They can't take this power away from us. **#HiveJusticeIsTheBestJustice**

The government gave us the power of the Hive. They can take it back. It's not, like, written into the Bill of Rights or anything. **#LawStudent**

Weird that **#CassieMcKinney** looks so much younger in real life than she did in her BLINQ photos. Was someone Photoshopping to make her look older, more guilty? **#ThingsThatMakeYouGoHmmmm**

Ask yourselves: How does a Level 6 perp evade **#TheHive** for this long AND manage to hack into government-controlled databases? The 📞 is coming from inside the house, **#sheeple**. Wake up! **#HasCassieSurfacedYet?**

I seriously cannot believe no one has killed **#CassieMcKinney** yet, ya girl is like a ninja. Makes me kinda respect her now.

Consider this: What is an apology, anyway? If the regret is there, do we need her to fall on her sword? She said "Sorry." Is that enough? What else does Cassie McKinney owe us?

Idea: **#LeaveCassieAlone** since she apologized and, like, that's what she needed to do, right?

I will chase Cassie McKinney for the rest of my life if she gets downgraded. IT'S NOT FAIR. **#PowerToThePeople**

Maybe if someone's been able to outrun a **#HiveMob** for this long, we should just let her go? Should we **#LeaveCassieAlone**?

R u kidding me???? One word??? She says ONE WORD & every1 is all **#LeaveCassieAlone**?

What else do you want her to say? You want her to dissect every word? It was a dumb joke and she said sorry. Get a fucking life. **#LeaveCassieAlone**

Gotta give it to **#CassieMcKinney**, she just issued a master apology in less than a dozen words. I know some politicians who should take lessons from her! 🎯

That shrug tho! WTF? **#Level64Ever**

Uh, "that shrug" was like saying, "Yeah, OK, I'll apologize." What stream were YOU watching? **#LeaveCassieAlone**

Can't believe **#CassieMcKinney** just hacked into the ad system LOL. Girl's got bigger balls than POTUS. **#TooSoon?**

#BLINQReaderPoll4390: Who thinks we should **#LeaveCassieAlone**? Vote: bl.inq/poll4390

ENTERTAINMENT NEWS ALERT: Level 6 perpetrator **#CassieMcKinney** spotted with fresh new haircut; issues apology. We're live with crowd reactions at the top of the hour!

I just voted NO in **#BLINQReaderPoll4390**, join me: **#LeaveCassieAlone**? Vote: bl.inq/poll4390

While you're all distracted by **#CassieMcKinney**'s apology, remember that POTUS just announced coalition for new drilling in protected Indigenous land in Canada. Sign the petition here: li.nk/pet.itionly754

It's kinda weird that first we all wanted Cassie alive and then we all wanted her dead and now I have no idea what I want. Someone tell me what I want! **#LeaveCassieAlone #KeepCassieAt6**

I just voted YES in **#BLINQReaderPoll4390**, join me: **#LeaveCassieAlone**? Vote: bl.inq/poll4390

Just catching up on the **#CassieMcKinney** apology now. Damn, I forgot she's just a kid. **#LeaveCassieAlone**

I just voted YES in **#BLINQReaderPoll4390**, join me: **#LeaveCassieAlone**? Vote: bl.inq/poll4390

I just voted YES in **#BLINQReaderPoll4390**, join me: **#LeaveCassieAlone**? Vote: bl.inq/poll4390

#HiveAlert: Level 1 Justice happening rn over in Capital Park, join me for the fun!

I just voted NO in **#BLINQReaderPoll4390**, join me: **#LeaveCassieAlone**? Vote: bl.inq/poll4390

I just voted YES in **#BLINQReaderPoll4390**, join me: **#LeaveCassieAlone**? Vote: bl.inq/poll4390

I just voted YES in **#BLINQReaderPoll4390**, join me: **#LeaveCassieAlone**? Vote: bl.inq/poll4390

I just voted YES in **#BLINQReaderPoll4390**, join me: **#LeaveCassieAlone**? Vote: bl.inq/poll4390

This whole thing is really showing me how weird Hive Justice can be. Anyone else? **#IsThisTheWorldWeWantToLiveIn?**

*

Livestream from the White House Press Briefing Room (In Progress)
Dean Hythe, President of the United States:

"I'm not going to answer that question. No. It's a bad question, very bad. Look back at the beginning. I never said I wanted this girl to die. And now she won't. I don't … There's nothing to talk about. She's fine. And the baby is doing great, by the way. You notice how no one is asking about my daughter and my grandson? Very suspicious.

"I'm going to bring — get her in here — I'm going to bring Alexandra Pastor up here. And let her explain all of this to you. Because clearly you all need some explaining."

"Mr. President, as always, it's such a pleasure to be here, to speak to your great policies and plans for this great nation of ours. Thank you so much.

"Isn't this an exciting day? We're witnessing a first: a Hive Justice reversal. We always thought that this might happen, but we never anticipated it would happen in such dramatic fashion.

"Approximately thirty-eight hours ago, Cassie McKinney livestreamed an apology for the actions that led to her assignment of Level 6. We observed a shift in online discourse roughly ten minutes after the apology, which immediately went viral and soon had penetration into most social media streams, including Facebook, Guessom, YouTube and, of course, BLINQ.

"The livestream itself was propagated across multiple platforms, but BLINQ did as it was designed to do and aggregated responses. What was most interesting, we found, was that people who had not originally voted on the initial Cassie McKinney post went back and voted on it after the fact, Liking it as a way of showing acceptance of her apology. Currently, the new Likes have offset enough Condemns that Ms. McKinney is at Level 3, and we project she will bottom out at Level 2 or even Level 1 within the next forty-eight hours.

"Of course, I'm sure you're wondering, did we anticipate something like this? Is this how Hive Justice is supposed to work? Does this mitigate the effectiveness of Hive Justice? Won't people simply apologize publicly and beat the rap?

"Well, we believe that the Hive will now take such an idea into account during the initial judgment period. Individuals will Condemn based not just on what was done but also based on their willingness to accept an apology.

"As to whether or not this is how the system was designed: of course it was. Ms. McKinney's apology went viral fast enough that it triggered an exoneration protocol. Most Hive matters are local and action is swift — there isn't enough time for a change of heart on the part of the Hive, and so the exoneration protocol never kicks in. This case was different.

"Think of it this way: the initial ramp-up of Condemns was the trial and verdict. Then came the sentencing … and the court was lenient. It's an imperfect metaphor but one that I've found helpful as I think over these events. Or, if you want, think of Cassie McKinney's new status as probation. Certainly the country will be watching her from now on, and she may not be so lucky next time.

"The motto of BLINQ is Trend Positive! We encourage all of our citizen-users to take that motto to heart. And thirty-eight hours ago, Cassie McKinney gave them the opportunity to do just that.

"We're witnessing the birth of something unique — not merely an artificial intelligence, but a *mass* intelligence, one that can do more than simply process information and respond intelligently but that is also developing its own morality.

"Isn't it amazing?"

10010310010 1

Something broke inside Cassie, some vital thing that had kept her adrenaline pumping for all these days. She felt it — snap! — and then, in its absence, a release. A warmth. Carson's bedroom looked brighter, like the sun had somehow angled its way around the blackout curtains, coating his gray walls with twinkling lights.

She could see it now: a future. A life. *Her* life, returning. Her body tingled.

"Am I hallucinating this?" she whispered. The president's face, spackled with a sour expression as he stood behind Alexandra; Alexandra herself, looking taller than she did in person; her name flashing across the chyron: "Breaking News: Cassie McKinney, first Level 6 perpetrator in history, currently at Level 3."

Carson spun his chair around. "Some damn fine drugs if you are, because I'm seeing the same thing."

The tingling in Cassie's body changed, converting into a weakness so sudden and overwhelming that she collapsed onto the nearest soft landing — Carson's bed, the blankets still rumpled from her sleep.

"Hey," he went on, "have you noticed that Gorfinkle guy is nowhere to be seen? It's the Pastor Show, and he's not —"

"Oh, my God," she breathed, not caring about Gorfinkle or much of anything else, really. The walls began to wobble, and she pressed her eyelids, trying to get them to stay still, to make the room stop spinning. "Is it really hot in here or is it me?"

"Put your head between your knees," Carson instructed, jumping over to a kneeling position next to her, placing one hand on Cassie's shoulder. "You're going to faint, and you do *not* want me responsible for administering first aid. I don't even know how to put on a bandage."

Cassie bent over, resting her forehead against her thighs, counting her breaths. *In, out. Life, death. In, out. Life, death.*

Carson's hand was still on her shoulder. "You OK, McKinney?"

She nodded.

"Good. Woulda sucked if you'd kicked it right when they announced you're a free woman."

She snorted through her knees, which unleashed a guffaw that set the room on fire. Carson joined her and together they crouched next to each other, half on the bed, half on the floor, laughing so hard that Cassie's throat started to hurt.

"From Level 6 to Level 2. Or even 1." Carson heaved, his shoulders shaking from the laughter, his words barely decipherable. "That's so fucking ridiculous, I can't even."

"Five minutes ago, I was a dead woman!" Cassie could barely get the words out.

"Now you'll just have to wear some kind of stupid sign for

a day, or some shit like that." Carson rolled back on his heels. Cassie liked his laugh — almost maniacal, incongruous with his easygoing vibe. It opened up his whole face.

"I'll take it!" Cassie cried gleefully. "I'll take it," she repeated, this time to herself.

And then her laugh got twisted up on its way out of her throat, and she choked. She was suddenly, unexpectedly, crying. Sobbing. The tears flowed fast and loose, like they had been waiting for permission to escape, and now they couldn't stop.

"Oh, Cass," Carson said, his voice now serious. He rubbed her shoulder. "Let it out. Let it out."

Like she had a say in the matter. Every molecule in her body was crying. Even her fingernails had tears. Carson's hand, warm and steady, ran circles over her shoulders, her back. On Carson's computer, the livestream had switched over to a group of news-heads talking about the groundbreaking change to Cassie McKinney's Hive status.

"Unprecedented, from the first second to the last," one of them was saying, and the words reverberated in Cassie's head. "We'll be studying this in history books."

A fresh wail broke from Cassie. History. Rachel. Someone had to have told her mom, right?

She gripped Carson's wrists. "We have to find my mom."

"Already on it." Carson's voice was quiet, serious. He looked intently into Cassie's eyes. "I pinged the local news. Your mom will be released any second now, if she hasn't been already — the DA is dropping the charges. We should probably wait a couple of hours, maybe even a day. Let things settle down. Who knows, there might be some groups protesting the reversal."

Cassie nodded, her convulsions subsiding. Soon she'd be home. Home, with her mom. The thought was … dizzying.

Carson was studying her again. She hiccuped, catching her breath. "What?"

"Nada. Just … goddamn, you're a *really* ugly crier."

"Carson!" She grabbed his shoulders, intending to push him away, but his hands found hers and he held her steady, their eyes locked.

"Seriously. You're gonna be OK, McKinney. Do you believe me?"

She nodded once, afraid to move too much, to burst the moment into pieces when all she wanted was to stay in it, keep it shiny and whole and revel in its possibilities.

"Good." He nodded once, too.

She held on to his hands, even though there was no real need to. But he was, Cassie noticed, holding on to hers, too.

Well, good. Because she didn't plan on letting go anytime soon.

100103200101

The sun was setting reluctantly, sending wavy plumes of tropical colors over the sky, as if to remind everyone who was in charge. Cassie tried to commit them to memory, pinks and oranges and faint purples, before they disappeared. She was learning how fragile things could be.

Carson escorted her, his arm tightly locked around her shoulders, as if he could protect her from any Hiver who might notice her, not like that she'd reverted to Level 1. He'd even insisted she wear a hat, but Cassie didn't think anyone was going to try anything. Not now. Everyone had moved on. Rowan, in her way, was right.

She didn't have her phone, of course, so the apartment's smart lock couldn't see her. Cassie had to knock. She stood at her own front door, waiting for it to open, and marveled at the anxiety boiling away at her insides. A horrible thought occurred to her: Would Rachel be pissed? Angry that she'd risked so much, that Cassie had started all of this? Would she glare at Cassie and say, "I told you so?" Would she —

The door opened.

Cassie's eyes widened in surprise. It was Bryce. In her house. With her mother.

He quickly looked around Cassie and Carson, up and down the hallway. "Just checking," he said before ushering them in.

The apartment was a wreck. Furniture was smashed. The sofa had been cut open. There were holes cut in the walls. The whole place had been tossed — thoroughly — and yet Cassie thought their cramped, cheap apartment had never looked so homey or so welcoming. Carson smartly stepped aside just in time, and when Rachel leaped toward her, arms outstretched, nearly knocking her over, she let herself get caught up in the riptide.

"Cassie!" Rachel cried.

"Mom," Cassie whispered, melting into the embrace, her knees buckling. Her mom held her up until she found the strength to stand again.

"Oh, my God, my girl." Rachel's voice, muffled against Cassie's cheek, was hoarse from crying. "You're OK. You're OK. You're OK, right?"

She pulled back, holding Cassie's cheeks, turning her head this way and that, examining every angle of her face. She touched one of Cassie's bruises, the purple one in full bloom on her chin.

"I'm OK," Cassie said, smiling through her tears. She sniffled, suddenly embarrassed. Carson and Bryce had tried to give them some space, but the small living room didn't offer much in the way of it, and they stood awkwardly to the side, Carson pretending to check the scene out the window, and Bryce discovering a sudden interest in the couch pillows, which he was inexplicably picking up, fluffing, putting down and then repeating.

"There's a nice coffee shop down the block," Rachel suggested. Bryce immediately picked up on the hint.

"Let's go, bro," he demanded, opening the door.

"I'm not your bro," Carson grumbled on his way out. He flashed Cassie a grin, a raised-eyebrows-I'll-see-you-soon smile, and Cassie wanted to say something — thank you, I owe you, how can I ever repay you — but she had all that and more to say to her mom, too. And to Bryce and to so many others, but there would be time enough for that.

Her mother held her at arm's length and they stared at each other for a long, silent moment.

"So," Cassie said. "Hashtag mom army. For real?"

Rachel hiccuped a laugh. "Oh, you saw that?"

"The *world* saw that. My mom went viral. Words I never thought I'd put into a sentence."

Rachel sniffled and wiped her wet eyes with the heels of her hands. "Yeah, well … I told you — lionesses will do pretty much anything to protect their cubs."

Cassie nodded, her throat suddenly too thick for words. She pulled her mom in close for another hug. She felt the sharp angles of her mother's body, the worry-thinned flesh, the protrusion of her shoulder blades. Her mom had aged a year in just a few days.

"I'm sorry," Cassie whispered. "I'm so sorry. I screwed up. I'm sorry."

She would have gone on apologizing for minutes, hours, days, if her mom hadn't stopped her with a quiet shushing sound.

"You screwed up. And you fixed it. And maybe you changed

things for the better." Rachel pulled back and kissed Cassie on the cheek, carefully avoiding her bruises. "I'm sure someday I'm going to be incredibly pissed about all of this, but right now I'm just so relieved. And so proud."

They curled up together on the remains of the couch, mother and daughter, entwined in a way Cassie couldn't remember having done since she was a kid. Rachel made them some tea, and other than getting up for the kettle, they didn't let go of each other for hours. Between tears punctuated by long moments of silence, Cassie told her everything, every single second and word and action she could remember. It was more words than she'd spoken to her mom in the entire previous year.

Cassie told her everything except for the deepest truth — the ghost accounts that haunted BLINQ and the internet, the easy way justice could be manipulated. It was too disconcerting, too real, too extant. It was a horror movie monster that could reach up out of the grave even after being killed, and Cassie couldn't bear to inflict that knowledge on her mother.

*

As the sun fully set and shadows crawled around the apartment's walls and corners, Cassie snuggled in closer. As she breathed in Rachel's familiar scent, Cassie realized she hadn't showered in days, and still her mom held her close.

"I couldn't have made it without you, Mom," Cassie admitted, a half-dream confession made with her eyes closed and sleep lurking. "Dad taught me everything I needed to clear my name, and I'm so, so lucky I got to be his daughter. But you ..."

Rachel held her breath, but Cassie didn't finish her thought, succumbing to a sleep that would seize her body for nearly a full day. Rachel stroked her choppy, uneven hair as she slept.

Cassie let her. That was everything.

10010330010l

Do you remember Alexandra Pastor?

Cassie had a new phone, and with it came access to her dad's digital self once more. She'd been without him for days on the run, then even longer as she waited for the publicity around her Hive Level drop to die down a bit so that she could take the risk of going online again. But now she was back, with a brand-new phone that had been gifted to her by a big tech firm that was courting her to work with them. She wasn't sure about their real intentions — she suspected they wanted a rebel mascot more than a coder — but she was happy to accept their bribes with a smile and her fingers crossed behind her back, along with a promise to consider their offer once she graduated.

The phone ran a custom OS she and Carson had tweaked based on an old Android fork. She swapped out all the bright colors for dull; she never wanted to get lost online again.

She also had her bracelet back, the one she'd tried to go back for when Rachel had dragged her out of her bedroom that early morning, the day the world changed. Whatever the NSA had been looking for, her jewelry hadn't been on the list. She planned never to take it off again. It wasn't the only thing that tied her to her father, but it was precious nonetheless. It was solid, not ephemeral like memory or code.

Do you remember Alexandra Pastor? she'd asked, hoping that maybe somewhere in the bot, her dad had left something she could use. She thought about the code that undergirded the digital Harlon, how it had an array of nicknames and endearments and chose one based on a very sophisticated algorithm. It seemed so real, but there was no way to compare it to her actual father, so who knew? Maybe it was just close enough.

Maybe that was all that mattered.

Do you remember Alexandra Pastor? Such a simple question. For a human being. A human being would say yes or no in an instant.

It took the bot a while to get back to her. She imagined it thought it was busy with something.

Alexandra Pastor is the deputy attorney general of Hive Justice. She was born on February 10, 1981. Is that what you mean, sweetie?

She sighed. The bot could do a lot, but it couldn't remember Harlon's life for her. Harlon's connection to Alexandra would remain the sketch Alexandra had given her, the lines blurry and indistinct, the white spaces devoid of tones and shadows and colors.

Colors …

The color is the code.

She stared at her bracelet. It hit her like a thunderbolt.

No. No way.

Ten stones. Each one a different color.

She almost dropped her phone in her eagerness to text the bot.

The color is the code, she sent.

The answer was almost immediate: **That's right, sweetheart. I guess you've met Alexandra. Be patient with her; she's a work in progress. But we all are, right?**

Holy.

Shit.

Ten stones. Ten colors.

The NSA had insisted to her mom that Dad had left something behind. A perfect encryption. A purloined letter.

And they'd been right all along. Harlon *had* left something. But it wasn't tech. It was something else. A code. An encryption key in solid form, unhackable.

Her father had been there at the beginning of the Hive and then had walked away. But the guilt and self-recrimination lingered. She remembered his uncharacteristic quiet when the Hive launched, his equally uncharacteristic outburst at her mother.

He'd had regrets. And he didn't know what to do about them.

But he *did* know. He'd hacked the Hive. Of course he had.

It had taken years, but he'd gotten inside, into the dirty heart of the Hive, dumped the data on a hidden server … sent Alexandra on a wild-goose chase to a secret website packed with data, the data that even now resided in the Superman USB key. And then the bracelet. Putting the pieces out there. Just in case.

What did Harlon think would happen? That Alexandra would visit her old, dead friend's family? That she would work with Cassie? What were the odds?

Or maybe the bracelet's secret had never been intended for her. Maybe it had been for her dad, a good hiding place. Stashed away in case he needed it. He didn't know he would die before he could use it.

In the end, there were some things she would never know. She would just have to live with that. The AI could tell her almost anything, processed through what it knew of Harlon. She still hadn't told her mother about the deep, deep truths that had led to her exoneration. She would tell Harlon, if she could think of a way to do it that would give the bot enough data to synthesize something meaningful. Because her digital dad wouldn't feel any emotions. She didn't have to worry about scaring it or freaking it out.

Her mom was another story entirely. Rachel had been through a lifetime's worth of "enough." No more.

Hey, what's new, sweetheart? the bot prompted.

She permitted herself a slight smile. She missed her dad so much.

I think I have a boyfriend.

The response was immediate: **Is he good to you?**

Tears welled up in her eyes. Stupid bot. It was just a stupid bot because even the smartest bot was still just a bot. But, dammit, it's exactly what her dad would have said.

Wiping away the tears, she typed back: **He saved my life.**

A long pause. She started to put her phone back in her pocket, figuring this was just one of those times when she wouldn't get a response. How could an AI ever —

Her phone pinged.

I'm glad. I want you around for a long time.

*

She spent hours online, comparing the colors of the stones to digital swatches. When she was sure she had them right, she ended up with a string of ten different hexadecimal codes. Each code represented a stone's color.

There were ten different possible combinations, assuming the codes were supposed to line up in the order of the stones on the bracelet. There was 1-2-3-4-5-6-7-8-9-10, then 2-3-4-5-6-7-8-9-10-1, then 3-4-5-6-7-8-9-10-1-2, and so on.

She hit pay dirt halfway through. The sixty-character string was a decryption key that unlocked the Superman USB key.

Cassie stared at the data as it scrolled past, then she started to laugh.

Everything about the Hive. *Everything.* Its past. Its construction. The flaws deliberately introduced into the system. The who, how, what, where, why and when. All of it, at her fingertips.

Every last drop of it.

*

The **#Westfield** Homecoming Queen ballots are being distributed this week. Odds that **#CassieMcKinney** will be on it? LOL **#WestfieldQueens**

The usual suspects will be on the court: Rowan, Madison, Indira, Livvy and then someone from the tech crowd and student council. Yawn. **#WestfieldQueens**

Who feels like having fun with the Court this year? Maybe we throw some unexpected names in the mix? **#WestfieldQueens**

Here's an idea: CASSIE MCKINNEY FOR WESTFIELD HIGH HOMECOMING QUEEN. **#WestfieldQueens**

Wait. Is Cassie really coming back to Westfield? **#WhatsUpWestfield**

Can you imagine a Level 6 convict being in your classes? How would anyone ever concentrate?
#LikeAnyoneCanConcentrateNow #WhatsUpWestfield

#BLINQReaderPoll416010: Does **#CassieMcKinney** deserve to be Homecoming Queen? Vote: bl.inq/poll416010 **#WestfieldQueens**

There's no way she's coming back to **#Westfield**. Right?

Is a Level 6 convict even eligible for Homecoming Queen? There are rules. **#WestfieldQueens**

She's gotta graduate from somewhere … why not Westfield? Hey, I like that hashtag! **#WhyNotWestfield**

God, you're so tragic Elena. **#WhatsUpWestfield**
LOL — RB **#RowanSpeaks**

I just voted NO in **#BLINQReaderPoll416010**, join me:
Does **#CassieMcKinney** deserve to be Homecoming Queen?
Vote: bl.inq/poll416010 **#WestfieldQueens**

I just voted YES in **#BLINQReaderPoll416010**, join me:
Does **#CassieMcKinney** deserve to be Homecoming Queen?
Vote: bl.inq/poll416010 **#WestfieldQueens**

Seriously, is she gonna come back to school? I'd like to buy her lunch. **#WestfieldQueens #CassieIsMyQueen**

*

Weeks passed. Cassie returned to Westfield, an occasion she was surprised to find she did not dread. After she'd evaded Hive Justice and the threat of death, a new high school was nothing.

Sarah had transferred elsewhere. Rowan and the Homework Coven studiously ignored her. Whatever. She could pull straight A's without them. See how well they did on the comp sci final without her, though.

One weekend, a couple of days after she'd returned to school, she lingered at the breakfast table with her mom, the two of them luxuriating in the quiet and the solace. There were no cops knocking on the door and no mobs screaming for her head.

She'd fallen off the headlinks and trending topics a while back. But this morning, her phone blew up with alerts about members of OHM who'd been caught in the raid. Trials were starting soon, for cyberterrorism, for evading Hive Justice, for obstruction of justice. Cassie skimmed the names, but they were real names, and all she knew were hacker handles.

"What's going on in the bean, teen?" Rachel asked, gazing at her over the top of her tablet.

Self-consciously, Cassie patted her head. Her hair was growing back in and she was letting it do what it wanted. She was tired of fighting and that included fighting her hair, her closet, her reflection every time she looked in the mirror.

"Just thinking."

"I know. About what? You look troubled."

She sighed. The night before, Carson had sent her a link to a page on his own web server. It aggregated data from a series of sources, including Cassie's BLINQ account and the secret ghost accounts they'd uncovered. According to Carson's calculations, her Likes had risen high enough that — even if the government decided to turn *all* of the ghost accounts against her — there were still enough real accounts Liking her that she would Trend Positive.

Meaning … maybe she should release that data from the Superman USB key. Maybe it was time to give the Hive a taste of Hive Justice.

Or maybe play along. Be a good girl. Sit on the data and wait. Alexandra had seemed disaffected with the Hive now. Maybe *she* could and would do something to change it from the inside.

Or …

Or.

Or.

Too many ors.

"So here's what I'm wondering, Mom. Say you can't be hurt. But other people can. Should you step in front of a bullet, then?"

Rachel put down her tablet and gazed at Cassie thoughtfully. She considered it for a long time. Cassie had regarded the question as an easy one.

"Step in front of a bullet? Maybe. It depends."

"Mom! Ugh. Can't you just answer the question?" Cassie sighed. After a moment she asked, "Depends on what?"

Rachel shrugged. "Well, what if your invulnerability wears off? Or what if it turns out nothing can hurt you *except* bullets, and you're about to find out in a very inconvenient way?"

Cassie frowned. She craved a simple, direct answer, and her analogy was screwing everything up. Alexandra's passive-aggressive warning — *she may not be so lucky next time* — tiptoed with burning feet through her thoughts.

"Forget about the bullet. What if you had a lot of power and you saw something you knew was wrong? Should you use that power to protect yourself and only yourself? Or should you risk it and use it to break the thing that's wrong?"

Rachel thought about that one for a lot less time. When she answered, it was with a sad smile. "You know what, honey? Your dad had a saying ..."

100103400101

Dad, I have a question for you.

Go ahead, baby.

Cassie took a deep breath. Her thumbs moved rapidly over the screen.

Should I be a sledgehammer or a drill?

And then she sat back.

And waited.